Praise for Mary Daheim and her Emma Lord mysteries

THE ALPINE ADVOCATE

"The lively ferment of life in a small Pacific Northwest town, with its convoluted genealogies and loyalties [and] its authentically quirky characters, combines with a baffling murder for an intriguing mystery novel."

—M. K. WREN

THE ALPINE BETRAYAL

"Editor-publisher Emma Lord finds out that running a small-town newspaper is worse than nutty—it's downright dangerous. Readers will take great pleasure in Mary Daheim's new mystery."

—CAROLYN G. HART

THE ALPINE CHRISTMAS

"If you like cozy mysteries, you need to try Daheim's Alpine series. . . . Recommended."

—*The Snooper*

THE ALPINE DECOY

"[A] fabulous series . . . Fine examples of the traditional, domestic mystery."

—*Mystery Lov*

By Mary Daheim
Published by Ballantine Books:

THE ALPINE ADVOCATE
THE ALPINE BETRAYAL
THE ALPINE CHRISTMAS
THE ALPINE DECOY
THE ALPINE ESCAPE
THE ALPINE FURY
THE ALPINE GAMBLE
THE ALPINE HERO

THE
ALPINE
HERO

Mary Daheim

BALLANTINE BOOKS • NEW YORK

Copyright © 1996 by Mary Daheim

All rights reserved under International and Pan-American Copyright Conventions. Published in the United States by Ballantine Books, a division of Random House, Inc., New York, and simultaneously in Canada by Random House of Canada Limited, Toronto.

http://www.randomhouse.com

Library of Congress Catalog Card Number: 96-96831

ISBN 0-345-39642-1

Manufactured in the United States of America

First Edition: January 1997

10 9 8 7 6 5 4 3

Chapter One

MY HAIR WAS three inches too long and my bank balance was thirty dollars short. I wasn't due for a paycheck at *The Alpine Advocate* for another two days. As the newspaper's editor and publisher, I could have given myself an advance. But that was cheating, which I despised. I'd done it once, with somebody else's husband, and the price had been high. In this winter of my introspection, I'd finally closed that long-overdue account.

Waiting to cross Front Street, I pondered my old sin and my new attitude. The affair twenty-three years ago had given me a son, a broken heart, and a skewed slant on love. The object of my blighted affection was currently separated from his certifiably crazy wife. But divorce wasn't imminent. Waiting for Tom Cavanaugh to leave Sandra was like winning the lottery—there was always a chance, but the odds were terrible.

My patience with Tom had run out. I'd finally exorcised him on New Year's Eve. He'd called from San Francisco to tell me how much he loved me. I'd said that was nice. Tom was justifiably bewildered. I wished him a Happy New Year and hung up. Six weeks had passed, and I hadn't heard from him again. Maybe he'd gotten the message.

I had no regrets. I felt liberated, even exhilarated. On an overcast February day in Alpine, Washington, with

1

four feet of snow covering the ground and a sharp wind blowing down from Mount Baldy, I felt buoyant. It didn't bother me that the buildings along Front Street were small and drab, with piles of dirty snow hugging their facades. I ignored the jarring sound of a drill at the corner of Front and Second. All it meant to me was a two-inch story, about a frozen pipe across the street at City Hall. I could sniff the sweet cedar smoke from the sawmill and the heady aroma of chicken soup from the Venison Inn. As far as the eye could see on the main thoroughfare, there were no more than twenty vehicles in transit. With not quite four thousand residents, the town neither hustles nor bustles. While I often missed the city, Alpine's quiet, arctic isolation suited my present mood just fine.

The thought of submitting my unruly brown locks to the capable hands of Stella Magruder was very appealing. Heedlessly, I allowed a logging truck to fling slush on my boots. Recklessly, I crossed Front Street before one of its two traffic lights changed. Giddily, I entered Stella's Styling Salon and greeted her assistant, Laurie, at the counter.

Laurie is pretty, pleasant—and dumb as a rope. As usual, she couldn't remember my name. This might be common in a busy metropolis, but Stella's Styling is the only beauty parlor in town.

"Emma Lord," I said with a big smile. Nothing was going to shake me from my newly acquired sanguine state.

"Umm." Laurie scanned the appointment book. "Would that be a haircut or a facial?" Her bland blue eyes gazed beyond my left ear.

The salon had recently begun offering facials. There were rumors that massage might follow. I kept smiling. "A haircut, with Stella. Two o'clock."

Miraculously, Laurie found my name. "Ms. Lord," she said, with doubt in her wispy voice. Reaching under the counter, she handed me a black smock. "You can change next to the facial room. It's in the back, by the rest room. Okay?" Laurie sounded as if it probably weren't.

The smock-changing routine was new, along with the facials. Vaguely, I recalled where the rest room was located. As I passed by the two workstations, Stella's reflection smiled at me in the big mirror that covered most of the wall. She was putting the finishing touches on an elderly woman I'd met somewhere around town. The blue rinse bordered on the garish, but the soft curls looked nice.

"Hi, Emma," Stella said in greeting. "I thought you'd died. You should have been in here before the end of January. Now I'll have to get out the hedge clippers." She laughed, a husky, happy sound that followed me through the door that led to the salon's nether parts.

The rest room was clearly marked. But there were four other doors. One of them was ajar, but I could hear the swishing sound of a washer and the hum of a dryer. I remembered that this was the salon's laundry and linen room. Uncertain as to which was the changing area, I opened the door opposite the rest room.

I'd made a mistake. This was the facial room. It was lighted only by a pair of thick aromatic candles. A woman was lying on the table, swathed in a sheet and a couple of towels. Her face was covered with dark green cream, and there were cotton pads over her eyes. I intended to apologize for the intrusion. But before my brain could connect with my voice, I saw that the woman's throat had been cut from ear to ear. There was no doubt that she was dead.

I screamed.

My sanguine mood was shattered.

* * *

Stella was the first to hear me. She rushed into the dimly lighted corridor gripping a comb. My initial reaction was that it was a weapon, and Stella was going to stab me. I screamed again, took in the alarm on her face, and tried to calm down.

"The woman in there is dead," I said, gulping and gesturing. "Her throat's been cut." My unsteady legs forced me to lean against the wall next to the facial-room door.

Stella visibly steeled herself, then pushed the door all the way open. Dropping the comb, she put both hands over her mouth to stifle a cry. Laurie appeared at that moment, along with a dark-haired young woman I didn't recognize. Stella whirled, grabbed her assistants by their shoulders, and spun them back down the narrow corridor.

"Becca! Call the sheriff!" Stella gave herself a shake. "Better yet, run over and get him or whoever's there. Hurry!"

The Skykomish County Sheriff's Office was almost directly across the street from the Clemans Building, which houses the salon. Becca, who I knew only by sight, now hurried away. Laurie stood dumbly by the rest-room door, watching her employer with uncomprehending blue eyes.

"Let's go back into the salon," Stella said, firmly closing the door on the dead woman. "I don't want to see *that* again."

Still shaking, I followed Stella and Laurie. The bright lights of the main salon hurt my eyes. Indeed, I seemed to hurt all over.

"Who is it?" I finally breathed as I half fell into the vacant chair at Laurie's station.

Before I could get an answer from Stella, she saw her Blue Rinse waiting patiently at the front counter. I suddenly remembered that the woman's name was Ella Hinshaw. She was a shirttail relation of my House & Home editor, Vida Runkel. Ella was about seventy, and deaf as a post. It appeared that she hadn't heard my screams, though she was eyeing all three of us with curiosity.

Stella arrived at the counter. It sounded as if she was trying to get rid of Ella before the sheriff arrived. Laurie was leaning against the shampoo bowl, looking bewildered.

"Who was it?" I hissed at her.

Laurie turned her wheat-colored head in my direction. Every time I saw her, both her style and shade were different. "Ms. Whitman," she said in a hushed voice. "You know—that woman from Startup."

I knew Honoria Whitman very well. She and Sheriff Milo Dodge had been seeing each other for about three years. Honoria lived twenty-five miles west of Alpine in a converted summer cottage off Highway 2. She was a potter who was confined to a wheelchair. I admired her courage and her independence. I liked her, but was sometimes put off by what I considered a faintly patronizing manner. Laurie's words caused me to start shaking all over again.

Stella had gotten rid of Ella Hinshaw. Watching the sheriff's office through the front door, Stella spoke sharply to Laurie: "Did you say that was Honoria Whitman?" Stella's usually husky voice was thin and strained. "Good God, Laurie, it's not *her*—it's Kay Whitman, Honoria's sister-in-law."

I felt dizzy with relief. I'd never heard of Kay Whitman; I vaguely recalled that Honoria had a sister-in-law. The only reason I knew that much was because the brother had killed the husband who had pushed Honoria down a flight of stairs and turned her into a cripple. After putting my head between my knees, I looked up to see Milo Dodge loping into the salon with Becca and Deputy Jack Mullins right behind him.

"Okay," Milo said, his usually laconic voice a trifle loud and fraught with authority. "What do we have here?" One hand was at his sidearm.

Stella took command, her full-figured body positioned in the middle of the salon where the reception area ended and the workstations began. "Emma went into the facial room by mistake. She found our client with her throat cut. It's true. I saw her myself. She's dead."

"Who is she?" Milo asked with a swift, reproachful glance at Becca. "This one couldn't remember her name."

"She was new," Becca began in an apologetic voice. Becca was new, too, at least to me. Stella seemed to have surrounded herself with employees who didn't know their clients, dead or alive. "In fact, she wasn't—"

Milo cut Becca off with a slashing motion of his hand. "Who is it, Stella?"

Stella was keeping her composure remarkably well, though she was pale under her carefully applied makeup. Still, she swallowed hard before answering. "Kay Whitman. She took Honoria's appointment."

Now the color drained from Milo's long face. He turned jerkily, staring out into Front Street. I had finally managed to get out of the chair and had edged close enough to see through the window. Sure enough, Honoria and her wheelchair were being pushed out of the sheriff's office by a man I didn't recognize. They appeared to be heading toward the Clemans Building.

Milo gave Jack Mullins a small shove. "Stop them. Don't let Honoria or her brother in here. Damn!" With a sharp shake of his head, Milo turned back to Stella. "I'm going to have a look. You call Doc Dewey and get him over here. Tell him to send an ambulance. They can go in the back way, right?"

Stella nodded. "The fire exit for the building is on Pine Street."

"Right." Milo's long-legged stride took him through the salon. He passed me without so much as a glance. "Show me the room, Stella," he ordered.

Becca was crying. She had sat down in one of the two chairs in the reception area and was hunched over like a child. Laurie regarded her coworker with mild dismay, but didn't move. I forced myself to join Becca. Doing something other than thinking about the dead woman would help me regain my equilibrium. Only now did it dawn on me that this was a major news story. I had to become Emma Lord, journalist, instead of Emma Lord, twittering ninny.

At first I didn't say anything, but merely patted Becca's plump shoulder. Mentally, I was trying to place her. She wasn't a newcomer, but she was a stranger to me. Vida had written a small article about Becca in early January. Rebecca Wolfe—the full name came back to me. She was an Alpine native, but had left town after high school. That was six or seven years ago, before my time. Vida had made some acerbic comment about Becca, but at the moment I couldn't remember what it was.

Becca continued to sob. I reached for a box of tissues and handed it to her. She fumbled with a single sheet, then began to hiccup just as Edith Bartleby, the Episcopal vicar's wife, entered the shop.

"Oh, dear," exclaimed Mrs. Bartleby, who was out of breath. "I'm late! I do hate tardiness, but there's some sort of giant drill around the corner where I usually park. When people are late for communion service, I sometimes can't help but feel disapproval—" Mrs. Bartleby stopped, taking in the scene. "My goodness! Whatever's happened? Is someone distraught over her haircut?"

Jack Mullins returned. I tried to see where Honoria and her escort had gone, but they'd disappeared. Two or three Alpiners had gathered on the sidewalk, however, apparently drawn by the unusual activity between the salon and the sheriff's office.

Jack went directly to the vicar's wife. "Mrs. Bartleby," he said in an unusually meek voice, "you have to go outside. I'm sorry. There's been an . . . accident."

"An accident! Oh, my!" Mrs. Bartleby's eyes grew very wide behind her rimless spectacles. "Nothing serious, I hope?" When there was no answer, she put a hand to the lapels of her drab brown raincoat. "Is it one of ours? Should I call Regis? Shall I . . ." Her high voice trailed off.

Stella had come back into the salon, without Milo. She rushed over to Mrs. Bartleby. "I'm afraid we'll have to reschedule. Could you call us later today?"

Mrs. Bartleby had glimpsed Laurie, still standing by the shampoo bowl, wearing her bovine expression. "But Laurie looks . . . as usual. My appointment is with her. It's a standing Monday. But of course you know that." She gave Stella a gently reproving look. "The rest of the week is so . . ." Again, the words faded away.

Putting a firm hand on Mrs. Bartleby's arm, Stella steered her out of the shop. "It's nothing for you to worry about, Mrs. Bartleby." Still soothing, Stella left her puzzled client outside just as a few flakes of snow began to fall.

"Laurie, start calling our three o'clocks," Stella ordered, as she drew the shade on the door and turned the CLOSED sign to the street. "The rest of them, too, I suppose." Her sixty-year-old face suddenly showed its age; even her usually firm body sagged. "Oh, my God, this is awful!" Shielded now from onlookers, Stella collapsed in the chair next to Becca. I moved out of the way.

Becca's tears had dwindled into sniveling. Laurie had wandered to the phone, but appeared to be having problems coping with the appointment book. Feeling useless, I paced around the display stand with its products that promised eternal youth, beauty, and hair to die for.

The fleeting phrase made me feel queasy all over again. But I had to keep in control. There was work to be done. I turned to Becca.

"Where were you? I mean, while your client was in the facial room alone?"

Becca looked at me with a blotchy face and reddened eyes. "I'd put the hydrating mask on, so I went down to the Burger Barn to get a Coke." She stared at me as if I were a circus freak.

"Ms. Lord owns the newspaper," Stella said, to give me credentials. "Do you remember Ms. Runkel?"

Becca did. Everyone remembered Ms. Runkel. Vida is a big woman, in many ways. At sixty-plus, she is tall, broad-shouldered, and full-busted. Her commanding presence has been known to make grown men weep and strong women cringe. Alfred Cobb, one of our three county commissioners and a Purple Heart hero of World War II, once said of her that "I'd sure as hell rather get run down by Vida's Buick than get hit by her hooters. If she'd been with me at Bastogne, we could have taken out a Panzer division between us." I love Vida dearly, but upon occasion, she still overwhelms me.

"Ms. Lord works for her," Stella said, then realized her slip, and flushed. "I mean, Ms. Runkel works for Ms. Lord." The mistake was easy to make. Sometimes I couldn't tell the difference, either.

"Oh—right." Becca managed to come up with a ghost of a smile. "The mask takes fifteen minutes," she explained. "I always leave the room, because my clients need the quiet time to relax and maybe even nap. Stella doesn't mind if I run out to get pop or something from the Upper Crust Bakery." There was a defensive note in Becca's voice as she looked at her employer for confirmation.

"That's right," Stella asserted as a siren wailed in the distance. "Becca doesn't always take a regular lunch break. She's already built up quite a clientele, since we're the only salon offering facials from here to Sultan."

In a way, I was surprised by Becca's success. Alpine's economy was still in a slump. As a typical Northwest logging community, the environmentalists had had their way with the timber industry. The result was out-of-work loggers, impoverished families, and an impending sense of doom. Federal programs had been offered to retrain the displaced workers, but logging is a vocation almost as ingrained as a religious calling. By the 1990s, fourth- and fifth-generation woodsmen found themselves not only without a job, but torn from tradition. The only bright spot on the horizon was the proposed construction of a community college.

"So the original appointment was made for Honoria Whitman?" I asked, discreetly taking a notebook out of my purse. Somewhere, in the rear of the building, I could hear a series of noises. Doc Dewey and the ambulance had probably arrived.

Stella answered for Becca. "That's right. Honoria called this morning. She doesn't usually come here, you know. It's easier for her to go to Sultan or even Monroe to get her hair cut. But she wanted to try the facial."

Honoria's choice struck me as odd. It was likely that her regular hairdresser, either in Sultan or Monroe, would provide facials. Why drive an extra twenty miles to Alpine?

I was about to ask that question when the front door to Stella's Styling Salon shook, rattled, and rolled. Stella, Becca and I all jumped. Even Laurie, who was still trying to cope with the appointments, seemed startled.

The glass in the door threatened to shatter. Stella was on her feet, but before she could reach the front of the salon, a voice reverberated from outside.

"Yoo-hoo! Yoo-hoo-hoo! Are you there? Open up, please! It's me—Vida Runkel!"

Stella obeyed. She could hardly do otherwise. My House & Home editor had spoken, and in Alpine, her word was law.

"Half the town is outside, gawking and freezing to death," Vida declared after we had informed her what was going on. Not that she needed informing—having heard the ambulance siren, Vida had rushed to the sheriff's office. Bill Blatt, another deputy who is also her nephew, had sketchily filled her in. "Really, people are such ghouls! From what I hear, this poor dead woman isn't even from Alpine!" Vida made it sound as if the death of a nonresident couldn't possibly count in any official census.

"It's Honoria's sister-in-law," I said, surprising myself with the note of apology in my voice.

Vida bristled. "I didn't know Honoria had a sister-in-law! Really, now! Why is she so secretive? Is it because she's from California?"

"Her brother's here, too," I noted. "Did you see them at the sheriff's office?"

Under the brim of her blue derby, Vida rolled her eyes. "They're being held incommunicado. Jack Mullins sent them into Milo's office until all this is sorted out." She lowered her voice and shot me a conspiratorial look. "Is this the brother who was in jail for you-know-what?"

I blinked. "I don't know. Honoria could have ten brothers. Whoever it is must be visiting. I haven't heard anything about it from Milo."

Vida snorted. "Maybe Milo didn't know. He and Honoria haven't been quite as cozy as they used to be. Or so I've been led to believe." From behind her big tortoiseshell framed glasses, Vida gave me her gimlet eye.

I felt the color rise in my cheeks. "The romance is a little rocky," I admitted.

There was no opportunity for Vida to expand on her remark. Jack Mullins reappeared from the rear of the salon. He was looking official—until he saw Vida. I knew he was about to ask her how she had gotten inside the shop. But of course he thought better of it, and zeroed in on Stella.

"Sheriff Dodge is still with Doc and the body," Jack said, running a hand through his short red hair. "We've got quite a crowd out back on Pine Street, including Janet Driggers, who is yelling her head off."

Janet was the wife of the local undertaker. A brassy, ribald woman, she worked part-time at Sky Travel, which was also located in the Clemans Building. I marveled that she, too, hadn't tried to barge through Stella's front door.

"So," Jack went on, "would you prefer to come over to the sheriff's office, or stay here?"

Stella drew back in the chair. "For what?"

"Questioning," Jack replied. Seeing Stella bridle, he offered her a placating smile. "It's just routine. We have to take statements. You, too, Emma," he added, glancing in my direction.

Stella sighed, then heaved herself out of the chair. "All

right. I'd rather do it across the street. Laurie, are you finished with your calls?"

Laurie wasn't. She couldn't reach Dot Parker or Lois
Hutchins. Neither had answering machines. What should
she do? Her helplessness was almost touching.

Stella ruffled her dyed blond locks with an agitated
hand. "Try again from the sheriff's. Let's get this over
with. I want to go home and have about four martinis."

"I don't drink martinis," Laurie protested.

"I don't care," Stella said abruptly. "Good God, what's
Richie going to think?"

Among other things, Richie Magruder was Stella's
husband and the deputy mayor. The latter title was
mostly honorary, except when the real mayor, Fuzzy
Baugh, was out of town or suffering from a heart attack
or in the bag. Dutifully, I followed Stella and Jack out of
the salon. The snow was now coming down hard, which
was just as well, because it apparently had sent most of
the curious onlookers scurrying for cover.

We trudged across Front Street, with Becca and Laurie
bringing up the rear. Once inside the sheriff's office, Jack
turned to Vida.

"Ah . . . Ms. Runkel, we don't need to question you.
You weren't involved in finding the body or on the
premises at the time of the murder."

Vida nodded sagely. "So it is murder, then?" She
nodded again.

"What I'm saying," Jack went on after clearing his
throat, "is that . . . well . . . you don't need to be here."

Vida smiled blandly. "But I do. This is news."

"Emma—Ms. Lord—is already here," Jack pointed out.

Vida's smile was ingenuous. "Of course she is. But
she can't be objective." Her gray eyes raked Jack, then
landed on me. "She found the body. She could be a

suspect. I'll be handling this story." Her smile turned into a simper. "Isn't that right, Ms. Lord?"

Even I never argued with Vida.

The previous year, Skykomish County had passed a bond issue for renovations to the sheriff's office, along with additional equipment and a much-needed deputy. While I had aggressively pushed the proposition from its inception, I hadn't been optimistic. There were too many families living in borderline poverty and too much concern over jobs to squeeze extra monies out of the taxpayers. But local residents had risen to the occasion and voted yes in a close election. Construction had begun in May, with completion by September 1. The usual delays and obstacles had pushed the date to mid-November. Now Milo Dodge had expanded office space, more secure jail facilities, an updated computer system, a fulltime receptionist, and the extra deputy. Dustin Fong had joined the Skykomish force the previous spring, and was slowly but surely easing into the job. As an emigré from Seattle, he was considered a bit strange; as an Asian-American, he was definitely labeled exotic. But like all nonnative Alpiners, including me, he would try to meld with the rest of the community. So far, he seemed to be achieving his goal with quiet determination.

Dustin had been given the task of keeping Honoria Whitman and her brother from going nuts. While they awaited official news, the duo had stayed in Milo's office, drinking coffee and asking unanswerable questions. By the time the rest of us arrived from Stella's Styling Salon, the Whitmans had guessed the worst. They knew something terrible had happened to Kay, but they weren't sure what or how or why.

The salon group was taken one by one into the sheriff's new interrogation room. This was a more formal, officially intimidating area, but it didn't spare us from Milo's swill-like coffee. I passed. The truth was, like Stella, I would have preferred a drink. Or at least a soda from the Burger Barn. I've never understood Americans' dependence on coffee or the British reliance on tea in times of crisis. Installing a brandy machine would be more helpful.

Having discovered the body, I was the first to be questioned. Jack Mullins had been assigned to the task, at least temporarily. We hadn't gotten past the time of my appointment when Milo entered the room. He looked disconcerted and immediately lighted a cigarette. Jack made his exit, with a self-deprecating nod for me.

The sheriff glanced at Jack's brief notes. "Okay," Milo said with a sigh, "you got there a little after two. What happened next?"

I told him. It didn't take long. My gaze kept falling on Milo's cigarette. He had been responsible—thus I rationalized—for my resumption of smoking over a year ago. But I'd managed to quit—again—the previous summer. Now I was beginning to think that had been a bad idea.

"You didn't see anybody in the corridor?" Milo asked, exhaling a small blue cloud.

"No." For the first time I considered the corridor itself. "I'm not even sure where it goes. I've used the women's room a couple of times when I've been at Stella's, but I never paid much attention to the rest of the building's rear area."

Having gotten control of himself, Milo was now very much the no-nonsense law officer. "It runs the width of the building," he explained without inflection. "There's a men's room at the other end, by Sky Travel. The fire exit is used for deliveries. All the first-floor tenants have direct access to the back corridor except for the optician on the corner. They have to go around through the travel agency."

I pictured the Clemans Building floor plan in my mind. The building was old, and named for the town founder, Carl Clemans. Its three stories included Stella's, Sky Travel, and the optician, all of which faced Front Street. The local medical supply store was at the rear, with its entrance on the side street. In the center of the structure was a small foyer, an elevator, and a staircase. The second floor was occupied by the Doukas law firm, an architect, and an accountant. The third and top story housed several small offices, including a loan company, an environmentalist group, a consignment shop, and an antiques store.

I had a question of my own for Milo. "Are you saying anybody could have come in off the street and gone through the back way to get to the facial room?"

Milo shook his head. "No. That's kept locked, except for deliveries. Whenever UPS or whoever comes by, they have to buzz from a box on Pine Street. The tenant getting the delivery comes to unlock the door. I had to ask Will Stuart at the medical supply place to let Doc Dewey and the ambulance drivers in."

Almost unconsciously, I made the connection: Will Stuart was Nancy Dewey's brother. He had owned Alpine Medical Supply almost as long as Nancy's husband had practiced medicine in Alpine. It was a fortuitous arrangement, especially for Doc Dewey and his brother-in-law. It was also profitable in an area where many loggers had lost more than their jobs over the years. Even strangers unfamiliar with Pacific Northwest lifestyles can tell they're in a timber town by the number of men with missing digits and limbs.

"You're certain she was dead when you opened the door?" Milo inquired on a cloud of smoke.

"I didn't take her pulse. Jeez, Milo, she was limp as a rag. . . ." I paused, vividly recalling Kay Whitman's bloodied body.

"You didn't touch her?" Milo's hazel eyes were fixed on my face.

I winced. "I sure didn't. I got as far as the threshold. I was looking straight at her. Her head was propped up on a pillow or something. It didn't take long to see that her throat had been cut and . . ." I shook myself, trying to erase the awful picture from my mind's eye.

"Did you see anyone at all—somebody who didn't belong in the building?" Milo's expression was even more stolid than usual.

"No." I knew the sheriff had to go by the book, but his attitude annoyed me. "If I had, wouldn't I have said so?"

Puffing on his cigarette, Milo shrugged. "Witnesses get hysterical. They don't always remember what they've seen. Or else they think it isn't important."

I leaned across the almost new pine table. "Milo—it's me, Emma. Not some dizzy goof like Laurie or maybe Becca. Perception is part of my job."

"You're still a witness." Milo's expression was inscrutable.

"I've told you everything I know," I said, trying not to sound testy. "Why don't you tell me about the weapon?"

"What's to tell?" Milo stubbed out his cigarette with great care. "We don't know anything about the weapon yet. I can only tell you that it was sharp." A glint of irony showed in the sheriff's hazel eyes.

"No kidding." I wasn't amused. "That rules out an emery board or an orange stick, I suppose."

Milo frowned. "What's an orange stick?"

"Never mind. Get a manicure someday. Then you'll find out."

Glancing at his reasonably well-kept nails, Milo made

a face. "What's wrong with clippers?" he muttered, then resumed his official attitude. "Did you go into the women's room?"

"No, I never intended to. I was heading for the changing room."

"Did you go in there?"

"No. I found the body first. What would you expect me to do—walk away, change into a smock, and have Stella tend to my tresses while another client is lying dead in the back room?" Now my tone was definitely sarcastic. " 'Oh, by the way, Stella,' " I said, mimicking myself, " 'did you know there's a stiff on the facial table? I wouldn't try pushing that neck-firming cream you're selling out front if I were you.' "

"That's not funny." Milo had turned severe. "Did you recognize the victim?"

"I don't know the victim," I answered, no longer caring if I sounded waspish. Noting that Milo's color was deepening, and aware that it signaled an impending outburst, I tried to simmer down. "Frankly, it would be impossible to recognize anybody—even if I knew them—when they're all covered with goop and wrapped like a mummy."

"That's what I figured." The color was still in Milo's face, but he didn't sound angry. In fact, his words were leaden. Watching him closely, I could see the worry in his eyes. Indeed, his attitude seemed to verge on fear.

Suddenly I knew what the sheriff was thinking. But before I could say so, he spoke again:

"Honoria and her brother stopped by to inspect our new quarters. She mentioned that her sister-in-law had taken her appointment at Stella's." Milo's voice began to drag. "My point is that the victim was unrecognizable. So did the killer make a mistake?"

I waited for Milo to continue. But either he wouldn't—

or he couldn't. Still, I knew what he meant and why he looked so troubled. At the last minute Kay Whitman had taken her sister-in-law's appointment. If the murder was premeditated, the killer might not have known of the change. Under all that cosmetic camouflage, he or she wouldn't have been able to tell one Whitman from another.

Maybe Honoria shouldn't have been drinking Milo's bad coffee in the sheriff's office down the hall. Maybe someone had intended to put her in the hospital morgue instead.

Chapter Two

VIDA WAS SO angry that she sat on her derby. We had finally returned to *The Advocate* around three-thirty. When Milo was finished questioning me, he insisted that Vida and I both leave. Naturally, we protested, arguing our rights as members of the press. But Milo was firm—we couldn't sit in on the interrogations, we weren't allowed to disturb Honoria and her brother, and we were in the way. Whatever hard news came out of the initial interviews would be passed on to *The Advocate* in plenty of time for our Tuesday-afternoon deadline.

I'll admit that it wasn't easy for me to concentrate. I've covered my share of homicides, both in Alpine and during my sixteen years with *The Oregonian*. When I first started on the metro beat in Portland, a veteran reporter told me never to think of the victim by name. You can't take any kind of personal interest in the deceased, he'd advised. He always referred to the dead person as The Stiff. But I'd never quite been able to dissociate myself. This time it was even harder. I didn't know Kay Whitman, but I knew her sister-in-law and I'd found her body. Nevertheless, we had a paper to put out. When Vida returned to the office, I considered reminding her that we had other things to do in order to meet our Tuesday deadline.

Vida, however, was in no mood to be diverted. She

had stomped back to the office in her splay-footed manner, banged the door open, removed her derby, flung it across the room, where it landed on her chair—and then sat on her hat. The crushed felt object that now reposed in her hands curbed her temper. But she was still indignant.

"Imagine! My own nephew, Billy, sitting right there guarding the door to Honoria and her brother, Whoozits! Whatever is the matter with Milo? Ooooooh!" Vida dumped the crumpled derby under her desk, whipped off her glasses, and began to rub violently at her eyes.

My ad manager, Leo Walsh, came into the news office with a folder of promotional mock-ups cradled in his arms. Taking in Vida's distress, he grinned.

"What's wrong, Duchess? Has the Burl Creek Thimble Club been unmasked as a front for hookers?"

Vida was not amused, either by the nickname or the remark. "Where have you been, Leo?" she demanded. "You've no right to behave in such a flippant manner when someone has been brutally murdered two blocks away from this very office."

Leo's seamed face registered disbelief. "What are you talking about? I've been doing the car lots on the other side of town. We've got Presidents' Day promotions coming up, remember?"

"Of course I remember," Vida snapped. "I can even remember when we celebrated our presidents' birthdays separately."

"You can probably remember the presidents," Leo quipped. Seeing the fire flare in Vida's eyes, he quickly backtracked. "I mean, which ones we honor, Washington and Lincoln. Most younger people—kids, that is—think it's a generic holiday, for all the presidents." Leo was speaking faster and faster, obviously trying to save himself from Vida's wrath. "You know—like All Saints. But they don't know what that is, either. And you're a Presbyterian anyway." Now virtually mumbling, he went to his desk, where he opened the big folder and began studying his vehicle ads. "I got the trucking place, too," he said in a more normal voice. "The trouble is, who's going to buy those secondhand logging rigs these days?"

"Vida's not kidding," I said, sitting on the edge of Leo's desk. "A woman got her throat slit at Stella's Salon this afternoon."

Leo was absorbed in his layouts. "Is that a new service? Eye tucks, boob jobs, putting hot wax all over yourselves, so you feel like a freaking eel. What does this one do, get rid of the turkey wattle? You women have the damnedest things done to your—" His head shot up and he stared at me with his world-weary brown eyes. "Shit! You're not kidding! Who was it?"

I started to explain, but Carla Steinmetz breezed into the office before I could get out more than two words. Unlike Leo, my reporter obviously had been someplace in town where the news of Kay Whitman's death had already been received. To my amazement, Carla didn't start with a barrage of questions. Instead, she shrieked, flew across the office, and hurled herself at me with such force that I almost fell on top of Leo's ads.

"Emma! I thought it was you! Emma! You're alive! Emma, Emma, *Emma*!"

Carla's concern was flattering, but she was smothering me. Gently, I pried her loose. "It was Kay Whitman," I said. "Honoria Whitman's sister-in-law. I gather that Kay and Honoria's brother are visiting from somewhere."

Both Carla and Leo looked blank. My reporter was the first to recall Honoria. "Oh!" she exclaimed, brushing the long black hair off her pretty face. "The sheriff's main squeeze! I know her."

"The sheriff's occasional squeeze—if you'll pardon

the rather crude term," Vida put in with a sharp glance for me. "I don't believe that their romance is flourishing as it once was."

"They've had some problems," I conceded, avoiding Vida's gaze. "But that's not important now. We've got a homicide story on our hands."

Vida and I explained what had happened at the salon. My ad manager and my reporter were sobered by the news. Leo held his head in his hands, cursing a world gone mad.

"It's never been sane," Vida remarked with some asperity. "You ought to know, Leo. You're from Los Angeles."

For once, Leo didn't take the bait. Instead, he concentrated on a photo of a 1974 Kenworth logging rig.

Carla, however, was watching me expectantly. She is eager to please, and sometimes does. But as a journalist, she is a better photographer than a reporter.

In the recent past Carla had chided me about not giving her meatier assignments. Back in October, I'd caved in and assigned her to a public hearing on giving Skykomish County property owners more control over federal lands. The issue was relatively complicated, and I couldn't blame Carla for being confused. But when one speaker referred to environmentalists as Mafia enforcers and another labeled bureaucrats as Nazis, Carla's story took off on a tangent. By the time she was done, it sounded as if the Godfather and Adolf Hitler had moved to Alpine.

Thus, I wasn't about to give Carla the Kay Whitman homicide assignment. Nor did I have much choice. Vida was clearing her throat loudly at the corner desk.

"You promised," she said with a wag of her finger.

"But, Vida, you never do hard news," I protested. "I

didn't argue at Stella's because everything was in such
confusion."

Vida had resurrected her derby and was making an
unsatisfactory effort to block the crown. "It's not up to
me to tell you how to run your newspaper, but it's quite
clear that you can't cover this story."

"Why not?" I was mildly annoyed. Vida may presume,
but she is never presumptuous. "Just because I found the
body . . ."

"I don't mean that." Vida dusted off the derby, which
remained sadly misshapen. She had put her glasses back
on and now gazed at me over the tortoiseshell rims. "I
mean you and Milo. His girlfriend is involved. *One* of his
girlfriends. It seems to me that your coverage of the
investigation would be unethical. Under the circumstances." Vida jammed the mangled hat back on her head.

In my office cubbyhole, I quietly fumed. Milo Dodge
and I were not a romantic item. We never had been. Over
the years we'd become good friends, and a couple of
kisses had resulted. Admittedly, in the past few months,
as I sorted through my feelings for Tom Cavanaugh and
Milo wrestled with his for Honoria Whitman, we had
grown closer. In fact, I'd finally confided the whole story
of my relationship with Tom. Milo had responded with
the details of his broken first marriage, and his current
problems with Honoria. We'd given each other a shoulder to cry on, but not much else.

Maybe we had been spending more time together. But
we'd always gone out to lunch and dinner and for drinks.
Sometimes I invited Milo to my place for a meal, alone,
or with others. He and his three grown children had spent
Thanksgiving and Christmas with me, along with my
son, Adam, and my brother, Ben, and a few other guests.
Upon reflection, I realized that instead of the once-a-

month dinner *à deux,* Milo and I had been eating together a couple of times a week. The frequency hadn't occurred to me until now. But if anyone had noticed, it would be Vida.

That didn't mean that Milo and I were in love. What we were trying to figure out was if we were out of love—with other people. Neither the sheriff nor I was prone to impulsiveness. I had always considered Milo a plodding sort. I was more generous in describing myself, calling it caution.

Thus, Vida's comments nettled. I trusted her to handle the murder story, though the assignment really wasn't fair to Carla.

And Carla was quick to tell me so. Five minutes after I went into my office, she came in and asked if she could close the door. That request from a staff member usually meant trouble.

"Look, Carla," I said after she had stated her case, "you're doing double duty as it is with Ginny gone on her honeymoon." Our office manager, Ginny Burmeister, had become Mrs. Rick Erlandson the previous Saturday night. The newlyweds had flown to Hawaii for a week. Carla had been saddled with covering the front office for her close friend and coworker.

"This is Monday," Carla said, raking a hand through her hair. "Ginny will be back a week from tomorrow because you gave her Presidents' Day which the rest of us don't get but I don't mind because you pay us overtime."

"Which," I interjected, "means you're getting overtime on the holiday for both your job and Ginny's."

Carla nodded. "Right, that's great. But once we get this week's edition out, all I really have to do is answer the phones and take a few classified and personals ads. Ginny can do the rest when she gets back."

There was some truth in Carla's words. But I wasn't going to let her cover the murder story. I was sufficiently piqued at not doing it myself. As far as I was concerned, Vida and I still hadn't played our final inning in that journalistic game.

"What about that tip we got from Cal Vickers about the big new house that's being built along the Skykomish River on the other side of Index?" Cal, the owner of the local Texaco station, had called me Monday morning about what looked like the foundation of an elaborate residence. He had come across it while on a fruitless steelheading expedition.

"I'll call the county this week to see who's applied for a permit," Carla replied, pouting. "That's no big whoop. It's probably some commuter place or a summer cabin. I want something with meat in it for a change."

Carla had forced my hand. "The fact is," I said, "I do need you for something else. I've decided to go ahead and reopen the back shop." It was only a small lie, since the plan had been festering in my brain for almost a year. "We won't print the paper here, at least not at first. But we can do desktop printing. Look what Ginny had to pay for her wedding invitations. I'm sure we could offer better prices. I'd like you and Ginny to be in charge. You can start by checking out what kind of equipment we'll need."

Carla brightened. "Computers? Desktop? Wow! I'd like that! Ginny will, too, I bet."

In all honesty, the idea was long overdue. The back shop had lain idle ever since I'd taken over *The Advocate* six years earlier. The space was used only for storage, and wasn't earning us a dime.

My inspiration not only buoyed Carla's spirits, but galvanized me as well. I'd procrastinated too long. As

Carla left my office, I silently thanked her for goading me into action.

I goaded myself into work. My editorial on a new bridge over the Skykomish River was ready to roll, as was most of the front page. But now I had to consider the space that would be allotted to the homicide story. The phones had been ringing ever since Vida and I returned from the sheriff's office. I wasn't used to not having Ginny there to answer them. No doubt there were two dozen irate subscriber messages on the voice mail that we ordinarily used only on weekends and after hours.

When I went back into the news office, Vida was gone. Leo informed me that she was lurking outside the sheriff's office. I nodded. That was good. Maybe Vida would worm something out of Milo or Bill Blatt before the end of the business day.

As it turned out, Vida wormed Honoria and her brother into *The Advocate*. Just after four-thirty, the trio arrived, with Honoria's wheelchair gliding across the threshold.

"I couldn't let these poor people go back to Startup without a few comforting words," Vida said. "They've had a terrible afternoon."

The Whitman siblings' demeanor attested to the fact. Honoria's customary self-possession was badly shaken. Her fine features seemed strained and her short ash-blonde coiffure had lost its flair. Everything about Honoria seemed different, including her lack of vitality, her tailored clothes, her wheelchair. She greeted me with a pathetic smile and an outstretched hand that somehow struck me as clawlike instead of graceful.

"Emma!" she said in her low voice. "It's been some time since I've seen you. And now, like this . . ." Her hand fell away into her lap.

The man who stood behind her wheelchair bore a

passing resemblance to his sister. He, too, was fair, though there was gray at his temples and he was beginning to bald. The bone structure might have been as aristocratic as Honoria's, but there was too much flesh on the face. Trevor Whitman looked puffy, and his color was poor. Prison pallor, I thought fleetingly, and offered my hand as Honoria introduced us.

"I'm terribly sorry for your loss," I said, the trite words sounding typically inadequate.

Trevor Whitman didn't respond. For an awkward moment, the only sound in the editorial office was the distant wail of the Burlington-Northern, slowing as it passed through town on its way to Seattle.

Trevor finally transferred an Alpine Medical shopping bag to his left hand and shook his head several times. Then he reached out to shake my hand. And shake it until I felt my arm would fall off. The shopping bag bounced weightlessly at his side as he stared somewhere past my right ear. After another strained pause, I gently squeezed his fingers. He still didn't let go. I had the impression that he was utterly dazed.

I turned to Honoria. "How are you going to get home?" In times of tragedy, I embrace mundane matters. It's easier that way.

"My car's here." Honoria paused; Trevor finally released my hand. I had seen Honoria's car parked in the space reserved for handicapped persons outside the sheriff's office. The Nissan sedan was specially rigged for her needs and also had been equipped with snow tires for winter in the Cascade Mountains. "We should leave right away, before the snow gets too heavy. Mother's all alone at my house."

Vida made a sympathetic noise. "Your poor mother! I didn't realize she was visiting you, too. You've talked to her, I assume?"

Honoria nodded. "But only about twenty minutes ago. We had to wait and wait for official word, and then we debated about whether to phone or tell her in person. It was snowing so hard for a while that we thought we'd have to put the chains on. It was even possible that we couldn't leave at all because Milo needed us to make arrangements or . . ." Her voice trickled off.

Vida was awash with compassion. "Then you must be off. My goodness, I didn't realize you had such a houseful! You should have told us about your company!" In any other context except this grief-stricken atmosphere, I would have taken Vida's words for reproach. But she went on, oozing comfort. "If there's anything we can do, let us know. Remember, Honoria, we're all your friends here in Alpine."

Honoria started to offer Vida another pathetic smile, but then her thin mouth abruptly turned down. "Not everyone," she said grimly.

Honoria didn't need to remind us that somebody in Alpine had killed her sister-in-law. Maybe that somebody had meant to kill her. Still without saying a word, Trevor Whitman pushed his sister out into the cold, darkening late afternoon.

At five-oh-five, the lights were still on at Stella's Styling Salon. Carla had relayed the information before leaving work. *The Advocate* is located across Front Street and two full blocks east of the Clemans Building. We couldn't see the storefronts from that distance, so Vida had sent Carla on a brief scouting expedition.

"That's good," Vida said after Carla had made her final exit. Leo had also left for the day. "I'll stop by Stella's on my way home." She began to gather up her belongings.

So did I. "You're not going without me," I declared, shrugging into my duffel coat.

Vida didn't protest. She had often tagged along with me on important stories, and usually I was glad that she did. My House & Home editor had a way with her when it came to eliciting even the most intimate confidences. Sometimes she badgered, sometimes she cajoled, sometimes she exuded almost saintly sympathy. Whatever the ploy, it was rare that she didn't find out what she wanted to know.

The snow had stopped, but a thin layer covered the ground and the rooftops. Alpine is nestled in the Cascade Mountains at the three-thousand-foot level, which means that winter lasts almost half the year. The town climbs up Tonga Ridge, its man-made roosts looking awkward in full sunlight, but melding into the trees under rain and snow. Mount Baldy's twin crests brood over the Sky-komish River Valley, the snow line marking time with the seasons.

Mining brought the first outsiders to the area, back before the turn of the century. The whistle-stop on the Great Northern Railroad was known as Nippon until Carl Clemans came from Snohomish to build a logging camp. He renamed the site Alpine, built a mill and another camp, and eventually erected small houses for the families who wanted to join their husbands and fathers in the woods.

The original mill had been shut down by Clemans in 1929, after the timber harvest was complete. When the mountainsides were scarred and shorn, there was talk of abandoning Alpine, of letting nature reclaim its own. But Vida's father-in-law and some enterprising Norwegians had spared the cluster of family cabins and fledgling enterprises by putting up a ski lodge. As the second-growth forest matured, new mills had sprung up. But

now, with the threat to the spotted owl and other endangered species, the timber industry was once again suffering death pangs. Only one sawmill remained, though
the ski lodge continued to flourish, especially during the
winter. A surge of commuters in the past decade had
helped keep the town's heart beating, and now the proposed community college promised to inject new blood.

Unfortunately, it was Kay Whitman's blood that com-
manded my attention after Stella let Vida and me into the
salon. She was alone, isolated behind crime-scene tape.

"Milo said I could come in to close up, as long as I
didn't touch anything except the counter stuff." Stella
grimaced. "I've canceled the morning appointments.
Even after all the money we sank into that bond issue,
Milo can't handle a homicide. He still has to ask for help
from Snohomish County."

The sheriff's expanded facilities included a small lab
and funding for a part-time forensics pathologist. Kay
Whitman's death was the first murder in Skykomish
County since the renovation had been completed. It
appeared that Milo still had to rely on Everett, which was
the seat of our neighboring county. Situated some fifty
miles away, SnoCo personnel were naturally not inclined
to give SkyCo problems priority. That was understandable, if distressing.

"Who'll want to do business here after all this?" Stella
demanded, waving a hand at the rear of the salon. "I've
spent over thirty years working my butt off in this town.
What do you bet they'll turn on me like snakes?"

I couldn't answer Stella's question. But Vida gave it
a try.

"Nonsense, Stella. Women aren't like that. If they're
satisfied with the way you cut their hair or give them a
permanent or do their nails, they'll still come here. It's
too far to drive to another salon, especially in bad

weather. In fact," Vida added slyly, "they'll probably line up for facials, just to see where the murder
occurred."

Stella eyed Vida with disbelief, but a hint of amusement tugged at her full mouth. "Vida, you're a ghoul."

"Perhaps." Vida shrugged. "Most people are. That's
why your business won't suffer. Be glad of it."

It seemed that Stella had been about to leave when we
arrived. "The sheriff wants me out of here," she said,
putting a zippered money bag into a woven satchel. "Is this
an official visit, or did you just come to commiserate?"

"Both," Vida replied.

"In that case," Stella said, "walk with me to the bank.
They're closed, so I'll make a night deposit. Then we can
go over to the Venison Inn and talk. I sure could use a
drink."

Stella turned heads in the bar of the Venison Inn. For
different reasons, so did Vida, who rarely frequented the
nondining area of the restaurant. The owner and bartender, Oren Rhodes, hurried to our small, round table to
take our orders and to offer his sympathy to Stella.

"That's the trouble with out-of-towners," Oren said,
leaning confidentially against Stella's chair. "They show
up in town, and the next thing you know—whammo!
There's trouble. Is it true that this woman came from
California?"

California had become a dirty word to a lot of Wash-
ingtonians, but I didn't number myself among them. I'd
hired a Californian in the form of Leo Walsh. The father
of my son lived in California. I'd always enjoyed Dis-
neyland, and it was in California. I rolled my eyes at
Vida as Stella informed Oren that she wasn't sure where
Ms. Whitman was from, but could he please hustle his
butt and get her a double martini?

Oren complied. I'd ordered a bourbon and water; Vida primly asked for a glass of shooting sherry. The other customers in the dimly lit and unatmospheric bar were again absorbed in their drinks, their conversations, and themselves.

"You understand," Vida began in a serious voice, "that we have a deadline of tomorrow afternoon." Stella nodded. She knew about deadlines because of the weekly ad she ran in *The Advocate*. "Milo may not release details until it's too late for us to print them. I—Emma and I— would like to hear your version before we get something distorted or not at all."

Stella fingered her unnaturally golden curls. "Okay, like what?"

Vida rested her cheek on one hand. "Well . . . *like,* as you put it, the basic facts. When did Honoria call to make her appointment?"

"Saturday." Stella's answer was prompt. "Late morning. I took the call myself, in between Shirley Bronsky and Darla Puckett. I was surprised, because this is only about the second time—Honoria, is it? That's a weird name, if you ask me—that Honoria's come to us. She said she wanted to try the facial. I wasn't even sure who she was until she gave me her phone number and I realized the prefix was in Startup."

Vida never took notes. Her memory was as comprehensive as it was infallible. "Did she mention her guests?" Vida asked.

Our drinks arrived. Oren tried to linger, but the silence enforced by Vida sent him back to the bar.

"Her guests?" Stella repeated the question after taking a deep sip of her martini. "No. She didn't say anything except that she wanted a facial. She'd heard it was something new that we offered. She sounded like a very fussy person, the kind of client who asks a million questions.

Product ingredients, deep-cleansing methods, how much of this is used, how long does that take, is this person you've hired trained, are you sure your cosmetics don't contain animal fats or the fur off some monkey's behind? People are getting too damned wrapped up in all this environmental stuff. Look what it's done to this town." Stella took another big gulp.

"But Honoria changed the appointment later." Vida daintily quaffed a drop of sherry.

"This afternoon. Well," Stella amended, "just before noon, actually. Laurie took that call. Honoria asked if it was all right if her sister-in-law came instead of her. I guess Honoria had changed her mind. Laurie said yes."

The tone of Stella's voice indicated that Laurie probably said yes to everything, including war, pillage, and pestilence. The double martini was half-gone. Stella turned toward the bar and jerked her head at Oren. I hoped he didn't assume we all wanted a second round. I was trying to concentrate. Unlike Vida's, my memory isn't perfect.

"Now, that's very odd," Vida was saying as she tipped her rumpled derby off her forehead. "You either want to have a facial or you don't. Why would Honoria substitute her sister-in-law?"

Stella uttered a little laugh. "I don't know. It doesn't matter to me as long as it's not a cancellation. Honoria, Kay, Queen Elizabeth—it's still twenty-five bucks."

Vida was looking thoughtful. "Did Becca know the difference? Between Honoria and Kay, that is to say."

Oren had appeared with Stella's second drink. She asked if he was running a tab. He said he was. Vida and I both protested, but Stella waved her perfectly mani-cured hand.

"My treat. Or bribe." She turned to me. "You still need a haircut, Emma." Then she looked back at Vida. "Becca didn't know either of them. Hey, Vida, what happened to your hat?" Stella giggled. The first double was taking effect.

"Never mind," Vida snapped. "Tell me this, Stella— did you have any calls or did anyone come in to inquire about either of the Whitman women's appointment?"

Stella started to giggle again, apparently thought better of it, and suddenly sobered. "You know, that's a strange question. Milo asked me the same thing. Laurie said somebody did call while I was out to lunch. Around one, maybe. I forgot about that because I wasn't there."

Vida had stiffened in her chair. I felt myself tense, too, as I found my voice before Vida did. "What did this caller want?" I asked.

Stella had set aside the empty glass and was drinking from the fresh martini. "I'm not sure," she replied after taking a swallow. "You know Laurie—she's kind of spacey. I guess he just wanted to make sure that Ms. Whitman had an appointment."

" 'He'?" Vida pounced on the pronoun.

Even in her alcohol-induced haze, Stella seemed to understand the significance of the question. "That's right, it was a man. As I said, I didn't think much about it at the time. I suppose it was because I figured he was picking her up or something."

"Picking up who?" Vida was leaning into the table, her bust brushing the sherry glass.

Stella shot Vida a hostile look. "Who? What do you mean 'who'? The Whitman facial, who else? Oh!" Suddenly Stella looked chagrined. "You mean which Whitman! My God, I never . . . Damn!" She stared at the olive floating in her drink.

"Did Laurie recognize the man's voice?" I asked, hoping to divert Stella from her self-reproach.

But the hairdresser shook her head, slowly, sadly. "I don't know. You'll have to ask Laurie."

That sounded like an impossible task. But I could tell from the set of Vida's jaw that she was up to it. It looked as if it was going to be a long Monday night.

Chapter Three

LAURIE MARSHALL STILL lived with her parents. I found it embarrassing to discover that I knew so little about the young woman I'd seen at Stella's for the past five years. Vida, of course, had the knowledge tucked inside her omniscient brain. Laurie was approximately twenty-five, had attended beauty school in Everett, and had been engaged twice, but never married. Her parents lived on Cascade Street across from the middle school. Her father, Martin Marshall, owned Tonga Sales and Rental, a heavy-equipment company located on River Street. Her mother, Jane, wrote god-awful poetry that she occasionally submitted to Vida for the House & Home section. Both senior Marshalls were familiar to me, yet I had never connected them with Laurie. On the way to their house, I admitted as much to Vida.

"It's not entirely your fault," Vida said magnanimously from behind the wheel of her big white Buick. "Laurie is such a cipher. She simply doesn't register as a real person. You probably won't believe that her half brother goes to Princeton on scholarship. Obviously, he got all the brains. But that was before your time in Alpine."

Over the years I'd learned that ignorance was forgivable as long as it pertained to events that occurred before my arrival. Taking comfort in the knowledge, I got out of

the car and gingerly walked through the new inch of
snow that covered Cascade Street. The Marshall residence was a reasonably handsome conversion of what
had probably been one of the original company houses.
The one-story cabin had been expanded to two floors,
with a deck, picture windows, and a shake exterior that
blended nicely with its woodsy surroundings.

Jane Marshall came to the door with a wooden spatula
in one hand. I'd never dealt directly with her at the paper,
so this was my first close viewing. She wasn't much
older than I was, late forties at most, though there were
fine lines around her eyes and mouth. Perhaps she had
once been as pretty as her daughter, but unlike Laurie,
Jane disdained cosmetics. She apparently also rejected
Laurie's scissors, for Jane's light brown hair hung
long and loose around her shoulders. Her thin, angular
body moved awkwardly, as if all the parts were loosely
connected.

"Ms. Runkel! What a surprise!" Jane let us in, though
her manner was tentative.

Vida formally introduced me. Jane's hazel eyes grew
wary as it dawned on her that this wasn't a social call.
Her husband, who entered the paneled entryway carrying
the TV remote, guessed at once why Vida and I had
come calling.

"Oh, hell," he said, more in exasperation than in anger.
"We're not going to be in the damned paper about this
killing, are we?"

Cocking an eye at Martin Marshall, Vida accepted the
challenge. "Should you be? Emma and I merely wanted a
few words with Laurie. Is she at home?"

"Yes," Martin said.

"No," Jane said, almost at the same time.

The Marshalls exchanged swift glances. Martin
seemed puzzled, then shrugged. "I thought I heard her

upstairs. Oh, well." He nodded his curly gray head at us and returned to wherever he could exercise the remote control.

Jane gave us a silly smile. "Men! They never pay attention to what's going on. I'm sorry you missed Laurie. If you'll excuse me, I'm just about to serve—"

At that moment Laurie appeared from around a corner, presumably where the staircase was located. She stopped and stared. Her mother blanched, then spoke in an unconvincing voice:

"Why, Laurie! I didn't realize you'd come back!"

Laurie blinked. "Where was I?"

Jane made a helpless gesture with the spatula, accidentally smacking it against the paneled wall. "Why, I didn't know. I was sure I heard you go out again." The spurt of color in Jane's cheeks definitely improved her looks, if not her demeanor. "Honestly, I never know who's coming and going around here! When Josh is home from college, it's a regular madhouse!" Calming herself, she put a hand on Laurie's arm. "Why don't we all go into the kitchen to visit while I get dinner ready?"

"We won't take up much of your time," Vida said, following Jane and Laurie down the hallway.

The kitchen smelled of garlic. It was small, but had been recently updated, with a skylight and white oak cabinetry. Jane immediately pulled a saucepan off the burner and began stirring its contents with the spatula.

"Ms. Runkel and Ms. Lord have just a couple of quick questions," Jane said, no doubt intending the cue for us as much as for Laurie.

Vida had positioned herself next to a refrigerator that was finished in the same wood as the cabinets. "We're doing background for our newspaper story," she explained, speaking more slowly than usual. "We need all the available facts about the homicide so that we can inform our readers accurately and fully."

Laurie said nothing. She was wearing jeans and a big sweatshirt, but it looked as if she had recently applied makeup. I suspected that Laurie spent much of her leisure time in front of a mirror. Her reflection might be the only thing she really understood.

"You took a phone call this afternoon around one," Vida said in an uncustomary soothing voice. "Or so Stella told us. It was a man, who was asking about the two o'clock facial appointment for Ms. Whitman. Can you tell us what he said?"

Half sitting on a kitchen stool, Laurie gave her imitation of thinking, which was indicated by shielding her eyes with her hand. "He asked what time Ms. Whitman's appointment was and when she'd be finished. I said it was at two. But she'd come a few minutes early, so she'd probably be done before three." Laurie tilted her head to one side and looked pleased with herself.

Vida nodded approval. "Excellent, Laurie. What did he say when you told him that?"

"Ah . . . I think he said fine, and hung up."

Still at the stove, Jane smiled at her daughter. "You have such a wonderful memory for details, Laurie. That's what inspired my poem 'Picayune.' " She turned to Vida. "You remember it, I'm sure, even if you didn't have space to run it."

"I remember," Vida murmured, trying to conceal the fact that she probably wanted to forget. "Lovely. So . . . detailed." She regarded Laurie with an almost sincere smile. "Did you recognize the man's voice?"

Laurie shook her head, in wide, languorous sweeps. "No. The sheriff asked me that already. It was a funny sort of voice, kind of croaking." Leaning down, she adjusted the cuff of her thick wool sock. "We don't do men. They go to Herb's."

Herb Amundson owned the barbershop in the Alpine Building directly across the street from *The Advocate*. At almost seventy, he refused to retire, and had been giving Alpine men the same U.S. Army–issue haircut for almost fifty years. If they wanted something different, they had to come when his son, Bo, filled in for his father, or go to Sultan.

I wasn't sure if Laurie could recognize anyone out of context, but I gave it a try. "Was the man who called someone you might know in Alpine? His voice, I mean."

Laurie's forehead wrinkled under her perfectly spaced bangs. It appeared that Milo hadn't asked this question. "You mean like somebody who lives here?" She didn't look at me, but instead gazed off in the direction of the far wall, where a big corkboard displayed messages, snapshots, and what appeared to be some of Jane's latest poetical jottings.

"Yes, a local." My smile was probably phonier than Vida's.

"Good heavens!" Jane cried, staring into her saucepan. "This is going to curdle! I really should get dinner on now." She gave Vida and me an apologetic look. "I'd love to ask you to stay, but I really didn't fix enough. Maybe some night when I do Mexican. Do you remember my poem 'Taco Madness'?"

"Yes," Vida replied grimly. "I'd never heard anyone try to rhyme *taco* and *Waco* before."

Even as she led us out of the kitchen, Jane nodded solemnly. "It was after that terrible tragedy with the Branch Davidians. The poem was my attempt to make sense of it all."

"Yes," Vida responded, still grim. At the door, she

made one last effort with Laurie. "You're certain that you don't know who called about Ms. Whitman?"

Laurie looked blank, which wasn't unusual. "I don't think so."

"I've written a new poem, about the baseball strike," Jane put in, now sounding faintly frantic. "I've tied the owners into the cosmos."

"A good place for them," Vida retorted, without looking at Jane. "Tell me one more thing, Laurie—did this man who called on the telephone ask for Honoria or Kay Whitman?"

The question seemed to send Laurie's brain into a paroxysm of labor. "Oh ... I ... Sheriff Dodge asked me ... but I don't think he said ... the man who called on the phone ..."

"It begins, 'O thou sky so infinite, weep not for the parasite; the universe counts not the winner, nor cares a fig for George Steinbrenner.' What do you think, Ms. Runkel?"

Reluctantly, Vida turned to Jane. "I think that's ... apt." She looked again at Laurie, still trying to coax the words out of her. "Did he actually give the first name?" Vida coached.

Laurie's shoulders slumped. "No," she admitted in defeat. The failure caused her to avoid Vida's gaze. "He just asked for Ms. Whitman."

"Ms.? Not Miss or Mrs.?" Vida never gave up.

It was too much for Laurie. She simply didn't know, or couldn't remember, or think for another second. Her mother shielded her daughter with one arm, and though Jane's smile was bright, her eyes were hard.

"So good to see you. Drop by another time when we're not in such a muddle. Good night." Jane Marshall waved us off. Or brushed us off, depending upon the interpretation.

"Rats," Vida muttered, tramping through the snow to her Buick. "That girl is impossible!"

"We didn't find out much more than Stella already told us," I said, getting into the passenger side of the car.

Vida gathered her tweed coat closer and squeezed behind the wheel. "Yes, we did," she said with fervor. Before turning on the ignition, she gazed at me through her glasses. "We found out that Jane Marshall isn't merely protective of her daughter. Laurie's mother is also scared to death *for* her. Or perhaps *of* her. Which do you think it is?"

Vida's remark had distracted me just enough that at first I didn't realize we weren't headed back to *The Advocate* so that I could collect my aging Jaguar. "Obviously, Jane's frightened for Laurie," I agreed. "But how could that poor girl scare anybody? She's not only dim, but exceedingly meek."

"I didn't mean it that way," Vida replied as a few flakes of new snow dusted the windshield. "I got the impression that Jane was afraid of what Laurie might reveal. Why else was she so determined not to let her daughter see us?"

"We can see Laurie anytime we want at Stella's," I pointed out. "Frankly, I got the impression that Laurie isn't just dim, but a little evasive."

"She's not clever enough to be evasive," Vida retorted, then, after a pause, murmured, "Perhaps."

"Perhaps what?" I inquired.

But Vida merely shook her head. We had continued driving along Cascade, passing St. Mildred's Catholic Church on the right and now, Holy Trinity Episcopal Church on the left. Vida began to slow down by Sky Robics. The building next door had been through several guises in the past eighty-odd years. Originally a bunkhouse, it was Holy Trinity's first site of worship, later a pool hall and allegedly a brothel, that—for no apparent reason, though Vida hints otherwise—became the Elks Club. Thirty years ago it assumed its current incarnation as an apartment complex with some eight units crammed into its two stories.

Vida maneuvered the Buick into a parking place near the covered entrance of what is called Orr House. The name isn't derived from the rumored brothel of yore, but in honor of an early Alpiner who managed the first pool hall. While Orr House's history may be complicated, our reason for climbing the wooden stairs to the second floor was not: Rebecca Wolfe lived in Apartment 6.

Stella's skin-care expert took her time opening the door. As is often the case, Becca recognized Vida at once, but seemed to have some trouble placing me. I was used to that, and introduced myself.

"I was Stella's two o'clock today," I said, hoping to enhance Becca's memory.

"Oh, wow!" Becca exclaimed, ushering us inside what looked like a very basic three-room unit. "You were the one who found the body! And—" She stopped, obviously embarrassed at her emotional collapse. "I was a mess. Oh, wow, it should have been you instead of me!"

I assumed she referred to her crying jag. "I may have been in shock," I said, which was possibly true. But I wasn't given to tears. The last occasion I'd lost complete control was when Tom Cavanaugh announced he couldn't leave his wife. That was the first time he'd made that statement. It had taken place twenty-three years ago. I'd cried so much that I became physically ill, which alarmed the OB-GYN who was caring for me in the first trimester of my pregnancy. The thought of my emotional outburst harming my unborn child taught me a tough lesson: I would never, ever let anything or anybody upset me so much again. And I hadn't. Perhaps I'd lost part of myself in the process, but at least I hadn't given it away.

With her eagle eye, Vida scanned the small living room's appointments. I did the same, if less swiftly. Becca had only recently moved back to Alpine, and the unit had a temporary air, along with the scent of incense. It was furnished with what looked mostly like castoffs, devoid of order or harmony. Judging by the clutter, there wasn't much sign of housekeeping, either.

Becca moved a stack of magazines from an ancient armchair and a pile of clothes from the brown-and-white-striped sofa. "Sit down, please. I was just going to walk over to the Grocery Basket and get something for dinner. I didn't feel like eating until now."

Vida chose the armchair. I was stuck with the sofa, and after I sat down, I realized I might be stuck in it as well. The springs were nonexistent, and I sank so low that my knees almost obstructed my vision. I realized why Vida had selected a different seat.

Becca got a folding chair that was propped against one wall. After she set it up, she asked if we'd like something to drink. Vida declined for both of us.

"We aren't staying long," she explained. "I'm sure Sheriff Dodge asked you a great many detailed questions this afternoon. But we may not have access to his official reports until it's too late to meet our deadline for Wednesday publication. Do bear with us if we go over tiresome ground." Vida was suddenly uncharacteristically self-effacing.

Becca picked up a bottle of mineral water from behind a haphazard pile of CDs. "That's cool. What can I tell you?" Unlike her coworker Laurie, Becca seemed eager to talk.

"You were informed about the appointment change?" Vida inquired, loosening the fleecy scarf around her neck.

After taking a drink of mineral water, Becca nodded. "Sure. But it didn't matter. I didn't know either of those clients. I'm just getting reacquainted with Alpine."

"Yes," Vida said with a tight little smile. "You left town for several years."

"It's good to be back." Becca didn't look at either of us, but seemed fascinated by a poster showing the harbor of Rio de Janeiro.

Vida's eyes followed Becca's. "You didn't go to Rio, did you?" she asked in a faintly startled voice.

Becca laughed. "No. But I worked for an airline for a while." She shifted on the chair, perhaps uneasily. I couldn't be sure. "I like working with people. That's why I decided to train as a cosmetician."

Deciding it was time to act like I was something other than Vida's ventriloquist's dummy, I asked Becca if she'd had an opportunity to chat with Kay Whitman.

"Sort of," Becca replied. "It was the usual stuff—I ask what problem areas they have with their skin, if they have any allergies to skin-care products, then I explain about the facial. I try not to talk too much. A facial should be mellow, relaxing."

Vida looked disappointed. "So Kay Whitman didn't tell you anything about herself?"

"Not really. She said she probably had spent too much time in the sun." Becca's hand automatically strayed to her own smooth cheek. "I said she must not be from around here. She just laughed."

Vida was sitting with her elbow on one knee and her hand propping up her chin. "Tell us this, Becca. You're an expert. What can you discern from a woman's face?"

Becca was puzzled. "You mean—about how she takes care of her skin? Or—what?"

"Let's put it like this." Vida sat back in the armchair.

"A person's face is a road map of life. Where do you think it had taken Kay Whitman?"

Becca sucked in her breath. "Wow! I've never thought of it quite like that! But you're right, Ms. Runkel—skin's a true indicator. It can show how much you drink, eat, smoke, do drugs—whatever." Letting her head fall back, Becca gazed up at the ceiling, which could have used a plastering job. "Ms. Whitman—Kay—is—was—in her midforties. Northern European ancestry—I can tell that from skin tones. She was right about spending time in the sun, but I don't think it was lately, maybe when she was younger. No drugs, no smoking, but she drank some. Small broken veins you can only see under the big magnifier indicate that. She didn't take extra care with her skin as a rule, but so many women don't. Good diet, though, fresh fruit, not too much red meat. She should have drunk more water. Most women don't, especially the ones over fifty. She didn't exercise, either—I could tell that just from looking at the rest of her—very little muscle tone. She had a basic T-zone problem, which is common—oily around the nose area, much drier in the rest of the face. She worried—her forehead was too wrinkled for her age. Not a really happy person, because she didn't have the laugh lines." Becca lowered her head. "How am I doing?"

"Marvelous," Vida replied, and sounded as if she meant it.

"Thanks." Becca took another drink of water, living up to her own advice. "Let's see—what else? Sex is a puzzle. You can't tell much, only that if a woman cares about her looks, she's getting some. Or wants to. That's about it, I guess. Except for the two little scars."

"Scars?" I echoed.

Becca nodded. "There was one over her left eyebrow and another at the corner of her mouth, same side. They

were hardly noticeable, except under the light. Ten years
old, at least. She didn't mention them, and neither did I.
It's not my business to ask unnecessary questions."

Briefly, Vida and I looked at each other. In our business, we had to ask all the questions—necessary, embarrassing, provocative, insipid.

"What time did you leave her alone?" Vida queried.

Becca shook her head in a forlorn manner. "Sheriff
Dodge asked that, too. I'd done a mini-facial on Dixie
Ridley at one, so she was gone by one thirty-five, one-
forty. Ms. Whitman came in about a quarter to two. I told
Stella it was fine to take her early. We must have started
about ten to. It takes twelve minutes to do the prelim
stuff and apply the mask. I told the sheriff I left the room
a couple of minutes after two o'clock."

That made sense to me. I'd been almost ten minutes
late for my appointment. I'd probably discovered the
body at two-eleven, two-twelve. The window of opportunity for the killer was very narrow.

Vaguely, I recalled my own euphoric feeling as I
crossed Front Street. "You left the salon through the
front door?" I asked, wishing I'd been more observant.

"Sure," Becca replied. "That's the only way out. The
rear entrance is always locked, except when the deliveries come."

I was trying to conjure up the scene on Front Street
during my two-block trek between *The Advocate* and
Stella's. "You didn't see anyone unusual when you went
to the Burger Barn?"

Becca laughed again. "Unusual? In Alpine? I saw
Crazy Eights Neffel, wearing a sombrero and mukluks.
Does that count?"

It didn't in Alpine. Crazy Eights was our local loon.
His antics weren't worth much, even for Vida's gossipy
"Scene Around Town" column.

Vida put both hands on the frayed arms of the chair and got up. "You've been very helpful, Becca. We both thank you. Would you like a ride to the Grocery Basket?"

Becca preferred to walk. She said she needed the exercise. "Usually, I work out at the gym next door," she explained. "But tonight—well, I was still kind of disturbed. You know what I mean?"

Unfortunately, Vida and I did.

"Becca's wrong," Vida asserted as we headed down First Street to *The Advocate,* where my Jag was still parked. "There are other ways to leave the salon. And thus, to enter it."

"You mean through Sky Travel or the medical supply place?" I said, noting that the snow was getting thicker again.

"Exactly," Vida agreed as we passed the darkened public library. "Not to mention the foyer door. If you use the stairs entrance instead of the elevator, you can get into the rear of the building. The law office and the rest of the tenants on the other floors have their own rest rooms, but that wasn't always so. Besides, they still have to come down to take their deliveries out back on Pine Street."

I hadn't thought of that. "In other words," I said slowly, "almost anybody could have come in that way without being noticed."

Vida nodded. The rumpled derby stayed in place and I absently wondered if she'd be able to set it right again. "You were going to Stella's about the time that the killer must have gone into the building. Unless, of course, he or she had been hiding out someplace inside. What—or who—did you see?"

We were passing the post office and the forest service offices. At the next corner and across Front Street loomed the solid if unimpressive granite bulk of the Clemans Building. As we kept moving I also saw the Skykomish County sheriff's headquarters. The lights were on and Milo's Cherokee Chief was still in its usual spot. It was now covered with new snow. Milo was probably covered in confusion, as well as paperwork.

"I didn't see a damned thing," I finally admitted. "I was thinking about Emma Lord, Free Woman."

"Oh, dear." Vida stopped for the red light at Front and Fourth. "Well, I'm not going to offer advice."

Of course Vida already had. Having met Tom Cavanaugh four years earlier, she had developed what I now considered an inexplicable affection for him. With a complete disregard for her usual hardheaded common sense, Vida had decided that Tommy, as she called him, and I were made for each other. In early January, when I'd first told her of my irrevocable decision to move on with my life, Vida had insisted I was being hasty. It was useless to remind her that I'd waited over twenty years for Tom to leave Sandra. "Life's not a measuring stick," she'd declared. "It's like a river, running wherever the current takes it. You can't count the years, you simply move with the ripples and rapids."

For once, I had no idea what Vida was talking about. In fact, I figured that she'd succumbed to some romantic influence under her recently acquired suitor, Buck Bardeen. Buck was the brother of Henry Bardeen, the ski-lodge manager. Colonel Bardeen was also retired from the air force, a widower, and courageous enough to take Vida on her own terms. They had met in a roundabout way through our personal ads, which made me feel vaguely responsible for their future. With less reason, Vida always acted as if she were responsible for mine.

"There's no point in talking about Tom and me

anymore," I said pointedly. "I'm starving. Let's go eat at the Venison Inn."

Vida had parked next to my Jag, which was also covered with snow. There was a light on at the newspaper office. "Did you forget to flip the switch?" Vida asked.

"No." We got out of the car. The door was unlocked. Cautiously, we went through the front office where Ginny usually held sway, and entered the newsroom.

Leo was at his desk, working on the computer. He looked up in surprise. "Hey—what's up?" Leo asked around the cigarette he held between his lips.

"Investigative reporting," Vida replied tersely. "My, but you're diligent."

Leo ignored the sarcasm in Vida's voice. "I have to be. At the last minute Platters in the Sky decided to hold a post–Valentine's Day sale. They took inventory over the weekend and came up with a bunch of old tapes they couldn't unload."

I'd forgotten that Tuesday was St. Valentine's Day. We'd run a special insert the previous week featuring ads with the usual hearts, cupids, and amorous lovers. Vida had written a feature on local couples who had been married for over fifty years. Carla had put together a photo story on newlyweds. I'd coaxed Father Dennis Kelly, my pastor at St. Mildred's, to write a piece on the real St. Valentine, or both of them, since historical data indicated there were two saints with the same name.

"We're going to dinner," I informed Leo. "Want to join us?"

Leo shook his head. "Thanks, but I was in the middle of my Cordon Bleu cheese sandwich when they called from Platters. I'll take a rain check, okay?"

"Sure." I started for the door. Vida was already there.

"Hey," Leo called. "Some guy came in about ten minutes ago with a personal ad. He seemed a little weird.

You might want to check him out when he comes back tomorrow. I'm not sure Carla can tell the difference between normal and otherwise."

I was puzzled as to why Leo hadn't taken the ad himself. While Ginny handled all our classifieds, Leo was, after all, our ad manager. "What's he coming back for?" I inquired.

"I couldn't find the forms in Ginny's desk. Carla's moved everything. Ginny will be pissed." Leo put his cigarette out and shifted his concentration to the computer screen.

I was still curious. "Was his personals ad kinky?"

Glancing up, Leo almost managed to conceal his impatience. "*Personal* ad, not *personals* ad." The distinction was made between the standard classifieds and our special matchmaking section inaugurated by Ginny the previous spring.

"What was it?" I pressed. " 'Thank you, St. Jude'?"

"No." Leo was again eyeing his computer graphics. "That was part of the weirdness. The message was, 'One down, one to go.' The guy seemed to think it was hilarious. He thought everything was hilarious, including the fact that I had a deadline to meet. That's why he was so damned weird." Leo turned to glare at Vida and me.

Vida, however, was looking owlish. I knew what she was thinking. "Who was he?" she asked.

"I don't know, Duchess." Leo was no longer hiding his exasperation. "We didn't get to the name-and-address routine because I couldn't find the freaking form. I've never seen him before in my life. Average height, average weight, brown hair, jeans, parka, boots, and six bricks shy of a load. Now go stuff yourselves and let me get this little hummer put together."

There was no point in being miffed. Vida and I

understood deadline pressures. We headed through the snow to the Venison Inn.

"That's very suggestive," Vida declared after we were seated in a booth by the windows.

"It's probably a coincidence," I said, but without conviction. " 'One down, one to go' could mean anything. Our imaginations have been stirred by Kay Whitman's murder."

Vida had picked up a menu. Over the top of the plastic-covered offerings, all I could see were her eyes and derby. "That may be so," she said dryly. "But isn't it enough?"

Chapter Four

On Tuesday, Vida wanted to go to Startup to interview Honoria and the other surviving Whitmans. But we were up against deadline, and a round trip would have taken too much time out of her workday. She had to content herself with a telephone call to Honoria's converted summer cabin down the highway.

Unfortunately, Honoria couldn't talk long. She and her brother and mother were trying to make arrangements for sending Kay's body back to California. There was a delay by the sheriff's department, which Honoria found hard to understand. She and Milo were good friends. Why couldn't he expedite matters for her?

"Naturally," Vida informed me after Honoria had rung off, "I couldn't answer her question, except with the obvious reply that Milo has to follow procedure. It strikes me that Honoria doesn't realize a crime has been committed."

"That's ridiculous," I said, looking up from the front-page layout on my computer screen. "Honoria's very intelligent. She must understand that Milo has to treat this like any other homicide."

Vida, who had exchanged her derby for a maroon slouch hat, seemed intent on defending Honoria. "It hasn't sunk in. Shock, I should guess. It isn't up to us to judge how she reacts. She's had more than her share of grief over the years."

That was indisputable. Honoria had moved to Startup from Carmel. She had been married to an abusive man who had pushed her down a flight of stairs, crippling her for life. Her brother, in turn, had exacted revenge by killing the husband. Apparently, Trevor Whitman had gone to prison for his deed.

"You know, Vida," I said in a musing voice, "we don't really have all the facts about Honoria's background. It occurs to me that what we do know is pretty sketchy."

Vida fingered her chin. "That's true. Honoria is a very private sort of person. I respect that. I think."

So did I. While I didn't consider myself as tight-lipped as Honoria, I also tended to keep my private life to myself. Honoria's reticence could be annoying, but I understood her feelings. While it wasn't unusual for people to keep their misfortunes to themselves, Honoria was also secretive about good news. The previous September, she had won a ten-thousand-dollar award from the state for her pottery. The only reason I ever learned about it was that I received a press release about the prizes from Olympia. When I called to congratulate her and ask why she hadn't informed us, Honoria had said she didn't think anyone in Alpine would be interested. Her reaction had struck me as more narrow than modest. But what I admired most was her courage and determination. Thanks to the specially equipped car, the electric wheelchair, and the alterations she had made in her house, Honoria was able to lead an active, independent life.

"Milo must know more about her past," Vida mused. The thought seemed to annoy Vida. She didn't like it when someone knew something she didn't. "Tomorrow is our easy day. Why don't we drive down to Startup?"

The suggestion sounded good to me. We would have the basic news story for this week's edition, then follow up next week with the latest developments and an in-depth article on Honoria and her sister-in-law. If possible, I would spare the family any mention of the seamier background details.

"That's fine," I agreed. "Unless you want to go tonight after work?"

I could have sworn that Vida blushed. Of course she didn't, but there was certainly a twitch in her face. "I can't. I . . . ah . . . have an engagement."

I couldn't help but grin. "Buck?"

Vida nodded once. "We're going to Everett for dinner at the yacht club. It's Valentine's Day." She actually ducked her head, the slouch hat covering most of her face.

"That's great," I said. It was. Vida had been a widow for almost twenty years. She hadn't dated in all the time I'd known her—until she met Buck last June.

"Let me relate the essence of my phone conversation with Honoria," Vida put in quickly. "Kay and Trevor live in Pacific Grove, which I gather isn't far from Carmel, where Honoria came from. They had been married for seventeen years. Kay was forty-three last November. She worked out of the home. I don't know what she did. There weren't any children, which is a blessing, I suppose. The Whitmans—Kay and Trevor, along with the mother, Ida—arrived to visit Honoria a week ago Sunday. They'd planned to stay until this coming Saturday." Vida paused for breath.

I made a face. "They were all staying with Honoria? Two weeks is a long time for four people to be cooped up in that place of hers. Especially this time of year. I'd go nuts."

Vida appeared to frown. Under the slouch hat's brim, it was hard to see more than the bottom of her glasses.

"You have Adam for weeks at a time when he's home from college."

"That's different. He's my son. I don't have to entertain him." It was true. I merely had to provide unlimited funds so that he could entertain himself and whichever girl he hit on in Skykomish County.

"You have your brother Ben visit for long periods, sometimes with Adam." Vida now seemed determined to prove some obscure point.

"I don't feel forced to amuse Ben, either." Nor did I. Ben was a priest, and often spent much of his visit with other priests—or, these days, ex-priests—in the vicinity. He had also recently taken up skiing, thanks to Father Dennis Kelly, who some parishioners insisted spent more time on the slopes than he did in the rectory. Ben had skied fitfully in our youth, but his previous assignment in Mississippi and his current parish in Arizona hadn't given him much opportunity to swoosh or schush or whatever skiers do when they aren't breaking various limbs along with their necks.

"What I mean is," Vida finally clarified, "Honoria's houseguests are—were—family. I'm sure they had a lovely time."

I lifted both eyebrows. "Oh? You mean right up until the brutal murder? Vida, what's with you?"

"Nothing." Vida bridled, then stood up. "I must write this story and finish my pages. I'd like to leave a few minutes early tonight."

Buck, I thought. St. Valentine's Day. Romance in the air, and spring, waiting somewhere around a four-foot snowbank. "Sure, why not?" I said as Vida made her exit.

The holiday meant nothing to me. I expected no flowers, no candy, no phone calls, no dinner dates in Everett. But that was all right.

And I was all wrong. Milo called two minutes later

and asked if I'd like to have dinner at King Olav's in the ski lodge. I was so startled that I said yes.

"My treat," he said, further surprising me. "You had a bad shock yesterday, Emma. You could use a break."

I don't know whether I was more astounded by the invitation or Milo's concern for my welfare. Even though our meals together had become more frequent, we usually went dutch. To my amazement I actually felt a flutter of excitement as I hung up the phone. Talking vigorously to myself, I decided that the rush came from the prospect of learning more details about Kay Whitman's murder. Surely Milo would reveal more than official statements after he had a Scotch or two.

When Vida turned in her homicide story, I discovered there were a few items she hadn't told me. Perhaps she'd gotten them from Milo or Bill Blatt or even Honoria. Whoever the source, I concentrated on the facts as well as the writing. Unfortunately, Vida had written the piece in a variation of her House & Home section's style. Before I applied my editor's pencil, the lead article read:

A woman visiting the area was found brutally murdered in the facial room at Stella's Styling Salon Monday afternoon shortly after two P.M. Stella Magruder, who has owned the salon since 1967, is married to Richard (Richie) Magruder, Alpine's deputy mayor and a former bull cook at Camp Two.

The slain woman was identified as Kay Beresford Whitman, 43, of Pacific Grove, California. She and her husband, Trevor, and mother-in-law, Ida Frickey Smith, were visiting the deceased's sister-in-law, Honoria Whitman, at her charming home in Startup.

The Whitman relatives arrived from California by car February 5. They planned to stay with Honoria Whitman until February 18. Their favorite sightseeing stops on the trip included the Oregon coast, Mount Rainier (though the road to Sunrise was closed due to snow), and Seattle, where they stopped at the Pike Place Market. They also visited the Ballard Locks, where they watched fishing boats, pleasure craft, and other vessels go between Puget Sound and Lake Union.

According to Skykomish County Sheriff Milo Dodge, Kay Whitman's throat was slit by a sharp instrument. The weapon has not yet been found. The victim's faux alligator handbag is also missing.

Ms. Whitman, her husband, and Ms. Honoria Whitman, who is an award-winning potteress from Startup with a recent successful showing in Tacoma, had come to Alpine to run errands. Sheriff Dodge and his deputies are investigating the murder, with the cooperation of Snohomish County law-enforcement officials.

Services are pending, probably somewhere in California.

I dashed into the news office, where Vida was laying out her page by hand. She not only refused to enter the computer age, but wrote all her copy on an ancient battered typewriter.

"What's this about Kay's handbag?" I demanded. "You didn't tell me it was missing. Milo didn't mention it, either."

"Oh." Vida pursed her lips. "Well. Milo probably forgot. I may not have said anything, because it seems like an obvious ploy. Do you really think anyone would come into the salon to kill a woman for her faux alligator bag?"

"No," I agreed. "But it's pretty stupid of the killer to try to make it look like a robbery."

"Killing is stupid," Vida declared. "In any event, Milo isn't fooled. Not this time."

I returned to my office before Vida could ask my opinion of her story. Hopefully, she wouldn't resent my editorial changes. I rarely had to alter much of her House & Home copy, but she wasn't accustomed to covering hard news. Carla had taken pictures as Honoria and Trevor emerged from the sheriff's office Monday. I'd let her write the cutline, which was brief and had only required one correction. Carla had identified Trevor Whitman as "Walt."

On my way home, I stopped at Bayard's Picture Perfect Photography Studio. Buddy Bayard does all our photo work. Normally, Carla deals with him, but this evening I was finally able to pick up the finished portraits that Adam, Ben, and I had sat for at Christmas. It had been an impulsive idea that hit me on Christmas Eve when I was feeling most nostalgic. Having lost our parents in an automobile crash twenty-four years ago, Ben and I had realized that we'd never had a family picture taken since. I'd made the appointment with Buddy for the thirtieth of December. By the time the proofs were ready, it was the second week of January. My son and brother had returned to Arizona. This meant sending the proofs to Ben in Tuba City, then on to Adam at ASU in Tempe. Ben typically couldn't make up his mind which pose he liked best, and Adam typically lost the proofs for almost three weeks. But now the finished product was ready.

Buddy was in the darkroom when I arrived. His wife, Roseanna, was closing up for the day. With her blonde pageboy swinging at her wide shoulders, Roseanna went to the filing cabinet behind the antique mahogany desk that served as the reception counter. She presented the three portraits with a certain dramatic flair.

"Well? Aren't they gorgeous?" she enthused. "Aren't you and your menfolk gorgeous?"

We weren't quite that, but I was pleased with the result. Ben had debated whether or not to wear his clerical collar, but to my surprise, Adam had talked him into it. My brother's sun-bronzed face, engaging grin, and warm brown eyes looked out at me. His features are sharper than mine, and his brown hair crinkles. Ben is just above average size for a man, while I am a bit under for a woman. Still, the resemblance is there, particularly in the mouth and eyes. No, we are not gorgeous, but we do have our charms.

Except for Adam's eyes, which are also brown, he doesn't look like Ben or me. As his face grows leaner and becomes more chiseled, he bears a remarkable likeness to his father. Adam is also tall like Tom, six-foot-two at last measuring. The mother in me was proud of my handsome son; the cast-off lover in me was suddenly saddened.

"What's wrong?" Roseanna asked in obvious disappointment. "Don't you like it?"

"Oh, yes!" I exclaimed, forcing a big smile. "It's great. I was just thinking how Adam has . . . changed."

Roseanna uttered a small laugh. "Babies one day, grownups the next. Don't I know it?"

The Bayards had three children, all but one now out of high school. Their own family portrait was proudly displayed in a gilt frame on the opposite wall.

Since Wednesday was payday, I felt safe writing a check for the pictures. Roseanna would mail Ben and Adam's copies to their respective residences in Arizona. I was putting my checkbook back into my purse when Ed Bronsky burst through the front door.

"Hey, hey!" cried my former ad manager and Alpine's newest millionaire, courtesy of his late aunt in Cedar

Falls, Iowa. "Just in time! I've been having cocktails with Mayor Baugh at the country club."

"Ed," I said, "we don't have a country club in Alpine."

Ed pulled back, creating three chins where there were usually only two. "Well! That's what you think, Emma Lord! We do now. Fuzzy Baugh and I have decided to turn the caddy shack into a country club."

If it was true, that was news. If it was news, I didn't want to hear it. Not just now, thirty minutes after *The Advocate* had gone off to be printed in Monroe. Besides, Ed's pretentious manner irked me these days. I actually preferred his preinheritance sloth, pessimism, and obsequiousness.

"We'll have to do some fund-raising," Ed went on, whether I wanted to hear it or not. "Oh, sure, I'm willing to fork up some big bucks as seed money. But what's a golf course without a country club? Where can you go for a couple of drinks and maybe a big steak after you finish that last hole?"

For Ed, the last hole was probably on the fifth green. I couldn't imagine him playing a full round of golf, even with a caddy. Furthermore, Ed was the only man I knew who had broken three ribs in a head-on collision with a golf cart. He'd run into Durwood Parker last September, which wasn't entirely Ed's fault. Durwood is the worst driver in Alpine—nay, in the world—and has had his license pulled by Milo Dodge.

I was determined not to discuss Ed's plans. "I must run," I said, glancing at my watch. It was shortly after five-thirty. Milo wasn't picking me up until seven, but nobody, especially Ed, needed to know that.

"Now hold on, Emma," Ed said, putting a pudgy hand on my arm and suddenly looking serious. "I need some advice. You're a publisher, you must have some contacts in the book business. How should I go about getting my autobiography published?"

It was all I could do to keep from screaming. I know I didn't do a very good job of hiding my dismay. "Your autobiography? Why, Ed?"

Ed's round face frowned at me. "What do you mean, *why*? It's a Horatio Alger rags-to-riches story. Small Town Boy Makes Good. People love that stuff. It inspires them." He and his cashmere overcoat turned to Roseanna. "Where's Buddy? He was supposed to have those prints ready by five."

"He's working on them now. I'll go check." It was to Roseanna's credit that she kept a straight face and a businesslike demeanor.

"You see," Ed explained even as I edged toward the door, "I've had Buddy blow up several photos from my early days. Baby pictures, first tricycle, altar boy, high-school football, the prom, graduation, wedding—you know, a retrospective. That would go in the middle of the book."

I was still trying to envision Ed in a football uniform. He was shaped more like the football. Perhaps he'd been slimmer then.

"That sounds . . . swell," I said, trying to smile. "Listen, I've got to scoot. As you know," I continued, appealing to Ed's ego, "Tuesday is always such a wild day at work. And this week, with that homicide at Stella's . . ."

"Yes." Ed grew confidential, moving closer and pinning me with my back to the door. "I don't like saying this, Emma, and I wouldn't, except that . . . well, you and I go way back. But people around here are beginning to *talk*."

My eyes grew wide. "About what?" Surely no one was

gossiping about Milo and me. We hadn't done anything yet, except eat.

"It's like this," Ed said, lowering his voice another notch. "You see, I'm in a position now where I hear things. That happens when you hang out with the top dogs. No offense, but this was a quiet, peaceful little town until you came along. There were maybe two, three murders in the ten years before you bought *The Advocate* from Marius Vandeventer. Since you moved to Alpine, we've had—what?—eight, nine killings in six years? And this time I hear you even found the body! How do you expect people to react to those kind of statistics?"

While I didn't quite understand Ed's insinuation, his words were still appalling. "Ed, you aren't seriously blaming *me* for the increase in homicides, are you? Violence is growing all over America; everywhere, for that matter. All I do is report it. You know that."

Ed gave me a helpless look. "All I know is what I hear. People—important people—are beginning to wonder." Clumsily, he patted my arm. "Just a word to the wise, Emma." He turned as Roseanna and Buddy entered the reception area.

Fuming, I left. I was still irritated when Milo picked me up more than an hour later. He wasn't in a much better mood, so I let him gripe first.

"This case is a pain in the ass," he announced before we got as far as the turn onto Alpine Way. "Honoria and her brother and mother insist Kay didn't have an enemy in the world. The woman was a saint, if you believe her husband."

"Do you?" I asked, turning just enough to observe Milo's profile. It was long, particularly the chin, but otherwise undistinguished. The sandy eyebrows grew almost together, and the nose was rather blunt. Still, it was an agreeable face, especially when Milo smiled. He had good teeth, even great teeth, big and strong and white. I checked myself, wondering why I felt like Leo Walsh, trying to sell a double-truck ad to the Grocery Basket.

"I never believe anybody, let alone the spouse of a murder victim," Milo said in answer to my question, which I had actually forgotten in my perusal of his features. "Trevor Whitman seems like a stand-up guy, but he's an ex-con, and never mind how he got that way. Oh, sure, I'm sympathetic as hell, on a personal level. If I had a sister, instead of that stuck-up biologist brother of mine in Dallas, I might have whacked her lout of a husband, too. But I can't let emotions run my job. I'm trying to keep with the facts."

Milo always did. It was his greatest strength—and sometimes his worst weakness. I didn't make any comment, since we were now turning off Tonga Road for the ski lodge.

The lodge is over fifty years old, but Rufus Runkel and the Norwegians had built for the ages. The solid log-and-granite exterior, soaring lobby, and flagstone floors almost seemed to grow out of the mountainside. Over the years there have been renovations and additions, including King Olav's itself, which opened only about four years earlier.

While the lodge's basic decor is Pacific Northwest natural embellished by Native American masks, totem poles, blankets, and carvings, the restaurant itself evokes the blue and white of Norway's fjords, mountains, and valleys. The overall theme is Scandinavian, and so is most of the menu. Milo chose meatballs. I went with the salmon. But first we ordered drinks.

"We didn't get much information out of you regarding the crime scene," I noted after our waitress took the bar requests. "Can't you do that in-house now?"

"We can, but we had to wait until this afternoon," Milo replied, lighting a cigarette. "Dale Quick had to come over from Wenatchee, you know."

I did know. Quick was the part-time forensics pathologist who worked for Skykomish, Chelan, and Douglas counties. His surname didn't suit him. As Jack Mullins once put it, "Quick may not be fast, but he sure is slow." He was, however, thorough.

"So? Has Dale come up with anything yet?" I inquired, trying to sound artless, and failing. It didn't matter. Milo was rarely fooled by my clumsy attempts at subterfuge.

"Nothing startling," Milo replied. "There's quite a bit of foot traffic in and out of that rear area, including the facial room. Becca had six other clients already that day. Stella figured another six had used the rest room, and eleven in all had traipsed back to the changing area. That doesn't count anybody from the optician's, the travel agency, and the medical supply who might have used the women's room. And in this weather, with snow and slush and water getting tracked in, footprints are hard to come by."

"The facial room is carpeted, isn't it?" I hadn't really noticed, but somehow assumed it must be so.

Milo nodded. Our drinks arrived, and he waited until the waitress was gone before speaking again. "It's that indoor-outdoor stuff, the same thing Stella's got in the rest of the salon. We've got it, too, since the remodeling. It's made to *not* show dirt or prints. The most we vacuumed out of it was the usual, including a bunch of cosmetic gunk."

"Fingerprints?" I asked hopefully after tasting my Jack Daniel's and water.

"Lots of those. Mostly Becca Wolfe's." Milo sighed

into his Scotch. "We've got one thing, Emma, but it's not much help."

I gave Milo an interested look. "What's that?"

"A towel." Milo paused. "Stella didn't find it until this afternoon when we let her go back into the salon so she could open up tomorrow. Jack Mullins and I should have noticed, but you women are always dyeing your hair and—"

"I don't dye my hair," I interrupted, shaking my shaggy brown locks.

"You know what I mean." Milo seemed peeved, though more with himself than with me. "Anyway, Stella took the wet stuff out of the dryer this afternoon. She couldn't do it Monday, because we told her not to go beyond the reception area, and the laundry room is in back. She noticed that one of the towels still had stains on it. Jack had glanced in the washer and dryer, but didn't see anything odd. Stella said they always add bleach and let it soak before they start the wash cycle. According to her, this towel had to have been thrown in after the bleach process because it was still dirty. Dale Quick isn't sure because he hasn't run all his tests, but he thinks the stains are human blood."

Milo and I both ordered a second drink. We finished our first ones while he theorized about the bloodstained towel. Wanting to avoid getting blood on his or her person, the killer had grabbed a towel, committed the murder, then thrown the towel into the washing machine, which was already turned on.

"I heard the washer and dryer," I said, feeling a bit shaken. "They were both going just before I went into the facial room. The door was ajar."

Milo grew thoughtful. "You're sure?"

"Absolutely. That's why I knew that door didn't lead to the changing room."

"I wonder if the killer heard you coming and that's why the door was ajar."

I shivered. It hadn't occurred to me that Kay Whitman's murderer might have been only a few feet away from me when I discovered the body. He or she might have been in one of the rest rooms, or the changing room, or even the laundry room itself.

There was no point in being terrified after the fact. "Did you ask Stella if she kept that door ajar? I would. The room must be very small, and the heat from the dryer might cause a fire hazard. That's a very old building."

"I'll ask her tomorrow," Milo said. "What I'd like to know is that if this perp used the towel as a shield, where did it come from? The laundry room, the facial room, or some other place?"

Sipping my second drink, I nodded. "I see your point. If the towel came from the laundry room, it would indicate that the killer knew his or her way around the building."

"It could," Milo allowed. "But Stella said Becca kept a stack of towels on a stand right by the door. We just have to make sure the stained one came from there."

"Would Becca know? I mean, did she keep close count?" I waited for Milo's answer while our salads arrived.

"I haven't talked to her today," Milo said, lavishly applying salt and pepper to the iceberg lettuce and small mound of shrimp. "We spent the morning back at the salon and interviewing potential witnesses."

I thought of Ella Hinshaw, who would have been getting her blue rinse curled and furled when the murder occurred. She was deaf, but she certainly wasn't blind. "Did anybody see anything odd?" I asked.

"Hell, no," Milo responded. He'd raised his voice just enough to attract the attention of a young couple at the next table. Like most of the other diners, they were skiers visiting from out of town. Milo's status as sheriff meant nothing to them. "There was a three-man work crew, fixing that busted pipe off Pine Street, but the damned drill is new and they were having problems, so they didn't pay any attention to what was going on around them. Even Janet Driggers, who's got an eagle eye along with a dirty mouth, didn't see jack-squat from her angle at Sky Travel. She was helping some ski bum figure out how to get from here to Sun Valley for next to nothing."

I considered telling Milo about the man who had come into *The Advocate* Monday evening asking to run a personal ad. But he hadn't shown up Tuesday, and I knew how much Milo disliked speculation. Instead, I asked what kind of plans the family was making for Kay Whitman's body.

Milo sighed, then wiped a dab of Roquefort dressing off his chin. "Honoria's pretty annoyed with me about that. The autopsy should be done tomorrow, according to the folks over in Everett, but you never know. If they have a hot one come along in the next twenty-four hours, poor old Kay will stay in the freezer. Honoria wanted me to promise they could leave by tomorrow night."

I wrinkled my brow at Milo. Of course he couldn't see my brow because my bangs were so long that they covered my forehead almost to my eyes. "I thought Honoria's relatives drove from California to Startup."

"Yeah? Well, they're flying back. Maybe somebody can retrieve the car later. They can't haul Kay eight hundred miles in the trunk." Milo speared the last shrimp on his plate and washed it down with Scotch.

"I hope you didn't say that to Honoria," I remarked dryly.

Milo started to look a trifle sheepish, then squared his shoulders and assumed an unusual air of bravado. "Hell, no. But I would if I'd thought of it. I can't tippy-toe around Honoria just because she and I . . . well, just because." Deflating, he mumbled into his glass.

I laughed. "Don't act coy with me, Dodge. We've revealed all sorts of shocking secrets to each other in the past few months. Are you trying to tell me now that you and Honoria are still hitting the sheets? I thought not."

"You're right. We're not. And don't talk like that. It doesn't sound like you." Milo's expression was full of reproach.

"Sorry." If I hadn't had two bourbons, I would have been embarrassed. I finished my own salad, then set the fork on the empty plate. "So I gather," I finally said after a lengthy but not entirely uncomfortable silence, "that you hadn't met her relatives until yesterday."

"That's right. I met her mother when I drove down to Startup this afternoon. Honoria brought her brother to see me while his wife was getting the facial. And getting herself killed," he added on an ironic note.

I couldn't help but wince. "What's her mother like? Mrs. Smith, isn't it? She must have remarried."

"Often," Milo replied. Again he paused, this time as the waitress whisked away our salad plates. "She seems like a nice woman, though. Honoria's father left them when the three kids were small. He was a circus acrobat."

"No kidding!" I laughed some more. "Did you know that before . . . this happened?"

Milo nodded as his meatballs and my salmon arrived. "He was never home much even while the Whitmans were still married. The circus wintered in Florida, which is where Honoria and her brother and sister were born. After the divorce, they moved to California. Ida married a guy in the Merchant Marine, a chef or a cook, and finally, some young guy, whose hobby was motorcycles. He got himself killed on I-80 outside of Oakland."

"Gosh," I murmured. "The family has had more trouble than I realized. It's a marvel that Honoria is so stable and sensible."

Forking up a meatball, Milo glanced across the linen-covered table. "Oh, yeah? That's what I always thought, too. But not anymore. Fact is, I'm beginning to wonder if Honoria is all there."

Milo seemed to swallow the meatball in one gulp. I gulped, too, but for a different reason. Slowly, but surely, it was dawning on me that Honoria Whitman wasn't just a casual friend, but a complete stranger.

Chapter Five

MILO TURNED DOWN my offer of a nightcap. I was mildly disappointed, but it was almost ten, and he not only had to get up before six, but felt obligated to check in with his night deputies, Dwight Gould and Sam Heppner. The most romantic part of our Valentine date came when he slapped me on the back and said, "Good night, kid."

I'd finally told him about Ed Bronsky's comments. Milo had snorted. He figured that Fuzzy Baugh probably had made some crack over a second martini. I decided Milo was right, but Ed's silly remarks still rankled.

The next morning I intended to relate Ed's prattle to Vida, but she was in such a euphoric mood that I kept my mouth shut. The dinner in Everett had been "delightful." The yacht club was "elegant." Buck had been "so gallant." I wanted to throw up. Vida was acting like a moonstruck teenager.

By noon, however, she'd pulled herself together. Maybe Leo had teased her, though I doubted that she'd confided in him about her date. As for Carla, she was too self-absorbed to notice anyone else's aberrations.

We were still getting calls about the murder. The numbers would skyrocket as soon as *The Advocate* hit the streets and the carrier boxes. By that time Vida and I would be in Startup. Milo had informed us that Kay's body couldn't be released until Thursday. Snohomish County had had a double murder late Tuesday night. Our homicide was put on hold.

While we were under less pressure on Wednesdays than any other day of the week, I still worked through my lunch hour. If Vida and I were going to be out of the office for a couple of hours, the least I could do was sort through my backed-up in-basket and think about next week's editorial.

About ten minutes before we were to leave, I called Milo to see if he had any news for us. It wouldn't appear in the paper for another week, but I didn't want anything to slip between the cracks.

"I thought Vida was covering this story," Milo said, sounding vaguely amused.

"She is, but I have to keep on top of things," I responded, feeling defensive. "I *am* the editor and publisher."

Milo didn't quibble. "Okay, but don't tell Vida I told you—I'll have Bill call her when I hang up. Stella and Laurie didn't leave the main part of the salon after one forty-five Monday. Stella was working on Ella Hinshaw, and Laurie had finished Charlene Vickers right around then."

Charlene was married to Cal, the service-station owner. She and I belonged to the same bridge club. I considered her a reliable person.

"Charlene didn't notice anything odd, like when she went back to change out of her smock?" I asked.

"She was gone before Kay Whitman arrived," Milo answered. "The other news is that Stella insists the towel doesn't belong to the salon. It's white, it's the right size, but when she gave it another look, she noticed that the brand was different from what they buy."

"Hmm." I grew silent, trying to imagine a would-be

killer sneaking around town with a white towel. "This sounds like the murder was carefully planned."

"You bet," Milo agreed. "Dale Quick is in the lab right now. He's found hair and he's found fibers, but what would you expect in a beauty salon?"

"No sign of the weapon?"

"Nope."

"Or the alligator purse?" My voice took on an edge. At dinner the previous night, I'd given Milo a hard time about neglecting to mention the handbag.

"Nope. It's occurred to me that the purse was taken for a different reason than to make it look like a robbery. Don't print this," Milo cautioned, "but I'm wondering if the killer didn't put the knife in the purse. According to Honoria, Kay's bag was pretty big."

I gnawed at my index finger. "That suggests a woman. Men—in Alpine, anyway—don't carry purses around town."

"They sure don't take them into the Icicle Creek Tavern," Milo agreed, referring to the loggers' favorite local hangout. "Anyway, we're searching the Clemans Building, a four-block radius between First and Fifth and Pine to the river. We're having the garbage sifted, which is a pain in the ass, since Monday was pickup day—all day. Oh, yeah, we dragged the Sky from the UPS loading dock to the bridge. But we didn't expect any luck there—the current's too damned swift this time of year. If I wanted to get rid of a murder weapon, that's where I'd pitch it."

I didn't ask about progress with the autopsy, which I knew was a sore point with Milo. He, more than anyone, resented having Snohomish County move him down the list of priorities. Urging him to have Bill Blatt call Vida right away, I hung up.

Ten minutes later I was riding in Vida's Buick and listening to the same recital I'd heard from Milo. She agreed with his theory about the handbag.

"Examine the knives at Harvey's Hardware," she said, driving carefully along the recently plowed highway. "Most of the ones he sells are under a foot in length. A knife that size could be easily concealed in a woman's purse."

We were stuck behind a moving van that bore Idaho license plates. "That indicates a man," I said, wondering why the thought hadn't dawned on me earlier. "A woman would have had the knife in her own purse. She wouldn't have needed to take Kay's."

Vida, however, wasn't convinced. "What if she was stopped? She'd have to open her purse, and—bingo! There's the bloodstained knife. She could throw Kay's purse away. No, I think the killer could be of either sex. But where did the purse and the knife go?"

"Where did the towel come from?" I asked. Traveling west, we were now below snow level. The fitful flakes had been replaced by a steady rain on the Buick's windshield.

Vida could merely speculate. "I carry a towel under the seat of this car. It was helpful when Roger used to get carsick."

The mention of Vida's eleven-year-old grandson made me feel a bit queasy. Roger was a terror, though Vida found him perfect. While I longed for him to grow up, I dreaded the thought of him as a teenager. If I had one wish for Roger, it was that he would go straight from pre-pubescence to midlife crisis. If I had a wish for myself, it would be to never lay eyes on the little wretch again.

Vida was still talking about her towel. Even after dear little Roger stopped puking on her upholstery, she had kept a towel in the car for unexpected spills. Her daughter, Meg, always carried two towels. Meg wasn't the mother of Roger, but perhaps some of her own offspring were inclined to motion sickness. Darla Puckett was never without a beach towel, due to her advanced age and frequent incontinence. As for Grace Grundle . . .

"Stop!" I cried. "I get the point. Lots of people carry lots of towels. I use rags, and they're in the trunk." Or boot, I thought absently, since I owned a Jag. "Why white?" I asked suddenly.

"Why not?" Vida frowned, but kept her eyes on the road.

"I don't own any white towels," I pointed out. "These days, everybody has colors. Solids, stripes, patterns—but no whites. They're boring and they're too hard to keep up unless you bleach them like Stella does."

"I have two sets of white towels," Vida said. "One is monogrammed."

I stopped arguing. I was still convinced that most households didn't use white towels. Motels, hotels, restaurants, hospitals—and beauty salons—had white towels. The point seemed small, but it bothered me. Milo, of course, would scoff.

We had passed Gold Bar. The thick stands of western red cedar, Douglas fir, Pacific silver fir, and western hemlock now gave way to cottonwood and vine maples, stripped bare by autumn winds. Turning off onto the unpaved road that led to Honoria's house, I noted a few patches of dirty snow tucked in the shade of heavy under-brush. The creek that in summer moved at a sluggish pace was now recklessly coursing through the property, making its way to the Skykomish River on the other side of the highway.

A blue plume of smoke spiraled out of Honoria's tin chimney. The wide porch, which Honoria called a veranda, looked deserted except for the covered summer furniture that was stored at one end. A gently sloping ramp led from the paved path to the front door. It had been several months since I'd seen the converted cabin in daylight. The rich brown shakes had weathered, turning a dark, streaked gray.

Honoria's Nissan was parked in the carport. A Dodge Caravan with California plates stood in a small clearing by the house. I assumed the vehicle belonged to Trevor Whitman.

Vida had called ahead, so Honoria was expecting us. That didn't mean that she was pleased by our visit, however. Given the circumstances, I couldn't blame her.

"There's fresh coffee," she said as we entered the small but comfortable living room with its adroitly placed examples of Honoria's pottery and that of other Pacific Northwest craftsmen. Honoria's throaty voice sounded peevish and her gray eyes didn't convey their usual serenity.

Trevor, who had come to the door with Honoria, was now standing by a wire-and-wicker chair that had been made by one of his sister's artisan friends. A woman about Vida's age stood in the doorway to the kitchen. Honoria introduced her as Ida Smith. Honoria and Trevor's mother crossed the room to shake our hands.

We offered condolences, which Mrs. Smith accepted with a brave smile. Her much-married reputation hadn't prepared me for the real woman: Ida Frickey Whitman Smith was about my height, a trifle overweight, with clear blue eyes that were framed by huge white-rimmed glasses on a chain. Her short white hair was highlighted by a streak of jet black that started at the side part and rippled to the flip that rested against her left cheek. She wore a minimum of makeup, and despite the well-earned wrinkles, she was still pretty in an ordinary, if self-conscious manner.

Vida and I seated ourselves on the genuine leather

couch. Honoria's cat, Dodger, meandered over from his place on the braided rug by the Franklin stove. He sniffed at Vida's boots, then rubbed his head against her ankles. Vida pulled away, giving the cat a disapproving look. She isn't fond of animals.

Mrs. Smith had retreated into the kitchen, presumably to fetch the coffee. Honoria allowed Trevor to move her between the couch and the wire-and-wicker chair.

Honoria let out a long sigh as she adjusted the striped serape that cushioned her back. "I'll be so glad to have my own wheelchair again. It's terribly inconvenient having to depend on other people. I despise that. Besides, this rental doesn't really fit me. But every so often, there's a problem, just like a car. You think you've got one thing fixed, and a few days later something else goes wrong."

Trevor offered his sister a feeble smile. "Your chair cost almost as much as a car, sis."

"Being handicapped is expensive," Honoria allowed.

"It saves on shoes." Trevor's attempt at a joke was met by an awkward silence. Honoria usually could find humor in her situation, but apparently not under the present tragic circumstances. Fortunately, Mrs. Smith re-entered the room, bearing a tray with four mugs, sugar, cream, and a carafe of coffee. All the blue earthenware vessels looked handmade.

"So much rain!" Mrs. Smith exclaimed in her small, light voice, which was very different from her daughter's husky tones. "And the snow, of course, though we haven't had much here. But everything is so gray. Don't you find it depressing?"

The question was intended for both Vida and me. "We're used to it," Vida replied in a manner that dismissed the weather as unimportant.

"I like it," I chimed in. It was true. I'd grown up in

Seattle's grayness, where rain is frequent, but falls almost unobtrusively, like a soft caress. As a child, I thought of rain as a shelter, protecting me from a grown-up world I often feared and didn't understand. Later I realized it was more like a barricade. I could withdraw behind that curtain of water, shielding my emotions and guarding my heart. The rain's patter was a comfort, an old song that told me I was safe under my roof, safe in my own house, safe from the intrusion of others in the private inglenook of my soul.

But Ida Smith hated the rain. "It's not that we don't have rain in California," she declared, passing out steaming mugs of coffee, "but I enjoy sunshine. It makes everything look better, brighter. Cream? Sugar?"

I took sugar; Vida requested both. Usually, she wasn't much of a coffee drinker, preferring tea or hot water. In Honoria's home, she was being polite, even as she tried to nudge Dodger away from her feet.

"When are you returning to California?" Vida asked, still wearing her sympathetic expression.

Honoria, who was encased in a flowing pants costume that matched her ash-blonde hair, glanced at her brother. "If possible, Trevor is flying back with the body tomorrow night. He can ride with the hearse from Everett to the airport at Sea-Tac. Then Friday, Mother and I will leave in Trevor's van. I'll fly back after the services."

"Very sensible," Vida said while I perused the house itself. I'd never been farther than Honoria's living room, but I knew she had a guest room in addition to her bedroom. That was probably where Trevor and Kay had stayed. Ida must have been forced to bunk with her daughter.

". . . parted with her less than half an hour," Vida was saying. In my musings about Honoria's hospitality, I'd missed part of what Vida had said. "The news of Kay's death must have been a terrible shock."

"Terrible," Trevor repeated, hanging his head. "That's the word." He looked up just enough to gaze at his sister. "We didn't believe it when the sheriff told us."

Honoria nodded slowly. "It wasn't real. As ridiculous as it sounds, I thought it was a trick so that Milo could show off his new equipment. You know, like a fire drill." Apparently racked by the memory, she pulled at her short, wavy hair. "It simply didn't sink in."

Mrs. Smith was placing the coffee tray on a table with a twisted-vine stand. The telephone and a petal-shaped lamp also sat on the table. The phone rang just as Mrs. Smith put the tray down.

Her face brightened as she held the receiver to her ear. "It's for you, honey," Mrs. Smith said, pointing the phone at Honoria. "It's your . . . friend."

Honoria stiffened in her wheelchair. "I'll call back." She snapped off the words.

In honeyed apology, Mrs. Smith relayed the message. Honoria continued speaking: "I don't believe in guilt when you're truly not to blame. But I can't help it—the same questions keep plaguing me. What if I hadn't let Kay take my appointment at Stella's?"

Instead of commiserating, Vida leaned forward on the black leather couch. "Indeed. What if you hadn't?"

Honoria's gray eyes widened. "Why—she might still be alive. Is that what you mean?"

"No." Vida now sat up very straight, unconsciously displaying her majestic bosom. "Surely another possibility has occurred to you." She paused, waiting for enlightenment to dawn.

Instead of crying out in protest or looking bewildered, Honoria tipped her head to one side. "You mean that I should be dead rather than Kay? Yes, of course. That's why I'm so distressed. There was no more reason to kill Kay than to kill me. It was a random, wanton act. At least that's the only way I can view it. Kay had no enemies, certainly not around here. As far as I know, neither do I." In an uncharacteristic nervous gesture, Honoria again fidgeted with the serape.

The phone rang again. This time Trevor picked it up, frowned, and buried his face in the receiver. The rest of us kept quiet so that he could hear. But a moment later he looked at his sister, and then his mother.

"It's Cassie," he said, sounding as if he were asking for help.

Mrs. Smith got up from the cane-backed chair where she'd just sat down. "I'll take it in Honoria's room," she said with a tight smile. "Poor Cassie. She must be fretting so."

Trevor spoke again into the phone. "Mother's coming. She'll explain. Hold on." He waited until Mrs. Smith had picked up the extension, then replaced the receiver. "Our sister," he explained. "Cassandra. She lives in Castro Valley."

"She married a lawyer who has his practice there," Honoria put in, carefully folding her hands and placing them in her lap. "They've been there for fifteen years. It's a good location, away from many of the big-city problems, but still close enough to the Bay Area to drive in for cultural events."

"Very nice," Vida murmured, then turned back to Honoria. "You must have been very fond of your sister-in-law. Not every woman would give up a facial to someone else. I can't say that I would."

To my knowledge, Vida had never had a facial in her life. I watched the exchange with interest.

A slight hint of color rose in Honoria's usually porcelain skin. "I rarely have one myself. But it was something new, and I felt . . . well, it would be an opportunity for Kay to see Alpine. We'd run most of our errands in Sultan and Monroe. Then Kay said how much she'd enjoy a facial, and since she was my guest, I couldn't help but give her my appointment. I didn't expect that the salon would have any other openings on such short notice." Suddenly Honoria was speaking at a much faster clip than her usual leisurely pace.

"Probably not," Vida agreed, stepping on Dodger's paw. The cat arched his back, hissed, and finally slunk back to the braided rug. Vaguely, I recalled that in more amiable, intimate days, the animal had been named for Milo Dodge. "Such a cosmetic novelty in Alpine, since Becca returned to town," Vida enthused. "Did you know her, by any chance?"

Honoria looked blank. "Who?"

"Rebecca Wolfe," Vida replied, doing her best to appear ingenuous. "The skin-care specialist. I believe she got married, but unfortunately, it didn't last. I don't know her ex-husband's name. She went back to using her maiden name. As you have done, Honoria." The statement held the hint of a challenge.

"Oh—yes, I did. No," Honoria continued, in some confusion, "I didn't actually know the name of the person who gives the facials. Not then. I think she was the one who came to the sheriff's office to tell them about Kay."

I confirmed Honoria's guess. Vida had gotten to her feet, and was looking rather abject.

"Dear me," she said, "this is a bother, but might I use your bathroom? It's such a long drive back to Alpine, and all this coffee . . ." Her hand trailed in the direction of her unfinished mug.

"Of course," Honoria said, pointing to the open door

through which her mother had exited a few minutes earlier. "It's between the bedrooms."

Vida tromped off, leaving the burden of interrogation on me. "You mentioned that Kay's murder was a wanton act," I stated. " 'Random,' I believe you said. You don't think that robbery was a motive?"

Honoria glanced at her brother. "Trevor says that Kay didn't have much cash in her purse—forty, fifty dollars. They'd brought traveler's checks and used credit cards. Robbery doesn't strike me as a serious motive, but of course anything is possible."

"Drugs," Trevor said. "You never know with these crackheads. Trust me, I've seen men knifed for less than fifty bucks."

The gaze that Honoria gave her brother would have put frost on the Sahara Desert. "We read all about such senseless crimes every day in the newspaper," she declared through lips that barely moved. "It doesn't do any good to speculate. We aren't the type of people who can get inside the ruined minds of drug addicts."

Mrs. Smith returned to the living room. "My! Cassie is so worried about us! I'm so glad she called. I tried to put her mind at ease."

"How are the children today?" Honoria inquired in a strained voice.

"They're fine," Mrs. Smith answered blithely, then hesitated. "Well, they were upset, too. But youngsters at that age—" She turned to bestow a grandmotherly smile on me. "Early teens, you see. They haven't yet gotten outside of themselves. Which is good, really. Children should be protected when they're growing up. They find out all too soon that the real world is so very hard." The corners of her mouth drooped, and she suddenly seemed absorbed by the beringed fingers that were clasped in her lap.

I didn't have a chance to respond. Vida was back in the room. It was clear that she didn't intend to sit down again. Her brow rose clear and high under the hunter-green turban.

"Mr. Whitman, I must again extend my deepest sympathy to you," Vida said. "I lost my husband in a tragic accident almost twenty years ago. No doubt he wasn't much older than your wife. My Ernest was a paragon of a man. It seems that Kay was a wonderful woman. I assure you, I know how you feel."

Trevor bobbed his head, the slack flesh jiggling under his jawline. "Kay was a really outstanding person. I couldn't have asked for more in a wife."

"A treasure," Mrs. Smith added firmly. "She was just like a real daughter to me."

"We were all very fond of Kay," Honoria declared. "That's why Cassie and her family are so upset, too. We'll be glad when all this . . ." She made a helpless gesture with one hand, the folds of her flowing tunic drifting around her arm. "You know what I mean, I'm sure." She bowed her head.

We trudged through the rain to Vida's car. Once the doors were shut and we saw the Whitmans disappear inside the cozy cottage, I uttered a cross between a laugh and a snort.

"Well? What did you overhear in the bathroom?"

"Nothing," Vida snapped. "Honoria must have had those walls reinforced with concrete."

I laughed. "What did you expect to hear?"

"The truth." Vida was waiting to reenter the highway. Traffic was fairly heavy this Wednesday afternoon on the cross-state route. "I never heard such piffle in my life. Cassie, or Cassandra, all in a stew. Shock and confusion and guilt on Honoria's part. They laid it on with a trowel, especially when we got to Kay. Why, you'd think she was perfect!"

"People often talk that way about the recently deceased," I pointed out as Vida finally pulled onto Highway 2. "You called your late husband a paragon." Vida had called him a number of less flattering things over the years, including a big fool. But that was usually in reference to his fatal attempt to go over Deception Falls in a barrel.

Vida still insisted that the Whitmans were trying to hoodwink us. "Honoria kept steering the conversation away from the incident itself. She was as bad as Jane Marshall, preventing anyone else from getting in more than a few worthless words. I think Honoria knows something about Kay that we don't."

"Undoubtedly," I agreed. "The woman was her sister-in-law for sixteen years."

"I don't mean just that," Vida said, dismissing my logic with a shake of her head. "I think she knows why Kay was killed."

Jarred, I stared at the wet ribbon of road. Outside of Gold Bar, we had passed the first of the chain-up areas. The sign indicated that the road was clear, at least until we reached the higher elevations.

"But who?" I asked in a perplexed voice. "That would mean that Trevor or Mrs. Smith killed her. Honoria couldn't have done it. She's an invalid. Kay had no connection to Alpine. As far as we know, she'd never been here before."

Vida was looking grim. "Precisely. We *don't* know. The other day, you mentioned how everything we know about Honoria and her background is strictly on her say-so. What if it's not true? Some of it, all of it, even a small part of it. What we don't know could be the key to Kay's murder."

The raindrops were growing heavier as we climbed among the Cascade foothills. Through the trees, we could glimpse the Skykomish River, a tumbling gash of gray and white, surging dangerously close to its banks. There could be flooding, if we had a sudden thaw coupled with more rain.

I mulled over Vida's words. It was true that I felt Honoria might not have told us the whole truth about her life. Certainly she had revealed only the barest facts. The suggestion that Kay's death was somehow linked to Alpine wasn't completely implausible. Jane and Laurie Marshall came to mind. Jane, at least, had behaved strangely. Becca Wolfe had seemed straightforward enough. But Becca had been gone for several years. And who was the friend who had called Honoria during our visit?

"How should I know?" Vida replied when I posed the question. We were stuck in a long line of traffic, perhaps behind an eighteen-wheeler that found the increasing grade a difficult pull. "I'll tell you one thing," Vida said, resigning herself to the snail's pace. "As I'd hoped, the linen closet was in the bathroom. Honoria doesn't own any white towels."

A quarter mile west of Index, we came to a complete stop. Vida got out of the car, taking her camera with her. "There must have been an accident. I'll hike up a ways to see if I can get a picture."

"Vida, wait." I didn't want my House & Home editor trudging along a cross-state highway in mixed snow and rain. But Vida was already at the bend in the road. I didn't catch up with her until she was standing on the verge, taking pictures of a blue sports car. Two other vehicles had pulled off to the side, and a half-dozen people were milling around in confusion.

I got the name of the sports-car driver, who turned out to be a seemingly unharmed but dazed young man from Everett. He'd been going too fast to take the curve, he mumbled. He'd skidded and gone into the ditch. After we determined that someone with a car phone had already called the state patrol, Vida and I returned to the Buick.

"We're stuck for a while," she said, wiping moisture from her face. Turning this way and that, she broke into a smile. "Where did Cal Vickers say that new house was being built?"

"Right above the spot where the North Fork of the Sky joins the South Fork," I said.

Vida opened her window, making peculiar motions at the car in back of us. The next thing I knew, she had angled the Buick onto the shoulder of the road and was backing up.

"With any luck, we can reverse until we get to that gravel road that goes up to Sunset Falls. I'll bet anything that's where the new construction is located. The North Fork comes in on the other side of the highway by the last bridge."

"That gravel road is on the other side of the bridge," I pointed out. "How are we going to back across that with all these cars?"

"We'll walk." Vida inched along; the bridge came into view through the rear window. She stopped the car and got out again. I had no choice but to follow her.

I'd never been on the road to Sunset Falls before. While it was indeed made of gravel, it appeared to have been recently improved and widened. A network of vine maples grew over the road, and tall evergreens flanked both sides. The air smelled damp and fresh, but the peaceful setting was disturbed by a loud, harsh noise.

In another fifty yards, we found the source of the noise: a cement truck was spewing its contents into a large wooden platform. Farther off, by the river, we could see an already-laid foundation that was even bigger. Vida waved at one of the workmen.

"Yoo-hoo! Press!" She trudged through the muddy ground, sinking almost to the top of her ankle boots.

The workman pointed to another man who was standing off to one side, studying a blueprint. Vida changed her path, and I dutifully followed. The man couldn't hear us coming over the noise. He didn't look up until we were within four feet of him.

"Press!" Vida shouted again. *"Alpine Advocate!"*

"What?" The man cupped his ear. He was wearing a hunting cap, a heavy brown jacket, and dark work pants. I assumed he was the foreman.

Vida motioned for the man to move away from the cement truck. He didn't seem pleased by the suggestion, but complied. Just as we reached another truck that bore the Nyquist Construction logo, the cement pouring stopped.

"We're from *The Advocate*," Vida said, offering the man her warmest smile. She also gave him our names, which seemed to cause some alarm. The man drew back a couple of steps, colliding with the truck.

"I don't talk to the media," he said. "Please leave."

Vida was dumbfounded, or as close as she ever got. "Now, see here, young man—" she began.

For once, I interposed myself between Vida and her would-be victim. "This is quite a project," I said pleasantly. "I see Nyquist Construction has been hired. They're an Alpine firm, and one of our advertisers. I'm surprised they haven't mentioned this job to us."

The man frowned at me. "I asked them not to. I don't do interviews."

I kept the pleasant expression pasted on my face. "Oh? Then maybe you could tell us who owns this property so that we can talk to them. It's so big that I assume it must be a new business. That's news in this part of the world."

The man's features loosened just a fraction. "I own the property. It's not a business. It's my house." He nodded curtly at the second foundation. "There, by the river. They're pouring for the garage and workshop now. If you want to know any more, you can contact me by E-mail."

We didn't have E-mail at *The Advocate*. Not yet, anyway. No doubt we'd get it along with other state-of-the-art innovations when—and if—I actually converted the back shop.

"How about the U.S. mail?" I suggested. "I'd be glad to do that, if you'll give me your name and address."

This time the man actually recoiled. "*My* name? You don't know *my* name?"

Vida couldn't stand being left out. "We certainly don't. We thought you were in concrete."

The man began to laugh. And laugh and laugh. Vida and I stared at each other. Finally, he stopped, literally holding his sides.

"I can't believe it! That's hilarious! I'm Toby Popp!"

We still didn't know who he was. When I said as much, Toby stopped laughing. He was incredulous. "Then why are you here?"

Vida waved a gloved hand at the foundations. "Because of these," she said testily. "Any structure of this size around here is news, especially if an Alpine contractor is involved. Emma already told you that, Mister . . . Popp."

"Well, now you know." Toby's mirth had faded. He was again looking stern. "You'd better leave."

"Certainly," Vida said, turning away.

"Thanks, anyway," I said, trying not to sink into the mire.

Back on the gravel road, Vida demanded to know who

Toby Popp was. I didn't hear her at first, because a second cement truck was now growling away.

"I've no idea," I replied. "A rock star? A TV personality? A psychopath?"

"He's not from around here," Vida asserted. "There've never been any Popps in Skykomish or east Snohomish counties." Her tone dismissed Toby Popp. I decided to do the same, except for having Carla check with Nyquist Construction so that we could run a small article. Their client seemed of no importance, except that he was bringing much-needed dollars into Alpine. I, too, put Toby Popp out of my mind.

That was foolish.

Chapter Six

WE DIDN'T GET back to Alpine until just before five o'clock. Carla had left, though Leo was still at his desk, going over some of the Presidents' Day ads. As expected, the phone messages had piled up, most of them in reference to the murder at Stella's.

"Vida," I asked as my House & Home editor sorted through her own calls, "you must know Stella fairly well. Is there anything in her background that might link her to Kay Whitman?"

Vida shot me a triumphant look. "So you've been thinking about what I said. That's progress. Perhaps." But she turned rueful. "Stella's life is an open book. The only connection might be through Becca. You see," she added in apology, "I don't know much about Becca's life outside of Alpine."

Leo glanced up from his ad copy. "Jeez! There's something you don't know, Duchess? I thought you had everything filed away inside that awe-inspiring head of yours!"

"Go to the dickens, Leo," Vida said with dignity. "I do know that in high school Becca was seeing a very nasty young man from Skykomish." She pointedly ignored Leo, and spoke directly to me. "He was involved in all sorts of unfortunate activities, including a motorcycle gang. That's when Stella became involved. She's always pitched in to help young people with problems."

I was well aware of Stella Magruder's compassion for troubled youth. It was said that she had saved many a teenager from getting in too deep. Apparently, Becca Wolfe was one of them.

"When Becca graduated—barely," Vida went on, "Stella advised her to leave Alpine. Imagine! That was a very daring idea." I kept a straight face, knowing that many adolescents couldn't wait to head for the Big City. "Becca moved away, with her parents' blessing. They simply couldn't handle the girl. Later, I heard she married. Then it seemed that the groom wasn't much better than the biker from Skykomish. That happens so often— young women making the wrong choices, over and over again."

I felt my face stiffen. I hadn't fallen into that particular trap. Instead, I'd clung to the same man for over twenty years. Maybe we all went to extremes when it came to mating. For some women, love had to be found, tested, lost, and found again. The cycle never stopped. Not being in love, or in the act of pursuing it, was tantamount to death. I, however, had found love early. The man I'd chosen had been both dangerous and safe. He had cast me adrift, which frightened as well as suited me. I'd never had to make promises I couldn't keep; there was no need to search for a new love. Until now.

"Anyway," Vida continued, "Becca divorced him, attended beauty school in Seattle, and returned to Alpine. I gleaned that much from the brief interview I did with her in January when she went to work for Stella."

"It's a weak link," I admitted.

Leo was on his feet. "Weak? It doesn't exist. You two are pushing it."

Vida's gaze was filled with disdain. "We didn't ask for your opinion."

"It's still free." Leo was putting on his raincoat. "If you're trying to tie this Whitman broad into the locals, dig into her past first. I used to work with a guy out in the San Fernando Valley who retired to Carmel. You want me to call him tonight?"

I thought it was a good idea. The offer also seemed to smooth Vida's ruffled feathers. "By all means," she said, gathering up her belongings. "Assuming, of course, this chum of yours is in the know."

Leo shrugged. "He's got contacts. Carmel's just south of Pacific Grove. Jake's bored spitless these days. He'll probably be glad to have something to do."

After Leo was gone, Vida heaved a great sigh. "I wish I had kinfolk in Carmel. They'd know something. Do you realize that I have only three California addresses on my Christmas-card list? None of them are in that part of the state." My House & Home editor sounded as if she were owning up to one of the Seven Deadly Sins.

I grinned at Vida. "That's okay. I thought of something just now while Leo was talking about his former colleague. Remember the environmentalist who stayed with Honoria last spring? She and Honoria went way back. Why don't we call her?" Proud of my brainstorm, I kept grinning.

Vida, however, was stalking across the room to the door. "I already did. The environmentalist moved to Brazil to save the rain forests. Good night, Emma."

Deflated, I wandered into my office. The phone calls could wait until morning. My editorial for next week was already outlined. I'd decided to write about the proposed sale of timberlands that had been charred in the previous summer's devastating fires. The blazes had roared through three of eastern Washington's national forests, and federal officials were still debating how to offer salvage logging. Supposedly, parcels of timber that hadn't been seriously harmed by the fires would be put up for bid. The plan was controversial, with the environmentalists arguing that the once-protected areas should stay that way. Timber-industry leaders couldn't agree whether the selected trees would be worth the effort. My point was that the government was dragging its feet.

I was doing the same thing. My buoyant mood of two days earlier had changed into listlessness. Maybe I was suffering from frustration over the seemingly fruitless interview at Honoria's house. Or perhaps the slow drive back to Alpine had dampened whatever enthusiasm I had left for the remainder of the day. I couldn't force myself to make up my mind whether to grocery-shop or eat at the Venison Inn.

The phone rang. It was after five-thirty, too late for anyone to expect an answer. I let it ring twice more, then noticed that the call was coming in on my direct line. I grabbed the receiver before the answering machine switched on.

"Mom—how come you're still at work?" Adam demanded. "Don't you usually cut out early on Wednesdays?"

I was surprised that Adam remembered any details of my job schedule. "Vida and I had to go down to Startup. What's happening in Tempe?"

"Not enough," Adam replied in an unusually mournful voice. "Just like everywhere else. People are indifferent. They don't care. You know what's wrong with the world? Selfishness. Everybody's too inner-directed."

I sucked in my breath. How had my son come to this conclusion when he, too, was guilty? Given his youth and my doting maternal instincts, Adam was in the vanguard of contemporary self-absorption.

"Selfish, yes," I agreed. "But some of it's fear. What gave you this sudden insight?"

"Nothing. Everything." Adam sounded world-weary. "It's been sinking in for a long time, maybe starting with the Navajo. The Hopi, too. Uncle Ben knows what I'm talking about."

So did Mother Emma. But a parent's opinions are rarely worth more than five cents on the dollar. "You've talked to Ben lately?"

"He called me a week or two ago about those family pictures," Adam responded, still solemn. "I was in the middle of making out my class schedule for next term. He advised me to take a lot of sociology and philosophy. That way, I can work with the Inner Person. Otherwise, change is useless."

I hesitated before asking the obvious: "Did Ben suggest beginning with you?"

Adam's laugh was patronizing. "He's always told me that. I made up a slogan. I've got it on the wall of my dorm. 'It all starts with I.' " Taking my silence for lack of comprehension, Adam went on, somewhat impatiently. "The word *it*—that begins with an *i*. Which means that if a person is going to make a difference—"

"I get it," I said. "Ben's right. You're right. But how do you intend to go about changing the world?"

"Mom," Adam said in his familiar tone of exasperation, "you're out of it. Change is made in ways that seem small, even unimportant. You have to go one-on-one with other people. That's why I want to be a social worker."

For the past few months Adam had been digressing from his previous goal, which was to become an anthropologist or an archaeologist, whichever was easier to spell on a résumé. He had spent two summers working the Anasazi digs with Ben, which had inspired my son to live in the past. That had been fine with me, as long as he worked at preparing for the future. Social work didn't seem to suit him.

"How many credits do you need to graduate in social work?" I inquired.

"Graduate?" Adam now sounded vague. "I don't know why a diploma is such a big deal. It's understanding and experience and compassion that mean the most when you work with people. Getting a so-called degree will take forever. I figured that after this next term I'd quit school and start doing something. Think of all the people I could be helping instead of staring at a computer screen or listening to some disorganized prof drone on about theories."

Whatever appetite I'd had earlier now turned into a knot in my stomach. "Adam, you've gone to three different universities, all at great expense. You've finished the basic requirements for most degrees. You've spent two years at ASU. Surely you can't need more than thirty or forty credits to graduate. Another year or so won't make that much difference to civilization as we know it."

"You don't sense the urgency," Adam asserted, still condescending. "If you hung out with Uncle Ben the way I've done the last couple of summers—"

"What does Uncle Ben say about this latest scheme of yours?" I interrupted.

"It's not a scheme. It's a blueprint." Adam paused, then lowered his voice. "I haven't told him yet."

Deciding that Ben might have more influence on Adam than I would, and realizing from twenty-two years of experience that it was pointless to argue, I tried to relax.

"Talk it over with him when you're in Tuba City for Easter break," I said. Then, because a mother never can resist giving unwelcome advice: "Meanwhile don't do anything . . . precipitous." I'd almost said "dumb." "That degree is your ticket to helping more people in better ways than you could do otherwise."

There was a brief silence at the other end of the line. Maybe my son was actually thinking about what I'd just said. But when Adam spoke again, he had gone off in a different direction.

"Are you pissed because you think my father wouldn't fork over any more travel money if I was out of school?"

Tom had been providing Adam's transportation for the past three years. He and my son—our son—had never met until Adam was in college. In my war of independence, I'd kept them apart. I had gone for twenty years without any contact with Tom. Then, after we met again and eventually ended up back in bed, we had discovered that time hadn't diminished our passion. In the meantime I'd let Tom get acquainted with our now-grown child. The two had seemed to forge a tentative bond. If Adam thought about it at all, he probably figured that Tom and I were nothing more than friends. We were no longer even that. I hadn't told Adam that I had again excised his father from my life.

Nor would I tell him now. I'd already uttered words he'd rather not hear. "I'm not concerned about your father's contributions," I said stiffly. "We got along before he made them, we can get along without them again. But I suspect he'd like to see you finish college."

"Do his other kids have degrees?" It was the first time I'd ever heard Adam refer to Tom's two children by Sandra.

"Not yet," I hedged. Tom's daughter, Kelsey, was threatening to quit Mills College to become an actress. The last I heard, his son, Graham, was finishing at USC.

"He won't care," Adam said easily. "He's told me that I should be whatever I want. He's not a dictator."

The implication was clear. Mom was the Black Hat. "You can be a bricklayer or a dentist or a warlock, if that's what you want. But you'd damned well better do it with a diploma in your hip pocket."

The vigor in my voice must have made a dent on Adam. "I'll talk it over with Uncle Ben at Easter," he mumbled, not sounding happy at the prospect.

"Good," I said, tempering my tone. "How's it going otherwise?"

It was going, sort of. There was yet another new girl, whose name I didn't bother to file in my brain. Classes were hard, and most of the instructors were boring. The roommate that he'd acquired in the fall had turned out to be a drug user and had left the campus the previous week. Without asking for money, clothes, or other merchandise, Adam finally rang off. He sounded glum, and that made me unhappy.

I'd call him back tomorrow night; maybe I'd insist that he come home for Easter. But that would disappoint Ben, who couldn't desert his parishioners during Holy Week. My brother and I were lucky to get together twice a year.

My spirits plunged still deeper. On weary legs, I finally left the office. The Jag had sat too long in the cold weather. It didn't want to start. Given my mood, I could empathize.

I went back into the office to call Cal Vickers and ask for a tow. Fortunately, he was still open. Alpine's merchants are whimsical when it comes to keeping hours. Cal said he'd be there in about ten minutes. It was six straight up, and he was about to close. He offered to give me a ride home in the tow truck.

I killed five minutes by trying to balance my checkbook. It had been payday, and I'd gone to the bank in the morning, but forgotten to enter my deposit. Grimly, I wondered how much the car repair would cost. There were only two other Jaguars in Skykomish County. I doubted that Cal would have parts, if they were needed. Usually, they were.

It was still snowing when I went outside to stand beside my precious, if aggravating, car. Traffic on Front Street had begun to dwindle. Most of the shops and businesses were closed. I glanced down the street toward the sheriff's office, but saw no sign of Milo's Cherokee Chief.

My teeth were beginning to chatter when Ed Bronsky pulled up in his Mercedes. "Emma!" he called. "Got a minute?"

"No," I shouted back. "I'm waiting for a tow from Cal."

"Then you've got more than a minute." Ed backed into the space usually reserved for Vida. He got out of the car, walking slightly pigeon-toed in his hand-tooled leather boots. "I've been thinking since we talked yesterday at Buddy's studio. Ever realize how you can be too close to see something for what it really is?"

"Don't start that again, Ed," I warned. "I'm not responsible for anything in this town except myself and *The Advocate*. Nobody in their right mind could accuse me of—"

"No, no, no." Ed waved his gloved hand. "I don't mean the murders. You're going to have to fend for yourself when it comes to—"

It was Ed's turn to be interrupted. Cal was slowing down in the middle of the street, amber lights flashing on top of his tow truck.

"I've got to go," I said with a toothy smile for Ed.

"Wait." Ed's voice conveyed his recently acquired self-confidence. Money, especially unearned, often bestows imagined attributes that are taken seriously by both the beneficiary and the beholder. "What are you doing for dinner?" Ed inquired. "Shirley's putting on one of her gourmet meals. An extra mouth won't matter."

As far as I knew, Shirley Bronsky's idea of gourmet cooking was roasting hot dogs on an imported fire poker. Going to the grocery store suddenly held enormous appeal. Except, of course, that I couldn't get there and back under my own power.

Cal had gotten out of his truck. Apparently, he'd heard the last part of my conversation with Ed. "Let's see if I can start this thing. Maybe you flooded the engine."

I brushed snowflakes from my eyelashes while Cal slid inside the Jag and Ed drummed his fingers on the Mercedes's ice-blue hood.

"Nope," Cal announced, getting out of my car. "Dead as a doornail. Go ahead, Emma. I won't be able to look at your Jag until morning anyway. I'll take it over to the station now and call you before noon."

I was trapped. Trying not to look like gallows bait, I turned back to Ed. "Okay, thanks. But you'll have to drive me home later."

Ed beamed. "No problem." He patted the Mercedes's front fender. "This baby runs like a gem in any kind of weather. Hop in and feel what it's like to travel in style."

Maybe the dig at my ailing ten-year-old Jag wasn't intentional. The Mercedes was beautiful and did indeed drive like a dream. But the pearl-gray leather interior was all Bronsky: sticky fingers had plied the upholstery; the ashtrays overflowed with gum and candy wrappers; the floor was littered with paper cups and bags from fast-food outlets. Absently, I wondered if Ed traveled with a towel. He could use one, along with a mop and a shovel.

The Bronskys still lived in their crowded split level on Pine Street. Ed had bragged about buying a new house ever since he'd inherited his fortune from Aunt Hilda a year and a half ago. Shirley wanted to build her "dream palace" from the ground up. It appeared that they hadn't yet come to a meeting of the minds.

The Bronskys had, however, acquired new furnishings, mostly of Italian Provincial design. The result was that they had less room to move around in, but more surfaces to clutter. Ed, Shirley, and their five children surrounded by ornate credenzas and naked Roman deities gave me something akin to the vapors.

So did Shirley's gourmet meal, which turned out to be a random assortment of microwavable entrées from the higher-priced end of the Grocery Basket's frozen-food section. On my left, Molly Bronsky was eating a pot pie; to my right, Joey was gulping down lasagna; I had what passed for creamed turkey on a wedge of something that looked like a small sponge, but wasn't as tasty.

The Bronskys eventually got around to talking about their future home. Shirley had won the war. They were going to build on property just past the golf course and across the river.

"The county commissioners are still dragging their butts about the new bridge," Ed stated, oblivious to the trickle of chicken Kiev sauce on his chin. While my host liked to eat just about anything that didn't come marked with a skull and crossbones, he fancied himself a gourmand. His tastes, however, remained lowbrow; Ed was merely paying more for better-looking boxes. "I'm going to have to do a little arm-twisting with the local engineering folks. I'd like to see the road branch off closer to our house. Not that I want to be right on a main drag—we'll have a tree-lined drive. And a gate, of course."

"With lions," Shirley put in, her banana satin-covered bosom jiggling. "You know, one on each side, sitting on a pedestal."

Ed nodded solemnly. "The family coat of arms can be worked into the gate itself. Wrought iron, I suppose.

Gold tarnishes. We're hiring a Seattle architect. The best. But we'll let Nyquist Construction do the building. If they're good enough for Toby Popp, they're good enough for us."

I stared at Ed, trying to keep eye contact instead of watching the cheese sauce run onto his shirt. "Toby Popp? You know him? Who is he?"

Ed stared back. "Emma! You don't know who Toby Popp is?" Obviously, he found my ignorance appalling. "Toby Popp," he said, lowering his voice as if the revelation might shock his children or whoever else spied on Ed and his riches, "is a former computer executive who retired this fall at the age of forty-two. He's worth billions. Toby's been written up in the business and investment publications, including *The Wall Street Journal*. I subscribe, you know." Ed puffed out his chest, so that it met his stomach.

In my job, I try to keep up with the met dailies out of Seattle, Everett, and Wenatchee, as well as the weeklies from Snohomish and Chelan counties. Occasionally, I read *The New York Times*. But there weren't enough hours in the day to catch more than a rare peek at *People* or *Newsweek*, let alone *The Wall Street Journal*.

Ed, however, was more than willing to educate me about Toby Popp. "He dropped out of Stanford in his sophomore year, got a job in Silicon Valley, and took off like a rocket. Software, that was his strong suit. Toby was always a hundred miles ahead of everybody else. About ten years ago he moved to Seattle to revolutionize one of the fledgling companies on the East Side. The man's a genius, but he's been there, done that, and now he wants to kick back and enjoy life. What a guy!"

Shirley, who had been nodding her gilded curls, giggled in her squeaky manner. "Just like Ed! It's so terrific to be able to give up the drudgery when you're still young."

I refrained from pointing out that Ed's idea of drudgery at *The Advocate* had involved drinking coffee, eating sweet rolls from the Upper Crust Bakery, and digging through his dog-eared clip-art file.

"So," I remarked, relinquishing the rest of the sponge, "Toby Popp's building a snazzy house down by Index." I wasn't about to confess that Vida and I had met the man and not known who he was.

"Yes," Shirley said, her plump body writhing some more under the satin pantsuit. "We've seen the architectural drawings. It's going to be fabulous."

"Big?" I kept my tone casual.

"Huge," Ed responded as the Bronsky offspring began to leave the table in relays, returning with large bowls of ice cream topped with various syrups. "The main house is four bedrooms, a living room, a dining room, five bathrooms, den, video-viewing room, and sunroom. There's a pool and an exercise room, too. Then he's got a separate triple garage with his computer lab attached, and another bathroom with an adjoining sauna and whirlpool. It's all cutting-edge stuff, solar heating, the works."

"Does Popp have a Mom Popp and some Poppettes?" I asked.

Ed grimaced. "I haven't gotten *that* chummy. In fact, we haven't exactly met yet. But we will. We have so much in common."

I assumed Ed had garnered his knowledge of Toby Popp through the media and Nyquist Construction. I was vexed. A retired billionaire software king was news. Index was less than twenty miles from Alpine. Ed should have passed the tip along to his former boss. Toby Popp might not like the media, but his presence was still worthy of a story. I'd ask Carla to step up her news-gathering efforts.

Shirley's efforts in the kitchen apparently ended with pressing the buttons on her microwave. I wasn't offered dessert, which was fine. I was anxious to get home. The Bronskys made feeble protests about my early departure, but Ed put on his cashmere overcoat before I could reconsider. When we were back in the Mercedes, he sprang his next surprise.

"Remember what I was saying when I stopped in front of the office this evening? What I meant by being too close to a thing is this book deal." Ed pulled onto Seventh, where the snow was falling harder. "I'm not sure I've got the perspective to put my life on paper. I can organize all the facts, the highlights, the insights, everything like that, but I need an outsider to capture the real me."

A butterfly net would have captured the real Ed about now, as far as I was concerned. We passed the Lutheran church. I knew what was coming. The sponge turned over in my stomach. Throughout my career I'd been approached by many leeches who wanted to collaborate. "I've got a great book in me," they usually began. I always tried to think of a tactful way to tell them that's where the book should stay.

"So what I mean, Emma, is that you're a pretty decent writer," Ed rattled on. "You can make the county commissioners' meetings sound sort of interesting, and some of your editorials aren't bad, either. You could write my biography. I'd give you credit, of course. You know, *My Rise to Riches and Beyond* by Ed Bronsky and Emma Lord." Even as he spoke, my name came out in much smaller type than his.

"Ed, I'm flattered, but—"

"I'll tape everything, then you can transcribe it and make it into a—what do you call it?—a narration style?"

"Narrative," I said in a weak voice.

"We can start this weekend," Ed asserted as we turned off Spruce Street to climb the final block to Fir, where my log house was situated at the edge of town. "I'll start tonight with my baby days. By Saturday, I should be up to third grade."

While the Mercedes handled beautifully, even a 400 E is only as good as its driver. Ed was looking at me instead of at the road. Despite the studded tires, the car was skidding ever so slightly because Ed wasn't following in the tracks laid down by other vehicles. We just missed hitting a Ford pickup parked by the high-school baseball field.

"Let me think about it," I hedged, knowing I should have said no outright. But I was nervous, and didn't want to upset my self-absorbed chauffeur.

"There'll be some money in it for you," Ed declared warmly. "Publishers pay big bucks up front, right?"

"They give advances, yes," I agreed, regaining my nerve as we glided along Fir Street. My house would have been in sight if I could have seen through the thick snow. "It's not the money, Ed. It's that I'm not sure I'll have the time. Right now we've got this murder story on our hands."

Ed aimed for the driveway, missed, and almost hit my mailbox. He slid to a stop, and I started to get out of the car.

"Vida's covering the murder," Ed said, leaning in my direction. "Like I told you, it doesn't help your reputation to associate yourself too much with these killings. People get the impression that you enjoy them."

Having arrived on my own property in one piece, I had the luxury of losing patience. "That's rot, Ed, and you know it. Good grief, you've worked on newspapers. Even if Vida's assigned to the investigation, I still have to oversee her coverage." Now out of the car, I gave Ed what I hoped was a friendly smile. "Thanks for dinner and the lift. I'll talk to you later, okay?"

"I'll call Friday," Ed promised. "Remember, this is the chance of a lifetime. You won't ever get another offer like this one."

Thank God, I thought. I kept smiling until my back was turned and I was headed for the sanctuary of my snug log house. I certainly didn't enjoy murder, but death warmed over held more charm than coauthoring Ed Bronsky's biography. Presently, the only story that captured my imagination was Kay Whitman's. Her life might not have been any more eventful than Ed's, but her manner of dying had given her notoriety. Too often that was the case: an ordinary person, living out routine days, without special talent or burning ambition, holding down a job, paying bills, going to the dentist, taking an occasional trip. Then, for some terrible reason, or none at all, death hurls the unremarkable victims into the limelight. They don't know, they don't care, which is as well. Still among the living, the rest of us are left to pick over their bones, like vultures.

Ed Bronsky was silly. Kay Whitman was dead. In all probability, I couldn't escape either of them.

Chapter Seven

VIDA AND LEO had both left messages on my answering machine. Figuring that the call to Leo wouldn't take long, I dialed his number first.

"No big meetings tonight," Leo remarked in a strained voice. "I was beginning to wonder if you'd run into an icy patch—or a hot stud."

"I ran into Ed Bronsky," I replied dryly. "He runs neither hot nor cold, but always at the mouth."

Leo chuckled. "Ed probably wants to run for mayor. I'll vote for him, if only because the job might keep him out of my hair." His voice had relaxed. "I wanted to tell you that I called my old buddy Jake Spivak in Carmel. Unfortunately, he wasn't home. His wife said he had to go up to San Francisco unexpectedly. Jake probably won't be back for a couple of days. Shall I try him then?"

"Oh . . ." I had sunk onto the sofa and was kicking off my boots. "That's up to you, Leo. Do you think he can help much?"

"He can dig up backgrounds," Leo said. "Honoria's from Carmel, and Pacific Grove's within spitting distance. There's always gossip. Maybe Jake knows somebody like Vida."

I appreciated Leo's willingness. "Sure, let him try. It probably won't do any good as far as solving the murder is concerned. Milo will be checking out the suspects, too."

"Will he?" There was irony in Leo's voice. "Face it, babe, your favorite sheriff is on the hot seat. How hard is he going to push this thing when it comes to his bed partner?"

"*Ex*–bed partner," I said, a bit too sharply. "Don't underestimate Milo. We're talking about his job. He'll do what he has to."

"Sure." Leo didn't sound convinced. "But he won't go for the gossip. He never does."

That much was true. Milo dealt strictly in facts and evidence. But I didn't defend the sheriff any further. I knew Leo wasn't a great admirer of our local lawman, an attitude I chalked up to journalistic cynicism. In thirty years of newspapering, Leo had seen it all, and not liked much of it.

On the other hand, Vida was full of enthusiasm. "I dropped in on Stella," she said before I could get in any more than "Hi." "A courtesy call, in a sense, because she's been through a great deal. Naturally, I got her to talk about Becca."

"Naturally," I murmured, carrying my gypsy phone to the cupboard where I kept my meager supply of liquor.

"Becca's been legally divorced for over a year," Vida continued. "Her husband's name was Eric Forbes. I'm told he has a pleasing way with women, all charm on the outside. When Eric worked, which wasn't often, he drove a truck for some firm in the south end of Seattle. He drank and beat her. An awful person, but apparently very good-looking. So was the unsuitable boy from Sky-komish. Becca and Eric stayed together for three years, which means she married him about a year after she left Alpine. Now here's the interesting part." Vida took a deep, audible breath. "He *stalks* her, mostly by phone. Doesn't that beat all?"

"Ahhh—well, not these days. It happens." I'd poured myself a small amount of bourbon and was adding ice. Quietly. I didn't want Vida to know that I was imbibing an alcoholic beverage. My House & Home editor was Presbyterian to her toes, and didn't approve of strong drink, except on rare occasions.

"Of course it does!" Vida suddenly sounded impatient. "But in this case, I mean the connection with Kay Whitman's murder. What better way to get back at your ex-wife than to kill off one of her clients?"

I took a quick gulp of my drink. "Vida! That's preposterous!" My House & Home editor wasn't showing sense, one of her favorite attributes.

Vida harrumphed. "I didn't say that's what happened. I'm merely pointing out that it's a possibility. Have you got a better idea?"

I didn't. But at least I could tell her about Toby Popp. Vida dismissed the software magnate with a sniff. "So silly, all these Windows and Apples and Macs and DOS. Indeed, until five years ago, the only Doss I knew was a stool softener. Not that I use it, of course, but Darla Puckett—"

"Ed wants me to ghost-write his autobiography," I interrupted.

"What?" Vida's voice was a predictable squawk. "Don't tell me! Ed's an utter ninny! What on earth could you write about *him*? He hasn't done a single thing in his life worth putting into a two-inch cutline! Oh, Emma, I hope you refused!"

"I tried to," I replied meekly.

"Say no. Now." She paused fractionally. "It's just after eight. Shall we try Laurie again?"

"Laurie?" I blinked into my bourbon. "What for? We came a cropper there already."

"We could invite her out to dessert. It's imperative that we see her alone. It would be our way of apologizing for intruding on her family's dinner hour."

The idea of putting on my boots again and surrendering my bourbon wasn't appealing. "It's snowing like mad," I pointed out. "Jane Marshall won't let Laurie meet us. I've got a better idea."

"You do?" Vida sounded surprised.

Accustomed to Vida's lack of confidence in anyone but herself, I ignored her response. "I still have to get my hair cut. Stella's appointment book must be crammed because of all the cancellations. I'll ask for Laurie, and make it sound as if I'm doing Stella a favor by freeing her up."

"Well . . ." Doubt surfaced in Vida's voice. "I'm the one who should talk to Laurie. After all, I'm covering the story."

"Do you need a hair appointment?" I knew Vida was better at prying.

"I could use a shampoo set," Vida replied thoughtfully. "Ordinarily, I go on Saturday morning, but I could pretend that I have an important engagement tomorrow night." She paused, then brightened. "Indeed, I might ask Buck to dinner. I haven't yet cooked for him."

I shuddered. Vida's cooking was just one notch above Shirley Bronsky's. Despite all the recipes and kitchen tips Vida had run over the years, her attempts at the stove were always doomed. I felt that serving Buck Bardeen a home-cooked meal was a bad idea. But I didn't dare say so.

"Okay, you ask for Laurie and I'll stick with Stella." We cut the deal. Pumping Laurie was a dirty job, but nobody could do it better than Vida Runkel.

*   *   *

"Why," Carla demanded, stamping one of her Doc Marten–clad feet, "does a retired billionaire in Index have to be a computer nerd? Why can't he be a basketball player or a movie star?"

Under my overgrown bangs, I narrowed my eyes at Carla. "You wanted a tough assignment, you got it. Toby Popp hates the media. Go get 'em, Steinmetz."

"Oh, *wow*!" Carla was sarcastic. "I can see it all now. Funny glasses, complexion problems, dresses like my father. Plus, he'll talk about macros and the Internet and all that boring junk. The only thing he'll have to eat is Ding Dongs. How do I find this dweeb?"

I drew Carla a map, advising her that Toby Popp might be on site. "I suspect he enjoys watching his mansion's progress," I said, checking my watch. It was eight twenty-five, and I'd conned Stella into taking me half an hour early, before her official opening at nine. "If he's not around, the workmen should know where to find him. Call Nyquist Construction first. They'll have an address." I shouldn't have to lead Carla by the hand. After almost five years of experience she should know how to track down a potential interviewee.

I left Carla looking confused while Vida hummed at her typewriter and Leo tried to talk Alpine Appliance into a four-color insert for next week. Out on Front Street, the fresh snow had been plowed, and some of the sidewalks were shoveled. Ours wasn't among them, and wouldn't be cleared, unless our next-door neighbors at Cascade Dry Cleaning had a charitable impulse. I trod carefully until I reached the corner. I'd walked to work, taking the treacherous downhill streets slowly. By sunrise, the clouds had lifted and the temperature had risen to almost forty. It would probably rain later in the day.

My route took me past the sheriff's office. Milo's

Cherokee Chief was parked in its usual slot. I'd drop in on him later. Maybe. I didn't want to infringe on Vida's territory.

Stella was alone when I arrived. She still seemed frazzled from her ordeal, though she was doing her best to keep up appearances. There was a fresh bouquet from Posies Unlimited, the valentine displays had been replaced by shamrocks for St. Patrick's Day, and Stella looked as if she'd lightened her own hair color and changed the hue of her makeup.

"Vida's right," she declared, handing me a smock. "The ghouls are coming in droves. I've had eleven calls from people I never heard of around here, and six more from Snohomish County. People are really strange."

I agreed. Then, hesitating only a split second, I marched back to the changing room. I had to put the shock of Monday's discovery behind me. Kay Whitman's blood and her lifeless body would always haunt me, but memories can be tamed. They must or life wouldn't be bearable.

This time I made no mistake about which room to enter. But after I had put on the smock, I couldn't resist a peek into the facial room.

The door was locked. I refrained from mentioning the fact to Stella because I didn't want her to know I'd been snooping. Maybe the room was always locked before Becca arrived. Or maybe Stella and her crew were taking safety precautions too late.

"I don't suppose you've had any brainstorms about the murder," I remarked as Stella shampooed my hair.

"A dozen of them," she answered. "Drug addicts. Vagrants from the train. A serial killer working his way across the state. One of those crazy hermits." Stella gently massaged my temples. "I like the hermit idea best. Those old guys wander into town every six months, and nobody pays any attention. I said as much to Jack Mullins. Do you know what he told me?"

"Uh-uh," I replied, feeling more relaxed than I'd been in days.

"Jack says he figures there are at least a couple of murders every year in this county that nobody ever knows about. Men, mostly, oddballs who wander the woods and sleep under the trees or in caves or abandoned shacks, and eventually meet up with some other oddball, like the hermits. One of them kills the other, and does God-knows-what with the body. They're never missed by anyone, because they have no family or friends. They simply disappear, and whoever kills them is never caught. Gruesome, huh?"

I'd heard a similar theory from Milo. The incidents weren't peculiar to Skykomish County, but apparently occurred wherever there was enough open country to accommodate wandering weirdos.

"That would be a convenient solution," I said as Stella rinsed the conditioner out of my hair.

Stella understood. "I know, it's too easy. But it *is* possible." Sitting up straight, I saw the anxiety in her face.

"The problem is that there's no motive," I said, following Stella to her workstation. "Thus, no suspects. The only people who knew Kay Whitman were her husband, her sister-in-law, and her mother-in-law. They all seemed to adore her."

In the mirror, I could see Stella frown. "Don't I know it? Even if somebody made a mistake, and thought Kay was Honoria, who'd want to kill her? She's an invalid who makes funny little jugs. What did she ever do to get her throat slit?"

For one awful, fleeting moment a phrase flashed through my mind: *spurned lover*. That would be Milo. That would be incredible. Then there was *jealous rival*.

That could be me. Had anyone considered the possibility? I felt a little sick. My head drooped, and Stella gave me a nudge.

"Hey, Emma, sit up! I can't do this if you're going to stare at your knees."

"Sorry." I offered Stella a ghostly smile.

Intent on her task, she didn't notice that I'd also gone pale. "What bothers me," she said, snipping away, "is that people are talking. Oh, I haven't heard anything firsthand, but I know this town. As long as the sheriff hasn't fingered anybody, suspicion is bound to fall on the salon—Becca and Laurie and even me. It doesn't make sense, it doesn't have to, all the rumor mongers need is—"

The phone interrupted Stella. With a sigh, she hurried to the front counter. Her practiced cheerful greeting died on her lips after the first two words.

"She's not here, and even if she were, I wouldn't let you talk to her. If you call again, I'm putting a trap on this line." Stella slammed the receiver down. Halfway back to her station, she stopped. "I'm going to do it anyway. I'm sick of that creep bothering Becca and the rest of us." Wheeling around, Stella returned to the phone. "Who should I call, Emma? The phone-company business office?"

"Dial the toll-free number, then ask for security," I responded. "Bear in mind that if they do it, you have to agree to prosecute."

Stella removed her hand from the receiver. "Really? I'm not sure that'd be smart. This guy's a real trouble-maker."

I shrugged, feeling snippets of hair tickle my nose and cheeks. "Maybe they've changed the rules. But that's what I found out ten years ago in Portland when Adam and I were getting a lot of crank calls. We decided it wasn't worth it because we figured they were from some dippy thirteen-year-old girl whose parents were doing so much pot that they didn't know if their kids were in the same state." As I babbled on I noticed the lines deepen on Stella's forehead. I remembered what Vida had told me about Becca's ex-husband. "Who is it?" I asked, though I had a feeling I already knew.

I was right. "His name's Eric Forbes and he's a walking time bomb. He damned near killed Becca once— in fact, he put her in the hospital, and that was when she finally left him." Wearily, Stella returned to her post. "As soon as she got back to Alpine, he started sending letters, mostly having to do with legal stuff and property—not that they had any—but you know what I mean—who bought this dish, who paid for that table. Becca didn't care if he got everything. She just wanted out. She wouldn't write back. That's when he started calling her here. She's got an answering machine at home so she can screen her calls."

Vida's outlandish theory suddenly made a little more sense. "Has this Eric ever been in Alpine?"

"I don't think so." Stella flipped my hair this way and that, then began cutting again. "If he has, Becca doesn't know about it. I'm sure she'd tell me if he showed up in town."

"What about her parents?" I inquired. "Have they heard from him?"

Stella gave a rueful shake of her head. "Marlene Wolfe drinks. Oh, she's sweet enough when she's smashed, but completely wrapped up in herself and the bottle. Monty Wolfe sits around in his so-called workshop and reads dirty magazines. How do you think Becca got into trouble in the first place? Your thirteen-year-old in Portland isn't the only one with parents who are permanently AWOL."

My mind veered in the opposite direction, to Laurie's mother. Jane Marshall stood on guard over her daughter, the epitome of the protective parent. Had she always watched her child so closely? Or was Jane's attitude newly acquired? I was about to pose that question when Laurie wandered into the salon.

"Good morning, Laurie," Stella said cheerfully. "You've got a full day. We had to squeeze in Nancy Dewey and Mrs. Runkel. Nancy's going into Seattle with Doc for some bigwig medical dinner, and Mrs. R has a social engagement." Stella winked at both Laurie and me in the mirror.

"Mrs. Runkel has a *date*?" Laurie's usually blank expression took on a hint of life. "With a *man*?"

Stella gazed at my reflection. "That's what it sounds like. Am I wrong, Emma?"

"No." I was noncommittal.

"Good for her," Stella declared as she made a final pass at my bangs. "Vida spends too much time with other women. That's bad. You lose perspective on life. If anything ever happens to Richie, I'll be out square-dancing with every unattached man in Skykomish County. God wouldn't have made two sexes if He hadn't intended for them to mingle." Wielding a hairbrush, Stella created a cascade of billowing chestnut waves that she sprayed into submission. "There! You won't be able to manage that for yourself, so you'd better schedule a body perm in three weeks. Do it now, or I won't see you again until May."

Sue Anne Daley entered the shop with a baby in a carrier. I knew her in-laws from church, so I smiled and waved before going back to change. Alone in front of the mirror, I turned my head this way and that. The new cut was reasonably attractive, but Stella was right: I had no talent for hairstyling beyond washing it and drying it with a towel. Stella's handiwork would be lost in twenty-four hours.

Back at the counter, Laurie was welcoming Molly Freeman, the high-school principal's wife. Becca arrived at the same time that the mailman came in. The salon was suddenly a-bustle. I waited to pay my bill and make the next appointment.

Becca whisked Molly away, leaving me with Laurie and the mailman. The post office was half a block from the Clemans Building, so the businesses at the west end of Front Street always received their mail before we did. Laurie handed the carrier what looked like three outgoing bills, gave him a vague smile, and then turned to me.

"That's thirty dollars, Ms. Lord. Do you need any hair products today? We have a special this week on frosted nail polish." Laurie's voice was mechanical; her head bobbed like a wobbly doll.

"I'm okay," I replied, opening my checkbook. "But I need another appointment. Three weeks from now, for a cut and a perm." Now I, too, was reciting like a robot, parroting Stella's instructions.

The request seemed to flummox Laurie. I couldn't blame her, since I never scheduled an appointment in advance, and was notorious for coming in at least two weeks late. Laurie dropped the mail, which she had been in the process of moving under the counter.

"Three weeks?" she said, all but disappearing as she crouched to collect the scattered envelopes. "That would be early March—"

Laurie screamed. I jumped, then leaned over the counter to see what had happened. She was kneeling , her stylish wheat-colored hair hiding her face. From the rear of the salon, Stella came at a run.

"Good God! What is it now?" she gasped.

But Laurie had regained her composure as quickly as

she had lost it. "Nothing," she said sharply, brushing the
side bangs from her forehead and regarding Stella with
eyes that were startlingly hard. "I thought I saw a spider.
One of those big ones, about the size of a compact."

Stella looked both annoyed and puzzled. "It's too cold
for spiders," she said in a vague voice. Then, with an
unsteady hand on Laurie's shoulder, she spoke more softly:
"Don't do that again, Laurie. I can't stand any more shocks,
and neither can our clients." Stella's buxom figure sashayed
back to Sue Anne Daley, who wore an understandably terrified expression while the baby in the carrier started to cry.
"We're still suffering from nerves." Stella laughed in a
forced manner. "You know, Sue Anne, I've been thinking
that you could use some auburn highlights. . . ."

Laurie was again standing up, flushing under her carefully applied cosmetics. "I'm sorry, Ms. Lord. Spiders
scare me, even the harmless ones." She lowered her gaze,
which had somehow struck me as unusually cunning.
"How about Thursday, March ninth, at three?"

Having added a six-dollar tip for Stella, I slid the
check across the counter. "Make it the eighth, same time.
Wednesdays are better for me to leave early."

Laurie consulted the appointment book again. "Three-
thirty?"

That was fine. I thanked Laurie, called out a farewell
to Stella and Sue Anne, then left the salon. My hair
looked better, but I felt worse.

I decided to visit Alpine Medical Supply. Will Stuart
couldn't improve my state of mind, but maybe he'd be
able to answer some questions.

Janet Driggers accosted me before I'd gone six feet.
She was on her way to work at Sky Travel, and her usually raucous spirits were not in evidence.

"You know, Emma," she began in a serious voice I
hardly recognized, "murder is bad enough. But when the

victim is from out of town, and Al doesn't get the burial business, we can't help but be pissed off. I did a slow burn yesterday when I read the story in *The Advocate*."

Janet sounded as if she had fallen in step with Ed Bronsky. It didn't seem likely. The two almost always chose opposite sides of any issue at Chamber of Commerce meetings.

"Kay Whitman's place of residence is my fault?" I tried to inject humor into the remark.

But Janet remained unamused. "Winter's usually our best season—for funerals, that is. The old farts can't take the cold. But this year there's been a downturn in dying. It's all these Scandinavians—they live to about a hundred, and they've got ice water in their veins anyway. No wonder I have to work part-time at the travel agency. Otherwise we'd be broke about now."

While Janet's green eyes conveyed candor as well as annoyance, I didn't quite believe her. Al Driggers had a monopoly on the undertaking business in Skykomish County. I figured that Janet worked because she enjoyed it, especially the occasional perks that allowed the Driggerses to take trips at a discount.

The thought reminded me of Milo's comment about Janet and the ski bum. "Say," I said brightly, "I hear you missed seeing anything Monday because you were stuck with some stranded skier. Was he worth the sacrifice?" For once, I lowered myself to Janet's level and leered.

Janet rolled her eyes. "Lordy, no! He was homely as a pig's butt. In fact, he looked like a pig, with little squinty eyes and a nose that could have passed for a snout. I wouldn't have spent a nickel on *après*-screw togs for that guy. But he had money. So many ski bums do. He was the type who lands somewhere, discovers the snow isn't quite what he expected, and wants to move on. They're looking for the perfect powder, like a druggie searching for the ultimate fix. They're incredibly spoiled and fixated. Screw 'em, I say. But not literally in his case."

"Do you remember his name?" I inquired, hoping to sound casual.

Janet's pretty face turned shrewd. She was hard to dupe, and I was inept at subterfuge. "Not offhand, but Milo already asked me. It was something like MacKay or MacKey or MacQuaid. His so-called address was in Utah." She glanced beyond my shoulder. "Here comes Carrie Starr. She's off to Europe next week. I wish I were married to a dentist like she is. There's more money in teeth than there is in death. Not everybody takes their choppers with them. Bob Starr buys back the gold fillings."

Swiftly changing gears, Janet greeted Dr. Starr's wife with a chipper smile. I continued on my way to Alpine Medical Supply, wondering if Milo had checked out the alleged ski bum. He probably had; I'd mention MacWhoever to Vida.

Will Stuart was over six feet tall, though his shoulders were slightly stooped under his professional light blue cotton jacket. He gazed at me from behind rimless bifocals and smiled benignly.

"Ms. Lord," he said in his soft, soothing voice, "I haven't seen you in here since you returned those crutches a couple of years ago after you sprained your ankle. How can I help you?"

"I don't know if you can," I said with a girlish laugh. "I'm helping Vida investigate the murder story."

Will Stuart chuckled, another soothing sound. "I can't imagine Vida needing help when it comes to investigating." He grew serious, resting one arm on an arch-support display. "That was a terrible thing. What's this world coming to?"

Will didn't expect an answer. "I'm sure that the sheriff or his deputies have talked to you," I said.

"My, yes." Will nodded his balding head. "I'm afraid I wasn't much help. I didn't hear or see anything unusual. No strangers, no one sneaking about. Everything was very ordinary."

"Except," I noted, "you waited on the murder victim's sister-in-law."

An elderly man entered the store, giving Will a faint nod. He began to browse along the middle aisle. I got the impression from the proprietor's lack of salesmanship that the man's visit wasn't unusual. Maybe he perused therapeutic items the way women search through clothing racks. The old man disappeared into the far aisle next to the opposite wall.

"Honoria Whitman is a lovely person," Will said, lowering his voice. "She always comes here for her special needs. I believe Sheriff Dodge recommended me."

"Her wheelchair had a problem," I remarked, my eyes roaming to various artificial limbs hanging from the near wall.

Will sighed. "Those electric wheelchairs have to be sent out of state for servicing. They're wonderful, but with more features, there are more things that can go wrong. A wheelchair is like any other appliance, you see."

I did, sort of. "You met Honoria's brother, Trevor." It was a statement, not a question.

"Yes," Will answered gravely. "He seemed like a very pleasant fellow. I feel extremely sorry for him. And for Ms. Whitman and the mother." Will gave the elderly man a slight smile as he rounded the end of the aisle and began to study bedpans.

"Neither of them seemed upset while they were in the store, I gather." Taking Will's hesitation for lack of comprehension, I clarified the comment: "Honoria and her brother, that is."

Will nodded. Apparently, he was deliberate by nature.

"Well—Ms. Whitman wasn't happy about her wheel-chair, especially when she found out it would take three to four weeks to get it back. I'm sure that's why she was so . . . touchy."

I frowned at the word. " 'Touchy'? As in, out of sorts?"

Again, Will didn't reply at once. "Annoyed would be more accurate, or perhaps impatient. We had to fill out a rather tedious service order, and I was a bit slow reading through it. I hadn't yet had the opportunity to collect my new glasses from next door." He removed what I assumed were the new spectacles and admired them at arm's length. "They're quite an improvement. I've never had bifocals before."

The browser had picked up a commode and was jug-gling it experimentally. He nodded once, then put it back, and moved on to bath chairs.

"It was that Driggers woman." Now Will was whis-pering. "She stopped me just as I was about to step out to see the optician. Ms. Driggers comes in from the travel agency every so often, asking for the most outrageous items, often of a prurient nature." The proprietor exuded an air of revulsion.

I didn't dare inquire what Janet might have wanted, but my eyes strayed to the spare parts on the near wall. Fortunately, none of the prostheses resembled a dildo. There was, however, a nice selection of massage vibrators in the glass case behind me.

"Then Ms. Whitman and her brother arrived," Will went on in his painstaking manner. "After they left, I received two phone calls from customers. The next thing I knew, there was all that excitement about the poor woman at the beauty parlor. I didn't get my glasses until almost four o'clock." Sadly, he shook his head.

The elderly man departed without a word. Maybe he stopped in to ponder the items he didn't need. Yet.

"How long were Honoria and Trevor here?" I asked.

Another pause ensued. "Oh—twenty minutes. I had to check out the loaner chair, of course. Ms. Whitman didn't care for the first one I brought out. The seat bothered her. She's very slim, and needs all the padding she can get."

A couple I recognized but couldn't place entered the store warily. They were around sixty, and the man wore a particularly anxious air. Taking in my presence, they both stopped in their tracks.

"Mr. and Mrs. Eriks!" Will greeted the newcomers warmly, as well as soothingly. "How was your surgery, Mr. Eriks?"

"Fine," Mr. Eriks replied tersely, his full face reddening. "That's why we're here." He glared not at Will or me, but at a doughnut-shaped object near the door.

"Of course!" Will exclaimed, all smiling sympathy. "My brother-in-law must have performed that procedure a thousand times. What you need is a soft yet firm support so that you can sit comfortably while the tissue heals. We have three different models, but—"

On that appropriate note, I murmured thank you and farewell. It was after nine-thirty, and there was work to be done. I skipped calling on Milo. I'd already invaded Vida's turf by talking to Will Stuart. I hadn't learned anything, but Vida would be displeased when she found out that I'd meddled. And of course she would find out. She always does.

There was no message yet from Cal Vickers about my car. I took that as a bad sign. The office was empty, with my staff members off on their appointed rounds. Not wanting to leave the front desk untended, I sat down in Ginny's usual spot and went over the news coverage for the upcoming Presidents' Day edition.

Carla had written a surprisingly sprightly piece about

George and Martha Washington. While she leaned a bit heavily on romance-novel language, the feature was cohesive and interesting. I tried to avoid suspecting her of cribbing.

Vida's contributions included three cherry-pie recipes, a fashion article on Civil War styles, and a peek inside the White House during Lincoln's presidency. I had reworked a three-part series I'd done long ago for *The Oregonian* on life in Virginia before the Revolutionary War. Though I'd shortened it considerably, it would still take up a page and a half. That was good. We needed filler for the special advertising section.

The mail arrived as I was editing Vida's account of Steve and Donna Wickstrom's Valentine's Day party for the high-school faculty. Steve taught math and science at Alpine High, and his wife, who was Rick Erlandson's older sister, and now Ginny Burmeister Erlandson's sister-in-law, ran a day-care center. I left off at the point where a blindfolded Principal Karl Freeman had pinned the heart on the wrong woman, namely Dixie Ridley, wife of the football coach.

Ginny and Rick had sent a postcard from Hawaii. The scene was cliché Diamond Head, but the message was a Burmeister original:

Dear Advocate *Gang,* Ginny wrote in her meticulous hand. *The sunshine is wonderful, the beaches are heavenly, and marriage is fun. Glad you're not here. (Ha-ha.) Love, Ginny & Rick.* It was typically Ginny; concise, honest, and uncomplicated.

The rest of the mail was unexciting, with the usual handouts, releases, and letters to the editor wherein I was generally described as a knucklehead. Three of the writers expressed dismay over the latest murder, but none of them blamed me directly. That was a relief. I've been accused of many vices in my tenure at *The Advocate,* though never of being an exponent of murder. Ed's remarks still rankled. I kept seeing myself as a modern-day Madame DeFarge, with computer keys clicking instead of knitting needles.

Vida came in just as I finished sorting the delivery. I was reminded of Laurie's strange reaction after dumping the salon's mail on the floor. When I related the incident to Vida, she stared at me with her owlish expression.

"You don't know why Laurie behaved so oddly?" she demanded.

I shook my head. "No. But I don't really believe she saw a spider."

Vida removed her velvet beret and ran a hand through her jumbled gray curls. "I'll have to find out when I go for my four o'clock appointment. Really, Emma, you should press harder."

Goaded, I confessed to calling on Will Stuart. To my mild surprise, Vida didn't seem upset. "I intended to talk to him on my way to Stella's. Do you think I should bother now?"

"Will didn't seem to have much to offer," I said. "Maybe you could get more out of him."

"Maybe." Vida's gaze roamed around the small reception area. "Will's a fussbudget with no imagination. It's a deadly combination." My puzzlement must have shown, for Vida shot me a faintly exasperated look. "He sees everything, but notices nothing. Or perhaps there was something he didn't see which he should have done. Yes, I'll talk to him." In her splayfooted style, she went into the news office.

As so often happens, she left me feeling inadequate. I couldn't help but suffer a bit of resentment, but it turned out to be a sensation I deserved.

Chapter Eight

IDA FRICKEY WHITMAN Pratt Foster Smith made her entrance at exactly one o'clock. She furtively slipped into the *Advocate* office with the collar of her faux leopard jacket turned up around her chin. Vida and I were the only staffers on hand; Carla was trying to track down Toby Popp, and Leo was consulting with advertisers.

"I came to say goodbye," Ida said in a nervous voice. "Honoria and Trevor are across the street, with Sheriff Dodge."

Professional etiquette required me to invite Mrs. Smith into my private office. But if I excluded Vida, I might as well throw myself off Spark Plug Mountain. Thus, I indicated Vida's visitor's chair to our guest, and seated myself in Leo's swivel model, which I scooted across the floor.

"So you're leaving immediately," I said with a smile that I hoped would put Mrs. Smith at ease. "Is Trevor still planning to fly to California tonight?"

Mrs. Smith nodded. She had taken a baby-blue handkerchief from her purse. "Honoria and I will start out tomorrow morning, very early. I'm so thankful there's a break in the weather. With any luck, we'll see sunshine by Friday. It's a short flight, but it takes two days by car. We can't drive straight through, so we'll have to stop along the way in Oregon."

"Grants Pass," Vida put in. "It's a logical break."

The suggestion seemed to float past Mrs. Smith, who was wringing the handkerchief. "I feel so silly, really. But there's something I want you to understand." Her blue eyes pleaded from behind the white-framed glasses. "Honoria may seem a bit reserved to you. Oh, I realize you've known her for several years, but I can tell by talking to her that except for Mr. Dodge, she hasn't formed any close friendships, especially with women. You must find that strange."

The truth was, I'd never thought about it. In five years the only real friends I had in Alpine were Vida and Milo. Leo might qualify if I didn't keep him at arm's length for professional purposes.

Vida, however, was nodding in an understanding manner. "There's a difference between being friendly and being friends," she pointed out. "Your daughter has always been quite friendly. But you're right, Mrs. Smith—she's never opened herself up to friendship."

Mrs. Smith sighed, a painful sound. "I know. Trevor isn't one for having chums, either. It's not their fault. I blame myself. I'm afraid I've had a rather rocky romantic history."

I said nothing. Vida said, "Oh?" The syllable was fraught with meaning.

"Their father was a circus acrobat." No hint of humor showed on Mrs. Smith's carefully made-up face. "Oliver Whitman lived the life of a circus performer, going on the road for eight months of the year, wintering in Florida for the other four. It's not conducive to family stability. I put up with it for ten years, and then I divorced him." Now her eyes glistened with tears, which made the handkerchief come in handy. "The fact is, I still loved him. But our home life was so unsettled. When a man's gone for so long, you never know what he's going to do with all those trapeze artists and magicians' assistants and elephant riders."

"Seal trainers," Vida put in, looking very solemn. "I understand they're most promiscuous."

I had no idea where Vida came up with such an idea, but Mrs. Smith nodded vigorously. "Oh my, yes! Marvela, that was her name—she was shameless! You wouldn't believe the rumors I heard out of Omaha!"

"Yes, I would." Vida nodded gravely, the beret slipping back on her gray curls.

"Then," Mrs. Smith went on, removing her glasses and dabbing at her eyes, "there was Dennis Pratt. He was in the Merchant Marine when I married him and we moved to Oakland. It was a terrible mistake on my part—Denny was never home, either. And when he was, he drank and . . . well, Honoria was a budding teenager by then. You can guess what happened." She put her glasses back in place and lowered her gaze.

This time I shook my head; Vida nodded in a manner that was both understanding and disapproving of the delicate subject. For my own part, I wondered why Mrs. Smith had been such a lousy judge of character. Apparently, she was the kind of woman who had to have a man—any man. I'd only wanted one.

"I had better luck with Dick," Mrs. Smith said, taking up her laundry list of mates. "Dick Foster was a cook, or a chef, depending upon who he worked for. The trouble was, you see, he didn't work very often." Her apologetic air may have been for her confession, or for Dick Foster's lack of stability. "I simply couldn't face another divorce, so I stuck by Dick for almost twelve years. Finally, I had to let go. Three years later I met Chad Smith." Mrs. Smith dimpled, reminding me how very pretty she must have been fifty years ago. "He was several years younger, you see, but so thoughtful and such fun! Chad drove a bus and rode motorcycles." The smile disappeared and the handkerchief returned to her eyes. "The motorcycles were his undoing. Four years ago he was killed in an accident. I was bereft."

"I lost my husband in an accident, too," Vida said, scarcely moving a muscle in her face. "Perhaps I mentioned it when we visited in Startup."

Mrs. Smith sniffed a bit, then offered Vida a sympathetic look. "You mentioned being widowed, yes. It's very hard, isn't it?"

"Terrible," Vida replied, still stoic.

Mrs. Smith nodded. "That explains it, you see."

I inclined my head. "Explains . . . what?"

"My children." Mrs. Smith's gaze was wide-eyed, apparently due to my lack of comprehension. "They've been through so much. It's why Honoria married so young. It's why Trevor has had . . . problems. And now this." She spread her hands in a helpless gesture. "The worst of it is that Trevor and Kay were so happy together. You can imagine how good it made me feel to know that somebody in the family had made a lasting marriage. Naturally, I've always hoped that Honoria would have better luck the second time around. I'm beginning to think she's afraid to get married again."

Vida had picked up a pencil and was idly twirling it. "That's possible. No one could blame her, given all the circumstances." She carefully laid the pencil next to a copy of this week's paper. "Honoria has never been one to ask for pity. I admire her courage greatly. But it might have been better for her if she'd been less reticent. Keeping things bottled up can make life harder in the long run."

The little speech had the desired effect on Ida Smith. "Oh, isn't that so? But Honoria was always like that. Even when she was a little girl, she kept things to herself. Every so often, I'd take her aside and say to her, 'Now, honey, it's time for us to have a mother-daughter talk. Tell me what's on your mind.' But she'd never open up. It was so frustrating!" Mrs. Smith's white hair with its streak of black waved around her ears. "That's why I'm telling you all this, so you'll understand. I wouldn't want you to think ill of Honoria. Or of Trevor, for that matter, even though you don't really know him."

I could tell from the way Vida sat, so seemingly at ease, but actually poised for combat, that she had a laundry list of questions for Mrs. Smith. But our visitor was getting to her feet, leaning with one hand on Vida's desk and suddenly looking very tired.

"I must go," Mrs. Smith declared. "Honoria and Trevor are probably waiting for me in the car. They didn't want to take up much of the sheriff's valuable time. It's so important to us that he finds poor Kay's killer."

Vida was also on her feet, practically shoving me out of the way as she followed Mrs. Smith to the door. "Just one thing," she said, placing a hand on the other woman's arm. "In my follow-up article, I should mention Honoria's married name. Newspaper style, you know."

It was no such thing, but it appeared that Mrs. Smith was ignorant of journalistic protocol. Still, she turned a puzzled face to Vida. "Well—Honoria never used her former husband's name after . . . afterward. She had it legally changed, you see."

Vida said nothing, but her hand remained in place.

"Oh, where's the harm?" Mrs. Smith murmured as her cheeks grew pink. "He's been dead for twelve years. It was Mitch Harmon. Mitchell Edward Harmon, to be exact. He was an airline mechanic. Do you need to know anything else about him?"

Of course Vida did, but even my House & Home editor has her limits. "That's fine, Mrs. Smith. Thank you. Do have a safe journey." Her hand finally slipped away, permitting Ida Smith to depart into the sunless afternoon.

"Well!" Vida shot me an ominous glance, then stalked back to her desk. "Now, what was that all about?"

"She feels guilty," I suggested. "Mrs. Smith wants us to think fondly of Honoria and Trevor. Now that Kay's been murdered, all those matrimonial escapades have come back to haunt her."

Vida arched her eyebrows. "The sins of the mother? Perhaps. Or is Mrs. Smith afraid that in the course of the investigation, we'll learn things that will harm her children's reputations?"

Replacing Leo's chair, I shrugged. "We know—" I caught myself. "We *think* we know that Trevor killed Mitch Harmon. Maybe Mrs. Smith doesn't realize that Honoria has admitted that much."

Vida was peering through the small window above her desk. "There's Honoria's car. They're leaving. Now, why didn't Honoria call on us as well as on Milo?"

Edging next to Vida, I watched the Nissan go down Front Street, heading for Alpine Way. "Honoria is coming back. She said so."

The right-turn signal flashed, and the specially rigged car headed for the bridge and the road that led to Highway 2. My eyes scanned the heart of the business district, taking in the Whistling Marmot Movie Theatre, Harvey's Hardware, the Bank of Alpine, Parker's Pharmacy, the Venison Inn, and, of course, the Clemans Building. Beyond those anchors of Alpine commerce, I could see the hospital, the medical and dental clinics, St. Mildred's Church, and a patchwork of houses, mostly small, some with tin roofs, others painted garish colors to defy the omnipresent leaden clouds.

The Whitmans were heading toward a different setting. I imagined palm and cypress trees, the roar of the ocean, the warm sun casting shadows on Spanish-mission architecture. If I'd ever been through Pacific Grove—and maybe I had, on some long-ago trip down the coast—I didn't recall the town. But it was home to Ida Whitman, and to Trevor as well. No doubt they would find some comfort there.

"Why Startup?" I asked, the thought seemingly born out of nowhere.

Vida, however, wasn't taken aback. "You mean Honoria? Yes, I've wondered about that. It seems an unusual choice. Milo might know," she added grudgingly.

"There are several arts-and-crafts enclaves in this state," I pointed out. "LaConner comes to mind. Port Townsend, the San Juan Islands, Stanwood, Seattle itself."

"Honoria didn't want to live in a big city." Vida had resettled her beret and was putting on her brown tweed coat. "She never said as much, but I'm sure it's true. The rustic life appealed to her."

So it seemed. But I still found Honoria's choice odd, since Startup is so small that it doesn't always appear on maps and isn't known for anything except its natural tranquillity.

"Where are you going?" I inquired as Vida started for the door.

She didn't break stride. "The sheriff's. Alpine Medical Supply. Stella's. The phone company." Vida was out of the office before I could ask any more questions.

Carla returned five minutes later, looking smug. "I got pictures," she announced, patting her camera. "The workmen didn't catch me until I'd shot almost a whole roll."

"Terrific," I said with enthusiasm. "What about Toby Popp? Was he there?"

Carla shook her head, the long black hair brushing her shoulders. "I didn't see him, and I would have known—I checked the library for mug shots in the Seattle papers. He's not as geeky as I thought he'd be."

"Good work, Carla." I felt it necessary to praise my reporter's initiative. "Did the workmen chase you away?"

"Sure," Carla replied cheerfully. "But they were sort of funny about it. I don't think they expected *me*."

Suddenly I felt old and ugly. Carla's implication was that the construction crew expected Vida or me to return, not a nubile twenty-five-year-old girl with raven hair. But at least Carla had her story and pictures. I quizzed her about Toby Popp's current residence, the price tag of the new house, and if there was a completion date set.

"He lives in a condo in Edmonds," Carla replied, still looking pleased with herself. "He used to live east of Lake Washington, near Issaquah, but he sold that place when he retired and moved north of Seattle so that he could be closer to Index. His estimated worth is right around one billion. I couldn't get an exact figure out of Nyquist Construction on the new house, so I sort of guessed high and low, and when they stopped saying anything, I figured it must be about three million. The property itself came pretty cheap. The house is supposed to be finished by the end of the year. They started in late January, which is when Nyquist estimated they wouldn't get much more snow at that level."

Located only about five hundred feet above sea level, Index's climate wasn't as cold as Alpine's. Still, the

January date was chancy. Even Seattle could get snow in March.

"Did you dig out any personal background?" I inquired as Leo returned from the advertising wars.

Carla wrinkled her nose. "Toby never talks to the media. According to the newspaper articles, on a scale of one to ten, his social skills are about zero. The only time he's ever seen in public is at baseball games. He was married once, way back before he dropped out of Stanford. It didn't last long, and if he's had any girlfriends since, nobody knows about them. Maybe he's gay."

"Maybe," I agreed. "He sounds more like a lone wolf, though."

"He is." Leo had chimed in as he removed layouts from his big fake-leather briefcase. "I remember him from when I was working for a paper in Santa Clara. He was a rising software star, except they didn't call it that then."

"Did he avoid the media in those days?" I asked, admiring Leo's handiwork on a mock-up for Francine's Fine Apparel.

Leo shrugged. "All I remember is that he was supposed to be some kind of future-shock genius. Guys like that don't buy ads to self-promote."

Back in my office, I worked on my timberlands-sale editorial. Usually, I try to assign myself a couple of news stories for each issue. Ed's remark about the proposed bridge over the Sky by the golf course goaded me into checking progress on the project. It had been rumored, discussed, and postponed for a couple of years. I also decided to look into the latest developments, assuming there were any, of the new community college.

The phone calls for both stories involved state agencies in Olympia. As usual, I was routed from one office to another. An hour and twenty minutes later I had collected material that would fill a maximum of ten inches—if I did a bit of padding. The bridge project was mired; the two-year-college site was being debated in the legislature. Our state representative, Bob Gunderson, a retired car salesman living in a mobile home by the fish hatchery where he allegedly paid a dollar a year rent, thought the best location would be west of Cass Pond, or maybe east of the ski lodge, or across Highway 2 north of the Overholt farm. In other words, he hadn't the foggiest notion where the campus should be built. Or maybe he didn't want to give *The Advocate* any news. During his last campaign swing through Alpine in October, Carla had described him as "a big, hearty man, wearing a brown shortcake." She'd meant sport coat. I had proofed the story, and my only excuse for not catching the mistake was that Adam had called to tell me his dorm was on fire. It wasn't, but the distraction had flawed my usually accurate eye.

Vida returned just before five. Her hair looked tidy, but otherwise unremarkable. "I must rush," she declared, hurriedly sorting through her phone messages. "Buck's coming at seven, so I'll have to grocery-shop on my way home. Pork chops sound nice, don't you think?"

As a concept, pork chops sounded fine. What Vida would do to them was another matter. "Did you learn anything new about the murder case?" I asked, avoiding the subject of dinner.

"Scads," Vida replied. "We'll talk tomorrow. Good night, Emma."

Vida left, practically running out the door before I could voice my objections. I was annoyed. Had our roles been reversed, she would have pinned me to the wall until I coughed up the latest information.

It was one minute after five, and the long distance rates were down. I called Adam in Tempe, but there was no answer. Carla had already left, planning to drop off the day's film at Buddy Bayard's. Leo had been in the front office, checking through the accumulation of classified ads. He was still there when I started for home.

"You get your car back?" he asked, looking up from a note Carla had made.

I nodded. "It was the battery." Relief had washed over me when Cal called just before lunch to say I'd be out a mere hundred bucks.

"I was going to offer you a lift home," Leo said. "You need a ride to Cal's?"

I'd planned to walk the seven blocks to the Texaco station on Alpine Way, but it was raining and I was tired. Downhearted, too, still not restored to my buoyant mood of Monday. As Leo and I drove along Front Street in his secondhand Toyota, I considered inviting him to dinner. But before I could issue the invitation, he voiced his intention of meeting Delphine Corson at Posies Unlimited. Delphine was Alpine's resident florist, and Leo's local squeeze. They were going out for drinks. Or something. I didn't pry.

Leo griped about the driving conditions. It had gotten colder in the last hour as evening settled in over the mountains. The rain had turned to sleet, and the black ice that remained was hard to see in the winter twilight.

"I'll never get used to this freaking weather," Leo complained, easing the Toyota into Cal's. "It's not the gloom that bothers me so much as the sudden changes."

I commiserated briefly, then thanked Leo and got out of the car. Cal waved at me from the garage area, where he was working on a minivan.

"Hang on just a sec," he called. "I'm all alone tonight, and I promised Jake O'Toole he'd get this baby back by six."

Most of Cal disappeared under the hood of the Grocery Basket owner's van. I wandered over to the office door, seeking shelter beneath the canopy that covered the gas pumps. A boy in his late teens was filling the tank of his rusted-out truck. He finished just as Cal came out of the garage.

"Go ahead," I said to Cal, nodding at the boy who was counting money from his wallet. "I'll wait." After all, I was in no hurry. I had nowhere to go except home, and no one was waiting for me there. The damp chill in the air made me shiver. If I ducked out from under the canopy, I could also get wet as well as cold. Obviously, I was feeling sorry for myself on this Thursday evening in February.

While Cal and his customer conducted their business inside, I spotted my Jag across the tarmac, between a Ford Taurus and Cal's tow truck. Out of the corner of my eye, I caught a blur of headlights as a car careened around the corner from Cedar Street, skidded, and crashed into a Jeep Wrangler on Alpine Way. The crunch of metal and the shattering of glass made me cringe. Two other vehicles stopped short, and a third swerved to avoid the collision but kept going. Cal and his customer came running out of the office.

"Jeez!" Cal cried. "What happened?"

I didn't reply. I was too anxious to see if the drivers were all right. To my relief, a young man got out of the Jeep and a woman in a very short skirt emerged from the sedan. They immediately began screaming at each other.

After Front Street, Alpine Way is the busiest thoroughfare in town. Both byways are regularly plowed during the winter, but the side streets aren't cleared as often. Compact snow and ice become a hazard, especially when they're interspersed with bare spots. After sunset the black ice is practically invisible. Despite the

sleet and the cold and the encroaching darkness, the accident was drawing a crowd. At least three people had hurried out from Itsa Bitsa Pizza next door to Cal's, and
across the street a man and a woman were gawking on
the corner by Mountain View Gardens, the local nursery.

Although I didn't have my camera with me, I got out
my notepad so I could take down names and damages.
Approaching with caution, I recognized both drivers: the
young man with the buzz cut was Tim Rafferty, part-time
college student and some-time bartender at the Icicle
Creek Tavern; the woman in the short skirt, knee-high
boots, and fuzzy red jacket was Amanda Hanson, who
worked at the post office.

"It's not my fault I skidded on that stupid black ice!"
Amanda was screaming. "You had time to get out of the
way, you idiot!"

"That's an arterial," Tim shouted back, gesturing at the
intersection of Alpine Way and Cedar. "I had the right-
of-way! You damned well better be insured all the way
up to your . . . butt!" Despite his anger, he couldn't resist
a glance at Amanda's exposed thighs. Idly, I wondered
why she wasn't shivering from the cold.

"I wouldn't even be here," Amanda railed, "if I didn't
have to wait on stupid customers who come into the post
office at four fifty-nine! Why don't those morons realize
that if they don't want a package they can just write
'Refused' on it and hand it back to their carrier? Look at
my car!" she raged on, jabbing a finger at her Subaru
Legacy. "The front end's a mess, and all because of that
dopey woman who thinks she's a poet!" She began
to cry.

"Hey," Tim Rafferty yelled, "I just came off my shift,
too! How would you like to put up with a bunch of half-
tanked losers who spend all their time bitching about the
spotted owl instead of trying to find another job? You sell

food stamps at the post office—why don't you tell those dumb bastards they can't use them to buy beer?"

Tim's tirade made no dent on Amanda, who was now leaning against her Subaru and sobbing. Cal had brought out some flares and was placing them around the accident scene. Traffic was now backed up in both directions from Front to Fir.

I was recording the Subaru's crumpled grill and fender when a vehicle with an amber flasher barged up Alpine Way. Milo's Cherokee Chief was easily recognizable. Apparently, he was off duty, because he was using his portable emergency light.

The sheriff took note of Cal first. Then he stalked over to the wreck, eyeing the drivers with an annoyed expression.

"I've got a deputy on the way," he announced. "Okay, what have we got here?"

Amanda stopped crying and began yelling again. Tim's rage resurfaced as he made a variety of accusations, stopping just short of asserting that the culpable Ms. Hanson had crash-landed atop his Jeep on her broom.

Milo, who was still wearing his regulation uniform and hat, glared at the combatants. "Shut up, both of you! Have we got an eyewitness around here?" He glowered at the bystanders, including me.

There was some muttering, but nobody volunteered. Finally, I stepped forward. "I saw it—sort of. This sleet makes things a little murky."

It appeared that Milo hadn't taken in my presence until I spoke. "Emma? Okay, come with me and I'll have you make a statement."

I protested, however. "Can't I do it tomorrow? I'm collecting my car."

The hazel eyes under the broad-brimmed hat were hard as marbles. I knew the sheriff well enough to recognize that he was in a bad mood that probably had nothing to do with the two-car collision.

"Witnesses forget," he snapped. "I want your information while it's fresh. Come on, let's go." Milo jerked a thumb in the direction of the Cherokee Chief just as Sam Heppner pulled up in his county car.

Cal called for me to wait. While Milo swore under his breath Sam took over at the accident scene. A moment later Cal reappeared with my car keys.

"We'll finish the paperwork tomorrow," Cal said, then turned to the sheriff. "Will either of these two need a tow? Or can I lock up and go home?"

"They're fine," Milo responded tersely. "Sam'll get them out of the way in the next few minutes. G'night, Cal." The sheriff loped back to his vehicle.

"Damn it, Milo," I grumbled, getting into the passenger seat, "you're going to have to bring me back over here after we're done."

Milo didn't say anything. He'd forgotten to remove the amber light, so traffic deferred to him as he headed up Alpine Way. When we reached Tonga Road, I realized he had no intention of going to headquarters.

"Okay, what's up?" I asked with an impatient sigh. "You don't give a rat's ass about Tim and Amanda."

The sheriff still didn't speak. A sideways glance told me that his long jaw was set and his eyes were focused on the road into the ski lodge. It was only when we arrived in the parking lot that Milo explained himself.

"I need a drink," he declared. "It's more private in the bar here than the Venison Inn."

"It'd be more private in my living room, you dunce," I chided. "The only reason I keep Scotch on hand is because of you and Ben."

"What about Leo?"

"What about Leo?" I didn't care for Milo's insinuating tone.

"You tell me," Milo shot back. He banged the car door open and awkwardly got out. He paused just long enough to remove the amber light and put it back inside the car.

I refused to budge. With my arms crossed and my mouth pursed like a prune, I stared fiercely through the windshield. There was snow coming down now, and its big, wet flakes accumulated swiftly. Milo was halfway to the ski-lodge entrance before he realized I wasn't with him.

He stopped and turned around, a tall, blurry figure in his drab brown sheriff's uniform. His shoulders were slightly hunched and he had lowered his head. But he didn't come toward me.

Angrily, I reached over and punched the horn. It let out a loud, blaring noise that made Milo jump. I didn't stop until he reached the Cherokee Chief.

"Goddamn it, Emma," he shouted, "what's the matter with you?"

"What's the matter with *you*?" I retorted. "Either stop acting like a prize jackass or take me back to Cal's!"

Milo's jaw still jutted, but he opened the passenger door. Then, instead of offering his hand, he started to get inside. "Move over," he mumbled. "Maybe we should talk here."

Clumsily, I got into the driver's seat. "Well?" My temper was still on a rampage, but Milo was suddenly looking so downcast that I felt a trace of sympathy. Or, given my own dark mood, maybe it was empathy.

"It's over," he said in a flat voice, staring straight ahead into the snow-covered windshield. "Honoria's not coming back."

My initial reaction was confusion. Milo and Honoria's relationship had been strained for months. The impression I'd gotten from the sheriff was that he was more upset by a change in the status quo than by any genuine sense of loss. Now, however, seeing the melancholy look on his face, I realized that I'd misjudged Milo's emotions. Maybe he had, too.

"Did Honoria tell you that?" I asked, rarely capable of finding the proper words of commiseration unless I could get them down on paper first.

Milo shook his head. "No, but I figure she came to say goodbye. The fact is—" He broke off, rubbing at his upper lip. "Honoria never felt at home around here. My guess is that the move was all a big mistake." Milo kept his index finger pressed against his lip, with the thumb propping up his chin. I was afraid that he might actually cry.

"Honoria's in shock," I declared. "Give her some time. Once they all settle down, she'll be back."

Removing his hat, Milo chucked it into the backseat. "I don't think so. You don't know how she operates, Emma. Once Honoria gets something in her head, it sticks."

I knew that was true, yet it could work to Milo's advantage—if that's what he really wanted. "Honoria made a big decision to move to Startup in the first place," I pointed out. "She must have had very good reasons to go through with such a drastic change. If this is how she wanted to spend the rest of her life, what makes you think that—in time—she won't return?"

"Because it felt like goodbye."

Between the snow outside and the vapor inside, the interior of the Cherokee Chief seemed cut off from the rest of the world. I felt isolated, not just from my surroundings, but from Milo. Sitting next to me, he seemed to have withdrawn into a place where I couldn't follow.

"So why *did* she move here?" I finally asked in an attempt to break down the barrier between us.

"Honoria wanted to start a new life." Milo spoke as if he'd memorized the reason. When I didn't say anything, he continued in a more normal tone. "She'd been married to a bum, she'd ended up a cripple, and it took her a while to put her life back together. When she got to the point where she could cope on her own, she decided to put the past behind her. That was four, five years ago. You know all that."

I did, and yet it wasn't enough. "She must have left Carmel while Trevor was still in jail."

Milo kept staring at the windshield. "Right. The disaster with Honoria's ex happened back in the early Eighties. Trevor was sentenced to twenty years on a second-degree homicide charge. He got paroled just before Memorial Day. I guess he actually served about ten years. The first trial ended in a hung jury." At last, Milo turned his head. My close scrutiny seemed to annoy him. "What's the matter—do I have crud on my chin?"

There are times when I marvel that I have ever even remotely considered Milo Dodge as a romantic possibility. It's not that Milo is ugly or even unattractive. Indeed, I have noticed that his receptionist, the young and pretty, if somewhat dull-witted, Toni Andreas, has a crush on him. But somehow he has a knack for spoiling any kind of potentially sensuous moment.

"No," I retorted. "You don't."

"Well, you do." Milo reached over and brushed at my jawline. "It's a potato chip. No," he contradicted himself on closer examination of the offending particle, "it's a piece of Frito."

I held my head. I never eat Fritos, but I must have gotten some residue on my hands during the ride with Leo Walsh. My present ad manager is tidier than his predecessor, but he's not exactly fussy, either.

Dismissing all notions of sexual tension between Milo and me, I pressed the sheriff about Honoria's recital of her tragic married life. "Is that it as far as Honoria and Trevor and Mitch are concerned?"

Milo frowned. "Mitch? Who's Mitch?"

I explained, recounting what Ida Smith had told Vida and me about Honoria's late and unlamented husband.

Milo was still frowning. "Honoria never said much about the guy, except that he was a skunk. They were together for seven, eight years. She was only nineteen when they got married, and at first, he—Mitch, is it?—seemed like an okay guy. But he was just a year older, and didn't like having to come home from work on time or paying bills or any of those other things that are part of real life. He drank and smoked pot and eventually started doing coke. When he couldn't afford the coke, he'd get mean and beat the crap out of Honoria. She put up with it for four or five years and then announced she was leaving him. That's when he threw her down the stairs." Milo grimaced. "She should have walked out a lot sooner, but the reason she married him in the first place was because she was fed up with her mother's parade of husbands."

Recalling Ida Smith's account, I could understand Honoria's feelings. "Still," I noted, "there must have been some close family ties in the Whitman family. Trevor—unfortunately for him—rushed to his sister's defense."

"I know." Once again, Milo was staring at the windshield, which was now covered with thick snow. "This is all sort of ironic. Now Trevor's wife has been murdered.

It has to make you wonder, doesn't it?" The sheriff slowly turned to look at me, his wide mouth twisted. "If Honoria ever finds out who killed Kay, will she return the favor?"

Chapter Nine

THE SOFT, SHIFTING curtain of lights behind the bar at King Olav's evokes the Aurora Borealis. Walls of rough granite, with mysterious recesses, and a graceful waterfall splashing into a small pool bring to mind the deep fjords of Norway. After a few drinks, it's been said that the brooding gods of Norse mythology can be glimpsed among the shadows. I wouldn't know: the scariest sight I've seen in the ski lodge bar was Ed Bronsky in a tux.

Milo and I sat at a small pine table, he cradling his Scotch, me fondling my bourbon. At six-thirty on a Thursday evening, the handful of other customers were mostly skiers. No one appeared to care that the uniformed sheriff of Skykomish County seemed intent on getting wasted.

To be fair, we were both sipping our first drinks. But Milo's mood was dark, and while he isn't a heavy drinker, I could tell that he had no intention of stopping until one of the other customers began to look like Odin.

I spent the first five minutes trying to convince Milo that Honoria wasn't homicidal, and that even if she were, her physical condition was limiting. The sheriff, however, alluded to firearms, poison, and homemade explosives. His former ladylove was clever, as well as determined. If she felt obligated to avenge her sister-in-law's death, she'd find a way. Honoria was like that. Milo took a deep drink from his highball glass.

"You know," I said, leaning back in my chair and wishing there was an easy way to slip off my boots, "you're missing the point. It isn't up to Honoria to figure out who killed Kay—that's your job. And when you finish doing it, and bring the perp to justice, that will be that. How's it going?"

My inadvertent attempt to catch Milo off guard actually worked. He started to shrug, then dug inside his regulation jacket and pulled out a package of cigarettes, which he shoved under my nose. I shook my head. Milo lighted up.

"The autopsy didn't tell us much," he said. "But Vida told you about that."

"No, she didn't." My pique returned. "Vida was too caught up in her dinner plans for Buck Bardeen."

Milo ignored my irritation. "Well, there wasn't much for her to pass on. Kay's throat was slit with something very sharp and fairly wide, which doesn't take a rocket scientist to figure. We can rule out a surgical scalpel, a butcher knife, or anything that Stella and her crew might have had lying around, like scissors or a razor. The ME's guess is a hunting knife."

I didn't want to think about the gruesome details that had prompted the medical examiner's opinion. "Hunting knives are pretty common in Alpine," I noted. Not only did a large number of locals hunt, but there were even more who fished. Most of them owned a knife.

"We checked with Harvey Adcock," Milo went on, puffing at his cigarette and referring to the owner of the local hardware-and-sporting-goods store. "Routine, but you never know. He's sold a couple of knives in the last ten days, but he didn't know either of the men who bought them. He figured one of the guys was going for

coyote or bobcat because he brought a new hunting
license. Not much else is in season around here, except
raccoons. The other one bought a steelhead card. He
already had a valid fishing license."

"So Harvey can identify them?" I asked.

"Neither was a local," Milo replied, signaling for
another round. "That's why he didn't recognize them.
But Dwight Gould had Harvey check with Olympia. The
hunter was some guy from Seattle, name of Brantley.
The steelheader was from Edmonds. Funny name—Pope
or Popp or Poop." Milo chuckled.

Without even thinking, I grabbed Milo's cigarette
pack. "Popp? Toby Popp?" My mouth was agape; the
cigarette clung to my lower lip.

Milo reached over and clicked his lighter. "Yeah,
that's it. Goofy name. According to Harvey, kind of a
goofy guy, too."

"When was that?" I suddenly remembered that if I was
going to smoke, I should try to look more like Bacall and
less like Bogart. I removed the cigarette from my lips and
attempted to hold it gracefully between my fingers.

"When?" Milo frowned at me. "I'm not sure Dwight
said. Saturday, maybe. No—it was Monday morning. I
remember now, because Harvey told Dwight that the
knife sales were over a week apart. The Seattle hunter
had come in Saturday before last. Harvey is closed on
Sundays, so it had to be Monday." The sheriff regarded
me with growing curiosity. "You know this Poop?"

"It's *Popp,* Toby Popp, and he's a billionaire software
king. Retired," I added somewhat crossly. "He's building
a big house near Index."

"Never heard of him," Milo remarked, seemingly
indifferent to the very rich and semifamous. "Hey, want
to look at a menu? I'm hungry. They'll feed us in here."

It occurred to me that I was starving. It also occurred

to me that Milo and I should both counteract our alcoholic intake with food. As the sheriff requested menus I tried to figure out if there was any connection between Toby Popp and Kay Whitman: California. The Monterey Peninsula. Stanford University. Silicon Valley.

"Milo . . ." I was having trouble putting my thoughts into a logical order that would make an impression on the sheriff. "Maybe you should do a little digging on Toby Popp. He and Honoria and Kay and Trevor all come from the same general area."

Milo's expression was uncomprehending. "So? If you're talking Northern California, that's probably about a zillion people. Hey, here's our drinks." He handed over his empty glass as if it were a sacrificial offering.

I decided that maybe this wasn't the time or place to badger Milo about Toby Popp. Even when he was concentrating on the job, his view tended to be unimaginative. Maybe I was crazy anyway. I sipped my second bourbon and studied the specials. The crab cakes sounded good. Milo went for the pot roast à la Ingrid. We stuffed ourselves and spoke of sports. The Sonics were an illusion, waiting for the play-offs to dash our hopes. The Seahawks were a eyesore, and we'd abandoned all hope entering the preseason. If the baseball strike ever ended, maybe the Mariners could provide some excitement.

By eight o'clock, we were full—and sober. Milo drove me back to Cal's and waited until he made sure my Jag would start. It did. I gave him a thumbs-up signal and went home.

My gloomy mood at the end of the workday seemed to have lifted. Retrieving my car had helped improve my spirits. Or maybe it was the crab cakes.

It didn't occur to me that it might have been Milo.

* * *

When Vida arrived at work the next morning, she was humming. I assumed that her cheerful mien was caused by the dinner date with Buck. But I was wrong.

"Buck didn't come after all," she said, adjusting the beaded backrest on her chair. "He came down with that twenty-four-hour flu. Or, I should say, he hopes it's the bug that lasts just a day. There's also that lingering flu going around where you think you're better, and a few days later, you're ill again."

"I hope you didn't cook the pork chops," I said, somewhat evilly. I'm not a morning person, and my perverse nature tends to surface before nine-thirty.

"No," Vida replied blithely. "Buck called just as I got in the house, so I froze them. Perhaps he'll be able to come Saturday."

Carla was making coffee, a duty that usually falls on Ginny. Leo was attending the monthly Kiwanis Club breakfast. When Carla went out into the front office, I sat down in Vida's visitor's chair.

"Okay, so tell me why you're so happy with the world," I said, keeping one eye on the burbling coffeemaker.

Vida evinced surprise. "Happy? I'm merely holding positive thoughts. I do sometimes, you know." Her gaze held a hint of reproach.

Wanting to get to the point, I ignored the remark. "You haven't told me what you learned yesterday afternoon. Give, Vida. I would have called you last night, but I thought Buck was there."

"Well, he wasn't." Briefly, Vida's sparkle faded. "However, I didn't waste the evening." Calmly, she picked up the phone messages that she'd given only a cursory glance the previous day. "I invited Jane Marshall over to help me write a birthday poem for my daughter, Amy. She's a leap-year baby, you know."

I did, in a vague sort of way, except that I could never

remember whether the February 29 child had been Amy, Beth, or Meg. There was no Jo. As far as I was concerned, Amy's main claim to fame—or infamy—was that she had given birth to Roger the Terrible.

"So you pumped Laurie's mother," I said, grinning at Vida's inventiveness. "What came of it?"

"First things first," Vida declared, apparently sorting the messages in order of their priority. "You'll recall that I also visited the sheriff yesterday afternoon."

I pretended that I hadn't dined with Milo. But, as usual, Vida knew all: "Marje Blatt and her friend, Jeannie Clay, went night skiing." Marje was Vida's niece, and the medical clinic's receptionist; Jeannie was Dr. Starr's dental assistant. I stopped grinning and waited for Vida to reveal my latest adventure with the sheriff. "It wasn't a good night for skiing—too wet. Marje and Jeannie decided to eat dinner in the ski lodge's coffee shop. They glimpsed you going into the bar with Milo, so I assume you're caught up on his report from the ME in Everett."

I nodded faintly. Vida continued: "Will Stuart is such a bore. You were right, he was no help at all. In fact, the killer could have walked right past the medical supply's front door and he wouldn't have noticed because he hadn't fetched his new glasses from the optician's. I made a brief stop there, too, but it was hopeless—they have all those displays of eyeglasses that completely block their view of the street. Then I went to Stella's." Vida fluffed her gray curls, which didn't look quite so tidy this morning. "I quizzed Laurie in a general sort of way about the murder—'Wasn't-it-awful-weren't-you-terrified-can-you-imagine such-a-blah-blah.' Then, somehow, I got her off on being shocked or startled by less lethal happenings. I must confess, I fibbed a bit, about a thank-you letter I received—except that I didn't, though I should have, if my grandchildren had any manners—

with a death's-head on the envelope. A prank, of course, I told Laurie—and really, not one in which my grand-children would indulge—but it put me off, all the same. Or so I claimed."

Vida paused to sip from a mug of hot water. "Now, you would expect that anyone who had seen something upsetting in the mail as recently as that very morning would chime right in with their personal experience. But," she went on, gazing at me over the rim of her glasses, "Laurie said nothing. Doesn't that beat all?"

Vida's attitude indicated that I should also be flabber-gasted. Instead, I tried to rationalize why Laurie might keep the incident to herself. "Maybe it *was* a spider," I suggested.

"Nonsense," Vida scoffed. "It's the wrong season, except for the smaller kind. Those big ones come inside during the late summer and early fall. You never see them the rest of the year."

I admitted that I was stumped. Vida, however, wasn't ready to give up. "Laurie definitely saw something in the mail delivery that disturbed her. It's her reaction to my inquiry that raises some very intriguing questions. Stella doesn't know anything about it, because I asked her on my way out."

"Point-blank?" Vida could be direct as well as oblique. She handled each person and situation in what she con-sidered the most efficacious manner.

"More or less," Vida answered. "I asked Stella—and this was a reasonable query—if the salon had received any hate mail or letters. She said not yet, though there had been a few anonymous hang-ups. Youngsters, I imagine, making mischief."

Laurie had not revealed anything else of interest during the hair appointment. Vida had no opportunity to speak with Becca. The skin-care specialist was completely booked, no doubt by curiosity-seekers.

The phone company held more promise. The local office deals solely with switching equipment and repair. While Vida doesn't have any relatives who work there, she can rely on Bill Blatt to ferret out information.

"I told Billy to have the phone company turn over Honoria's records from the week prior to her family's arrival. Milo had already asked for Stella's records at the salon. They should be available late this afternoon. Billy is having them faxed."

I didn't know what Milo or Vida expected to find in the phone messages, but the check was routine in a homicide. At last we had gotten down to Jane Marshall. As Vida squared her shoulders and adjusted her glasses, I sensed that the visit with Laurie's mother had been the most interesting.

"The poem we devised was rather clever, actually." Vida propped her chin on her hand, gazing up at the ceiling as if Jane had written the words on the aging plasterboard. " 'Though born in 'fifty-six/The calendar plays its tricks/Which makes you only nine/You're the child-woman of mine.' "

I swallowed discreetly. "That's very . . ."

Vida put out a hand, her eyes still on the ceiling. "I'm not done. 'Though birthdays mark mere years/Lives are passed in smiles and tears/Cherished is the leap-year baby/Ever young is our dear Amy.' " Vida's smile was downright sappy, which certainly suited the poem. I supposed that I couldn't expect anything better when it came to a celebration of Roger's mother. Nor did I point out that *baby* didn't quite rhyme with *Amy*.

"Amy will love it," I said, which was as close to the truth as I dared come.

Vida nodded. "Of course she will. I'm very pleased,

because usually Jane writes such drivel. Naturally, the collaboration created a mood of mutual confidences." My House & Home editor wiggled her eyebrows. "Now you may think me lax in not having delved more deeply into the Marshalls' background when they arrived in town seventeen years ago. But remember, I hadn't been on the job that long. Marius Vandeventer had me covering every coffee klatch, wedding shower, and dinner party in Alpine. There was much more social life back then, because there were jobs, and people had money to spend."

Briefly, Vida paused to reflect upon what I suspected she considered a happier era. "In any event, I hadn't yet honed my interrogatory skills. Jane and Martin seemed like a pleasant addition to Alpine, and we were all relieved to see that someone was going to buy the equipment company after Axel Swensen retired. To my untrained eye, the Marshalls were a nice young couple with a pretty nine-year-old daughter and an infant son who'd moved here from Weaverville, California. I didn't realize that Jane had been married before, and that Laurie was actually Martin's stepchild. The boy, Josh, is Martin's. He attends Princeton on scholarship."

Vida had paused for effect, and she got what she wanted: all sorts of whistles, buzzers, and alarms were going off inside my brain. "I know where Weaverville is," I said. "It's in the mountains, between Eureka and Redding. I wrote an article about other logging towns in the West for last year's Loggeramma edition, and Weaverville was one of them. Still," I added, losing steam, "it's not very close to Carmel or Silicon Valley."

"No, it's not," Vida agreed, "but you're on the right track. Jane went to Stanford, where she met her first husband. They both dropped out—she had a baby, and he got a job."

"In the fledgling computer industry?"

Vida nodded. "The marriage was not a success. Jane's first husband—Laurie's father—spent all his time playing with computers. Really, it reminds me of how young men used to tinker with cars and neglect their families. There's no excuse for any of them. After four years Jane filed for divorce, and moved to Weed, which is where she was from. It's not far from Redding, which is close to Weaverville. That's how she met Martin, who was not only looking for a wife, but a machinery shop to buy. And that's how they came to Alpine."

I was silent for a few moments. Something was missing. "We are," I said dryly, "talking about Toby Popp, aren't we?"

Vida yanked off her glasses and began rubbing her eyes. "Oooooh! I'd like to think so! But that silly Jane never actually mentioned her first husband's name!" She stared at me over her clenched fists. "Don't think I didn't try everything short of torture!"

I was sure that Vida had done all she could. I was also sure that it was enough. Nor could I blame Jane Marshall for not identifying Toby Popp: as his former wife and the mother of his child, it was understandable that she would shy away from publicity. Not only would she respect Toby's wish for privacy, but the daughter of a billionaire was a hot commodity on the ransom market.

"I wonder if the Marshalls know Toby is moving to Index," I said, getting up and going over to pour a cup of coffee. "If they don't now, they will when the paper comes out next week."

Vida had put her glasses back on and was making a face into her mug. I presumed that the water had gotten cold. "If Toby Popp is indeed Laurie's father, Jane made a dreadful mistake."

"What's that? Nerd genes?" I stood by Vida's desk, ignoring the ringing phones, which I hoped Carla was picking up in the front office.

Vida's mouth turned down. "Nerd genes ... Now, I wonder ..." She let the thought trail away. "Martin legally adopted Laurie shortly after he and Jane married. Toby—or whoever he was—didn't fight it. Children, it seemed, were a nuisance."

I was properly dismayed. "So Laurie will never inherit any of her real father's enormous wealth. Bummer, as my son would say."

"Maybe it's just as well. Money presents its own kind of problems." Vida spoke in an unusually distracted manner.

"I wouldn't know," I remarked, regarding my House & Home editor with curiosity. "What are you thinking about, Vida? Besides Laurie, the nonheiress."

"Genes," Vida replied promptly. "When I mentioned Laurie's reaction—or lack thereof—to my comments about disturbing mail, you didn't respond. That bothered me, because I felt Laurie's attitude was out of character." Apparently seeing my confusion, Vida hurried on: "You would have noticed if you'd been there. What gave me pause was Laurie herself—it was unnatural for her not to react. 'Is she really that stupid?' I asked myself. The answer was no. No one is *that* stupid. Laurie had screamed in response to something that upset her—even a moron wouldn't forget that, and in any event, intelligence has nothing to do with memory or emotions. Now, if Jane Marshall and Toby Popp are her parents, how could Laurie be an imbecile? Oh, it happens, but it's rare. Jane may write dreadful poetry—most of the time—but she got into Stanford and so did Laurie's father, whoever he may be. I think that Laurie is not as stupid as she pretends. Indeed," Vida added, her bust heaving under the red-white-and-blue-striped blouse, "I sense that she's clever and cunning. I can't help but wonder if Laurie Marshall isn't a genius."

I remembered the odd look in Laurie's eyes the previous morning. I'd thought of it as determination, but perhaps it was much more. Vida could be right. On the other hand, what did it have to do with Kay Whitman's murder?

"Possibly nothing," Vida admitted as Ed Bronsky charged through the door. "Oh, Ed, how nice!" The sarcasm was lost on our visitor. "Do you want to buy an ad or have you written a news release?"

Ed was wearing a different overcoat, black alpaca, with a fur collar. I could tell it was new, because the price tag dangled from the left-hand pocket. No doubt it was an oversight, since Ed couldn't see around his stomach. He looked like a big fat squirrel.

"I'm here to see Emma," he announced, offering me a conspiratorial smile. "Can you spare fifteen minutes out of your busy schedule?" Ed chuckled, pleased to have caught us seemingly taking our ease.

I agreed that I could fit Ed in, though I added that I had an interview scheduled at nine-fifteen with Principal Freeman. Ed helped himself to coffee, but showed disappointment when he couldn't find any sweet rolls.

"That's Ginny's job on Fridays," I said, leading the way into my office. "She's still on her honeymoon."

"Oh, well." With a disheartened sigh, Ed wedged himself into one of my visitor's chairs. It creaked ominously, reminding me that one of these days I'd have to get it fixed. It creaked again when he turned to stare at my open door. "Say, Emma, shouldn't we . . . ah, that is . . ."

As a former employee, Ed knew my policy regarding doors. Unless the discussion was extremely delicate, the door stayed open. I gazed at Ed with innocent eyes.

"Is something wrong, Ed? It's not trouble with Shirley, I hope?"

Ed drew back in the chair, causing it to retreat a couple of inches. "Shirley? Of course not! It's about the . . ." He gestured with his hands, indicating what I assumed was the size of a book. "You *know*," he whispered.

"Oh!" I all but shrieked, looking beyond Ed into the news office, where Leo had just arrived. "Your autobiography!" Picking up a Seattle phone book, I ignored Ed's wince. "I've solved your problem, Ed. I'm giving you the number and address of a writers' group. They've got members all over the state, and they're often looking for projects just like yours. I can imagine how excited they'll be to hear about your book idea."

Ed may be dopey, but he isn't dumb. "Now, just a minute, Emma," he said, sounding severe. "I don't want some freelancer who doesn't know me from Adam. The reason I asked you is because we go way back, both on the job and off. We're not just friends and former coworkers, we're fellow parishioners and members of the Chamber of Commerce. How could some hired gun out of Seattle or Yakima write about the real me?"

My brainstorm seemed to be backfiring. I rested the phone book against the edge of my desk. Ed's pudgy face showed signs not only of indignation, but of anguish. Puffed-up jackass that he might be, Ed was still human. I could see Vida fetching more hot water and pretending not to eavesdrop. Leo was almost as discreet, standing by Carla's desk, seemingly lost in admiration of some contact photos.

"Okay," I said, trying to inject camaraderie into my voice, "let's try this. When you get everything organized,

I'll go through it, and help you outline your own version. We've got two problems, Ed. One is that I honestly don't have the spare time to give a full-length book—especially one that's meaty"—I'd almost said beefy—"the attention it deserves. The other is that you are the only person who can write this story." Ed started to protest, but I held up a hand, which unfortunately allowed the phone book to fall on my foot. "It's not perspective," I emphasized, "that's so vital, but insight. You've written advertising copy, you know your way around words." I couldn't believe I was saying all this with a straight face. No doubt the pain in my foot helped. "When you start putting things down on paper, you'll make all sorts of discoveries, subconscious, latent, intimate, even spiritual sides of yourself that you—that all of us—don't think about on a day-to-day basis. It'll be a journey, Ed, inside of you, and the result will bring what you are out into the open for the benefit of the reader."

Leo spun around and had to lean on Carla's desk for support. I could see his shoulders shaking with mirth. Fortunately, Vida had returned to her desk and was out of my range of vision. I could imagine her rolling her eyes.

Ed was looking very thoughtful. "You have a point, Emma. Maybe I should keep the tape I brought along." He patted the breast pocket of his overcoat. "Actually, I only got up to the first day of kindergarten. It was a logical stopping place, though. You know how writers always end chapters with some kind of drama that makes the reader keep turning the page—at school nap-time, I got rolled up in my mat."

"Yes." I nodded solemnly. "That's just the thing. It sounds great, Ed." As if taken by surprise, I glanced at my watch. "Good grief! It's almost nine-ten! Principal Freeman will keep me after school if I'm tardy! Ha-ha."

Ed laughed, but it was perfunctory. I suspected that he

was already delving into his inner self. Escorting Ed out
of the office, I couldn't look at Leo or Vida. I managed a
wave for Carla, who was on the phone in the front office.
Accepting Ed's earnest handshake, I got into the Jag and
headed for the high school. I felt as if I were driving a
getaway car.

The snow of the previous night hadn't amounted to
much, and I was reminded of the collision between
Amanda Hanson and Tim Rafferty. I'd forgotten to stop
by the sheriff's office to fill out a report. I'd also forgotten what Amanda had said about the customer who
had returned the unwanted parcel. While Amanda had
mentioned no names, she'd said that the woman wrote
poetry. I had intended to pass the remark on to Vida, but
in the excitement of figuring out Laurie's parentage,
Amanda's complaint had slipped my mind.

The interview with Karl Freeman took longer than I'd
expected. Sometimes I forget how cautious and long-
winded educators can be. All I had wanted to find out
from the principal was if he'd heard anything new about
the community-college plans. Often, the local high
school serves as a springboard, sometimes providing
physical plant and a source for faculty.

The most that Karl Freeman could tell me—and he
hedged there, too—was that he felt a sense of interest
among several or at least a few teachers who might consider teaching at a higher level, depending upon various
other factors. As for the actual location of the new college, the principal didn't really know, but would guess—
if pressed—that it would be somewhere close to town.
The high school had formed three committees, one to
explore the impact of the college on the curriculum for
grades nine through twelve, the second to determine
which faculty members were qualified to teach at the college level, and the third to discuss whether or not a task

force should be set up to work at the local level between the high school and the college, or if it would be more appropriate for the legislature to make that decision, in which case, there was a subcommittee handling that specific issue. The one thing that Principal Freeman could say in all sincerity was that the quality of education at Alpine High would continue to be maintained at the highest standards, as long as the voters kept passing school levies, one of which would be put before the electorate in March of the following year, if board members agreed upon the timing and the amount. Both factors were being studied by ad hoc committees from the school board, and a decision should be forthcoming in the next few months.

My head was spinning as I drove down Highway 187 to Front Street. As usual, I noted the vacant storefronts. Some had moved to the Alpine Mall; others had simply closed their doors forever. Not much in the way of new business had come along to fill the vacuum. If Principal Freeman thought he could pass a levy before the community college began to sprout foundations and walls, he was doomed to disappointment. Alpiners needed a visible sign of new life before they'd agree to pay for so much as an unabridged dictionary.

I passed *The Advocate* and the sheriff's office. The post office was located in a brown brick building, wedged between the U.S. Forest Service and the state highway department. The architecture was so uninspiring that I assumed it had been a cooperative venture between the three agencies. Only the government could turn such a beautiful setting into something so drab.

Amanda Hanson was waiting on Grace Grundle when I arrived. Grace is a retired schoolteacher, and has an inner-ear problem that sometimes causes her to stagger. At present she was leaning against the counter, fussing over the cost of a package she was sending to a relative in Kansas.

"I simply don't understand," Grace said in her quiet but firm voice, "why there's so little difference between second class and parcel post. Are you trying to tell me that for six cents less, it might take up to five more days to deliver this to Hector?"

Amanda, who was wearing a frilly white blouse that probably violated several regulations handed down by the postmaster general, gave Grace a condescending look. "It's up to you. What's the rush?"

Grace bristled. "It's three loaves of banana bread. Hector loves my banana bread. I don't want it to get stale."

"Then send it express mail," Amanda said as her patience began to ebb. "He'll have it Monday."

"But his birthday isn't until Wednesday," Grace protested.

Amanda leaned her pert chin on one hand. "Then ship it first class."

"But that will cost me almost five dollars!" Grace looked horrified.

"Express mail will cost you fifteen." Amanda stood up straight, her contemptuous blue eyes regarding Grace as if she had her picture on the post office wall.

"Fifteen dollars! Oh, my." Grace reeled against the counter. "Why, I've never spent that much in my life to mail anything, including my husband's ashes!"

There were now three other people behind me in line and Amanda was the only clerk on duty. "Look," she said sharply, "make up your mind. If you want to think it over, step aside and come back when you're ready."

As classroom dictator to three generations of Alpine elementary students, Grace wasn't used to taking orders. "Now see here, young woman," Grace huffed, "your job is to accommodate me. If you don't wish to do that, then I must ask to speak to your supervisor."

"Oh, for God's . . ." Amanda grabbed the parcel from the scale and shoved it back at Grace. "Go ahead, talk to Roy. I'll get him for you right now." With a rustle of white frills, she left the window and hurried to the nether reaches of the post office.

Heather Bardeen, the daughter of Henry, was standing behind me with several large packages. We exchanged knowing looks.

"It's my break," she whispered. "Dad will think I've been kidnapped if I don't get back behind the desk at the ski lodge before ten-thirty."

Roy Everson appeared at that moment, his thin face wearing what I presumed was his customer-friendly expression. "Now, Mrs. Grundle—" he began.

"Roy," Grace interrupted with a wag of her finger, "posture, posture, posture! What have I always told you about keeping your shoulders straight and your head back? You'll have a crooked spine by the time you're forty!"

"I'm fifty." Roy sighed, beckoning for Grace to join him at the next window. "Let's see what we've got here, Mrs. Grundle. I take it you want to—"

"*Take* it? No, Roy, you aren't *taking* anything—not in that sense. What you mean is that *you understand*. . . ."

I smiled faintly at Amanda, who had resumed her stance behind the counter. Her gaze was conspiratorial—until she recognized me. "You saw the wreck," she said, lowering her voice. "Well? Was it my fault, or that jerk Tim Rafferty? He was going way too fast for that kind of road conditions."

"*Those kinds,*" Grace Grundle shot across the partition. "Plural nouns require plural adjectives and adverbs."

Amanda, who had moved to Alpine with her husband

only a year and a half earlier, didn't feel compelled to obey Grace's grammar rules. "Evil old bitch," Amanda mouthed. "Well? Wasn't that Rafferty guy speeding?"

The last thing I wanted to do was to get into an argument over the collision. "I haven't filed a report," I said truthfully. "I'm sure that black ice sent you into a skid. It's up to the sheriff to decide who was at fault. May I have twenty thirty-two-cent stamps?"

Amanda flipped open a book showing the various commemorative and regular issues. "Which kind?"

"Any kind," I replied. Amanda gave me a bunch of lighthouses. I gave her six dollars and forty cents. "Say," I said, not quite up to being ingenuous, "who was the pest with the parcel last night?" Seeing Amanda frown, I clarified my question. "You know, the woman who came in just before closing time."

Amanda handed me a receipt and gave an incredulous shake of her head. "That Marshall woman, the one who writes poems. Sometimes she puts them on the envelopes she's mailing. You know, like her light bill—'Utility rates are outrageously high/Who can afford to bake a pie?' Junk. The problem with people like her is that they spend all their time thinking so-called deep thoughts and not paying attention to real life. If she's got a package she doesn't want, just hand it over to the carrier. Don't bother us about it, especially not at one minute to five."

I managed to put on my most sympathetic face. "What was it, something she ordered from the TV shopping network?"

"QVC?" Amanda shook her head. "No. I wish it had been. Those are easy—so many people order stuff from that cable deal and then change their minds. But this one didn't have a return address. We don't know what to do with it. Dead Lettersville, that's where it'll go. Somebody wasted a lot of postage."

I felt myself tense, though I wasn't sure why. "Don't do that," I said, barely able to recognize my own voice. I saw Amanda's curious expression. "Humor me," I went on, feeling silly. "If you've still got that package, turn it over to the sheriff."

Amanda continued to stare, then shrugged. "Okay, why not?" She leaned across the counter and again lowered her voice. "Does that mean Dodge and you will admit Rafferty was at fault?"

Before I could answer, Grace Grundle spoke up: "*You and Dodge!* Really, I can't think what is happening to the English language! It's all this television." Apparently having finally concluded her business with Roy Everson, Grace Grundle went on her wavery way out of the post office. I followed, keeping my distance, but not making any promises to Amanda about the accident. She was on her own; I had to tell the truth as I had seen it.

But I couldn't dismiss my curiosity about the parcel that Jane Marshall had refused. The U.S. Post Office was delivering too much unwanted mail in Alpine. It couldn't be a coincidence.

Chapter Ten

MILO ALSO HAD forgotten about the accident report. He had Dustin Fong give me a form, which I dutifully filled out, trying to be both accurate and fair. When I finished, I tapped on the sheriff's door.

Milo was on the phone, but he motioned for me to come in. Since the remodeling, the sheriff's private quarters have been expanded, a skylight has been put in, and the walls have been painted a rich cream color. Milo's personal decor includes a mounted steelhead, a photograph of his children taken about ten years ago, a map of Skykomish County, a forged twenty-dollar bill, an ashtray made out of antlers, a mediocre painting of Mount Baldy, and a poster proclaiming that GUN CONTROL MEANS HITTING YOUR TARGET. Besides added space, Milo also has a new computer, extra shelving, and a separate door that leads to the rest room, the interrogation room, and the evidence room. It also allows Milo to slip out the rear exit, should he feel so inclined.

I had been sitting for a couple of minutes when Milo finally hung up the phone. Murder wasn't the only crime on the sheriff's agenda. A hubcap thief was loose in Alpine, and the sheriff had an informant who thought the stolen goods were being sold to a dealer in Lynnwood.

"I got a description," Milo said, jabbing his pen at an open notepad. "Young, but not too young. Average height, average weight, brownish hair, hazel or brown eyes, no visible marks." He yawned. "Tattoos are in. Why can't these guys have *crook* put on their foreheads? That's the only way we'll ever get anybody to give an accurate description."

I sympathized. Then, burrowing deeper into the sheriff's good graces, I accepted a mug of his pathetic coffee. "I'm meddling," I admitted, "but if I don't, Vida will."

Milo wore a pained expression, but didn't stop me from explaining about the Marshall women and their strange mail deliveries. "Laurie didn't receive a package at the salon—that must have been a letter, or at least nothing bigger than a ten-by-twenty envelope. But her mother refused a parcel that had no return address. Amanda Hanson will send it to the Dead Letter Office unless you confiscate it."

"As what? A parcel?" Milo made a face. "Hey, Emma, I really don't get this one. What do Jane and Laurie Marshall have to do with Kay Whitman's murder? At least I assume that's what's going through that curly little head of yours." He suddenly stopped and stared. "Whoa! You don't have curls anymore. What happened?"

"I got my hair cut," I replied peevishly. "Yesterday morning." It was typical of Milo not to notice such things immediately. "I lost all my permanent." I'd also lost all the styling that Stella had put into my thick brown locks. She might as well have stuck a bowl on my head and used pruning shears. "And yes, Laurie does have something to do with the murder—she was on the scene when it happened."

Milo now wore a musing expression. "Okay," he murmured, obviously humoring me. "So you think Laurie knows something and she's being blackmailed. Is that it?"

The thought had never occurred to me, nor did I believe that the sheriff was serious. "I'm not sure what I believe," I said, sounding sulky. Then, though I knew it would do no good, I told Milo how Vida and I had called on the Marshalls Monday evening. "Jane acted as if she didn't want Laurie to talk to us. We couldn't figure out why. At the time I figured maybe it was because Laurie is a mental midget, and her mother didn't want her saying something stupid that might mislead us. But now we think she may actually be much more intelligent than she pretends because her real father is . . . oh, dear." I was drowning in a sea of conjecture.

"Emma," Milo began, pushing himself back in his new leather chair and placing his feet on the desk, "let Vida handle the story. It's bad enough with her, God knows, but when you jump into the act, it's enough to make me want to turn in my badge. Go away now, and let me get back to work."

"The parcel," I said stubbornly. "The least you can do is have a look."

"You look," Milo said, lighting a cigarette. "I'll be damned if I can figure out why you think Jane Marshall has anything to do with the murder of Kay Whitman. Even with a big stretch, some damned package—which could be a dress she changed her mind about or a bunch of bulbs she doesn't want to put in the frozen ground right now—that doesn't ring any alarm bells with me. Go ahead, pretend you brought me the package. Open it, examine it, fondle it, then throw the damned thing in the trash. Garbage pickup's on Monday, so it'll be gone in seventy-two hours, and we can forget it, like a bad dream. G'bye, Emma."

Feeling like a flop, I left the sheriff to his hubcaps. Vida could collect the unwanted package from the post office. I told her so when I returned to *The Advocate*. In contrast to Milo, she was intrigued.

"Someone is harassing the Marshalls," she declared. "For how long, I wonder?"

"Good point," I said as Carla joined us in the newsroom. "Why not ask Jane? You two seem to have bonded."

Vida inclined her head. "Perhaps. Odd, isn't it, that both Laurie and Becca have worrisome elements in their lives. Laurie—and presumably Jane—receive unwanted mail. Becca gets annoying phone calls from her ex-husband. Do either—or both—of these situations have anything to do with Kay Whitman's death, or are they merely a sign of the times?"

"Speaking of *The Times*," Carla put in, "I had them send me this photo of Toby Popp from their files in Seattle. It's at least five years old, but we can use it with the house story."

Leo looked up from his computer screen. "That's Popp?" The furrows on his weathered face grew deeper as he stood up and leaned across his desk. "Hey! That's the guy who came in with the personal ad!"

Vida and I stared, while Carla looked puzzled. It dawned on me that my reporter didn't know anything about the strange man who had shown up Monday night with the ad copy. It was Leo, however, who explained what had happened.

"Weird science," he concluded. "Maybe all those computer guys really are nuts."

Carla was studying the photo, which seemed to have been cropped from a bigger picture. Toby was turned to his left, indicating that in the original shot, he'd been looking at someone else.

"I think he's kind of cute," Carla said. "For a nerd."

"A billion bucks' worth of cute," Leo remarked, sitting down again. "I met the guy. Trust me, he's weird."

"We met him, too," Vida declared, glancing in my direction. "He's not ordinary, I'll admit that." She adjusted her glasses, then shook her head. "No, he *is* ordinary. That's what's so peculiar about him."

"His ad was weird, Duchess. He acted weird." Leo wasn't giving in. "He never came back, which is the weirdest part of all."

"Evidence of a one-track mind," Vida countered. "That's how people become an enormous success. Toby Popp must be incredibly focused. My, my—I wonder what the ad meant?"

"Tell me again," Carla begged.

No one could accuse Carla of being focused. " 'One down, one to go,' " I quoted, exchanging yet another glance with Vida. "We thought it was kind of . . . odd."

"We thought," Vida said in a firm voice, "that it might pertain to Kay Whitman's murder, coming as it did only hours after the tragedy. I suspect that Emma and I were victimized by our own active imaginations."

"Occupational hazard," Leo remarked in an agreeable voice.

We were silent for a few moments, the only sound coming from the occasional rumble of a truck out on Front Street and the whistle of the Burlington-Northern as it began its steep climb through the Cascade Tunnel. Leo had returned to his computer screen, Carla was examining the photo of Toby Popp, Vida was ostensibly reading through a wedding story, and I was studying some of the advertising copy. I suspected that neither Vida nor I was concentrating on our work. My guess was proved right when my House & Home editor put on her brown tweed coat and announced that she was going to the post office.

I returned to my desk, making a valiant effort to engross myself in next week's edition. By eleven o'clock, I'd finished the brief (and dull) community-college article and the even briefer (and duller) new-bridge story. The timber-sales editorial was ready to roll. I cast about for another story idea, but nothing came to mind. The truth was, I should have been covering the homicide. It wasn't that I didn't trust Vida with the story, at least not the gathering of it—she was better at ferreting out facts than I was. The writing was another matter, though as long as I could edit her copy, that was all right, too. But I felt a personal as well as a professional void. I needed that story to fill a hole in my life. But I'd be damned if I'd give that empty nook a name.

Vida returned shortly before noon, suggesting that we eat lunch at the Burger Barn. Apparently, she was ignoring her diet. In the pre–Buck Bardeen era, Vida had periodically attempted to lose weight, either via the occasional fad route, or by consuming only carrots, celery, cottage cheese, and hard-boiled eggs. In between, she would binge. Neither extreme seemed to affect her figure. Nor did her more concerted efforts when she first started seeing Buck the previous summer. I had seen pictures of Vida as a young woman, and she had always looked the same, at least as far as her weight was concerned. She wasn't fat; she was big. But somehow, she clung to the notion that her destiny was being slim. Given her otherwise exceptionally good sense, I marveled at her self-delusion. The optimism about her ability to lose pounds and inches ranked right up there with her unshakable conviction that her grandson, Roger, was a well-behaved child.

Vida had brought her straw shopping bag along to the Burger Barn. As I suspected, it contained the parcel that Jane Marshall had returned to the post office.

"I considered opening it in front of Milo," Vida said as we sat down in a rear booth, "but he'd scoff. However, I went through channels and got Billy to authorize having me pick up the parcel. Amanda isn't exactly a stickler for rules. You can tell that by those skimpy skirts."

Jessie Lott, who always looks hot and tired even before noon on a forty-degree day, took our order. I was content with the burger basket; Vida requested the meatloaf sandwich, which came with mashed potatoes and gravy, a vegetable medley, and Jell-O.

"I'll skip dinner," she murmured after Jessie had gone. "Or have soup."

My sense of anticipation had grown. Vida seemed to relish prolonging the moment, which wasn't like her. Finally, I realized that she was waiting for the couple across the aisle to leave. When they did about three minutes later, Vida produced the package.

It was the size of a large dictionary, and wrapped in plain brown paper. Vida pointed out the address and postmark.

"Sultan, February fifteenth, which was Wednesday, day before yesterday. The requisite number of stamps, block printing, black felt-tipped pen, sent to Marshall, 522 Cascade Street, Alpine, Washington 98289. What does that tell you?"

"It'd tell me more if you opened the damned thing," I said dryly.

Vida sighed. "Be patient, Emma. I'm trying to gauge Jane Marshall's reaction. She did *not* open this package. Why?"

I hazarded a guess. "Because she knew what was in it?"

"Perhaps." Vida waited, the wise teacher hoping her dim pupil would come up with a better answer.

"Because she knew who sent it," I finally said.

"Exactly. Jane knew because she recognized the hand-writing." Seeing my incredulous expression, she waved a hand. "Not in the usual sense—but the fact that it's block-printed means Jane—or someone else in the family—had received other mailings addressed in a similar fashion. They were unwelcome, as was this one. Now, shall we open it?"

I held my breath as Vida undid the wrapping paper, which was sealed with strapping tape. To my annoyance, she folded the paper into neat squares, then placed it beside her on the worn vinyl upholstery. The box was white, the shiny kind that's usually reserved for gifts. A vase might fit, or a pair of bookends.

The rustle of tissue struck my ear at the same time that something repugnant hit my nostrils. Vida's head was bent over the box. She jumped, let out a shriek, and dropped the box onto the floor. Her face was white; her hands shook. Jessie Lott appeared with my coffee and Vida's tea.

"We're out of Jell-O," the waitress said. "Would you like sliced peaches instead?" At last, Jessie took in Vida's horrified expression. "Why, whatever's wrong, dear? Are you feeling sick?"

I could see Vida's self-discipline at work. She rested her hands on the table, squared her shoulders, and licked her lips. "I'm fine, Jessie." Vida actually managed a smile, though it mocked her usual manner. "Peaches sound very nice, thank you."

Though puzzled, Jessie Lott wasn't the curious type. She moved away again, just as Buddy Bayard and Dutch Bamberg sat down in the opposite booth. We exchanged greetings, though I know I sounded stilted and Vida was distracted.

The smell was beginning to make me feel queasy. "What is it?" I whispered.

Vida leaned forward, now holding on to her black pillbox hat. "It's a cat," she said under her breath. "A dead cat. If I had to guess, I'd say it was Dodger. I think we'd better get the sheriff."

Seldom have I admired Vida as much as I did when she put the lid back on the box and carried the feline corpse out of the Burger Barn and across the street to Milo's headquarters. I offered to go with her, but she insisted that I stay so that I could ask Jessie to move us to another, less odoriferous booth.

Since it was now into the noon hour, Jessie had only one seating available, up front. It was inevitable that she noticed the smell when she moved our place settings.

"Are you sure Vida isn't sick?" she asked, wrinkling her broad nose.

"That's not Vida," I replied, feeling protective as well as defensive. "It was something in a package she just opened."

"She ought to send it back," Jessie declared, putting down silverware and new napkins. "I'd ask for a refund. Whatever that was, it's worse than a dead skunk. Do you want me to hold your orders?"

I'd been holding my breath, as the smell had followed us almost to the Burger Barn's front section. Without knowing it, Jessie had come very close to the truth. But I made no comment on her observation, except to agree that she should wait before serving us. Sitting down, I breathed deeply, bravely. The dead-cat odor was almost masked by the usual film of grease that clung to the Burger Barn's atmosphere. I wondered if I was brave enough to drink my coffee. I also wondered if I was stupid enough to buy a pack of cigarettes. Until the previous night out with Milo, I hadn't smoked for six weeks.

Before I could let weakness overcome me, Becca

Wolfe stopped at the booth. "Ms. Lord!" she exclaimed. "You already changed your new haircut! Didn't you like the way Stella fixed it?"

At the moment I felt lucky that my hair hadn't fallen out in clumps. Trying to emulate Vida's staunchness, I offered Becca a feeble smile. "Have a seat, I'm waiting for Mrs. Runkel. She had to . . . run an errand." I almost choked on the words.

"I'm doing takeout," Becca said. "Let me put my order in and then I'll come back to wait. I wanted to ask you a question."

Anxiously, I kept my eye on the door. Several Alpiners I recognized, including Father Dennis Kelly, came in. My pastor didn't see me, since he was absorbed in conversation with his luncheon companions, Jake and Buzzy, the Brothers O'Toole.

Becca returned, sitting sideways in the booth. "I was wondering about something that's been bothering me," she said, looking unusually diffident. "You were so nice to me the other day when . . . you know, when that customer got killed. Usually, if I have a problem, I go to Stella. She's great. But Stella's got a good marriage—she and Richie have been together forever." Becca paused, running a hand through her short, dark hair. "I know you're a single mom. So what I'm asking is how do you deal with an ex-husband? Or did you get what they call an amicable divorce? That's the phrase, right?"

Next to a dead cat, the last thing I wanted to do was discuss my private life. "I'm not divorced," I said primly. "I was never married."

Becca's blue eyes grew wide. "But I thought . . . oh, excuse me!" Her flawless cheeks turned pink, and though she was embarrassed, she couldn't suppress her curiosity. "I heard you had a son, and I . . . well, you know."

"I do have a son," I said, lifting my chin. "I don't have

a husband." The smile I offered Becca felt brittle. "Go ahead, ask me anything. I love giving opinions on subjects I know nothing about."

Becca appeared as if she wasn't sure whether I was trying to be funny or sarcastic. I didn't know, either. To soften my words, I reached over and patted her arm. Becca bit her lip.

"It's my ex," she said. "He's trying to drive me crazy. Stella said I should get a restraining order, but I've heard they don't do much good. In fact, I think it would only make Eric mad. What do you think?"

I understood Stella's rationale, though I, too, had heard of cases where the restraining order was not only violated, but the woman involved had ended up dead. "What's he doing?" I asked, remembering the phone call Stella had received while I was in the salon Thursday morning.

Becca placed her dimpled, manicured hands against her mouth, then whispered through her fingers: "I don't know exactly what he's doing. But he's here in Alpine."

From the rear of the restaurant, a youthful male voice called Becca's name. She jumped, then realized it was the cook. "My order," she said, flushing deeply. "I'm sort of nervous these days. Thanks, Ms. Lord."

I'd done nothing to help Becca. Stella or Vida or one of the many divorced women in Alpine could offer more sound advice. I knew nothing of husbands or ex-husbands, except secondhand. Disconsolately, I watched Becca pick up her food and exit the Burger Barn. Jessie Lott refilled my coffee mug. I kept eyeing the door.

Vida finally appeared, looking grim. "Milo says the cat is—was—definitely Dodger. His neck had been broken. Ugh." She sat down and held her head.

Jessie returned, this time with our orders. Neither Vida

nor I had much appetite. I nibbled a french fry; she poked at her sliced peaches.

"They'll check with the Sultan post office," Vida said, still glum. "Surely someone will remember who mailed the box. Sultan isn't that big."

Sultan had just under three thousand citizens, but the outlying area took in at least twice that number, including Startup, Gold Bar, and Baring. "The package didn't have to be mailed from the post office," I pointed out. "Whoever sent it could have figured out how many stamps were required, and used a mailbox. It would've fit, barely."

Vida now looked thoughtful. "That's so. But why would anyone do such an awful thing?"

I had no answer, though a sudden idea occurred to me. "Vida—the postmark was Wednesday. The Whitmans didn't leave until Thursday, yesterday. Wouldn't Honoria have missed Dodger?"

"Maybe she had given him away," Vida replied slowly. "Cats are strange creatures. Perhaps he sensed that Honoria was leaving and ran off."

We didn't speak for the next few minutes, except for Vida's complaining that her meatloaf sandwich was dry, and my noting that my hamburger bun seemed stale. The truth was that we could have been eating at a five-star French restaurant and still found our entrées unappealing.

I finally remembered to tell Vida about Becca's visit to our table. "We should tell Milo," my House & Home editor declared as we figured out our separate bills. "I'm not saying that Eric Forbes had anything to do with Kay's murder, but he sounds like a danger to Becca."

"There are too many side issues," I grumbled, leaving a dollar tip and heading for the register. "It's like links in a paper chain—Kay was Becca's client, and this Eric is Becca's ex-husband. Laurie was present at the time of the murder, and she may or may not be the daughter of Toby Popp. There are connections all over the place, but do they mean anything?"

We were now out on the sidewalk where the rain was coming down in a steady drizzle. The clouds were so low that Mount Baldy had disappeared behind a gray curtain. Dampness permeated the air, with icicles dripping from storefronts and melted snow trickling along the gutters.

"The connections—I should say situations," Vida corrected herself, tromping across Front Street in her brown galoshes, "mean a great deal to the people involved. But if you're asking what they have to do with Kay Whitman's death, I must confess to being up a stump."

So was I. We were now in front of Parker's Pharmacy. *The Advocate* was a block away, at Front and Fourth; the sheriff's office was right across Third Street. Vida and I exchanged swift looks, then marched west.

Milo was behind the curving counter where Dustin Fong sat at a computer, Bill Blatt talked on the phone, and Toni Andreas held sway in her newly installed receptionist's slot.

"Now what?" Milo demanded, sounding exasperated.

"Don't be like that," Vida said crossly. "It gets my goat when you act as if we're a pair of pests. We've come to see if you've checked with the Sultan postmistress."

"Sam Heppner's out on patrol, so I sent him into Sultan," Milo replied, still sour. "If it makes you feel better, we've called Grants Pass. Honoria and her mother ought to get in around six. With any luck, the local cops can contact them at one of the motels. Then we can find out when Honoria last saw Dodger."

Vida gave a single nod. "Very good." She turned to her nephew, who had just gotten off the phone. "What about that fax from US West?"

Bill's fair skin colored slightly. "It hasn't come yet, Aunt Vida. They said it'd probably be late today."

Vida uttered a small snort. "No wonder they were divested. You'd think they'd be more efficient these days." Her eyes darted from her nephew to Milo to Dustin and back to Bill, who was squirming in his seat. "Well?" She spoke sharply. "What is it? I know when something's bothering you, Billy."

Nervously, Bill pushed a lock of blond hair off his forehead. "It's . . . it's just business, Aunt Vida. Honest." He gave his boss a helpless look.

Milo hooked his thumbs in his belt. "Okay, go ahead." He sighed. "What now?"

Bill pointed to the phone. "That was Stella Magruder. She says Becca Wolfe never got back from lunch. Stella's worried."

Chapter Eleven

ED BRONSKY'S WARNING buzzed through my brain as I sat across from Milo in his private office. If there was gossip about my voyeuristic involvement in local crime, maybe it was justified. For the third time in a single week, I found myself giving information to the sheriff.

"Look," I said, "Becca didn't say anything except that her ex-husband was in town. He scares her, but she didn't seem inclined to call you."

In the chair next to me, Vida was looking at her watch. Milo hadn't tried to keep her out of his inner sanctum; he knew such an effort would prove futile.

Vida looked up. "It's one-twenty now. How long has Becca been missing?"

Milo glanced at the notes Bill Blatt had taken over the phone. "Stella said Becca left the salon about twelve-fifteen. She hasn't come back." The sheriff turned to me. "What time did Becca leave the Burger Barn?"

I considered. "Twelve-thirty, twelve thirty-five? It was while Vida was here with . . . Dodger." I hated calling the poor dead thing by name. Somehow, it made the tragedy seem worse.

Milo picked up the phone and poked a button. He asked whoever answered exactly when the cat corpse had been reported in the log. "Twelve twenty-four," he said, making another note, then directing his attention at Vida. "You didn't see Becca on your way back to the Burger Barn, I take it?"

"No." Vida answered without hesitation. "If I had, don't you think I would have said as much?"

"Shit." Milo swore softly, ignoring Vida's reproachful expression. "What could happen to her in one block? She didn't even have to cross Front Street to get back to work."

The only businesses between the Burger Barn and the Clemans Building were the ski shop and the cobbler's. The most likely scenario was that Becca had been hailed by someone, maybe in a car. I made the suggestion and watched Milo roll his eyes.

"Hell, you think I haven't thought of that already? But would she go off with her ex-husband right after she's announced he's dangerous?"

"She didn't say that exactly," I hedged.

Milo had already requested an all-points bulletin on Becca. I could imagine Stella Magruder's reaction to the latest disaster. The salon owner must feel hexed.

"We need a description of this Forbes guy," Milo declared, his gaze on Vida.

For once, Vida couldn't help. She made a rueful face, then offered suggestions, as if to make amends for her inadequacy. "Ask Stella. She may have seen a picture. Or Becca's parents. Perhaps they knew their son-in-law, even if they didn't approve of him."

Milo gave orders to Dustin Fong to deliver the news. "I hate this part," the sheriff lamented. "Telling the relatives is harder than anything else."

"You've no reason to believe Becca is dead," I pointed out. "Vida—who was on the street when you went to and from the sheriff's?" I didn't doubt for a minute that Vida could recall not only names, but apparel, attitude, and family background.

Vida sighed. "Reverend Phelps, from the Methodist church. Heather Bardeen and Chaz Phipps from the ski lodge. The Peabody brothers. Georgia Carlson, Dr. Flake, Irene Baugh, George Engebretsen—one or two others I can't recall off the top of my head. But I saw no strangers."

Milo had been hurriedly jotting down names. "We'll find out if they saw Becca—or anybody else. What about cars?"

"I pay no attention to cars." Vida sniffed. "Cars aren't important—only who is in them. I did see my brother-in-law, Edward, passing by in his truck. He needs a new muffler. Such a racket it made!" She shook her head in disapproval.

Any law-enforcement official who didn't know Vida might have questioned her accuracy. But not Milo. "I'm going to see Stella," he said, getting up. "We'll keep you posted on the latest developments."

"Of course you will," Vida agreed. She was also on her feet. "That's because we're going with you."

Milo stopped at the edge of his desk. "Hold it! This is official business. I said we'd keep you posted."

"I need hair products," Vida announced blithely, then looked at me. "You need a permanent, but there's no time for that. Perhaps you could have Stella perk up your new cut. It looks a trifle . . . limp." She wore a genuinely apologetic expression.

"On the contrary," I said, suddenly feeling bold, "I'll see if Stella can fit me in this afternoon."

In defeat, Milo was a reasonably good sport. I was serious about the perm. There was nothing pressing on my calendar for the rest of the day. This week all the breaking news seemed to be coming out of Stella's.

Stella, however, had a busier schedule than I did. Laurie was not only working with her own clients, but she'd volunteered to take over for Becca in the facial room.

"I could do it tomorrow," Stella said, obviously trying hard to keep worry at bay. "Eleven-thirty?"

I nodded, then let Vida move in. But my House & Home editor deferred to Milo. "After you, Sheriff. Becca's situation is far more compelling than my need for a good conditioner."

Stella wasn't as gracious. "Make it short, Milo. I've got the mayor's wife with her head in a shampoo bowl, and Minnie Harris under the dryer."

Milo's questions were brief. Stella's replies were to the point: unless Becca had a client in the noon hour, she always brought her lunch back to the salon. She'd been booked until twelve, and had a twelve-thirty, with Irene Baugh. When Becca didn't show up, the mayor's wife had decided to have the facial after her hair appointment, instead of before.

"It meant Irene had to wait," Stella explained hurriedly, "because I had to set Minnie Harris first. Minnie was anxious to get back to the desk at the Lumberjack Motel. They're busy on Fridays during ski season. Anyway, I was sure Becca would be back. I thought the Burger Barn was slow filling her order. When Becca wasn't here for her one-fifteen with Darlene Adcock, I got nervous and called you. I felt silly, but what else could I do?"

"You did the right thing," Milo reassured her. "What do you know about Becca's ex?"

"World-class creep," Stella asserted, glancing anxiously in the direction of her waiting clients. "He called here yesterday." She gave me a nervous, quirky smile.

"You were here, Emma. That's the last time I heard anything of the jerk. Why do you ask?" Stella was again staring at Milo.

The sheriff explained that Becca had told me Eric Forbes was in Alpine. Stella gaped and leaned against the counter for support. "Jesus H. Christ!" she exclaimed under her breath. "Becca never told me that! Oh, shit!"

"Would she have told Laurie?" Milo inquired.

Stella was shaking her head in apparent disbelief over Milo's announcement. "Laurie? Oh—I don't know. Maybe. Maybe not. They work well together, but they're not exactly buddies. Oh, double shit!" Stella sat down in the swivel chair behind the counter.

For me, there was a fascination in watching Milo handle a witness. Stella Magruder was not only a businesswoman and the wife of Alpine's deputy mayor, but a voter and a lifelong acquaintance. Only in a small town is a public official exposed so rawly to the electorate. Yet Milo behaved as if Stella were a stranger who wouldn't know a polling booth if it fell on her. I had to admire the sheriff for his objectivity.

"Did Becca have a boyfriend?" he asked, seemingly indifferent to Stella's semicollapse.

Stella was staring not at any of us, but at the telephone on the counter. Maybe she was thinking about Eric Forbes's Thursday-morning call. Or perhaps her own, to the sheriff's office.

"A boyfriend?" Stella finally echoed. "I don't think so." Her voice was hollow.

"What about girlfriends?" Milo asked, keeping his poker face.

Slowly, Stella got to her feet. "Becca had turned her back on the old crowd from high school. They were the ones who got her into trouble in the first place. Some of them have moved on anyway. The only girl chum she ever mentioned was your receptionist, Toni Andreas." The information was delivered with a slightly chiding look for Milo.

"Okay," Milo responded noncommittally. "I'll check with Toni. We're already contacting her parents."

"Good luck." Stella's tone was ironic. Then, with a forceful movement, she came around the counter and stood toe-to-toe with Milo. "Listen, Sheriff, you'd better move your ass on this one. It's bad enough that a client gets killed on my turf, but to lose an employee—I swear to God I'll torch that brand-new snazzy office of yours if you don't come up with some answers pretty frigging fast!" With a flip of her hips, Stella marched off to tend to business.

"Hmm," Vida murmured. "I don't believe I'll get that conditioner after all."

But Milo wasn't finished. A moment later Laurie came out of the rear part of the salon, presumably from the facial room. The sheriff beckoned to her; she came forward with obvious reluctance.

Laurie knew nothing about Becca's former husband. She was almost certain that Becca hadn't been dating since her return to Alpine. If Becca had any close friends—including Toni Andreas—Laurie didn't know about them. Laurie not only knew nothing, but in the immortal words of Yogi Berra, she didn't suspect anything either.

Vida and I, however, believed otherwise. When Milo finished with Laurie, we lingered.

"Laurie," Vida said kindly, "I really must purchase some conditioner. What type would you suggest for my hair?" To prove her concern, she removed the black pillbox hat she'd been wearing.

Laurie wandered over to the hair-products display.

"You need a conditioner for permed, noncolored extra-thick hair," she said, as if by rote. "This is a good one," she continued, taking a large white plastic jug from the rack. "If you buy the biggest size, you save almost two dollars."

"How nice," Vida remarked. "How much is that, Laurie?"

"Fifteen ninety-five, plus tax." Laurie's pretty face was an absolute blank.

"With tax?" Vida asked.

In her typically vague manner, Laurie began to look at the sales tax chart that was taped next to the register. Vida leaned down and slapped her hand over the paper.

"Make a guess, Laurie." Vida wore a smile that would have made an angel blush.

"Seventeen-thirty," Laurie replied, those blue eyes bland. "I do this all the time. I can sort of memorize it." She looked away.

"Remarkable." Vida spoke without inflection. "Your father must be very proud of you."

The startled expression that passed over Laurie's face was almost imperceptible. "He wanted me to go to work for him at the machinery shop, but I said I'd like a career of my own. I really enjoy doing hair. It's creative."

If Laurie hadn't missed a beat, neither had Vida. "I didn't mean Martin Marshall, Laurie. I referred to your real father. Surely you've heard from him now that he's moving so close to Alpine."

If I'd glimpsed surprise on Laurie's face a moment ago, I could have sworn that it was now briefly replaced by alarm. Then her gaze hardened, that same agatelike look I'd seen the previous morning after she dropped the mail. "I hardly remember my birth father," she said carefully. "My dad's my dad. That's why I'm Laurie Marshall."

"Instead of Laurie Popp." Vida tossed off the line as if it were an aside in a play.

"Seventeen-thirty," Laurie repeated. "Do you need shampoo?"

Even Vida knows when to run up the white flag. "I have exact change," she murmured, rummaging through her purse. "No, I don't need shampoo, thank you."

I had assumed Milo would leave after he finished questioning Laurie, but apparently he hadn't. The sheriff now appeared in the rear of the salon, where he paused to speak to Stella.

"What's he been doing?" I whispered as Vida and I headed for the door. "I thought he went back to his office."

Vida wore a sour expression, no doubt smarting from her defeat at Laurie's hands. "He did. That is, he exited the salon." She paused in midstep, looking over her shoulder. "Interesting, that."

"What?"

But Vida didn't answer. Maybe she was taking out her revenge on me. I'd let her; she'd get over it. Vida's not a spiteful sort.

But I wondered what she meant.

While I didn't know Becca Wolfe very well, I was worried about her. For the next two hours I felt distracted, my mind constantly turning to Becca's whereabouts. My imagination was working overtime, inventing all sorts of grisly scenarios.

Around four o'clock, I went into the news office and sat down next to Vida's desk. "Have you heard anything from Milo?" I asked.

Vida shook her head. "I talked to Billy a few minutes ago. There's no news, not even from the phone company. Stella told Milo she's never seen a picture of Eric."

"I've been thinking," I said, trying to keep my hands from making nervous little gestures. "What if Becca saw something Monday? Or the murderer *thinks* she saw something. Isn't it possible that he or she might have taken steps to silence her?"

"It certainly crossed my mind," Vida agreed, putting aside the etiquette book she'd been consulting for filler on her page. "I trust it also occurred to Milo. But why would the killer wait five days to act? Becca has been interrogated thoroughly."

"Her subconscious," I said, more to myself than to Vida. "Becca hasn't told anybody what she knows because she hasn't realized it yet."

Vida whipped off her glasses and began rubbing her eyes. "That means the killer is still among us. Oh, dear!"

The phone rang, causing Vida to fumble for her glasses before lifting the receiver. Her whole body tensed as she listened, then rose from the chair.

"Don't read it to me, Billy. I'll be right over." Vida hung up and reached for her coat. "That was Billy. He has the phone-company information."

I rushed into my office. "I'm coming, too," I called, grabbing my duffel coat. Feeling a need to excuse myself, I gave Vida a wan smile as we went through the door. "I can't stand the suspense."

My House & Home editor was understanding. "It's the immediacy. You discovered the body. We all know Stella and the others at the salon, not to mention Honoria and her family. The killer has struck very close to home."

Vida's words struck home, too. As we walked through the rain I noted that Front Street was now virtually clear of snow, and so was Third, at least as far as where it crossed Cedar. In Alpine, looking south means looking up, viewing the town as it climbs Tonga Ridge. I could see all the way to the cul-de-sac off Fir Street, which is where my log house sits nestled among the trees. Until today, snow had clung to the evergreens that flank the mountainside almost to the crest. The steady rain had washed the branches clean. It occurred to me that I hadn't seen the trees so bare since November. Maybe spring was coming after all.

Bill Blatt's offer of a chair for his aunt was declined. "I can read standing up," Vida asserted with a wave of her hand.

I tried to look over her shoulder, but since Vida is almost six inches taller, my success was limited. "Interesting," she remarked, pushing the fax along the counter in my direction. "Don't you think so, Billy?"

Billy looked bewildered. There was no sign of any other sheriff's personnel except for Toni Andreas. I saw Vida dart a glance her way, and knew that Toni was next on the interrogation list.

But Vida bided her time. "See here, Emma," she said, pointing to the record of calls made on Monday, February 13. "There's only one long-distance charge, at four fifty-two, to Pacific Grove. That would be the undertaker. Isn't that correct, Billy?"

Bill Blatt was once again squirming under his aunt's scrutiny. "We haven't had time to check. Should I do it now?"

Vida nodded solemnly. "I should hope so, Billy. Or do you have a reason to wait?" The sarcasm was almost hidden behind her mild tone.

I, however, was beginning to feel a bit like Bill. Then Vida's point dawned on me. "There's no call to Castro Valley," I said. "That's where Honoria's sister lives, isn't it?"

Vida gave another nod. "Exactly." She pursed her lips, watching Bill dial the number in the 408 area code. "That means no one notified Cassandra of Kay's death until Tuesday. Doesn't that strike you as odd?"

"Honoria or Trevor could have called from Alpine," I pointed out. "Maybe from here."

Bill spoke a few words into the receiver, then hung up. "You're right, Aunt Vida. That was the Pacific Grove funeral home. They received Ms. Whitman's body last night."

"Ah!" Vida said in an undertone. "Trevor has arrived, then."

"The funeral is Monday at ten o'clock," Bill added, obviously eager to please his aunt. "Actually, it's a memorial service. Mr. Whitman requested cremation."

Vida had retrieved the list of phone calls. "Do you remember if Honoria or her brother telephoned their sister from here on Monday?"

Bill's face worked in concentration. "They made some calls," he said at last. "But I think they were trying to get hold of their mother in Startup."

Vida lifted her eyebrows. " 'Trying'? What do you mean, Billy?"

"Well . . ." Bill cleared his throat. "I don't think she answered the first couple of times. Ask Toni—she might remember."

Toni Andreas was pretty in an angular sort of way, with a boyish figure and close-cropped brown hair. During Adam's brief courtship of her, my son had decided that she was dim and had no sense of humor. With the arrogance of youth, he couldn't endure the lack of either. Milo, however, had informed me that Toni was reasonably bright and fairly efficient. Otherwise he wouldn't have hired her full-time. The sheriff apparently didn't care if Toni could keep the rest of the staff rolling in the aisles as long as she helped keep them on their toes.

I trailed along after Vida as she approached Toni's area at the far end of the curving counter. Toni looked daunted as my House & Home editor approached.

"We keep a log of all calls," Toni said, in answer to Vida's first question. "It's done by computer. I can print out the Monday list, if you want it."

"We do," Vida replied, at her most majestic.

Toni fiddled around with her computer keyboard, then went over to the printer, which was next to the far wall, close to Milo's office door.

"Here," said Toni, handing Vida a three-foot-long sheet of paper. "Incoming calls are on the left, outgoing in the right-hand column."

The gaze Vida riveted on Toni was enough to melt the snow on Tonga Ridge. "We should have access to this list all the time, not merely when a homicide has occurred."

Toni sat down again, virtually huddling in her chair. "You'll have to ask Sheriff Dodge about that," she mumbled.

"So I shall." Vida scanned the list. "My, my! I see you have some of the same cranks we have at *The Advocate*! Certain persons seem to have nothing better to do than bother the local law-enforcement agency and the weekly newspaper."

Vida, who probably had half of Alpine's phone numbers memorized, referred to the usual bothersome calls we received during the week. Some criticized our grammar, some objected to our content, some simply wanted to complain about something. And then there was Averill Fairbanks, who was always sighting a UFO in his backyard, atop Mount Baldy, or up his rear end. My staff and I knew the various types of pests, and accepted them as part of the job. Sometimes they were a nuisance; often they were amusing; only rarely were they helpful, though I held a secret theory that many journalists actually enjoyed the calls and letters because they added spice to what is often routine.

Vida was still studying the list. "Darla Puckett must have hardening of the arteries—she never used to be so silly. . . . Ellsworth Overholt is always insisting there's a cougar roaming his pasture—that's ridiculous this time of year. . . . Now, whatever is Elmer Kemp calling about? That one beats me. . . ."

But Vida finally gave up musing over the vagaries of Alpine residents and concentrated on the matter at hand. "No, there aren't any calls to California on Monday. There are three of them to Startup, however." She shoved the printout in front of me. "Is that Honoria's number? I must confess, I don't know it."

I did, and verified the fact. Switching gears, I gazed at the list faxed to the sheriff by the phone company. Stella's Salon registered only outgoing long-distance calls. The beauty parlor was a total blank, but a swift perusal showed that Honoria made quite a few out-of-area calls: Seattle, Tacoma, Everett, Bellevue, Edmonds, Issaquah, Kirkland, LaConner, Bellingham, Yakima, and, of course, Alpine. Though barely thirty miles separated the two towns, toll lines ran between them. I turned to Toni. "Can you tell if a call went through from this?"

Toni shook her head. "No, only that it was placed and at what time."

Vida was wearing a bemused expression as she handed the list back to Toni. "This is most interesting. Thank you, Toni. By the way, have you any notion of where Becca might have gone?"

Toni's aquiline features looked pinched. "I sure don't. Becca's solid. She'd never run out on her job. I've been majorly upset since she didn't come back to work this afternoon."

Vida was very serious. "We're all upset, Toni. Had she been seeing anyone?"

"Not really." Toni's limpid brown eyes glistened with tears. "There was some salesman she kind of liked, but they'd never gone out. Becca met him at the Venison Inn when he was on his way to eastern Washington. He gave her his card, but I don't think he's come back this way since."

"When was that?" Vida inquired.

Toni sighed. "A week or two ago? I honestly don't remember. I told Becca I bet he was married."

Vida recognized a dead end when she saw it. Thanking Toni, she started for the door. But Dustin Fong entered before we got that far. Vida pounced.

"Mr. and Mrs. Wolfe haven't any idea where their daughter might have gone," Dustin reported. "They're pretty upset. I got a search warrant to check out her apartment, but I didn't find anything."

"What about a description of Eric Forbes?" Vida asked.

Dustin wore a penitent expression. "They only met Eric once, when he and Becca came for Christmas. Mrs. Wolfe said he was tall, dark, and handsome. Mr. Wolfe said he was runty, brownish hair, and homely. The Wolfes don't agree on much, I'm afraid."

Vida inclined her head, the pillbox slipping precariously over one ear. "Neither of them is very observant, alas. I trust you found no photographs at Becca's apartment?"

"No, ma'am." Dustin sighed with regret. "Not even a wedding picture."

Adjusting her hat, Vida smiled warmly at Dustin. Obviously, she considered him an outstanding rookie on her roster of informants. "No doubt Becca didn't feel sentimental when it came to Eric or her marriage. It's a pity that her parents are so self-absorbed." For Vida, the comment was extremely charitable.

On the way back to the office, Vida couldn't contain her excitement. "What can it mean? I simply don't understand. Oh, dear—I so hate to be baffled!"

We were waiting to cross Third Street, with a brisk wind at our backs. I felt baffled, too. "Are you referring to Cassandra or the three calls to Mrs. Smith?"

"Both," Vida replied as we hoofed it to the next curb. "Don't tell me that Trevor or Honoria called Castro Valley from a pay phone. That makes no sense. Why would they do such a thing when the call could be made from Milo's office? The only communication between the Whitmans and Cassandra occurred when she called while we were visiting. Do you remember what Mrs. Smith said?"

I reflected back on our Wednesday visit to Startup. We had commiserated with the Whitmans only forty-eight hours earlier. Somehow, it seemed like weeks.

"Mrs. Smith talked about the grandchildren and how worried Cassandra was," I said, feeling the west wind pushing me ever forward. "She mentioned Cassie's concern a couple of times."

"Indeed she did," Vida replied. "If you ask me, Mrs. Smith put too much emphasis on her other daughter's concern." We had passed Parker's Pharmacy and were now crossing Fourth as a yellow school bus returned from its daily run. "But why was Cassandra worried? As far as we can tell, she was never notified of Kay's death." Turning into *The Advocate,* Vida gave me her gimlet eye. "I don't believe Honoria or Trevor or their mother bothered to notify Cassandra. I think she called her family in Startup by chance. What do you suppose that means?"

Leo Walsh was getting ready to go home. When he saw Vida and me return to the news office, his face took on a sheepish look.

"I'm off to eat some humble pie," he declared. "My hot-shit source in Carmel dried up on me."

At first, I couldn't think what Leo was talking about. Then I remembered his old pal, Jake Spivak, who supposedly was going to dig the dirt for us.

"That's okay," I reassured Leo. "Honoria probably moved away before Jake arrived in Carmel."

"That's true," Leo allowed, fastening the hooded down jacket that he'd acquired after his first winter in Alpine. "Jake moved there just a couple of years ago. Still, he might have asked around. But his wife, April, doesn't expect him back until Monday."

"We won't be back until then, either," I said, glancing at the clock, which stood at almost five. "Enjoy the weekend."

Leo flipped the hood over his head. "I'll enjoy it more than poor Jake will. He got stuck in San Francisco with our old boss." Snatching up an almost empty pack of cigarettes, Leo shook one out, clicked his lighter, and exhaled. "Jesus, sometimes I think I'm luckier than some people—all my wife did was run off with another man. That's *normal,* for chrissakes. But this poor bastard married a broad who's not only nuts, but now she tries to kill herself. It's too bad she didn't do it right. Her husband's a hell of a guy. Tom Cavanaugh deserves better. See you Monday."

Chapter Twelve

I READILY ACCEPTED Vida's offer to follow her home and have a cup of hot tea. The Buick's taillights led the way up Sixth Street to Tyee, while my windshield wipers seemed to keep time to an old folk song, "Delia's Gone." Except it sounded like, "Sandra's gone, one more round, Sandra's gone. . . ."

But she wasn't. Sandra had survived. It was Tom who had gone, out of my life and over the edge and free-falling into my past. What did it matter that his wife had slashed her wrists or swallowed sleeping pills or hooked up a hose to the Rolls-Royce exhaust pipe? I'd finished with Tom. He had no power to affect my life.

"Emma lies," went the wipers, "one more round, Emma lies. . . ."

Vida's tidy bungalow was filled with a different song, the melody spun by her canary, Cupcake. Vida greeted him with little cooing noises, then turned the burner on under the teakettle.

"You should have pressed Leo for more information," she said in faint rebuke. "It would have been natural enough. I almost quizzed him myself, but your reaction put me off. I'm glad Leo didn't notice how pale you turned."

I had now regained much of my composure. "It's

stupid. I've put all that behind me. But having Leo mention Tom out of the blue . . . I was surprised, that's all."

"Flummoxed," Vida agreed, setting two exquisite English bone-china cups on the kitchen table. "Flabbergasted. All those things. Do sit, while we wait for the kettle to boil. I've got some cookies somewhere. . . ." Vida twisted around, glancing at shelves, cupboards, and counters. "Danish shortbread, quite delicious . . . Now where . . . ? Aha!"

As I'd suspected, the cookie tin was decorated with merry elves and prancing reindeer. No doubt Vida had avoided the holiday offering because of her diet. If the contents had been tightly sealed, they might still be fresh.

But except for the pleated paper containers, the tin was empty. Vida's jaw dropped, and then she chuckled.

"Roger! I thought I heard him rustling around in here a week or so ago. So cunning, the way he figures out where Grams hides her treats! And so adorable when he nibbles away like a little chipmunk!"

Having seen Roger cram a mound of mashed potatoes into his kisser and create an illusion that he'd swallowed a softball, I didn't quite buy Vida's affectionate version of her grandson's eating habits.

"I'm not going to tell Leo," I declared. "There's no reason for him to know about Tom and me."

Vida had emptied the cookie wrappers into the garbage and resealed the tin. "Perhaps not. The question is, I suppose, why you find it so important to keep Leo in the dark."

I had no difficulty meeting Vida's steady gaze, but giving her an answer was much harder. "Well," I began as the teakettle whistled and Cupcake sang along, "it isn't just Leo. It's everybody else in this town."

Vida waited until I finished speaking before she got up and went to the stove. "Frankly, Emma, that doesn't make much sense. Nobody in Alpine knows Tommy," she said, using the nickname that my House & Home editor considered her exclusive prerogative. "Oh, he was here for a few days four years ago, but except for the *Advocate* staff and Milo and a handful of others, no one actually met him. Adam's existence is proof that he had a father. Why would you care if Grace Grundle or Harvey Adcock or Jack Mullins could put a name on him?"

Staring at Vida's plaid place mat, I tried to think through her query. "You're right," I finally said. "I don't care about Grace or Harvey or Jack. But I do care about Leo knowing, because he knows Tom. Maybe I'm merely guarding my privacy."

Having waited longer than usual for the tea to steep, Vida poured us each a steaming cup. "I can understand that. But I think you're being overly protective. You worry too much about what Leo thinks, perhaps because you don't want him to invade your life. Now, that's wise from a professional point of view," Vida went on quickly before I could interrupt, "but personally, I'm not so sure. You've built such sturdy walls around yourself, Emma. You're isolated." Vida lowered her eyes and picked up her teacup. "Just like me."

I'd expected Vida to compare me with Honoria, rather than herself. Or to say that small towns are good hiding places for the heart. Until that moment I hadn't thought much about the similarities between us.

Cupcake had stopped singing while the rain spattered against the kitchen windows. Buck Bardeen had been the first man in Vida's life since her husband's death. His arrival had led her out of self-imposed exile, and now it seemed that she wanted me to follow.

"I'm not in love," I said flatly. "Not with Tom, not with Leo, not with . . . anybody."

"That's not what I'm talking about," Vida replied

calmly. "Being 'in love' is a state of mind which comes unbidden and often goes in the same way. Nor do I refer to celibacy. Intimacy is so much more important. I'm speaking about friendship, about affection, about trust. None of us should cut ourselves off from these very basic human needs. I almost learned that too late. You still have time." Daintily, Vida sipped her tea.

I, too, drank, though I noted that my hand shook a bit as I raised the cup. "Change is tough," I remarked in a hushed voice.

"Oh, yes." Vida nodded. "Don't I know it?"

"You've done it, though."

"Perhaps."

I sighed. "I don't know how I feel. About Tom and Sandra."

"I know." Vida nodded again.

"I've tried to hate him."

"That only works for a short time."

"I've tried to forget."

"That takes much longer." Vida got to her feet. Cupcake was hopping around in his cage, flapping his wings and cheeping. "Dear me, he gets so fractious this time of night. I believe he needs a bath. Tomorrow, precious." Vida made a clucking noise with her tongue.

Resting my head on one hand, I tried to focus on my goals in life: Being a good person. Being a good mother. Being a good journalist. Surely they were worthy ideals, of which I'd often fallen short. Was something missing? Of course it was, and I'd always known it, but so what? Nobody has everything. That was part of the human condition.

Vida's phone rang just as she was about to pour more tea. She picked up the receiver from the extension by the refrigerator and uttered her usual imperious greeting.

And, as is also characteristic, her voice then fell into a conversational lilt:

"Why, Laurie—how nice! No, I came straight home . . . Well, certainly. No, that would be fine . . . Yes, take a right on Sixth, then a left on Tyee . . . Bye." Vida's eyes glittered with triumph as she hung up the phone. "Laurie and her mother are stopping in for a chat. Isn't that nice?"

It took a moment for the news to register; my mind was still bogged down with Vida's advice. "Laurie—and Jane? What are they going to chat *about*?"

"I can only guess," Vida said, whisking my teacup off the table. "You don't mind, do you? Leaving, that is. I didn't tell Laurie you were here." Vida had the grace to look sheepish.

I had no choice but to make my exit. By way of apology, Vida hugged me at the door. She is not a demonstrative person, so I felt partially mollified. Burrowing into the hood of my duffel coat, I trudged through the rain to my Jag.

I was almost there when Vida called out: "Stop! No, no! Keep going—but stop at your car!"

Confused, I reached the driver's side. Raindrops were rolling off my hood, impairing my vision. In the deepening twilight, Vida was a blur on her front porch. The next thing I noticed were headlights, pulling in behind the Jaguar. I didn't recognize the car, but I knew Jane and Laurie Marshall as soon as they got out.

"Oh, my!" Vida cried, waving her arms in apparent agitation. "Everybody is here at once! Hello, Emma! Do come in, Jane, Laurie! Hurry now! It's so very wet!"

I hid my smile. Vida's ruse had fooled me; maybe it had also fooled the Marshall women. The three of us went inside, while Vida exclaimed about the fortuitousness of already having made tea.

Neither Jane nor Laurie accepted Vida's offer,

however. After removing their raingear, they both sank onto the chintz-covered couch while I sat in a tufted club chair, and Vida enthroned herself in her late husband's favorite dark green wing chair.

To my surprise, it was Laurie who introduced the reason for the visit. If my presence put her off, it didn't show.

"I owe you an apology, Mrs. Runkel," Laurie said, then glanced at me as well. "You, too, Ms. Lord. I've been thinking about what happened to Ms. Whitman on Monday, and now what might have happened to Becca. I talked it over with my mother." She turned to Jane, who was twisting her hands and biting her lower lip. "There's something terrible going on at the salon, or at least with people who are attached to it in some way. I don't want to be responsible for hampering the investigation."

Laurie's precise, articulate speech was a far cry from her usual vague manner. Indeed, the attitude of mother and daughter seemed to have been reversed: it was Laurie who now appeared concerned for her mother's welfare, instead of the other way around.

"I never meant to mislead you," Laurie continued, "or anybody else, for that matter. But I've lived my life as Laurie Marshall for so long that I never think of being anyone else. My early childhood hardly exists, even in my memory."

At last, Jane managed to speak up: "If there's blame, put it on my shoulders. I didn't want Laurie to remember. It wasn't a happy time for either of us."

Thoughts of abuse—physical, verbal, sexual—ravaged my mind. Another ugly marriage, with mother and child battered and beaten. The theme kept recurring: Honoria and Mitch; Becca and Eric; Jane and—who?

But I wasn't quite right. Jane had now taken up the tale. "My first husband wasn't a bad man," she asserted, still unable to control her fidgeting fingers. "The worst thing I could accuse him of was selfishness. He simply didn't have time for us. I might as well never have been married in the first place."

There are worse things than not being married. The words tripped through my head, an old refrain of my mother's on one of those rare days when she and my father weren't getting along. Over the years I'd often found solace in the phrase. Apparently, Jane Marshall wouldn't agree.

"The truth is," Laurie put in with a wry glance at her mother, "Mom doesn't like to admit she let go of Toby Popp. Do you blame her for giving up on a future billionaire?"

Hindsight is a wonderful thing, as Vida had indicated in her comforting commentary. "You wanted a normal life for yourself and Laurie," Vida asserted, resting her hands on the leather arms of the wing chair. "Work can be more devastating to a marriage than a mistress. Toby Popp obviously cared more for his computers than his family."

"That's the point!" Jane exclaimed, her voice now taking on its usual excitable edge. "We weren't a family. And if we'd stayed married, if I'd nagged, if I'd made threats, if I'd been able to make Toby feel guilty, then maybe he wouldn't have become so rich and successful!"

Somehow, I suspected that Jane had tried all those tactics and failed. But maybe it made her feel better to think otherwise.

"So," I noted, "you divorced Toby, married Martin, and he adopted Laurie. Your story really does have a happy ending. I assume Toby didn't put up a custody fight."

Jane gave her daughter a quick, guilty look. "Toby didn't want to cause trouble. Really, he hardly noticed we were gone. I like to think he wanted what was best for us."

Toby didn't want anything except his software, I thought cynically. My reaction must have shown, because Laurie was again wearing her ironic expression.

"What Mom's not telling you is that whether or not she'd stayed married to Toby, he would have been impossible to live with. If we didn't live like a normal family while you were still married to him and he was holed up at work, things would only have gotten worse. Face it, Mom," Laurie said, poking her mother in the arm, "Toby Popp may be a genius, but he's also crazy."

Jane's face sagged. "Oh, Laurie! That's not fair! You can't understand the pressures he's had to put up with. He was always shy—I asked him out first. His idea of jokes and such may have been . . . unusual, but that's because his brain works on a much higher plane."

Laurie lifted her carefully plucked eyebrows. "Like outer space?"

In the wing chair, Vida was nodding. "I can imagine that Mr. Popp would be eccentric. Is that why you refused his parcel, Jane?"

Jane's pale face flushed slightly. "I've always refused his so-called gifts. So has Laurie. He can't buy his way back into our lives just because he decided to move nearby."

Now Vida and I exchanged swift glances. "Gifts?" Vida echoed. "What sort of gifts?"

Jane threw up her hands. "Money. Stock options. An Italian sports car. A house in Rancho Mirage. Toby must be going through midlife crisis. Now that he's retired, I think he wishes he had a family after all."

I found myself sinking into the soft club chair. Knowing it was Roger's favorite, I suspected that he had broken the springs. "Has Toby just started doing this since he bought the property at Index?"

Jane nodded. "He began last fall by sending these silly little notes, like riddles. He and I used to play word games, you see." The flush deepened as she avoided her daughter's gaze. "I was always better at them than he was. Mine would rhyme."

"How nice," Vida remarked tersely.

"Finally," Jane went on, "we—Martin, Laurie, and I— figured out that he was building a house at Index. I wrote him a letter, asking him not to bother us. After all, we hadn't heard from him in almost twenty years."

"But he wouldn't stop," Laurie said, with a vexed shake of her head. "In fact, he started sending the . . . bribes. I don't know what else to call them. I don't think Toby knows of any other way to win people over except with money. Naturally, we sent everything back." She paused, giving me a wry look. "Yesterday, in the salon, there was a letter addressed to me from Learjet. I never opened it, but I'll bet you anything it was my own plane. Now what on earth would I do with a private jet in Alpine?"

Vida had edged forward on the wing chair and was addressing Jane. "And the parcel you returned to the post office?"

Jane gave a forlorn shake of her head. "Who knows? Jewelry, maybe, or a rare edition of Lord Byron. I made the mistake of opening the first package Toby sent us. It was two dozen tins of Beluga caviar. They came the day before New Year's, and I was so angry that I served them to our guests New Year's Eve and nobody could tell the difference between Toby's high-priced stuff and the Safeway special. I'd loved to have told him that. The truth is, Toby wouldn't know the difference, either. His idea of exotic food is tuna fish."

"So," Vida said slowly, "you've no idea what he sent in the box yesterday."

"None," Jane answered promptly. "But in a way, I felt heartened."

"You did?" I turned wide eyes on Jane Marshall. "Why?"

"Because," she replied, meeting my gaze head-on and without apparent guile, "Toby must have delegated that one, which means he may be losing interest. You see, that wasn't his handwriting. His penmanship is a terrible scrawl."

Only the rain and a couple of chirps from Cupcake could be heard in Vida's living room. The silence encouraged Jane and Laurie to rise from the sofa.

But Vida wasn't finished with her guests. "You're certain?" she asked, barring the way with her imposing presence.

Jane, who had lost the flush from her pale face, eyed Vida quizzically. "I think so. I mean, the address was printed. Toby always wrote everything out in longhand. I don't know how anybody ever read it. But then I suppose he used his computer to communicate at work."

Vida stepped aside. "I must thank you both for being so candid. Though I wonder why you didn't contact Sheriff Dodge first."

Laurie uttered a little laugh as she put on her rain slicker. "We tried, but he'd just left the office. Besides, he never asked about Toby. You did. Mom and I didn't want to leave you with a bad impression. After all, you're the local opinion makers."

"Yes." Taking the statement as a matter of course, Vida wore a thoughtful expression as she opened the front door.

Jane turned under the porch light, her expression

pleading. "This isn't for publication, I hope? Laurie and I intended this as a private conversation."

Vida shrugged. "Emma and I are off the job. Don't fret. At this point, I see no reason to mention any connection between you and Toby Popp in print."

The qualified disclaimer seemed to satisfy Jane, who started down the five steps that led to the walkway. At the last moment Vida put a hand on Laurie's arm. "Laurie—are you going to go on pretending?"

The blue eyes revealed surprise, then understanding. "Why not? It's easier that way. Look what being brilliant did for Toby. He's a head case. I want to lead a normal life. I always have, since we left California."

"That makes a certain amount of sense," Vida murmured. "Good night. Drive safely."

After closing the door, Vida turned to me. "Laurie truly doesn't even think of Toby as her father. I can't say as I blame her. But I hate to see a fine mind go to waste."

"It's not wasted," I said brightly. "She's creating wonderful hairdos."

Vida looked askance. "Not for you. Maybe you ought to switch from Stella."

I turned down Vida's offer of whipping up a bit of supper. My stomach was growling, but I wasn't desperate enough to endure one of my House & Home editor's ill-got meals. Instead, I talked her into eating at the ski lodge's coffee shop.

Despite the rainy Friday night, the number of visitors was still up. Obviously, skiers who had already planned their weekend weren't following the weather report. Or else they hoped for a dramatic change, which would bring new snow. Vida and I had to wait ten minutes for a table.

We spent most of the meal talking about the

Marshalls. Vida still wasn't convinced that Toby Popp hadn't sent the dead cat to the Marshall residence.

"Who else?" she argued. "And if it were someone else, why?"

"Why send it at all?" I asked with a little shiver. "It's a gruesome stunt."

We were just finishing our dinners when Milo strolled into the coffee shop, wearing his civilian clothes and looking sort of lost. Halfway to the counter seating, he saw us and stopped.

"My microwave broke," he announced. "I decided to eat out."

We were at a table for two, but Vida was undaunted. "Why don't you borrow a chair from those people?" She pointed to a nearby gathering of five at a setting for six. "Emma and I have finished dinner, but we were just talking about dessert."

We'd been doing no such thing, but I kept my mouth shut. When the waitress brought Milo a menu, Vida ordered blackberry cobbler. I chimed in and did the same, though I usually disdain dessert. For some peculiar, amazing reason, I'm not particularly fond of sweets. Grease is another matter. Maybe—hopefully—it all evens out.

Milo chose the steak sandwich, which was what I'd had. As soon as he gave his order, Vida related the account of the Marshall women's visit to her house. Predictably, the sheriff showed minimal interest.

"Let's say Toby Popp actually mailed Honoria's cat to the Marshalls," he mused, looking around for an ashtray. "That might—*might,* mind you—be a federal offense, violating some postal law. That's none of my business. Then, let's say you two think Toby Popp is involved in Kay Whitman's murder because at one time he and Kay lived in the same state, which just happens to be one of the most populous in this country. Given that kind of tenuous connection, I could also haul in Leo Walsh and maybe a hundred other former Californians. That would cost the taxpayers a lot of money and drive me nuts. What's your point?"

Vida's gaze was steely. "That cat was named for you, Milo. Don't you care?"

Milo arched one sandy eyebrow at Vida. "I never liked cats much. I wasn't exactly flattered when Honoria named the damned thing after me." He motioned to the waitress, requesting an ashtray. The sheriff was informed that he was sitting in the No Smoking section. Milo swore and Vida smirked.

"Anyway," Milo continued after the waitress had drifted away, "since you'll find out Monday, I might as well tell you now. We ran a routine check on Honoria's bank account in Sultan. Last week—the tenth, to be exact—she withdrew twenty-five hundred dollars. The teller said she put it into a money order. That's weird, because Honoria always wrote checks."

Vida and I gazed at each other. "A major art purchase?" I finally suggested.

Milo shrugged. "Could be. There's no way of telling. The thing hasn't been cashed yet."

I'd sent Adam enough money orders to know that the payer always filled in the payee's name, usually after leaving the bank. "It's too bad Honoria didn't have close neighbors," I remarked. "How far is the nearest house?"

Milo sighed. "Not within shouting distance. One of the things she liked best about the place was the privacy. There's a woman named Paula who makes stained glass a few miles up the road, but I don't think they were bosom buddies. I'm having whoever's on patrol pick up her mail." The sheriff's expression turned a bit sheepish.

"That's both personal and professional interest, I guess. Anyway, nothing turned up today."

Milo's salad arrived, along with the blackberry cobblers. Without my noticing, Vida apparently had requested a side of vanilla ice cream. Doggedly, I dug into my dessert just as the sheriff's cell phone went off.

Milo juggled the phone and the salt-and-pepper shakers. After the initial, "Dodge here," he didn't say anything, but I could tell from his somber expression that this was a business call. Finally, he stood up and ambled over to the coffee-shop entrance, the phone glued to his ear. Vida and I watched him as he leaned against the wall next to the coatrack.

"Most vexing," Vida noted. "The least Milo could do is talk at the table."

"He's okay," I replied, deciding that even if the blackberries had been frozen, they were still delicious. Maybe dessert wasn't such a bad idea after all. "Have you nagged him lately about the weapon?"

Vida shook her head. "It's useless. If they'd found it, they'd tell us. I suspect that knife or whatever it was made its way into the Skykomish River."

"And Kay's purse?" The ice cream was pretty tasty, too.

Vida frowned. "I know what you're thinking. Ordinarily, the knife and the purse would have sunk. But that's not accounting for the swift current this time of year, particularly when it rains so hard and the snow at the upper levels melts. We'll be lucky if we get out of this weather without flooding."

I recalled other winters when the river had spilled over its banks and threatened adjacent businesses and residences. In years past, before my time, the Sky had gone on rampages that had actually swept away some of the older, flimsier structures in the vicinity.

Vida's sidelong gaze was fixed on Milo, who was still on the phone. "He does go on," she said. "Or someone does. I wonder if it's about Becca."

My own eyes scanned the coffee shop. I recognized only a half-dozen Alpiners. The rest were strangers. "It's too bad there are so many skiers in town over the weekend. Otherwise, somebody like Eric Forbes would stand out."

"True," Vida agreed. "I trust Milo has had his vis-à-vis in King County try to locate Eric in Seattle. If he's not there, then we could surmise that Becca is right, and he came up here. Dear me." She sighed deeply, then polished off the last spoonful of cobbler.

Milo returned to the table just as the waitress brought his entrée. He sat down with the usual awkward effort of arranging his long legs, then grimaced at both of us.

"That was Grants Pass. They put me through to Honoria. She and her mother are staying at the Holiday Inn Express." The sheriff was back at the salt and pepper, now doctoring his steak and fries. "Honoria says Dodger disappeared Wednesday morning after she let him out. He never came back. She figures he sensed that they were leaving and took off. Cats do that, I guess. Maybe they're smarter than I thought."

"They're not," Vida retorted. "It would have been more likely for Dodger to try to follow Honoria. What was she planning to do with him during her absence?"

Milo was eating hungrily, popping steak, fries, and toasted French bread into his mouth at once. "That woman in Gold Bar who makes stained glass—Paula Rubens. Honoria said she would have taken the cat."

I leaned closer to the sheriff. "Did you tell Honoria what happened?"

Milo looked pained. "I had to. She was appalled. Shit!" He forked in more steak and bread.

Vida gave a faint, reproachful shake of her head. "Did you ask her about the money order?"

The sheriff was now attacking his neglected salad. "I did. That's when I lost the connection." Milo kept his long face straight, then narrowed his eyes. "I didn't get a chance to ask about all those long-distance calls. But Dustin checked them out and they're mostly art types or galleries or studios. Except," he added with a sly expression, "for the one in Edmonds. It turns out that number belongs to Toby Popp."

The sheriff downed three fries at once. I almost swallowed my spoon. Vida looked like the cat that ate the canary. Except the cat was dead, the canary was alive, and it seemed to me that we had a viable suspect in Toby Popp. The only problem was that I didn't know what crime the billionaire computer king had committed.

Chapter Thirteen

CARLA HAD MENTIONED that Toby Popp lived north of Seattle. The suburb of Edmonds is just across the King–Snohomish county line, on Puget Sound. It's a relatively quiet area, with spectacular views of the water and the Olympic Mountains. If I were a computer king, I might want to live there, too—at least until my multimillion-dollar house in the forest was completed.

Milo's response to the obvious query of bringing Toby Popp in for questioning was ambivalent. He'd consider it, of course. He needed some grounds, other than a couple of phone calls. He'd never heard of Toby Popp until the last few days. But what he'd learned made Toby sound like some kind of god who probably had about two dozen six-figure lawyers at his beck and call. Unfamiliar with the rich and semifamous, the sheriff didn't know how such wealth and power would affect an investigation, but he figured to come out on the short end.

After that last remark, Vida excused herself to go to the ladies' room to freshen up, as she put it. I didn't just lean into Milo, I punched him in the arm.

"Listen, kiddo," I said, making sure my voice was low, "I've watched you interrogate witnesses. Nobody around here cows you. Are you going to let some computer nerd turn you into a wimp?"

Wiping a dab of Roquefort dressing off his upper lip,

Milo frowned at me. "What's with you, Emma? When was I ever a wimp?"

"About thirty seconds ago. You were waffling on Toby Popp. Don't. He's Laurie Marshall's father, he's more than a little weird, and for all we know, he and Kay Whitman may have had a torrid affair back in their California youth."

"Nerds aren't torrid." Milo tossed his rumpled napkin onto the table. "Okay, but I'll bet anything this Popp character wanted to buy some pottery from Honoria for his snazzy new house."

The suggestion was plausible. Now that Toby was retired, perhaps he was broadening his horizons. Jane Marshall had mentioned a rare edition of poetry. Perhaps she knew or guessed that her former husband would spend some of his huge fortune on collectibles. Art was often a sound investment.

Deciding not to badger Milo further, I reiterated my lament about Honoria's lack of friends and neighbors. "There must be somebody she knew fairly well besides you in the area," I said in a fretful voice. "Honoria lived in Startup for several years. Surely she got close to some of the people in the art community. What about the woman in Gold Bar with the stained glass?"

"Paula Rubens." Milo paused, chewed and swallowed before speaking again. "Oh, Honoria would talk about certain people from time to time—but not as if they were pals. Usually, they were Everett or Seattle types. I met some of them when she dragged me to those gallery deals. Face it, Emma—Honoria came up here to get away."

I could see Vida reentering the coffee shop. As usual, she recognized more of the diners than I did. Her return to the table was typical, a royal progress of greetings and exchanges.

"Everybody needs friends," I muttered, echoing my House & Home editor. A sudden thought struck my mind. I grabbed Milo's arm just as he was putting his silverware down. "Hey, I just remembered something! When were those calls placed to Edmonds?"

"Monday," Milo answered. "And Thursday. Why?"

Vida and I had been in Startup on Wednesday. Toby Popp had been at the Index building site that same day. "What about Wednesday? Are you sure a call wasn't made?"

Milo didn't think so. Judging from his indifferent expression, the topic didn't intrigue him. My perverse nature surfaced, though in a righteous cause. I played my trump card, which should appeal to his male vanity.

"You'd better look at Wednesday, after two o'clock." I gave Milo an arch little smile. "A man called for Honoria while Vida and I were at her house. Mrs. Smith answered. When she told Honoria about the caller, Mrs. Smith referred to him as her daughter's friend. Honoria indicated she'd talk to him later, so I assume the call was returned. Has it ever occurred to you that you might have had a rival whose name is Toby Popp?"

Out in the ski-lodge parking lot, Vida praised me for my cunning. "I can't think why we didn't jump on that phone call sooner. Mrs. Smith sounded downright unctuous when she was talking to whoever it was."

We had taken my Jag from Vida's house. Getting behind the wheel, I gave my House & Home editor a wry sideways look. "You mean she sounded the way you'd expect an ordinary middle-class woman to talk to a billionaire?"

"Precisely." Unused to the low roof of my car, Vida knocked her pillbox askew. "Awed by dollar signs. Moneybags dancing through her head. What I'd call the

Fat Cat Syndrome. Of course, you might also interpret it as the way a mother might speak to her daughter's suitor. Assuming, of course, that she approved of him."

"I don't think Mrs. Smith is the type who'd disapprove of a billion dollars." I put the car into gear, then drove out of the parking lot. Milo's Cherokee Chief was somewhere on the road ahead of us. He had reluctantly agreed to let us go over the list of phone calls a second time.

Crossing Burl Creek, Vida was muttering away. The "Fat Cat" reference had made her think of the late Dodger. "Fingerprints—Milo should have checked the parcel immediately. One couldn't expect much off the wrapping paper, because it was handled by so many people, including me. But the box itself is another matter. Oh, dear—of course I touched it, too, and I'd removed my gloves. Still, I wonder if Milo . . ."

"I'm sure he did," I interjected, taking the alternate route into town, along Alpine Way. "Speaking of gloves, I'll bet the cat killer wore them. Even if I didn't care who knew I'd sent the thing, I wouldn't want to touch poor Dodger with my bare hands." Involuntarily, I shivered.

Though Vida had attempted to right her hat, it now tilted in the opposite direction. "True. The heart of the matter is that we don't know if there's any connection between Dodger's demise and Kay Whitman's murder. Some people don't care for cats. I certainly understand that—they're such perverse, unfriendly, spoiled creatures. Dogs are more helpful, though I'm not fond of them, either." Vida was still speaking more to herself than to me. "This Dodger calamity strikes me as the kind of cruel prank a youngster might dream up. But why would someone mail the cat from Sultan to the Marshalls?"

We had arrived at the sheriff's headquarters, where Milo waited at the door. After he led us into his office, the first thing I did was study the wall map of Skykomish County and the adjacent areas. I knew Highway 2 by heart, but maybe I felt that staring at the place names would provide inspiration.

The town of Skykomish lies six miles west of Alpine. Coming down through the Cascade foothills, three more minutes takes the traveler to Grotto, and another three to Baring. The turnoff into the secluded town of Index is about five miles farther. Then, heading onto flatter terrain, the distance between Gold Bar, Startup, and Sultan can be covered in a quarter of an hour. The last, more populated, eight-mile stretch goes into Monroe, a virtual gateway to Seattle's suburbs. For those of us used to plying Highway 2, the ground was usually traversed quickly, with no annoying stoplights, arterials, or gridlock.

It was the corridor along the Skykomish River between Index and Sultan that captured my attention. Sultan was by far the largest of the little towns that dotted the highway. Who was the mystery mailer living in that still sparsely inhabited stretch? Or had someone traveled that twenty-seven miles of road from Alpine to mail a dead cat?

"This is stupid," I said flatly. "Are we getting hung up on something that's irrelevant?"

Milo shrugged. "Probably."

Vida was already seated, going over the complete list of phone calls to and from Honoria's house for the past week. My House & Home editor let out a little yelp before Milo or I could speculate further.

"Here!" She thrust the computerized list in front of me. "Three-oh-three, Monday afternoon, the thirteenth. Someone called Toby Popp's number in Edmonds."

Milo came around from behind his desk to hang over my shoulder. "So?"

"Think, Milo," Vida urged. "This call was placed while Honoria and Trevor were in Alpine."

Having always considered Milo to be slower on the uptake than I am, it was humbling to realize that at first, neither of us understood what Vida was saying. She was beginning to look peeved when we both stumbled into comprehension.

"Popp has an alibi for Kay Whitman's murder," Milo finally said with a faint nod.

Ironically, I was the one who wasn't willing to leap to any such conclusion. "We don't know that he actually answered the Monday-afternoon call. What we do know is that Monday evening, Toby Popp was in Alpine. He came into *The Advocate* and talked to Leo Walsh."

Vida had reclaimed the list of phone calls, turning it over. "Goodness!" she exclaimed. "I didn't realize there was anything on the back. These are the incoming toll calls. Seattle, Everett, Bellingham, Portland, Vancouver, BC." She tapped the page with her index finger. "What's this queer number? It says Index, but it's the wrong prefix."

Milo leaned across his desk. "That's a cell phone. The call was placed at two-oh-three Wednesday."

"Well now!" Vida was exultant. "We were at Honoria's then. She received a call that Mrs. Smith took. Who would have a cellular phone in Index except Toby Popp?"

I hadn't been able to convince Milo that Toby was panting after Honoria, and apparently Vida wasn't going to have much better luck. "It's possible," Milo allowed. "We'll check it out. But these days all sorts of people have cell phones around here, especially the logging crews. I still say Toby's in the art market."

"A simple question will do," Vida said, looking prim. "Ask Honoria."

Milo shrugged again, then ambled over to his phone. As usual, his desk was in disarray, as chaotic as my own. Still, he found what he was looking for almost at once—a pale green Post-it note with a phone number. I sat down next to Vida while the sheriff dialed.

Neither Honoria nor her mother was in at the Grants Pass motel. Leaving a message, Milo hung up and turned to us with a wry expression.

"They're probably out to dinner. Honoria knows she can call me late."

The sense of intimacy in Milo's comment was unsettling, at least from a professional point of view. I tried to glance at Vida to see how she was reacting, but my House & Home editor was fingering her strong chin and gazing at the ceiling.

"Milo," she said in a musing voice that fooled nobody, including herself, "I trust you've contacted people who know the Whitmans in Pacific Grove."

"I put Sam Heppner on that," Milo answered in a matter-of-fact tone. "He's tracked down some neighbors. None of them were home during the day, but he reached a couple last night."

"And?" Vida sounded expectant.

Milo made what I could only consider a slight grimace. "They weren't much help. Trevor and Kay live in a condo. Nobody sees their neighbors unless they show up at the monthly owners meeting. The Whitmans didn't do that. But then they've only been there about six months."

Vida looked disgruntled, then brightened. "Is that because Trevor got out of prison about then?"

"Trevor was released in May of last year." Again, Milo showed no emotion. "He'd served ten years of a twenty-year sentence for second-degree homicide. He was convicted in eighty-three, there were appeals, given the special circumstances of the crime, and he finally was put away in April of 'eighty-four. Trevor was sent to Soledad, which was pretty convenient for Kay and Mrs. Smith. It's not that far from Pacific Grove."

As Vida sat next to me looking thoughtful, I posed a question: "Did the neighbors know that Trevor was an ex-con?"

Milo shook his head. "Sam says they didn't. In fact, they still don't. Hell, it's not like he was some sex offender. The guy's entitled to his privacy."

I sensed that Milo was working hard to walk the fine line between his job and his concern for Honoria's family. As Skykomish County's chief law-enforcement officer, the sheriff not only knew most of the perps and their families, but in one recent case, he'd been related to some of them. Milo, with his natural tunnel vision, had managed to keep justice in his sights while putting kinship aside. He searched for the truth, which he called "facts," and any side issues were dismissed as irrelevant. But this case was different. To my knowledge, this was the first time that Milo had been sleeping with the enemy.

"How was Mitch Harmon killed?" I asked, my voice unnaturally quiet.

Milo didn't flinch or otherwise betray any emotion. "He was shot through the head and chest with Trevor's forty-five automatic. He'd served a hitch in 'Nam. Honoria said that her brother had warned Harmon more than once. After the . . . accident, Trevor tracked down Harmon and shot him." At last, Milo made a face, though I presumed it was more in disgust over Mitch Harmon's abuse than Trevor Whitman's retaliation. Sometimes it was hard to know who to root for.

"Did Trevor work?" I inquired, increasingly aware of how little I really knew about the Whitman family.

"Sure," Milo answered, sounding as if he were

giving references for Trevor Whitman. "He repairs air-conditioning equipment for a firm that's based in Sacramento. He's been with them since last July. His supervisor has nothing but praise for him."

"And Kay?" I inquired. "Did she work?"

Milo shifted in his chair. "Yeah, she did, but not recently. Actually, Honoria had mentioned that to me earlier. Kay tutored kids in math. She'd taught at one time, but she got burned out. When Trevor got out of jail, Kay decided to kick back for a while. They wanted to do some traveling, like coming up here. Trevor hadn't used any sick leave or vacation days since he started work last summer, so he had two weeks coming. He's due back on the job Monday, but that's the day of the memorial service."

Vida had been unnaturally quiet; now she turned her pensive expression on Milo. "A young and reasonably attractive woman—I imagine Kay was attractive, though I never met her—is left alone for ten years. Oh, I assume there were conjugal visits, but still . . ." She let the sentence trail off as her questioning gaze took in both Milo and me.

While I knew what Vida was suggesting, her train of thought triggered a different idea in my brain. "That's what we need for the Wednesday edition—a picture of Kay. I never thought to ask Honoria or Trevor for one when we were in Startup." I trotted out my most winsome look for Milo. "When you talk to Honoria, could you ask her to overnight a photo to us after she gets to Pacific Grove? We'll reimburse her for the cost."

Milo lifted only one shoulder this time. "Sure, why not?"

"Get two," Vida put in. "One with Trevor, or, if possible, a grouping—Kay, Trevor, Honoria, and the mother. Oh! I almost forgot—if Honoria can't manage it, ask permission for us to use something from her house in Startup."

Milo's subservience faded. "Oh, no you don't," he said with an amiable shake of his head. "You two aren't getting into Honoria's place. Hell, we haven't searched it either."

"You haven't?" Vida was horrified.

"Why should we?" Milo was still complaisant. "It's not a crime scene, and for now, none of the people who were at that house are suspects."

I saw Vida's jaw tense, and knew what she was thinking. My own thoughts were scattered. Honoria and Trevor had alibis for the crime. Depending on when the murder had actually been committed, they were either at Alpine Medical or with the sheriff himself. As for Mrs. Smith, she had been in Startup. Or so she claimed.

"Let me see that phone list again," I said. Gluing my eyes on the Monday-afternoon calls, I found only the calls to Toby Popp's number in Edmonds and the funeral home in Pacific Grove.

"Did Toby and Mrs. Smith connect?" I wondered out loud, then turned to Milo. "If Mrs. Smith can prove she made that call and talked to Toby, neither of them could have been in Alpine, murdering Kay Whitman."

"I never thought they did," Milo remarked a trifle grimly. "I'm not checking Toby Popp's calls. There's an easier way—asking Mrs. Smith if she talked to him Monday afternoon. That establishes alibis for both her and Popp. I'd like to erase that software guy from the picture."

"In more ways than one," Vida murmured.

Milo heard the comment and glared. "This isn't a love triangle," he growled. "Listen up, if Toby Popp's name is dragged into this homicide investigation, the media will be all over Alpine. Maybe he mailed a dead cat to his ex-wife—that's not my problem. Jane Marshall hasn't filed any complaints, she didn't even open the damned box. But tie this rich bird into a murder, and we've all got more than we bargained for. You read me?" The hazel eyes glinted as Milo stared first at Vida, and then at me.

Vida seemed to take the rebuke in stride. "Oh, very well, have it your way." Getting to her feet, she offered the sheriff a frosty smile. "I do hope you're being more aggressive about Becca. You've checked up on Eric Forbes, of course."

Milo finally lowered his gaze. "Yeah, right. KingCo can't locate him. Nobody's seen him since yesterday."

Vida sniffed. "Nobody in King County has seen him, you mean. I suspect he's been sighted in Skykomish County, though." My House & Home editor started for the door. "Let's hope," she added with a glance over her shoulder, "it wasn't by Becca. Good night, Milo. Come along, Emma. I must put Cupcake to bed."

Saturday dawned predictably gray and wet. I tried to think of a good reason to crawl out of bed, and thought of my son. I still hadn't talked with Adam since our gloomy conversation earlier in the week. After a shower and a cup of coffee I dialed Tempe.

Adam didn't answer. It was an hour later in Arizona, not quite ten o'clock. On a whim, I called my brother at the Tuba City rectory in the northern part of the state. Ben's crackling voice came through on the second ring.

"Hey, Sluggly," he said, greeting me with my child-hood nickname, "what's happening? I haven't talked to you since I got those gruesome pictures. I figured you were going to surprise me and take a midwinter break. It's sunny and sixty-five on the reservation. How about a visit?"

Why not? The thought lodged in my brain with

unexpected excitement. I didn't give a hoot about the sunshine, but I cared deeply for my brother. A side trip to Adam in Tempe was immensely appealing. To hell with debt and bank balances and deadlines and homicides and screwy wives who shackled their husbands to the bedpost.

"Early March," I said, breathless. "I'll take a four-day weekend. Are you sure you want me to come?"

"Hell, yes," my brother replied, as thrilled as I was. "Really? I'll make tacos. No, I'll buy tacos. Shit, I'll treat you to tacos at the Tuba City Truck Stop Café. They're the best. How come you finally decided to head for the great Southwest?"

"Oh," I replied, trying to sound casual, "maybe because two of my favorite fellas live there. Have you talked to Adam lately?"

Ben's voice dropped a notch. "Yeah, last night. He's going through A Crisis, capital *A,* capital *C.* The kid's serious about this social-work thing, Sluggly. It's not just a whim. Honest."

"Stench . . ." The familiar retaliation was borne on a sigh. "You don't know Adam like I do. Everything is A Crisis with capital letters. Maybe I've spoiled him. He'll work his way out of it, though. He always does."

"Well . . ." Ben's chuckle was almost a choking noise. "Adam's old enough to make some serious decisions about his future. I've had a chance to watch him work with people, and he's good. He cares. He listens. Oh, he's still too young to realize that you can't rush into solutions, or to accept the fact that sometimes there aren't any solutions. But that's okay. Whatever he does, it ought to involve people."

"He's likable," I allowed. "I can't see him in sales. Or teaching. He sure wouldn't want to go through medical school. Human resources, maybe."

"Maybe." My brother didn't sound very enthusiastic. "Look, we can talk about it when you get here. But let Adam have his say. Better yet, maybe you'll be able to see him in action on the reservation. He's learned some Navajo."

"He has?" I was surprised. Adam had struggled mightily with high-school Spanish, having neither an aptitude nor a liking for foreign languages.

"He's read a lot about their culture," Ben continued in a serious voice. "In fact, he's immersed himself in Native-American lore. That started when he worked on the Anasazi dig two years ago."

Adam, with a book. Adam, studying a language. Adam, listening to people whose problems were not his own. I was beginning to feel as if I didn't know my own son.

"You're biased," I said, irritated. My brother had invaded my maternal turf. "Adam's grades are strictly average. That's not because he's stupid—he's not—but because he's lazy. As far as I can tell, college—all three of them—has been one big kegger and dozens of girls."

Ben chuckled again, a more natural sound this time. "You're right—up to a point. But I've seen Adam change in the last year. He's growing up, Sluggly. He's discovered that the world doesn't stop at the end of his arms."

My child was becoming a man, and I wasn't aboard for the journey. Adam hadn't spent much of the previous two summers with me. He'd been with Ben, in Tuba City. Thanksgiving and Christmas always were so busy, so rushed. Maybe I'd treated him like a houseguest, instead of a son. A sense of loss swept over me, as if the rain had come indoors.

I didn't expect Ben to understand. He was childless, yet he seemed to know Adam better than I did. For twenty years I'd been unwilling to share my son with his father. Now, it seemed, I'd given him up to his uncle by default.

"I'm a crappy mother," I blurted. "It looks as if I'm the one who hasn't been listening."

"Stick it, Sluggly," Ben said cheerfully. "Adam is always going to sound like a kid to you. Even when you're about ninety and eating soup with your hands, he'll still be immature. I may not have children, but I've watched them interact with their parents. Mississippi, Arizona, wherever—it's a cross-cultural thing. It's called generations."

I tried to take comfort from Ben's words. But I still felt a void deep inside. "I'll see for myself," I mumbled. "Two weeks. I'll call Sky Travel right away."

"I'll order the tacos," Ben said. "Does Adam know you're coming?"

"Ah . . . no." I didn't want to admit that I'd made my decision so impulsively. "I tried to call him a couple of times, but he wasn't in. I'll try again later today."

"You're a lousy liar. Don't bother to confess it. Lame efforts like that don't count." Ben now laughed heartily, though his good humor wasn't entirely for my sake: "Veronica Whitegoose is here to arrange her grandson's baptism. I'll talk to you later when you know your arrival time. Chin up, Sluggly. You may not be smart, but you sure are dumb."

Usually, Ben lifted my spirits. But upon hanging up, I felt depressed. Instead of phoning Sky Travel, I decided to get dressed and drive downtown.

Janet Driggers was on duty, apparently having just opened the office at ten. A steaming cup of coffee sat on her desk as she listened to the accumulation of messages on Sky Travel's answering machine.

"Just a sec, Emma," she murmured, signaling for me to sit down.

I sat while Janet scribbled some notes. Her piquant features grew bored as Leonard Hollenberg droned on about his proposed trip to Hawaii. As one of our three county commissioners, Leonard was definitely a blabbermouth. I considered going across the street to the Upper Crust to fetch some coffee and maybe a sweet roll, but the call finally ended.

"One more," Janet said, holding up an index finger as the next voice played over the tape. It was female, vaguely familiar, and when Becca Wolfe called herself Mrs. Eric Forbes, I jumped in my chair. Janet turned pale and stared at me with startled green eyes.

". . . to go to Cabo San Lucas. I've got some coupons from when I worked at the airline in Seattle. . . ." Becca sounded perfectly normal, allowing for the usual answering-machine distortion. "We'd like to leave a week from today, if Stella will give me the time off. Call me tomorrow at my home phone. The number is . . ."

Chapter Fourteen

"JESUS!" JANET BREATHED after the message had played out. "I thought Becca was missing in action! It sounds like she's going on a second honeymoon!"

I was literally on the edge of my seat. "Where did she call from? When? Try her home number. I'll wait."

Janet dialed, a frantic series of motions. Then the travel agent spoke in an anxious voice. As usual, Janet Driggers didn't worry about tact: "Becca, you idiot, where the hell have you been? You've had the whole town worried sick! We thought you were dead!"

I gave another start as I heard Becca's voice; Janet had turned on the speakerphone. "I'm not." There was a faint giggle. "I feel totally stupid, but ... well, Eric and I reconciled. He's changed. Really, he has. That's why we want to go to Cabo. We can get married again there."

"Jesus." Janet's voice dropped this time as she shook her head in disbelief. "Listen, Becca, if you think any man can ... oh, fuck it, you spent the night in the sack, right? Where were you—some motel on Highway 2?"

Becca didn't seem to mind Janet's frank speech. She giggled again. "No, we went to the Lumberjack. At first, we were just going to talk everything out in private, but then—hey," Becca interrupted herself, apparently catch-

ing on to the amplified echo in Janet's voice, "is somebody listening in?"

"You bet," Janet replied. "Emma Lord's here, and if I
had my way, I'd call in Stella and Milo and Fuzzy Baugh
and everybody else in Alpine! Goddamn it, Becca, we
honest-to-God thought you were cut up in pieces and
lying in somebody's bait box! Why in hell didn't you tell
Stella where you'd gone?"

Becca's tone turned defensive. "I tried to. I called
Stella twice from the motel, but the line was busy. Then I
got . . . well, *involved*. Back off, Janet—it's none of your
business. Have you and your husband ever broken up and
then tried to get back together?"

For once, Janet seemed nonplussed. So was I. The idea
of the bloodless Al Driggers erupting with any kind of
emotion apparently stupefied us both.

Or so I thought. Janet, however, worked out of a different manual. "You don't reason with men, Becca," she
said after a pause to marshal her forces. "You haul out
the black lace goodies and *perform*, for chrissakes! Keep
'em loose, keep 'em hungry, keep 'em happy! Power?
It's not fists or guns or politics—it's *sex*. Remember that,
Becca. Where do you want to stay in Cabo? I'm recom-
mending the Finisterra."

Reeling in my chair, I scarcely heard the rest of the
conversation. Indeed, before Janet finished, I left Sky
Travel, motioning that I would return. Less than a minute later I was in the sheriff's office. Jack Mullins was
on duty, looking sleepy and less than his usual jocu-
lar self.

I gave him my big news. Jack's incredulity faded
swiftly as he contacted Milo, who apparently was at
home. After delivering the bare bones about Becca, Jack
winced as Milo exploded in his ear. I could hear the
sheriff's irate voice from where I was standing.

"You didn't need a phone," I remarked in a weak attempt at humor after Jack hung up. "What's Milo going to do, arrest Becca for deceiving an entire county?"

Jack's sleepy demeanor had disappeared. "I think he's going to personally check on the nonmissing Ms. Wolfe and her ex. It could be phony, some kind of setup."

It didn't seem to me that Jack believed what he was saying. And while it wouldn't do to take chances, I suspected that Milo's real intention was to confront Becca over her gross negligence. Maybe he'd haul Stella and the Wolfes along for good measure. I couldn't really blame the sheriff. Becca's behavior had been inexcusable.

I stated as much, but Jack merely shook his head in a bemused manner. "You'd be surprised," he said with an air of apology, "at how many women will take a man back, no matter how he's treated them. The hardest part of our job is convincing wives and girlfriends to file charges. Sometimes it gets downright dangerous when we get called in to break up a domestic brawl. We turn into the bad guys, while the couple shows a united front."

I was aware of the problem, though I'd never understood why women, in particular, defended abusive men. Loyalty should have no part in it, and love was not enough.

But then who was I to criticize? Abuse comes in many forms, along with broken promises. How long had I put up with Tom hurting me? Maybe I was an even bigger sap than Becca.

Returning to Sky Travel, I got down to business with Janet Driggers. We decided that my best route to Tuba City was via Phoenix, where I could rent a car and pick up Adam in Tempe. We'd have to drive over two hundred miles to Tuba City, but we could spell each other. Maybe I'd rediscover my son along the way.

Having completed my travel arrangements, the rest of Saturday loomed empty before me. Briefly, I considered driving into Seattle. I got as far as the bridge over the Skykomish River when I decided that I was starting out too late to accomplish much in the city and also cover a hundred-and-sixty-mile round trip.

But having gotten as far as the edge of town, I kept going. When I reached Highway 2, I automatically turned west. The Cascade Mountains divide the state of Washington into two very different halves. The eastern part is mostly rolling prairies, farmland, the coulees of the Columbia River, the wheatlands of the Palouse. It is drier in the summer, hotter, with a hint of the Great Plains. In winter, the weather turns cold and snow frequently covers the vast landscape under the broad, brumal sky. For at least half the year it is brown and gold, and would be arid, save for the great dams that provide enough irrigation to feed the masses and make a few farmers rich. The region is almost as foreign to me as the Dakotas or the Missouri River Valley. I am much more at home in western Washington, with its rain, its forest, its more temperate climate, and its rush-hour traffic jams.

Thus, I drove in the direction that was familiar, down the wet highway with its twists and turns and weeping waterfalls that splashed across the rocky face of the mountains. Somewhere around the Skykomish Ranger Station, I realized where I was going, at least in a vague sort of way: Paula Rubens lived in Gold Bar. The town was sufficiently tiny that she shouldn't be hard to find. When I pulled into Gold Bar Gas, I made the proper inquiries. Paula lived on the road to Wallace Falls State Park. I couldn't miss her place, according to the man with the jet-black goatee—she had stained-glass windows all over her house, her barn, and even her privy.

The *privy* turned out to be a separate building that was Paula's studio and hot tub. She laughed when I offered the service-station attendant's description.

"There *was* a privy on the site when I bought the place," Paula said, ushering me into what had apparently once been a farmhouse. She was a big, cheerful redheaded woman of fifty wearing a caftan that could have covered a small room. "That was eight years ago. I modernized. Hell, I could afford to, at the price I paid for this dump."

Paula's *dump* was virtually one big room with airy stained-glass windows from floor to ceiling. She had removed the walls, save for a few structurally required beams. The result was an open space that somehow still managed to be cozy.

"Drink?" Paula offered, the black-and-white-striped caftan swaying around her ample form as she moved across the uncarpeted terra-cotta-tiled floor. "It's almost noon, and I'm not against a good hit before lunch."

Not wanting to be ungracious, I said a small shot of bourbon with water sounded fine. Paula's bar was what looked like a very ancient armoire in the Spanish style. Or maybe it was Portuguese. My hostess poured herself an ample dose of gin and a slightly less hefty measure of bourbon for me.

"So you're the Alpine editor person," she said with an infectious grin. "I read your paper. It's pretty well done for a small-town weekly. But then I was raised on *The Washington Post*. My father was a minor-league spook."

Silently cursing myself for not knowing of Paula Rubens's presence along the Stevens Pass corridor, I made a mental note to send Carla out on an interview.

The stained-glass artist sounded like an interesting feature story.

But for now, I had to limit myself to questions concerning Honoria Whitman. Acknowledging that Paula was a no-nonsense type, I went straight to the point.

"Naturally, we're covering Kay Whitman's murder in Alpine. I gather you're friendly with her sister-in-law, Honoria. How did you react to the news of Kay's death?"

Paula chuckled richly. "Hey, Emma, this sounds like one of those TV encounters! You know, 'What was your reaction when the nuclear bomb fell on you?' Shoot, I didn't even hear about the murder until Honoria asked me to take her cat. Come to think of it, she never brought the animal over here."

As if on cue, a pair of Siamese sauntered out from behind the cushion-covered couch. To my surprise, Paula Rubens addressed the cats in French.

"My little conceit." She laughed as the cats climbed up on the couch beside her. "I named them Rheims and Rouen after two of my favorite cathedrals. The stained-glass windows, you know."

Acknowledging the remarks with a nod and a smile, I grew serious. "Honoria's cat—Dodger—had an accident. He's dead, I'm afraid."

"Oh, shoot!" Paula Rubens couldn't have looked any more distressed if I'd told her that the cathedrals in Rheims and Rouen had fallen down. "What was it—a car?" She picked up both Siamese and plopped them on her lap.

"No," I replied, trying to walk a fine line between candor and discretion. "Somebody strangled him."

Paula held her own pets close, though neither seemed pleased at the display of protectiveness. "Oh, good God!

What's wrong with people? Do you blame me for keeping these two indoors most of the time?"

"Is that because there've been other cats killed?" I
asked.

Paula nodded with vigor. "At least two have been shot
in the past couple of years, and once in a while some
animal gets them. Last fall I heard that a black bear was
coming right up to some of the houses around here and
mauling both cats and dogs. I wouldn't want to live anywhere other than in the country—cities are a canker—but
let's face it, there are dangers here, too." My hostess's
broad face still looked disturbed.

I could read nothing other than genuine anguish in
Paula's demeanor. There had been far less dismay in her
attitude toward Kay's murder than Dodger's demise. I
sensed that Paula was as open as she seemed, incapable
of dissembling. If she hadn't known Kay Whitman, she
wouldn't pretend to a grief she didn't feel. The cat was
another matter.

"Dodger was strangled and mailed to somebody
in Alpine." I didn't wait for the shock to settle in on
Paula. "It could have been some ghoulish teenager—
or not. In covering this type of story, we have to investigate on our own. Obviously, what I'm looking for is a
connection between Kay's killer and this cat business.
Have you any idea who might have done such a thing to
Dodger?"

Rheims and Rouen had managed to squirm out of
Paula's grasp. Their almost identical creamy-beige
bodies paraded into the kitchen. Disappearing behind a
birch counter that divided the two rooms, the animals
probably went in search of lunch.

Paula rose to freshen her drink, which seemed like a
daring thing to do at eleven-forty on a Saturday morning.

She tipped her head in my direction, with a questioning look, but I covered my glass and smiled a no-thank-you.

"There are kids around here who are ornery enough to do that sort of thing," she finally said, resettling herself on the couch. "No," she corrected herself, "not the part about mailing the poor animal. That takes time—and money. The kids I'm thinking of are the kind who torture animals and then let the owners find them stuffed in their mailboxes. How did Honoria feel about what happened to Dodger? She was very fond of him."

I explained how Honoria had left before learning Dodger's fate. "She was appalled when the sheriff told her last night on the phone. She thought he'd simply run away. I suppose that's why you didn't hear from her again before she headed to California." My tone had grown speculative; I waited for Paula to comment. When she didn't, I pressed a bit. "I never really knew Honoria that well. Were you good friends?"

"Casual friends," Paula answered after thinking the question through. "She wasn't what I'd call the chummy sort. We'd go to some showings together, dinner once in a while, maybe a movie in Monroe. But there'd be long periods where I wouldn't hear from her. If I'd called last, I'd wait. The phone rings at both ends, that's always been my motto. I don't think I'd heard from Honoria since the holidays, not until she called me about taking Dodger, and then, as a sort of afterthought, she mentioned that her sister-in-law had been killed."

Finishing my drink, I considered Paula's words. "You mean it was a throwaway line?"

"Yes." Paula's smile was cynical. "You got it. It was like, 'Would you mind keeping Dodger for a week or so while I attend my sister-in-law's funeral? She was murdered the other day, you know.' Which I didn't, and I let out a yelp, but Honoria just went on, cool as the proverbial cucumber, about how Dodger should have a mix of dry and wet food, and not to give him liver. Strange, huh?"

"Was it? For Honoria, I mean. She doesn't exactly boil over with emotion."

"Oh, that's true enough." Paula gave a little shake of her head, the burnished tangle of curls dancing on her wide shoulders. "Besides, Honoria is always up-front about her feelings. When you can pry anything out of her, I mean. Let's face it, she never liked her sister-in-law much. In fact, I was surprised when she told me they'd been visiting. I thought Trevor and Kay had split up years ago."

The Siamese cats returned to the living room, preened a bit, and slipped behind the couch. Against the far wall, a very old grandfather clock, stripped of its original finish, chimed the quarter hour.

"They split up?" I echoed, not trying to hide my surprise.

Paula nodded, another vigorous gesture. "Eight, ten years ago. It was while Trevor was in the slammer." With a grimace, Paula stopped speaking, then put a finger to her lips. "Damn, am I telling tales about Trevor out of school?"

"No, no," I assured Paula. "I know that Trevor went to prison for killing Honoria's first husband. But I thought Kay had waited faithfully for him."

Setting her empty glass on a side table made from a shiny cedar burl, Paula sighed. "One evening about two years ago I made dinner for Honoria. Afterward we drank some brandy. She's not much for the hard stuff, but that night she'd just had a very successful showing in Bellevue, and I guess she wanted to celebrate. Or unwind. Putting shows together, working with galleries, suffering through critics, dealing with customers—it drains you. Anyway, she had about three brandies, and opened up more than usual. She got off on Kay, and how she'd dumped poor Trevor almost as soon as he was sent to prison. Loyalty is one of Honoria's great virtues. She felt that Kay had betrayed Trevor, and maybe she did. Anyway, Honoria didn't think much of her sister-in-law. But if Trevor and Kay reconciled after all these years, Honoria might have forgiven her. Trevor obviously did."

I recalled Vida's remarks about Kay. A young, attractive woman with a husband serving a long jail term would certainly be vulnerable to temptation. As Vida had suggested, Kay could have found another man. Or several of them, over a twelve-year period. But perhaps Kay still loved Trevor. If he returned her feelings, then he'd take her back, forgive and forget. Just as Becca was doing with Eric Forbes.

Paula's revelation also shored up what I knew Vida had been thinking: that if Kay had taken a lover, or lovers, the motive for her murder might be passion scorned. I could believe that; in fact, I wanted to believe it. But why had Kay been killed in Alpine? Had she been followed from California, or was her murderer in our midst all along?

I didn't say any of these things out loud. Paula was glancing from her liquor cabinet to the kitchen and back again. Anticipating that she was about to offer another drink or a bit of lunch, I decided to take my leave. While I found Paula's company agreeable, I was anxious to speculate with Vida. Vida, of course, would be annoyed that I'd called on Paula without her. But she'd get over it.

There was one more question for Paula, however. "Did Honoria tell you if Kay had found another man?"

Paula had also risen. I thought I saw a fleeting look of

disappointment cross her face. She might have fled the city, but I suspected that her self-imposed exile had a price. Paula was probably lonely. While I didn't want to flatter myself, I figured that she found me a slightly more interesting guest than Dodger. Then again, as she fondly watched the Siamese weave in and out under the hem of her caftan, maybe not.

"Honoria didn't mention a man specifically," Paula responded. "As I told you, loyalty was her big hang-up. It was a quality that Kay lacked, and Honoria harped on it. I suppose you could assume that some guy was in the background, though. It would be a safe guess."

I nodded, then put out my hand. "It usually is. Thanks for everything, Paula. Stop and see me if you get to Alpine. The drinks will be on me."

Paula brightened, and for the first time I noticed her eyes, a gray green that wasn't a true hazel, but whose color seemed to shift and merge with the light.

"I'll do that," she declared. "I haven't been to Alpine since last summer. Maybe we'll discover more mutual friends, and we can trash them, too."

I grinned, pleased at the kinship we seemed to be experiencing. "The only problem in trashing Honoria is that she doesn't expose enough of herself to make it worthwhile. Then there's her handicap, which, when I remember she has one, commands nothing but admiration for overcoming it so well. I don't know if I admire that about her most, or the way she's been able to recover from that horror of a husband, and move on to have a relationship with men again."

The oddly colored eyes grew puzzled. "Mitch? Are you kidding? Honoria was nuts about the guy. Isn't that why she moved to Startup? She wanted to finally get over him."

I stared at Paula Rubens. The cats began to chase each

other across the hardwood floor. In the ensuing silence, I could hear the grandfather clock chime the noon hour. It sounded like a warning bell.

In the end I stayed for lunch. Paula had insisted, stating quite rightly that we couldn't stand out on the porch forever in the chill, wet air. Furthermore, she didn't want Rheims and Rouen to escape. They might end up like Dodger.

Initially, our conversation over mushroom-filled crepes stayed fixed on Honoria. Paula insisted that Honoria's feelings for Mitch Harmon were deep and abiding. My hostess was more vague about Mitch's brutality, however. He'd had a temper, yes, but Honoria had never blamed him directly for her accident. Confused, I abandoned further probing, and talk turned to an exchange of life stories.

My abbreviated version seemed dull by comparison. Paula had been raised in D.C., but had attended a Swiss boarding school. Indeed, she'd attended four of them, having been expelled from the first three for a variety of high jinks, including the seduction of a prim and proper Calvinist chaplain. She had studied painting in Paris, where she'd also learned to make crepes such as the ones she'd whipped up for lunch. She'd lived in Florence for six years with a sculptor who created nothing but cross-eyed stone frogs. In her early thirties she'd headed back to the States, and settled in Manhattan, where she'd become involved in selling artifacts from old buildings that were about to be demolished. That was when she had discovered her interest and talent for stained glass. Despite an off-and-on affair with a tuba player from the New York Philharmonic, she finally decided to move west. Oddly, or so it seemed to me, she chose Cheyenne, where she fell in love with a cattle auctioneer. When his jealous wife came after her with a shotgun, Paula left for Seattle. A year later she was in Gold Bar, where she felt not only at home, but as if she'd been there in another life, perhaps as a Douglas fir. Paula definitely believed in reincarnation. She also claimed to have been a cat during the reign of Amenhotep II in Egypt.

Extracting a promise that she would give at least some of this biography to Carla for an article, I left Paula around two. The rain had stopped, and the clouds were lifting. By the time I reached the turnoff for Alpine, a frail sun was following me up the mountainside.

I drove straight to Vida's house. The big white Buick was parked in the drive, so I knew she was home.

"Well," my House & Home editor exclaimed after I confessed to my latest incursion on her journalistic turf, "you might have called me! Really, Emma, I'm beginning to feel as if you lack confidence in my investigative abilities."

"Oh, Vida!" I tried to make a joke out of the mere idea. "That's like saying that Lou Piniella doesn't think Randy Johnson can pitch!"

It was the wrong metaphor. Vida wasn't interested in sports. "Lu and Ella who? Don't bring up your big-city friends! Goodness, I can't think why you have to go haring off on your own to talk to these people! I'm not sure I even want to hear about it! You probably got everything mixed up!"

Suddenly I felt about eight years old. It didn't matter that I was the boss. Vida's scolding reminded me painfully, longingly, of my mother. I hung my head, fingers entwined behind my back.

"It was a whim," I said, sounding suitably childish. "I just felt like getting out of town for a few hours. The next thing I knew, I was in Gold Bar."

"Of course you were," Vida snapped. "How could you not be unless you went east?"

I didn't try to argue the logic of Vida's statement. "Okay, I'm sorry. To be honest, I didn't think much would come of it, except that Paula might know who killed Dodger. She didn't. But she made a wonderful lunch." My usual perversity prodded me into a pugnacious stance. Vida might not admit it, but she knew that cooking was her domestic Achilles' heel.

"Oh, so your new friend is a wonderful cook, too! Well! She sounds to me like a bit of a know-nothing! Stained glass, indeed! However can you see through it? Why would you want such a thing except in a church?"

I didn't bother to point out that there was a great deal of clear glass in Paula's designs. To my mixed annoyance and pleasure, Vida was exhibiting jealousy. It wasn't an uncommon reaction on her part when I made a new woman friend.

"Paula knows something we don't," I said, casting off truculence. "She says Kay left Trevor years ago. And Honoria never stopped loving her late husband. Oh, Honoria despised Kay. G'bye, Vida. See you Monday." I turned toward the front door.

Naturally, I didn't get very far. I hadn't expected to. Vida let out a little shriek, then with surprising agility, she blocked my passage.

"Just a minute, young lady," she huffed. "You can't walk out on me now! You march right into the kitchen and start talking. I'll make tea." The command brooked no opposition; the offer of tea was grudging.

"It won't be some fancy English or Indian brand," she went on, entering the kitchen, "just plain old reliable Red Rose. Now sit down and go over all this—carefully."

I did. For most of the account, Vida's back was turned to me while she put on the kettle, got out the cups, and searched for a fresh box of tea bags. But I could tell from the tilt of her head how she was responding.

"The part about Kay and Trevor is understandable," Vida said when I concluded. "As you may recall, I wondered about that myself. Prison has taken a toll on many a marriage, especially if the spouse is gone for a long time." She was now sitting at the table. "Kay probably went off with someone else, and when that didn't work out, she took Trevor back when he got out of jail. That's the simplest kind of scenario, and would explain Honoria's earlier dislike of Kay as well as welcoming her to Startup with Trevor and Mrs. Smith. Honoria could hardly do anything else. But this business about Honoria's enduring love for Mitch Harmon is another matter. I've always gathered from what little she said, at least in my presence, that she feared and hated the man. Certainly Milo never gave us any reason to believe otherwise."

We discussed the point until the teakettle sang. Cupcake sang, too, a merry little canary song that somehow lifted my spirits. When Vida and I had talked the situation through and come up with no viable solutions, my House & Home editor suddenly took on a conspiratorial air.

"I was not idle today," she said, wiggling her eyebrows in what I took for a mysterious manner. "I spoke with Becca. And Eric."

"Aha!" I had to smile. "So you went off without me."

"*I'm* covering the story." Vida now looked smug. "Naturally, Billy called me after you told Jack Mullins about Becca contacting Janet Driggers. My nephew also informed me that Milo was going to see Becca, so I waited an hour or so, and then I went to her apartment, too. She seemed quite chagrined by then. So did this Eric, who is neither as handsome as Mrs. Wolfe claimed, nor as gruesome as Mr. Wolfe reported. In fact, he's rather nondescript, except for muscles. Perhaps I was mistaken in thinking he was as good-looking as the unsuitable boy from Skykomish."

"Did he seem dangerous?" I inquired.

Vida had returned to the stove. A patch of sunshine through the kitchen window turned the well-polished steel fittings to gold. "It's hard to tell. His manners are adequate. But that's often the case." Vida hadn't bothered to steep the tea this time, but simply dumped a bag in each of our steaming cups. "They seemed very lovey-dovey, despite being embarrassed over the furor Becca's disappearance had caused."

"How could they have been at the Lumberjack without anyone knowing?" I demanded, scooping my tea bag out with a teaspoon. "Minnie Harris should recognize Becca."

"Exactly." Vida smirked a bit. "Minnie was having her hair done at Stella's when Becca ran off with Eric. Don't you remember?"

I did, now that Vida mentioned it. "And Mel Harris doesn't know Becca. What did they do, use assumed names?"

Vida nodded. "They registered as Mr. and Mrs. Becker, from Seattle, a combination of their first names, Becca and Eric. Mel had no idea who Becca was because she hasn't been back in town very long, and the Harrises didn't move here until after she left Alpine."

Cupcake was still singing, emitting long trills as he hopped around his cage, going from rung to rung. I shook my head. "It doesn't sound right. Becca and Eric, I mean. She must have been very hostile to have gotten rid of her wedding pictures and souvenirs. Why would she take him back? Where," I asked, wondering about the practicalities, "did she run into him?"

"Right on Front Street, by the ski shop." Vida's expression was rueful. "Plain sight, wouldn't you know it? He drove up and honked, and she got in. They went off together. In fact, they rode all around town before finally agreeing to go to the Lumberjack. Isn't it strange how we can miss the obvious? Frankly, it gets my goat."

Before long, it would get mine, too.

Chapter Fifteen

By the time I left Vida's house, I was not only back in her good graces, but she was expressing excitement over my trip to Arizona. She was fond of Ben, even if he was a Catholic priest, and thus alien to her Presbyterian soul. As for Adam, she reserved judgment. Vida was convinced that I spoiled him. Since I thought Roger was rotten to the core, my son and her grandson were off-limits as topics of serious discussion.

At home, I couldn't resist calling Milo. He was in, and though I had merely intended to tease him about my visit with Paula Rubens, I blurted out a dinner invitation instead. Milo blurted out acceptance. He'd drop by around six-thirty. Was there any chance that I was cooking lamb chops?

There wasn't. I had a couple of New York steaks in the freezer. Milo liked beef just fine. Should he stop to pick up some booze? The offer took me aback. Milo usually didn't contribute much to dinners chez Emma except his appetite. I told him that my Scotch supply was still plentiful.

I was giving my housework, as my mother used to say, "a lick and a promise," when Martin Marshall arrived on my doorstep.

I almost didn't recognize him at first, because he was dressed in a suit and a tie. Like most Alpiners, Martin's everyday wardrobe runs to plaid flannel shirts and Sears work pants. The charcoal suit jacket looked a bit snug; I suspected it was usually kept in mothballs

"We're going to a wedding in Monroe," Martin explained, sounding anxious, "and I had to run over to the mall and pick up the present at Table Toppings. Jane bought it, but she walked out of the store without it. I was just passing by, so I thought I'd drop in."

Even with a stretch of the imagination, Martin's route from the mall wouldn't have taken him by my house. Since he avoided my eyes, I figured that he knew he hadn't fooled me.

"Do you mind?" He put one foot across the threshold, then darted a look of apology.

"No, come on in. What can I do for you?"

The implied offer seemed to relax him, though he declined to sit down. "I won't take but a minute, Ms. Lord." He smoothed his curly gray hair with both hands. "It's about this murder case. I appreciate—*we* appreciate—the fact that you didn't mention our names in your story the other day. But then Becca Wolfe pulled that disappearing act Friday, and it looks as if everything's going wrong at the salon. I can't begin to tell you how important it is to Jane and Laurie and me to keep us out of this."

I hadn't yet decided how to handle Becca's brief disappearance. It had been reported to the sheriff, and thus was a matter of public record. On the other hand, there was no crime involved and she appeared to be safe. Maybe it was a chatty item for Vida's "Scene Around Town" column.

"We'll do our best," I said. "So far there's no reason to bring in Laurie or you and Jane."

If I expected Martin to show relief, I was wrong. Instead, he ran a finger under the collar of his stiff white shirt. "It's not what you think. I mean, we know there's no connection between us and this Whitman woman who got killed. But it's the other business. . . ." His voice faded into misery.

"Toby Popp?" I gave Martin a sympathetic smile. "Your wife told me all about her first marriage. I understand why your family doesn't want the publicity. Toby probably doesn't either. He seems to shy away from the media."

Martin reddened and clenched his right fist. "I don't give a damn about Toby Popp! All I want is for him to leave us alone! He dropped out for almost twenty years, then he shows up like Santa Claus. I've worked hard, I've made a decent living for my family, I've been a real father to Laurie and a good husband to Jane. Of all the places in the world that Toby could have gone, why did that self-centered so-called genius of a jackass have to come here?"

I didn't blame Martin Marshall for being disturbed. His question wasn't merely rhetorical: I was afraid that I, like him, knew the answer.

"He hit middle age and suddenly realized the only thing he had was money," I murmured. "I suppose he's in need of family—or at least a daughter."

"That's it." Martin unclenched his fist and waved at the air. "*My* daughter. He gave her up a long time ago. She hardly remembers him. Then he thinks he can win her over with a bunch of expensive presents and big checks. Imagine, he wants to *buy* Laurie!"

Martin's voice had risen again. I tried to speak calmly, hoping to soothe him. "She doesn't seem to be for sale."

"She's not," Martin declared heatedly. "Oh, I'll admit, Jane almost fell for the first couple of gifts. She felt Toby owed her—and Laurie—something. But I put an end to that. In for a dime, in for a dollar. Take no part of him, I said. The next thing you know, he'll want Laurie to live with him in his mansion down on the river. Why else build such a big place for one lousy person?"

"Maybe," I said, still in a reasonable tone, "he wants to start another family. He's not too old for that."

Martin snorted. "He's too chicken for it. He doesn't have the guts to court a woman. His ego might be the size of Mount Baldy, but he doesn't have the heart. He doesn't *have* a heart, as far as I'm concerned. It serves him right if it got ripped out thirty years ago."

"He must have cared deeply for Jane," I said, wishing that Martin would either sit down or take off. I was getting tired of standing on the hardwood floor.

Martin seemed to have read my mind. His shoulders slumped in the suit coat as he turned to leave. "Jane broke his heart?" he murmured. "No way. She got him on the rebound. You bet it didn't work out. Even if Toby'd been a normal guy, the marriage would've flopped. Thanks, Ms. Lord. I've got to run or we'll be late for the wedding. I don't know why, but I feel better now."

I didn't know why Martin felt better, either. I'd hardly been able to offer much solace. I couldn't even promise to keep the Marshall name out of the paper. Maybe he just needed to vent his frustrations. Certainly he had them—a wife and daughter who were being courted by a billionaire was enough to threaten any ordinary man.

I had scarcely closed the door on Martin when Ed Bronsky showed up. He looked frazzled, but as usual, was full of himself. Nervously, I eyed my watch. The late afternoon was being swallowed up by my unexpected visitors.

"I've been working all day," Ed said, barging into the living room and thudding onto one of my armchairs. A hand-tooled leather attaché case dangled from one hand. "I got up to my college career. What's that line about being in Arcadia? It's got something to do with a university in England."

I refrained from holding my head. Ed's so-called college career had lasted two quarters at Central Washington State. "The quote's from Evelyn Waugh's *Brideshead Revisited*. It's not about the narrator's days at Oxford so much as the idyllic life that he and—"

"Whatever." Ed waved a beefy paw. "I've been thinking that I ought to have some references to the classics, maybe begin the book like Dickens did, you know, 'First of all, I was born.' Or however it goes. Have you got a copy of *A Christmas Carol*?"

"It's *David Copperfield*." Trying to control my impatience, I balanced uneasily on the arm of my green sofa. "If I were you, Ed, I'd stick to my own words. The author's *voice*, as they call it." I was choking on the suggestion.

"Hmmm." Ed looked thoughtful. "I suppose. What about using quotes as chapter headings? Like when I get into my advertising career, I could use what Churchill said about blood, sweat, and tears. That kind of phrase would add class."

But not accuracy, I thought, unless Ed was referring to me instead of himself. "See how the actual writing goes," I temporized. It was pointless to argue further.

Ed was still thinking, his pudgy face a mass of furrows and lumps. "That's the other thing, Emma. I sat down at my computer today and worked on the first chapter. It's kind of rough, but I thought you'd want to go over it. The editor's touch, as it were."

Surreptitiously, I glanced at my watch. It was after five-thirty, and Milo was due in less than an hour. I still had to finish cleaning, get dressed, and start dinner.

"Leave it with me," I finally said. Getting rid of Ed seemed like the lesser of two evils. "I'll proof it tomorrow."

"It isn't proofing exactly," Ed admitted. "In fact, we should read it together." He clicked the attaché case open and extracted a pile of computer paper. "Let's sit at the dining-room table. We'll have more room. I don't suppose you could spare a short one?"

Ed had gotten to his feet, but I stayed firmly on the sofa's arm. "Ed," I intoned, "I can't do this right now. I'm expecting company. Frankly, you ought to rework your first chapter so that it's all but press-ready. Otherwise," I continued, practically gagging, "it won't have that Bronsky touch."

"Company?" Ed's gaze darted around the room, as if my guest were hiding behind the furniture. "Who?"

It was none of Ed's business, but on the other hand, hosting Milo wasn't a state secret. Thus, I revealed the name of my dinner companion.

Ed's expression changed from inquisitiveness to disapproval. "Gee, Emma, that's not a good idea. You'd better cancel. Give Milo a call, and we'll get started." To my horror, Ed bustled over to the dining-room table.

"Ed!" I spoke sharply, my patience exhausted. "What the hell are you talking about? And don't you dare sit down!"

Rather than the annoyance I'd expected, Ed exhibited puzzlement. "Hey, I'm only thinking of your reputation! Come on, Emma, you've got to know what people are saying. I'm surprised at Milo—I thought he was a pretty smart guy."

At last, I slid off the sofa. Arms crossed, I approached Ed. "Now what? Have I gone beyond encouraging crime for the sake of circulation? Is Milo doing likewise to keep himself and his deputies in overtime? What's today's rumor, Ed? That the sheriff and I conspired to kill Kay Whitman?"

Ed actually looked as if the thought had never occurred to him, but it wasn't a bad idea. "Gee, not that—though it could work. You see," he went on earnestly, "most people think that the wrong woman was killed. It was supposed to be Honoria, not her sister-in-law. If you and Milo are seeing each other on the sly, then who had a motive to get Honoria out of the way?" Ed regarded me with genuine curiosity.

I was flabbergasted. While the twisted concept had crossed my mind earlier, it had never dawned on me that anyone would take it seriously. My initial reaction was to lash out at Ed, at Fuzzy Baugh, at whichever other so-called mover and shaker had bandied such an idea about over a third martini. Instead, I curbed my temper and tried to be reasonable.

"Okay, Ed—who's the suspect? Milo or me?"

Ed flushed and held up the hand that wasn't holding Chapter One. "Hey—*I* didn't come up with it. But you found the body. You were there. What's a person to think? Especially people who don't know you as well as I do?"

Under my breath, I uttered several words that would have uncurled Vida's gray locks. "This is ridiculous, Ed," I finally declared, feeling hopelessly at sea. "It's more than that—it's scurrilous. If I find out who's been saying such things, I'll sue his—or her or their—pants off. So will Milo, if he's implicated. These kind of rumors damage our professional credibility as well as our personal reputations."

Ed, who had been gulping a bit, began jamming the computer sheets back into the attaché case. "Don't blame me for idle gossip, Emma. You know what this town is like. You've got to admit, a triangle is always a motive for murder. Where there's smoke, there's fire. A man and a woman who spend a lot of time together are bound to get talked about. Nobody can believe that they don't ... well, *you* know." Ed lowered his eyes.

"And *you* know that they *don't*." I bit off the words.

"As I said, don't blame me." Ed had bumbled his way to the door, colliding with the vacuum cleaner en route. "I'll go home now and do some rewriting. See you in church."

I was so angry after Ed left that I practically reinvented my living room. Not only did I clean and dust, I threw out two wastebaskets full of accumulated items that I'd been saving for reasons that now eluded me.

While getting dressed, I called Vida to ask her if she'd been hearing any of Ed's so-called rumors. If they were real, I couldn't imagine that my House & Home editor's pipeline had failed her.

But Vida wasn't home. Vaguely, I recalled that she'd mentioned going to her daughter's for dinner. Or, if Buck had recovered from the flu, they'd eat out. It had all seemed up in the air, which was probably why I'd forgotten.

Finally calming down, I tried to deal with Ed's gossip in a rational manner. Except in the beginning, when the local citizenry learned that I had borne a child out of wedlock, I had never been the subject of ugly talk. If I backed away to give the current tales some journalistic objectivity, the rumors weren't as preposterous as they seemed. The public knew only what had appeared in the Wednesday edition of *The Advocate*. Any other information that had leaked out since was strictly hearsay, and a matter of speculation. If people discovered that Honoria had given Kay her facial appointment, it was natural that some would think the killer did in the wrong woman. Certainly that idea had been considered by the rest of us. There seemed to be no more motive for murdering Kay than for killing Honoria. If no one in Alpine or the rest of Skykomish County knew Kay Whitman, why did she die? It was more plausible to believe that Honoria was the intended victim. Honoria had dated the sheriff for three years; they were said to be on the outs. Who was Milo seeing since then? Emma Lord, that's who. It made sense, in a simplistic, weird, Alpine kind of way.

On the other hand, who was Honoria seeing? I liked that question better. Was it Toby Popp? Was it someone else? Was it anybody? Paula Rubens hadn't thought so. But except for Wednesday's phone call, Paula hadn't spoken with Honoria since New Year's.

I was still mulling and making a green salad when Milo arrived. He didn't bring Scotch, but he had a bottle of Drambuie.

"You like this stuff, right?" he said, delivering the gift in its brown paper bag. "It's kind of sweet, but the warming part is good."

"It costs the world, you goof," I said, grinning as I relieved the liqueur of its packaging. "Thanks, Milo. I'll save it for after dinner. I can drink to forget Ed Bronsky."

For starters, I limited my recital to Ed's autobiography-in-progress. I'd save the rumor mill until Milo was sitting down with Scotch in hand. He listened attentively as I made our drinks.

"Who'd want to read about Ed's life?" the sheriff asked when I had finished in the kitchen and we'd returned to the living room. "Ed's got too much time on his hands these days. Can't your priest keep him busy doing good works?"

"Ed does volunteer at church," I admitted. "But you're right—he needs a real project. God knows there's plenty to do in this community. The Food Bank is always crying for donations, and we haven't got a multipurpose shelter. Maybe I'll mention it to Father Den."

After Milo had downed some of his drink, I related Ed's latest, crazy rumor. I expected the sheriff to be angry; I had not anticipated his amusement.

"People are saying you'd kill for me? Hell, Emma, that's wild!" The hazel eyes sparkled with pleasure as the sheriff edged closer to me on the sofa.

"People are wacko," I retorted, my annoyance returning. "If we're going to talk about nonexistent love triangles, let's zero in on you, Honoria, and Mitch Harmon."

Milo didn't exactly recoil, but he definitely pulled away. "Mitch Harmon? You mean Honoria's late husband? What about him? What's he got to do with me?"

The perplexity on Milo's long face was so apparent that I took pity on him. But if my tone softened, I didn't mince words in relating Paula Rubens's account of Honoria's abiding love for her spouse.

Milo continued to look bewildered. "Honest to God, Emma, I never heard that. Honoria hardly talked about Harmon at all, and when she did, it was about how he banged her around and finally crippled her. Are you sure this Paula is reliable?"

"I told you, Honoria unloaded all this after a few drinks. Paula may have some eccentricities, but she strikes me as an honest, open person. Why would she lie?"

Naturally, Milo couldn't answer that question. He sat in silence for a few moments, swigging Scotch and shaking his head. "This is weird. I don't get it."

Nor, when I told him, did Milo get the part about Kay dumping Trevor. "Self-delusion, maybe," I suggested. "Honoria and Trevor and their mother may have put on a front. They wouldn't want to admit that Trevor's wife walked out on him while he was in prison. Mrs. Smith seems like the type who'd worry about what the neighbors would say. That's why she came to Alpine before she left for California—to apologize for her children. Her own marital track record is so patchy, she's ashamed of it. I think she feels guilty, too, for setting a bad example. Ida Smith is the kind of person who does exactly what she wants, but is always apologizing, as if saying 'I'm sorry' makes up for her flaws."

Again, Milo was quiet, apparently thinking through what I'd said. "Well, at least Kay came back to Trevor," he finally remarked. "She was willing to try for a fresh start. That's to her credit."

I regarded Milo over the rim of my glass. "Did it get her killed?"

The sheriff had finished his drink. Instead of waggling his glass at me in his usual way of asking for a refill, he set it down on the coffee table.

"It may have," he allowed, looking glum. "That triangle idea could work another way."

I tried not to look too pleased as Milo's thinking seemed to be following the same route as my own. He might not be inclined to detours on his straight and narrow path to Truth, but his slower starts usually led him to the finish line. "You mean a former lover of Kay's?"

But Milo shook his head. "No. I mean of Trevor's."

Admittedly, I hadn't looked at the case from that angle. Milo theorized that after Kay left Trevor, another woman could have entered his life. A former girlfriend, a well-meaning neighbor, even a stranger might have visited Trevor in prison.

"We're back to the beginning," I said with a sigh as we sat down at the dining-room table. "In fact, we seem to be going in circles. So is this former love in Alpine, or did she follow the Whitmans? If she's here, who is she? Nobody I know fits into the time frame, not even Jane Marshall, who married Martin and moved here before Trevor went to jail."

The comment reminded me of Martin's visit. Milo listened with an air of mild interest. In between big bites of steak, he chuckled.

"You like that part about the woman who broke Toby Popp's heart, I'll bet," Milo remarked. "Who was she? Kay Whitman? Or one of four million other California girls?"

"You know, Milo," I said, passing my guest a second baked potato, "it might not hurt to dig into the Mitch Harmon case. Why did Paula insist that Honoria didn't blame him for her handicap? And by the way, did you ever talk to Honoria again last night?"

"No." Milo looked sheepish. "By the time I got around to it, it was almost ten. I figured Honoria and her mother would turn in early to get a good start on the road this morning. They had to drive through the Siskiyous and the stretch by Mount Shasta. It could be dicey this time of year."

There was no point in needling Milo. He was in an awkward position, especially if he still cared for Honoria. But the backdoor approach remained open.

"I'm talking about an official inquiry," I said. "The police and court records. The trial testimony. Wouldn't you like to know the truth about Mitch Harmon?"

For once, the truth didn't seem to appeal to Milo. "I don't see what it has to do with Kay's murder."

"Oh, Milo!" Angrily, I swung my arms, knocking over the pepper mill. It fell to the floor and actually bounced.

The sheriff and I bent down at the same time. Our heads butted, and we both exclaimed in mild pain.

"Hey!" Milo was looking at me under the tablecloth. His eyes twinkled. We were so close that our noses almost touched.

I'm not sure how or why we both tumbled out of our chairs and onto the rag rug. Milo wrapped an arm around my neck and kissed me, hard. I kissed him back. Locked together, we rolled out from under the table. I lay on the floor, feeling his weight half resting on top of me.

"Emma." He kissed me again.

"Crazy," I mumbled, my lips against his cheek. He smelled faintly of shaving soap.

"Yeah. Crazy." He kissed my ear, my neck, my throat. My eyes were closed as I felt his big hands move down along my body. What the hell was going on? Should it? Could it? Did I want it? I was tingling in various places; there was a strange ringing noise in my head.

"Shit!" Milo yelled, rolling off of me and crashing into the sofa. "Where the hell's my coat?"

My eyes were wide open as I struggled to sit up. "Your coat? Where are you going?" I felt dismayed, panicky, hurt. Most of all, a terrible longing enveloped me.

The ringing had now translated into the sound of a telephone. Milo was pawing at his down jacket, which he'd left on the sofa arm. Finally he yanked out his cell phone and barked into it.

"Dodge. What now?"

Dazedly, I got to my feet. The second bourbon I'd poured for myself sat next to my empty dinner plate. The drink wasn't quite finished. I polished it off in a single swallow, disappointed that it was mostly melted ice.

"That's crazy!" Milo was shouting into the phone. "Are you sure? Okay, put her on."

The sheriff placed an unsteady hand over the mouthpiece. "It's the damnedest thing I ever heard. Sam Heppner's putting through a call from Sacramento. He swears it's Kay Whitman. Am I going nuts?"

Chapter Sixteen

IF MILO WAS going nuts, I was going with him. Literally. There was no way he could shake me after an announcement like that. I leaned against him, trying to listen to the voice on the phone. It was ordinary, matter-of-fact, and faintly amused. Unfortunately, I could catch only the nuances, not the actual words. Giving up, I flopped onto the sofa and waited for Milo to ring off.

"Jesus," he muttered, now putting on his jacket, "that's really weird."

I was on my feet again. "I'm coming, too, if you're headed for the office. What did she say?"

Milo was still shaking his head. "She swears she's Kay Beresford Whitman. She lives and works in Sacramento. She found out she was supposed to be dead from some friend in the state police office. She thought it was a joke, but decided to call up here just in case."

"Maybe," I said, scurrying into the kitchen to make sure the stove was turned off, "it's a different Kay Whitman."

"No. She divorced Trevor ten years ago and moved to Sacramento. She works for the state education association. We'll have to check it out, of course."

"He married two women named Kay," I offered. "It happens. Some guy from my high-school class married three Jennifers."

"So why act as if Kay Number One had stuck around? Besides, this explains why the victim's purse had to disappear. The killer wanted to get rid of her ID. The next question is, why?"

I had joined Milo at the door. A quick inspection of his worried face told me that he had all but forgotten about our interlude on the floor. At least temporarily. Maybe it was just as well.

"I'll take my own car," I volunteered as we stepped out into the cool night air. "That way, you won't have to drive me home if you get tied up."

Milo didn't argue, a confirmation of his single-mindedness. Steering the Jag down Fourth, I saw a quarter moon sitting above Baldy. There were stars out, bright and close, promising sun in the morning. False spring, I thought, a familiar sensation in late February. The temperature warmed for a few days, then dipped again, and brought new snow. Maybe it was like the unexpected passion that had erupted between Milo and me. The winter of our emotions would grip us again, and while we might remember, we wouldn't thaw.

Sam Heppner and Dustin Fong were on duty. Both looked shaken. By the time I arrived, Milo already had his jacket off and was sitting behind the reception counter at the computer.

"How do I work this damned thing to get data out of Sacramento?" he demanded.

Dustin hovered at his superior's elbow, giving instructions. Milo pressed keys, grumbled as the screen changed, fiddled with the mouse cursor, and finally swore.

"What's taking so damned long?" he asked in an angry tone. "How do you guys put up with this technical crap?"

"It's Saturday night," Dustin explained in an apologetic voice. "Everybody jumps on the network."

Milo looked aghast. "Everybody sits on their butts, playing with their computers? What happened to going out and getting drunk and beating up your wife and running over the neighbor's dog?" The sheriff slammed his hand against the computer monitor.

His comment seemed to conjure up an emergency telephone call. Sam Heppner took the message about a car going off the road just below the summit. Possible fatalities, ambulance dispatched, deputy at the scene.

Milo looked almost mollified by the report. "Okay," he sighed, gazing up at Dustin. "Now what? California's asking for a password."

"We set that up earlier this week to access their system, sir." Dustin bent down to type in whatever was required. "It's only good for five days. We'll have to make another request tomorrow."

"Jeez." Milo lighted a cigarette. "What is this, some kind of game?"

Edging around the counter, I tried to peek at the computer screen. From what I could see, a directory was scrolling down the monitor. Finally, a faint smile tugged at Milo's long mouth. "There! Monterey County divorce records. Do I put in Trevor and Kay's names?" Milo's big hands were poised awkwardly over the keyboard. Only minutes ago those same hands had explored my body. Like a silly teenager, I started to smile and had to turn away.

What seemed like a long time, but was probably less than a minute, passed before Milo struck California gold. "Here—final decree granted to Kay Beresford Whitman almost exactly ten years ago. Now, how do I find out if they remarried?"

I had moved around to the inside of the counter. Standing next to Dustin, I watched the screen bring up the marriage license heading for the state of California. Again, Milo typed in the Whitmans. Again, we waited.

The date was June 23, 1977. "The first time around," Milo breathed. "How do I get the second set of wedding bells?"

"You don't," Dustin replied, eyeing the monitor. "If they'd remarried in California, that would show under this heading. Try entering them individually."

But only the 1977 license appeared under Kay and Trevor's names. "Maybe they went to Reno," Milo said. "Or Mexico."

"Maybe they didn't bother," I put in. "It could be that they were living together since Trevor got out of jail. Why don't you try getting the transcript from Trevor's murder trial?"

According to Dustin, that information wasn't available on the database. The sheriff would have to request it from the Monterey County Courthouse on Monday. He might, the young deputy suggested shyly, try to bring up Trevor's criminal record. Assuming, Dustin added with an air of apology, that Mr. Whitman had one.

The proposal made Milo scowl. "I'll try Harmon first. Mitch—that'd be Mitchell, I suppose."

A full five minutes actually dragged by as the sheriff attempted to get at the California records. In fact, it took so long that Milo got up from the computer and ordered Dustin to take over.

"That damned thing doesn't like me," the sheriff groused. "All the money we've poured into this system, and it acts like some frigging prima donna! Screw it!"

Dustin's luck wasn't much better. He found two Mitchell Harmons, one in San Luis Obispo, and another from Bakersfield. The former was a thirty-one-year-old arsonist; the latter had a burglary career spanning forty years. Neither sounded like Honoria's late husband.

Milo surrendered. "We'll go back to the Stone Age Monday," he averred. "Phone calls, dusty files, feet-dragging clerks who don't give a damn about a two-bit law-enforcement agency in a podunk Washington town. But eventually, we might actually learn something."

Sam Heppner was on the phone again, taking down a report of an alleged theft at the bowling alley. Dustin Fong was looking guilty, as if he alone were to blame for the failure of the Computer Age.

With a wave of his arm, Milo signaled for me to follow him into his private office. At his desk, he examined what turned out to be notes Sam had taken from Kay Whitman.

"I've got her home and work address and numbers, plus her Social Security and California driver's-license IDs," Milo said, lighting another cigarette. "There's not much doubt that she's the Kay Whitman who was married to Trevor. The numbers check out. Damn!" He fingered his long chin, studying the notes some more.

"So who got killed?" To cover for asking the obvious, I gestured at Milo to give me a cigarette. If I were going to let my bananas flambé dessert molder, I might as well incinerate myself instead.

"God." Milo ran a hand through his graying sandy hair. "This is really awful, Emma. Do you realize what this means?"

I gave Milo a bleak look. "I'm afraid so. The Whitmans lied."

"Why?" Milo rested his chin on his hands. "The only thing that occurs to me is some kind of insurance scam."

My mind had been racing off in other directions, none of which seemed to lead anywhere. I was willing to hear Milo out. "What kind of scam?"

The sheriff sat up straight, puffing on his cigarette. "Let's say that Kay—the real Kay—had a big policy naming Trevor the beneficiary. I had one of those, through the county, and another personal one. It was only a couple of years ago that I realized I'd never taken my ex's name off. If I'd been shot in a brawl at the Icicle Creek Tavern, Old Mulehide would have gotten all of it. I changed it quick, believe me, and put in the kids' names."

I considered the theory. "It might work—if the real Kay never found out she was supposed to be dead. But now that's blown. Are you going to call Trevor? Honoria and Mrs. Smith ought to have arrived in Pacific Grove by now."

Milo sighed, a painful sound. "Yeah, I guess. Damn it, Emma, Honoria wouldn't be a party to a stunt like this. She's too honest."

A year ago, a month ago, even a week ago, I would have agreed wholeheartedly with Milo. But my opinion of Honoria had shifted in the past six days. There were too many things that didn't jibe: little things, like not mentioning her acquaintance with Toby Popp; big things, like telling Paula Rubens she'd genuinely loved her husband. And worst of all, asserting that the woman who got her throat slit at Stella's Styling Salon was her sister-in-law, Kay Whitman. Were they lies motivated by shame or were they deliberately intended to mislead? Or was some other factor involved that I hadn't yet recognized?

"Did she really say that?" The words popped out of my mouth.

"Huh?" Milo was justifiably puzzled.

"Did Honoria ever say that the woman who got killed was Kay Whitman? Who made the actual identification?"

"Trevor, at the morgue in Everett last Monday night. Honoria didn't go with him." The sheriff's expression indicated that the wheels were turning in his brain. "Dwight Gould was there. I'd ridden as far as Honoria's with him. He picked me up on his way back to town."

I recalled seeing Milo's Cherokee Chief parked on Front Street Monday night. I'd assumed he was in the office. Fleetingly, it occurred to me that we assume a great many things, some of which are not true. The thought lodged just long enough to disturb me for reasons that were elusive.

"So Honoria never saw the body," I noted. "But when you talked to her here, in Alpine, and later that evening, did she act as if it were Kay?"

"She did." Milo was now looking faintly distracted, as if he were trying to keep up with my comments while also sorting through something else. "Let's look at what we know," he said after a pause. "Honoria was entertaining her mother, brother, and—she said—sister-in-law for the better part of a week. I know that, because I called her last Friday night to ask if she'd like to go out for a drink. We hadn't seen each other for a month or so." Milo grimaced at the admission, though he'd already confided in me about the estrangement. Maybe he was still feeling the pain of parting.

"Anyway," the sheriff continued, extinguishing his cigarette and putting his arms behind his head, "Honoria said she had company from California. Her family, is the way she put it. But I pressed her on that—one of the things that always griped me about Honoria was that she was so damned private. That was when she said it was her mother, her brother, and his wife. I didn't talk to her again until she and Trevor showed up here Monday afternoon."

"Maybe the woman was Trevor's wife," I suggested.

"Maybe. But if he had remarried, why didn't it show up on the computer?"

"Because they got married somewhere other than California? You were the one who thought of that." Something else was niggling at me. This time I snatched the thought out of the air and brought it home. "Honoria didn't invite you to drive down to meet her relatives?"

"No." Milo wore a small, wry smile. "Right, I thought that was kind of odd at the time. On the other hand, we haven't been exactly cozy the last few months. But it crossed my mind that maybe she was ashamed of me. Now I wonder if she was ashamed of her family."

"Or afraid."

"Could be." Grimly Milo picked up the phone. "I'm going to call this Kay Whitman back. You shouldn't be here, but you are."

I wondered if our romp on the floor had changed Milo's attitude. It looked as if he'd finally have to yank off the kid gloves and challenge Honoria. I wasn't sure how men's minds worked, or if they worked at all when it came to the intricacies of male-female emotions, yet I sensed that Milo was somehow pushing Honoria and me around on his personal chessboard. If we hadn't traded places, we'd at least assumed different roles.

But no one except a machine answered at Kay Whitman's home. "She must have gone out," Milo said, sounding irked. "Or else she's tired of people calling her and asking if she's really dead. Damn."

The sheriff couldn't stall any longer. After searching through the piles of paper on his desk, he found what he was looking for: though he didn't say so out loud, I knew it was Trevor Whitman's number in Pacific Grove.

Again, there was no response, not even a recording. Milo looked both disappointed and relieved. "I don't have Mrs. Smith's number," he admitted. "I wonder if we could get it through Directory Assistance?"

"Smith?" I wasn't sure how many people lived in Pacific Grove, but I thought it was at least four times the size of Alpine. "You might try under Ida. The last husband's name was . . . drat, I forget. Vida would know, but she wasn't home when I tried to call her earlier."

"Nobody's home," Milo remarked gloomily. "So much for the idea that the whole world's sitting around on Saturday night, getting off on their computers."

Milo, however, wasn't giving up. He dialed the 408 area code and asked for Pacific Grove, then requested Smith, Ida. There was no listing. Identifying himself as the sheriff of Skykomish County, spelling S-K-Y-K-O-M-I-S-H twice, and adding in a tone of growing impatience that it was in Washington, Washington *State,* not D.C., he insisted that the operator read him the first names of all the Smiths in Pacific Grove. Milo repeated each one, glancing at me in the hope that one of the names or initials would trigger my memory. We were into the *C*'s when I remembered that Husband Number Four had been called Chad. There was no listing under that name, but there was a C. H. Smith. Milo wrote down the number and thanked the operator.

Ida Smith answered on the second ring. Milo put her on the speakerphone.

"Mrs. Smith," he said, after identifying himself, "we've had some disturbing news. Or maybe it's good news. It seems your daughter-in-law is alive. Kay Whitman called us tonight from Sacramento."

A hollow silence ensued. Milo waited. I held my breath.

Nervous laughter finally erupted at the other end. "I'm sorry, is this some kind of joke? Who is this?"

"I told you, it's Sheriff Dodge, in Alpine. When did you and your daughter get in from Grants Pass?" The question was intended to give Milo credibility, but I had the feeling he really cared.

"Around six." Mrs. Smith was hesitant. "We haven't quite unpacked. Oh, dear—what was that you said about . . . Kay?"

"A woman named Kay Whitman telephoned our office an hour ago," Milo reiterated, sounding calmer than he looked. "She insists she's your son's former wife. Can you explain that?"

There was another silence of sorts, though a muffling, shuffling noise echoed from the speakerphone. Milo and I exchanged frowns. It sounded as if Mrs. Smith had put her hand over the mouthpiece and was conferring with someone, possibly Honoria.

"No, I certainly can't," Mrs. Smith declared in an indignant tone. "There must be some mistake. Really, this is too much after all we've . . . ."

Dustin Fong poked his head in the door, wearing the apologetic air that I was beginning to find habitual. "Sir," he whispered, "we just got a call from that Whitman woman. She's at the Sacramento airport, waiting to board a Seattle flight. She'll be in Alpine tomorrow." The deputy withdrew and closed the door.

"Okay, Mrs. Smith," Milo said in mock defeat. "If you say so. We'll find out when the impostor gets into town. We understand she's on her way. Is Honoria around, by any chance?"

"No." The answer came too quickly.

"How about Trevor?"

"No. I'm alone." There was another pause. "That's why it's taking me so long to unpack." Again the nervous laugh vibrated through the speakerphone. "I'm not as young as I used to be, you know."

The sheriff rang off. "She's not a good liar, either. At least not when she's caught off guard."

I acknowledged the remark with a nod, but my mind was following a different track. "It's obvious now why the Whitmans didn't call Cassandra, the other sister— if it wasn't Kay who was killed, why would Cassandra care?"

Milo, however, didn't agree. "The victim was still a sister-in-law, or a live-in. She was being treated as family. Why else bring her along on this trip? Cassandra would want to know if the woman got killed."

"But they didn't tell her." I moved uneasily in the chair. The office smelled like stale smoke, scorched coffee, and gun oil. "Do you know Cassandra's last name?"

Regretfully, Milo shook his head. "Honoria never mentioned it, and I didn't think to ask. It didn't seem important."

"Maybe Mrs. Smith would tell you."

"I'm not calling her again. Not now. It looks as if I'm going to have to get Monterey County involved. How else can we ever identify the body?" The sheriff emitted a heavy sigh.

All kinds of crazy ideas were dancing through my brain. How obsessed was Mrs. Smith with appearances and the family image? Had she and Trevor picked up some hitchhiker and had her pose as the devoted wife of an ex-con? Or did Trevor meet somebody in an Oregon bar and bring her along for the ride? More likely, had he asked his current girlfriend to join Mom in visiting sis? That was the simplest explanation. But it didn't tell us why she'd gotten herself killed.

"Facts," Milo said, bringing me out of my reverie. "We've got to stick to facts. I wish we had some. We're plugged up until this Kay Whitman gets here. Then we'll have to wait until Monday to get any records out of Monterey County. Still, I can get their people going on missing persons. That'll help."

The sheriff got out of his chair and headed for the outer office. I joined him, watching as he gave orders to Dwight Gould to call Salinas, the county seat.

"I can contact the local papers Monday," I offered. "Mitch Harmon's murder should have been covered all over the area."

"Good," Milo responded, leaning an elbow on the counter. "That might be faster than having the court transcripts dug out."

"The towel," I said, from out of nowhere. "That's a *fact*. Have you any idea where it came from and how it got into Stella's washer?"

"The killer put it there," Milo answered reasonably. "It could have come from anywhere. Like your bathroom."

"Not *my* bathroom." I didn't want to go over the white vs. colored-towel issue again. "What are you going to do now?" The question came out in an uncertain voice, which surprised me. I thought I was sticking to business, but realized that pleasure was still lurking somewhere in the back of my mind.

Milo, however, didn't seem to notice that I sounded strange. "Wait to hear from Salinas. Call Sea-Tac and check to make sure Kay Whitman is actually on a flight from Sacramento. Take another look at alibis."

I regarded Milo with surprise. "Including Toby Popp's?"

"Maybe." The sheriff seemed disgruntled.

"And?" I prodded.

"Oh . . ." Milo grimaced. "Whatever comes to mind."

"You can't avoid it, you know." My glance bounced off Milo and fell on my shoes.

"What's that?"

"Honoria. You're going to have to talk to her tonight. And Trevor." I gave the sheriff a lame little smile.

Milo hitched up his belt. "I know." He uttered another big sigh. "You sticking around?"

I'd considered it, but I had plans of my own. "No. I've got to get hold of Vida, for one thing. It *is* her story."

"Okay." Milo turned to Dwight, who had just hung up the phone. "You talk to Salinas?"

I left the sheriff's office. As I'd said, I had plans of my own. Besides, Milo didn't seem to want dessert. Of any kind.

The bananas wouldn't keep. But I would.

To my relief, Vida was home. It was going on nine when I arrived, and she'd just gotten in the door. Buck was still ailing, so she'd had dinner with Amy, her husband, Ted—and Roger. The adorable little fellow had made a spaceship out of his ravioli. Unfortunately, he'd used his father's chair for a launching pad. Before Vida could fully launch herself on her grandson's antics, I interrupted with my latest bulletins. Kay Whitman's resurrection so startled my House & Home editor that she let out a loud squawk.

"Impossible! And she's coming *here*? Oh, good grief!" Vida all but staggered around her tidy living room before collapsing in her late husband's favorite chair. "This is incredible! Are you absolutely certain? Did you get this secondhand from Milo?"

"Now don't get mad," I said, seeing Vida's hackles rise as the shock wore off. "I tried to call but you weren't home. That's why I'm here now, to bring you up to speed, and to ask you to go with me to see Stella."

Vida glanced at her watch. "At nine o'clock? Well, maybe. This is all very peculiar. Honestly, Emma, I do wish you'd tried to phone me at Amy's."

I'd done that once, a year or so ago, and had gotten Roger, who'd used every orifice of his wretched little body to make disgusting noises in my ear. Nor had he let me speak with his grandmother, who, he insisted, was dead. I didn't bother to defend myself further with Vida.

Stella and Richie Magruder lived in a big old house on First Hill, across from the high school. It was a comfortable place, set among second-stand Douglas firs, a home that had raised children, and reflected Stella's down-to-earth personality.

Stella, however, greeted Vida and me as if we'd come from Mars. "What's wrong now?" she demanded, ushering us into the long hallway with its lily-patterned wallpaper.

"Nothing," Vida soothed. "That is, nothing that should distress you. Oh—do I smell pecan pie?"

"No. It's nail-polish remover." Stella wasn't taken in by Vida's comment. "Come on into the living room anyway. Richie's out playing poker with the boys, so I was experimenting with a new line of polish. It's expensive and the colors are too glitzy. I'm going to pass. How about a drink?" She flashed a hand that had three gaudily painted nails, all in different shades.

Judging from the empty highball glass on the end table, Stella'd already had a drink. Or two. Yet the salon owner was clear-eyed, and crisp of speech. Somehow, Vida and I ended up with apple juice.

"If you've come to commiserate about Becca's stupid stunt, don't bother," Stella said, sitting back down on the couch. "If she's serious about getting back together with this Eric creep, she'll probably quit before I can fire her. It looks like Becca is the type who learns the hard way."

Don't we all, I thought. But Stella was right. It was pointless to harp on Becca's apparent lack of judgment. The hour was late, and there were other, more pressing matters at hand. Since Milo hadn't sworn me to secrecy, I told Stella about the woman who said she was the real Kay Whitman. Stella's reaction wasn't as marked as Vida's.

"So who got whacked in my salon?" Stella inquired with a vexed expression.

"That's what we want to know," Vida put in. "When the woman came in, did she give her name?"

Stella ran a hand through her gilded locks. "God, I'm not sure. Why does Monday seem like six months ago? I suppose she said, 'I'm Ms. Whitman, I've got a facial appointment.' That's the usual drill."

"What did she look like?" The question was mine, and I felt foolish. I'd seen her, but recalled only a body, smeared with green cream, bloodied and yet bloodless.

Stella tipped her head to one side. "Average height, decent figure, early forties, light brown hair with red highlights, probably not natural, slacks and sweater under a barn jacket. Kind of plain, but she wasn't wearing makeup. Almost nobody does, when they come for a facial. I doubt I'd recognize her if I ever saw her again. Not that I will, of course."

"She wasn't remarkable." Vida frowned into her apple juice. "Not a femme fatale."

"God, no." Stella laughed in a strained manner. "If she gained thirty pounds, she could have fit right into Alpine."

Vida had assumed a pensive air. "Stella, you're very aware of people. Earlier on, it occurred to me that a woman—such as Honoria—wouldn't make a facial appointment unless she really wanted one. But I've been thinking, and now I realize that she might do such a thing if she had another reason for coming to the salon. Can you think why Honoria would have wanted to do that?"

"I don't know Honoria," Stella said, picking up her highball glass, which she'd refilled with what looked like a screwdriver. "Do you mean she needed an excuse to talk to Becca?"

Vida nodded, in an uncharacteristically vague manner. "Or to you or Laurie. But she wouldn't want to have her hair cut. Honoria has it done in Sultan, always the same style, very becoming. Women don't switch hairdressers for fanciful reasons. That's why I'm wondering if she didn't have an ulterior motive for scheduling a facial. It wouldn't alter her appearance, and she'd achieve her underlying goal."

This was the first I'd heard of Vida's idea. It made a certain amount of sense. Stella, however, was shaking her head.

"I can't think why Honoria Whitman would want to talk to me—or Laurie or Becca. The point is, she didn't come at all. Kay—or whoever she was—came instead."

"Exactly." Vida was looking slightly smug. "Let's conjecture that Honoria planned to come to Alpine alone. She made the Monday appointment on Saturday. Perhaps she thought her relatives would be gone after the weekend. Or perhaps she wanted to escape from them for a few hours. Houseguests can be trying, and Honoria is used to being alone. But on Monday, the company is still there. Trevor and this unknown woman insist on joining Honoria. Maybe the so-called sister-in-law announces she wants to come to the salon, too. Honoria's meeting plans are upset. She doesn't want to waste the opportunity, so she gives up the appointment, figuring she can do it later, after her guests are gone. But whatever Honoria had in mind, she didn't want her relatives to know about it. Especially, I would guess, not the alleged sister-in-law."

Stella was smiling. "That's very complicated, Vida. But I don't know what you're talking about. Becca and Laurie don't know Honoria, either."

Vida said no more. We seemed to have come up against a brick wall. "Did you ever figure out where the towel came from?" I asked Stella, deciding to get back to basics.

Stella couldn't begin to guess. Vida and I drank our apple juice, then left our hostess to finish removing her nail polish.

"Rats," Vida muttered as we walked back to my car. "I was hoping Stella would remember something—any-thing—that might indicate the victim didn't actually claim to be Kay Whitman."

"No, you didn't," I countered. "You wanted to see if she knew of any connection between Honoria and Laurie. Such as Toby Popp."

"There is one, of course." Vida's profile was set. "It may go back to Honoria's youth, or only six months ago. But it exists."

The moon was now overhead, a white, bright wedge in the jet-black sky. I could still see the stars, dazzling in number, and beckoning as if they were within touching distance of Tonga Ridge.

"Let's pack it in," I suggested, hearing the tired note in my voice. "We'll know more tomorrow when the real Kay Whitman gets here."

"I wonder why she's coming?" Vida ducked low to get into the Jag.

"Wouldn't you?" Fastening my seat belt, I turned the ignition key. "If I'd been reported as having my throat slit in Alliance, Nebraska, or Appleton, Wisconsin, I think I'd be curious enough to go to the source. For one thing, I'd be scared."

"Y-e-s." Vida drew the word out as she removed her glasses and rubbed her eyes. "Oooooh! This is all such a mess! I wonder how Milo is doing with his alibis?"

"I'm not going to think about it anymore tonight," I declared, heading past the high school, which stood dark and mute on its hill above Spruce Street. "I'm going to concentrate on seeing Adam and Ben in Arizona."

Putting her glasses back on, Vida sighed. "Arizona! All that sun and dryness! I've never been there."

"They have some kind of winter in the northern part where Ben is," I said. "I think."

"I should hope so." Vida was looking out the window as we headed down Seventh toward her house. "What are you going to do?"

"About what?" Puzzled, I glanced at Vida before I turned left onto Tyee.

"Tommy. Are you really going to abandon him?"

"Vida." My sigh turned into a groan. I couldn't understand why my usually sensible House & Home editor seemed determined to keep me tied to Tom Cavanaugh. Sometimes I wondered if she'd had an early love who'd gotten away. Maybe Vida had secret regrets. "I can't abandon what I never had. Twenty-three years ago, Tom abandoned *me*. This isn't revenge, it's common sense, the kind you admire so much. Tom's got grown kids, plenty of friends, business associates, and most of all, a wife. He doesn't need me." I'd pulled into Vida's driveway. "Not really."

"I see." Vida was staring straight ahead. "Yes. I suppose I do. You're quite serious. Well now." She picked up her purse and held on to her green toque. "The important thing, I think, isn't what you're running away *from*. It's what you're running *to*. Good night, Emma."

The porch light was on. I could see Vida walk up the stairs and across the porch. She bent down to unlock the door, then stepped inside. The light went off.

I was left with the moon and the stars and a strange sense of liberation.

I'd felt that way Monday; it didn't last.

Maybe this time would be different.

Chapter Seventeen

ARMED WITH A sugar doughnut and a paper cup of coffee, I cornered Father Den after Sunday Mass. Maneuvering him to one end of the school hall where St. Mildred's Altar Guild hosted its weekly postliturgical social hour, I unloaded about Ed Bronsky. Tact and subterfuge were unnecessary. In the past two years I'd become friendly with our pastor, not only through the usual parish channels, but because Dennis Kelly and my brother had grown close. Den and Ben shared more than a religious vocation: they were near in age, they enjoyed sports, they had some favorite authors in common, and they both had a sense of humor. I could be candid with Father Den.

He, in turn, allowed that there were opportunities galore for Ed. "We'll talk him into being St. Mildred's angel," Den said with his infectious grin. "An angel, as in Broadway show angels. He's got the time and money to back this parish. Let's see if he's willing to put both of them where his mouth is."

Hatching what I hoped would be a small coup buoyed me through the first half of the day. But after I'd read the Sunday paper, written a couple of letters, and given up on a best-seller somebody had recommended, I began to feel edgy. Vida was entertaining her daughter and family from Bellingham. Leo was probably with Delphine

Corson. And Milo was either working or had gone fishing. Of course it wasn't ideal weather for a masochistic steelheader: the sky was almost clear, the temperature had risen into the high forties, and there wasn't much wind. With the misery quotient so low, Milo might have decided that an outing wasn't worth it. At best, steelhead were elusive. Some fishermen waited ten years before landing the first one. They spent the next five years talking about it, which would be about the same amount of time that would pass before they caught another fish. In the world of sportsmen, they were a strange breed, as exotic as their prey, but more numerous.

Since it was almost three, Milo should have gotten back. The sheriff liked to hit his favorite holes at first light. I tried the office first.

Jack Mullins answered. "Dodge went into Seattle," he said. "That Whitman woman called this morning to say she was staying with friends. The sheriff didn't want to wait until tomorrow, and he figured he could save her a trip up here."

I was disappointed. Meeting the real Kay Whitman— if indeed that was who she was—had intrigued me. "Have Milo call me when he gets back." I thanked Jack and hung up.

Ten minutes later I was in my car. Maybe I'd drive down to see Paula Rubens. Waiting at the railroad crossing for the Burlington Northern to pass, I wondered if I should call her first. I wasn't keen on drop-in company, though in a small, informal town like Alpine, it was hard to avoid. I could phone her from Skykomish.

I watched the freight cars rumble by. Many were ghosts from the past—the Great Northern, the Northern Pacific, Union Pacific, Southern Pacific, Ashley, Drew & Northern, Milwaukee Road, Rio Grande, City of Prineville

Railway, and of course the more contemporary green of Burlington Northern. Like most Americans of a certain age, I am fascinated by trains. At night, when I'm going to sleep, I can hear the whistle in the darkness, and the slowing of the locomotives as they start the steep ascent through the eight-mile Cascade Tunnel. I am comforted, though whether it is because I could jump aboard and be somewhere else in a few short hours, or because the railroad evokes so much of this country's history, I don't know. Nor do I care. The siren call of the whistle can lead us into the unknown, without a preordained destination. Trains connect us with more than just place names. Maybe, as I sat waiting in the Jag, I was driving off into some great void, hoping that the excursion would open my mind to a killer's identity.

The boxcars rattled and clattered along the tracks as the warning signal flashed and clanged. Four cars were empty, a waste I always wondered about while watching trains pass. Maybe they'd been unloaded at an earlier stop; but why not send them off to a sideline? Or maybe they were going to take on freight somewhere farther along the route. My idle musings made the time pass faster. Maybe ... a fragmentary thought flitted through my brain and was lost.

The caboose, or crummy, as it's locally known, disappeared past Alpine's tiny smoke-smudged brick station. A moment later I crossed the tracks, then the river, and headed for the highway.

Sunday cross-state traffic was fairly heavy, especially with returning skiers. I decided not to turn off the road at Skykomish or Index, but to wait until I got to Gold Bar Gas. That way, if Paula wasn't home, I'd be close enough to Monroe to head for the strip malls and do some shopping. Travel items were on my mental list, mostly toiletries and panty hose. I didn't want to waste the trip.

It was exactly four o'clock when I pulled into the service station to use the phone. Paula answered on the third ring. She sounded surprised to hear from me.

"Emma! I figured you'd forget I existed! What's up? Do you want to grill me again?"

"Not really. Although," I added, "I've got some interesting news about the victim. I stopped here in Gold Bar for gas and I thought if you weren't busy, I'd . . . ah . . . drop in for a couple of minutes."

The pause at the other end unsettled me. "Oh, damn all, Emma!" Paula finally exclaimed. "It sounds great, but I'm in the middle of something. You ever work with glass?"

I said I hadn't, not in the way she meant, anyway. Paula mentioned temperatures and textures and other things I didn't understand. "How about Tuesday night? You could come for dinner."

Trying not to feel another surge of disappointment, I told Paula I'd rather do dinner on Wednesday, since Tuesday was our deadline. That didn't work for Paula; we compromised on Thursday. Like a sulky child, I withheld my information about Kay Whitman. If Paula wouldn't see me now, she could wait to read about it in *The Advocate*.

Back inside the Jag, I pulled out onto Highway 2. Suddenly driving the sixteen additional miles to Monroe didn't seem very appealing. There wasn't anything in the stores there that I couldn't buy at Parker's Pharmacy in Alpine. At the next turnoff, I'd reverse my tracks and head back home.

Ironically, the next turnoff was Honoria's drive. Going off the highway, I geared down and let the car creep among the trees. The vine maples' bare branches formed an arch over the narrow, rutted road. As the sun started to set somewhere out over Puget Sound, clouds moved in. No doubt there was rain coming, maybe even snow at the higher elevations.

Honoria's house wore a curious, lifeless look. I stopped where the drive broadened into a wider paved track that led to her empty carport. But the carport shouldn't be empty. Trevor and Mrs. Smith and the ersatz Kay had arrived by car; Honoria had her specially rigged model; Trevor had flown back to Pacific Grove with the body. Honoria had told Vida and me that she and her mother were going to drive Trevor's van. Not wanting to make the long return trip without her own car, Honoria would fly home.

That was it. Honoria must have left her car at the Sea-Tac airport. I nodded in agreement with my rationale.

But I was still uneasy. Getting out of the Jag, I walked up the path to Honoria's porch. Everything was as I remembered it, with the covered summer furniture and barbecue, and the storm door installed in place of the summer screen. Everything, that is, except Dodger. On other occasions, he'd been there to greet me, a surly presence who seemed to resent my intrusion. I missed him anyway.

The melancholy I'd sensed upon first seeing the house now returned as I tried to peer through the front windows. Honoria had pulled the drapes, obscuring all but a sliver of view. I left the porch and went around to the back. There, I could see through a small window that looked into the kitchen.

It was tidy. Too tidy, I decided. I jiggled the window sash. Nothing happened, except that I broke a fingernail. It looked as if the window was an original, unlike the large sheets of glass that Honoria had installed at the front of the house. Pressing my face against one of the four rectangular panes, I saw a simple hook and eye. The window should swing inwards. I gave the sash a hard shove.

The bottom pane cracked. Feeling guilty, I bit my lower lip. But instead of cutting my losses and going away to mind my own business, I tapped the broken glass. It fell onto the kitchen floor.

News *was* my business, I argued, feeling the need to placate my conscience. Maybe I could find the family photos Vida wanted to run in the next edition. Cautiously, I reached inside and lifted the hook. The window swung open. With the aid of a chopping block I found near the woodpile, I hoisted myself through the opening.

The kitchen hadn't been stripped, but several important items were missing: the microwave, the toaster, the coffeemaker, the breadmaker, the Cuisinart, and the finely glazed set of blue dishes Honoria had made.

In the living room, the furniture was in place, but all signs of personal effects were gone, including the art that Honoria had collected over the years. The same was true of both bedrooms. As for the bath, it was bare. The only reminder of Honoria was the alterations she'd made to accommodate her wheelchair—the widened hallway, the bathtub with its steel bars, the counters that were lowered to suit her sedentary lifestyle.

Back in the living room, it was growing dark. I switched on a light, but nothing happened. Apparently, Honoria had had the power turned off. No wonder her car was gone. So was she, and it looked as if there were no plans for a return trip to Startup.

There was no telephone either. That struck me as strange, until I realized that in this day and age of independent communications, many people owned their own phones. I smiled ruefully as I pulled out a desk drawer.

Honoria hadn't bothered to take her old bills or

correspondence. If this were a movie, I'd find a clue among the discards. But this was real life, and in the gathering gloom, I couldn't read anything smaller than eighteen-point type.

Under the bills and letters and gallery announcements, I felt something cold and hard. It didn't take a magnifying glass to see that it was a gun. Being fairly ignorant when it comes to firearms, I thought that maybe it was an automatic. At least it looked more like it would belong to a gangster than a cowboy.

I reminded myself this wasn't the movies. Honoria couldn't be blamed for owning a gun. She lived alone and was confined to a wheelchair. So why hadn't she taken the weapon with her? Was it because the gun wasn't hers?

I realized as I closed the drawer that Milo had been right all along. *Honoria wasn't coming back.* The sheriff knew his erstwhile lover better than I did. But none of us had known her very well. For Honoria, who had always seemed steeped in integrity if not in candor, told lies. What were lies and what were not? The woman who had been murdered at Stella's Styling Salon wasn't Kay Whitman. The real Kay Whitman was alive and divorced from Trevor. Honoria had loved her late husband. He may or may not have crippled her, depending upon which story could be believed. Honoria had said she was coming back to Startup, but it was obvious now that her intentions were quite different.

The previous evening in Milo's office, I'd wondered about Honoria's lies. I thought they might be motivated by shame—her mother had married often and badly; Trevor had taken to wife a woman who had proved disloyal; Honoria had made a poor choice, unless I believed what she'd told Paula. If I accepted that Honoria loved Mitch Harmon, the marriage had still come to a tragic end.

But if Honoria lied for other reasons, could she be covering up for someone else? It had occurred to me that she had lied to deceive, but all lies are a deception. Was it possible that Honoria was deceiving herself?

I pictured Honoria as I had last seen her in this very living room. She'd been edgy, fretful, and lacking her usual composure. She'd sat there in her billowy pajama outfit, fidgeting with the serape, keeping a wary eye on her mother and brother. She hated being dependent, she missed her wheelchair, she was uncomfortable, she was ... *afraid.* Fear wasn't part of Honoria's usual makeup. Courage was the trait I most associated with her. But last Wednesday, Honoria had been frightened.

Stick to the facts, Milo always said. *Don't go off on a tangent.* All along, we knew that Honoria had made a facial appointment and that she had given it up to her so-called sister-in-law. Only the Whitman ménage was aware of the change until "Kay" showed up at the salon. Ten to fifteen minutes later the woman was dead. The facts had been obvious from the start. All of us, including Milo, had ignored them. In a way, I couldn't blame the sheriff. Like Vida with Roger, Milo had a blind spot.

I stood by the buffet, which had been stripped of its artifacts and personal mementos. There were no family photos here, though I wondered why Honoria had bothered to take them. Her family had only brought her grief. A rustling noise startled me, but it was the Alpine Medical Supply shopping bag, dangling from a filigree knob. It swayed in the wake of my movements, and my brain began to spin. *Facts.* Verifiable information, dates, names, official records, tangible items—like that empty shopping bag. I wasn't sure why the woman at the salon had to die, but at last I knew who killed her.

I was eager to get out of Honoria's house, which suddenly seemed not only melancholy, but sinister. I used the back door to make my exit, turning the old-fashioned lock, but unable to do anything about the dead bolt. Across the herb garden, about twenty yards from the woodshed, Honoria's small studio sat among the cottonwoods. I had never been inside, but the front was built almost entirely of glass. There was also a skylight. A breeze stirred the trees as I followed the paved path up to the level entrance. Suddenly feeling cold, I pulled the hood of my duffel coat over my head.

Unfortunately, what little sun was left reflected off the long windows. It was all but impossible to see much inside. Or maybe there wasn't much to see. If Honoria had stripped the house, she'd probably removed everything of value from the studio, too.

"You're early." The voice floated out from behind me. "That's a change. You used to always be late."

Startled, I turned around. The sinking sun was now directly in my eyes, making it hard for me to see much more than the figure of a man on the path. He moved closer, then stopped and let out a strange little cry.

"You're not Kay!"

I recognized the voice before I could actually see the face. It was Trevor Whitman. Taking a deep breath, I moved quickly down the path.

"I was just leaving," I said, not breaking stride. As I started to pass him a swift glance showed me that he was as startled as I was.

Trevor grabbed my coat before I could break into a run. "Hold it!" he cried. "What are you doing here?"

I was beginning to tremble, now more from fear than from cold. We stood on the path, so close that my coat and his jacket touched. Forcing my brain to work, I took my cue from the first words out of his mouth:

"I'm meeting Kay." My voice sounded thin. "She called from Seattle."

"That's bull!" Trevor snatched at my arms, twisting them and turning me away from him. "She doesn't know you!"

"She called Alpine last night." It wasn't a lie, though I didn't know why I cared. Honesty didn't seem very important at the moment. "Where were you when I pulled in?" The question might seem irrelevant, but time was my only ally. Kay Whitman must be on her way.

"I went into Sultan for a drink. Your damned Jag is blocking my way." Trevor gave me a sharp little shake. "I thought it belonged to . . . someone else."

Vaguely, I recalled that Vida and I had driven to Honoria's in the Buick. Of course Trevor wouldn't recognize my car.

"Look," I said, trying to sound casual, and sure that I failed, "why don't I move the Jag? Otherwise, Kay will have to park almost on the highway." It was an exaggeration, but I couldn't think of anything more plausible.

"Let her," Trevor snapped. A sideways glimpse showed that his puffy, pale face was downright ugly. And terrifying. "We're going inside."

Trevor had a key that he made me use. The ramp to the back door was a few feet away from the broken window. Apparently, he didn't notice the shards of glass. Now he had wrapped one arm around my neck while the other gripped my waist. It took me a while to unlock the door. Even under the best of circumstances, I have problems with keys.

It was now almost completely dark in the house. Trevor propelled me into the living room, where we stood by the small opening in the drapes.

"She's always late. It's five. I know it's five. She should be here by now." Trevor's manner was growing agitated.

I thought of the gun in the desk drawer. If I could get

free for even a moment, maybe I could reach the gun. Was it loaded? Did it matter?

Even as I cast about for a way to break Trevor's hold, he hauled me over to the desk. When he opened the drawer, I realized that the gun was his. It must have been the service automatic he had used to kill Mitch Harmon.

"You're excess baggage," he said, taking out the gun. With his free hand, he spun me around. I stumbled and fell against the wicker chair. When I righted myself, I saw that Trevor held the gun in both hands, pointed straight at my head. "You got no business being here, fouling up my plans."

"Yes, I do," I said, sounding surprisingly firm. If I had figured out Trevor and Honoria and the rest of the Whitmans in the last few minutes, I knew there might be a way to divert my captor. "Family," I intoned, taking a deep breath. "You've got family. Lots of people don't have any close ties these days. Think of the example you're setting."

"What the hell are you jabbering about?" He gestured with the gun. "Move away from that chair, closer to the window so I can see out."

I obeyed. "I'm talking about loyalty. You've demonstrated that all your life. When your mother kept marrying and remarrying, you and Honoria formed an unusually close bond. You felt responsible for each other. You'd have died for each other. You would kill for each other. And you did. Twice."

"The so-called law doesn't see it that way," Trevor retorted, glancing through the drapes. "Damn! I wish the power wasn't turned off! It's getting pitch-black out there!"

"You're right, the law doesn't always take strong feelings into account." I was forcing myself to remain calm, which seemed to be working on an external level.

Internally, I felt hollow and vague and disjointed. My voice seemed to be coming from somewhere else in the room, as if I were a ventriloquist. "That's why you need somebody like me. As part of the media, I can tell your story so that people will understand what real family bonds are all about."

Until that moment I don't think Trevor had considered me as anything but an obstacle. It was too dark now to see his eyes, but I guessed that something new flickered in them, a self-serving spark that I needed to fan. As long as that little flame was kept alive, I might live, too.

"Newspapers and TV don't tell the real story," Trevor declared. "They hide stuff, the stuff that doesn't fit their cut-and-dried ideas of justice."

"That's right," I agreed. "Sometimes it's because they're lazy, sometimes it's because of legal . . ."

Again he gestured with the gun. "There's a candle on the mantel. Matches, too. Light the thing, will you?"

Honoria had owned a great many candles, most of them handmade. Only one remained on the mantel, a thick, round factory product that had been burned halfway. My hands were shaking so hard that I had to strike three matches before the wick caught.

"What really happened when Mitch Harmon got killed?" I asked, obediently returning to my place between the wicker chair and the window. "If Mitch wasn't an abusive man, why did he have to die?"

The candle was casting eerie shadows across the living room. Trevor's features became exaggerated, almost grotesque. "I warned him, over and over. He didn't own Honoria. She might be his wife, but she was still my sister. What made him such a big shot that he wouldn't let me drop in whenever I was in the neighborhood? Why couldn't I ask for Honoria's help when I had problems?

Why," Trevor demanded, his voice rising, "did Mitch Harmon have to get between us?"

"What did he do—try to throw you out?" The question crawled from my throat so low and raspy that it sounded like a handful of gravel.

Trevor nodded vigorously. "You bet he did! He even said he'd call the cops! Like hell, I told him! He came at me, right there at the top of the stairs to their fancy condo! He was going to pitch my ass into the street! God! I couldn't let him do that! Honoria was trying to explain how things were, but she sounded all upset and weird. I had my gun"—Trevor gripped the automatic even tighter, the skin on his knuckles now taut—"so I shot him."

Trevor lowered the weapon a scant half inch. "That was when Honoria fell down the stairs. That damned Harmon crashed into her. Jesus, I couldn't believe it!"

Envisioning the scene, I felt dizzy. Honoria must have tried to reason with Trevor, which would have sounded "upset and weird" to her irrational brother. Maybe she, too, had asked him to leave. When Trevor took aim at Mitch, Honoria might have tried to dive between the two men. Whatever had happened, the bullet had torn into Harmon, toppling him onto his wife, who had fallen down the stairs and ended up paralyzed for life.

I couldn't speak. I didn't need to. Trevor was like a bottle of carbonated soda that had been shaken and kept under pressure until it finally exploded. Maybe the years in prison had taught him to keep his counsel; maybe his only confidante was Honoria; maybe he needed to babble and blurt and defend himself.

"But Honoria realized I only meant to help her. She didn't want to see me go to jail. Oh, after she got out of the hospital, she talked to me about getting evaluated and all that shit to see if my mind wasn't unhinged from being in 'Nam. That was a crock. I *liked* serving my hitch in 'Nam. Except for being away from Honoria, it was the best part of my life. Mom thought Honoria's advice sucked, too. Nobody in our family had ever been crazy. Between us, we got Honoria to say that I was defending her, which was the truth. I didn't see how she put up with that Harmon guy. He wanted to cut her off from her family, like locking her up in a tower someplace. Better for me to be a prisoner, than her."

Except, of course, that Honoria had become a prisoner, not just of her body, but of the lies she'd told to protect her brother. She'd loved Trevor, but she'd loved her husband, too. The loathing for Mitch Harmon was feigned, a disservice to his memory in an unworthy cause. Honoria had taken back her maiden name, perhaps for professional purposes, perhaps to appease her family. No wonder she had fled California. The memories and the lies must have haunted her.

My dizziness had passed, but I felt weak. "So why did Kay leave you?"

"She was going to after the first year." Trevor opened the drapes another inch. "But Mom and Honoria talked her into giving it another try. Then, after I had to kill Harmon and went to jail for doing my good deed, Kay walked. Mom refused to believe it. She always thought that when I got out, Kay would come back. But she didn't."

"So who was the woman at the salon?" Slowly, I edged backward, moving toward the mantel. To what purpose, I wasn't sure. But I couldn't keep standing unsupported in one place any longer. Every nerve in my body felt as if it were about to snap. "Was she your wife?"

"Hell, no. She was Faye Harmon Peake, Mitch's sister. She'd always kind of liked me, before I married Kay and before I blew her brother away. Faye married someone else, got divorced, and then showed up last summer after I got out of the slammer. We dated each other for a few weeks, and then she moved in with me. When Mom and I mentioned our trip to see Honoria, she insisted on coming along. I wasn't for it—Faye was getting on my nerves. Mom said if she came, we'd have to pretend we were married. Mom's funny about stuff like that. She wants people to think everything's proper and classy. Faye said, Why not? She thought it was a gas. Then she got the idea to call herself Kay instead of Faye. The names rhyme, see? Mom thought that was great. Who'd know the difference in a backwoods place like this?"

"What did Honoria think?" I'd actually gotten past the wicker chair.

Trevor made a face. "Sometimes Honoria didn't have much of a sense of humor. But she decided she might as well go along with the gag. Then it turned out to be no laughing matter."

"That was when Kay—Faye—started blackmailing Honoria, right? What was it—greed, or revenge?" I saw the guess go home, though Trevor took it more calmly than I'd expected.

"Faye was kind of a weird person. Right after she moved in with me, she started in on Mom. Faye said she'd tell everybody that I was some maniac who went around beating up women and killing people just for the fun of it. Hell, I got paid to kill people in 'Nam. And Mitch Harmon didn't count—he was ruining our family. Anyway, I guess Mom got all upset, but I didn't know about it at the time. Except for what's left of Chad's insurance and her Social Security, Mom's tapped. I think Mom wanted Faye to come with us on the trip so she could keep an eye on her. Mom didn't trust Faye. Can you blame her?"

The question was asked in all innocence. Nobody ever

blamed Mom—not out loud. Mom never blamed herself. And her son wouldn't take the blame for anything, including murder. But Mrs. Smith—and Honoria— couldn't bear to have the truth come out. They were meaty pickings for a blackmailer.

"Of course," Trevor went on in his self-righteous, faintly portentous manner, "Faye never hit me up for hush money—I was her meal ticket. But she saw Honoria with all that artsy-craftsy stuff, and she knew my sis had some bucks. Then Faye found out that Honoria had a really rich guy chasing her. A billionaire, for chrissakes! Honoria paid the first installment, just to get Faye out of her hair, but there would have been more—and more, until she was drained. The next thing I know, Honoria's marrying that billionaire bastard, just to pay off Faye. I couldn't let that happen, not after everything Honoria's done for me."

I recalled the twenty-five-hundred-dollar withdrawal and the money order taken from Honoria's account. No doubt it had been a token payment as far as Faye Harmon Peake was concerned.

"You couldn't let Faye live with what she knew," I said, feeling the hearth tiles beneath my feet. "Not in the long run. I don't know how Honoria feels about Toby Popp, but I imagine your mother would love to see them marry. If Faye talked to the press, Toby would run like a scared rabbit. She would have been believed, because she was Mitch's sister. I gather that Faye realized what really happened."

Trevor's features twisted into anger. "How do you mean? I told you what really happened!"

He had, for a fact. It wouldn't do to point out that his account was skewed. Faye might have been conniving and greedy, but that didn't mean her vision was cloudy. She must have known that Honoria and Mitch were a loving couple whose lives had been shattered by an obsessed, mentally deranged brother. How ironic, I thought as my hand drifted to the mantelpiece, that Honoria and Trevor could be siblings and yet so different; how fitting that Faye and Mitch should also find themselves at opposite ends of the moral scale. Not much had changed since Cain and Abel.

"Hey!" Trevor shouted. "Get away from that fireplace! What are you trying to pull?"

"Nothing," I said in a tired voice. "I have to lean on something. Tell me how you'd like to have this written. We publish on Wednesday, so there isn't much time."

The practicality of the matter seemed to goad Trevor. He turned away from the window and squinted down the automatic's sight line. "Time? You're the one without any time! I can't let you—"

At the sound of breaking glass, I hurled the candle and dropped to the floor. The living room was plunged into darkness. Trevor swore, but his voice was lost in the shouted command of Milo Dodge.

"Hold it!" The glare of a flashlight captured Trevor's uncertain form. "You're covered! Put down your weapon and place your hands behind your head! Now!"

"Fuck you!" Trevor screamed. "I'm taking her with me!"

In the split second of silence, I could hear Milo warring with himself. The crazed man with the automatic pointed at my prone form was Trevor Whitman, the brother of the woman Milo had loved for the past three years. If the sheriff shot Trevor, the rift would never be mended. None of this was worked out logically in my brain, because I was absolutely terrified. But somehow I knew it, at some gut level, where my life hung in the balance between Milo's heart and his head.

His head won. He fired the King Cobra magnum twice. Trevor died within six inches of my staring eyes.

It was only after Milo had taken me in his arms that I sensed I'd been wrong.

Maybe Milo's heart had won after all.

Chapter Eighteen

KAY WHITMAN WANTED to see a doctor. She needed Valium or Lorazepam or some kind of pill that would calm her down. She insisted that she was still in shock from having to identify her ex-husband's body. Never mind that the bastard had deserved getting killed; her nerves were still a mess.

So were mine. But while Bill Blatt escorted Kay Whitman to Alpine Hospital's emergency room, I settled for some of Milo's restorative brandy. Almost two hours had passed since Trevor Whitman had died on the floor of his sister's house in Startup. Driving my Jag from Startup had forced me to keep the trauma at bay. Kay, whom I had met out on the shoulder of Highway 2 just as the snow began to fall, had ridden with me. Milo had stayed behind until Jack Mullins and an ambulance arrived.

On the way back to Alpine, Kay explained why she'd come north on such short notice. "After I called the sheriff, I phoned Trevor in Pacific Grove. I figured he had something to do with this mix-up. Frankly, Trevor was bad to the bone. I didn't know it when I married him, of course, but it didn't take long to discover he was a very violent person."

Kay—the real, living, breathing Kay Whitman—was about my age, my height, and my coloring. Up close, her features were more refined than mine, but I could see that at a distance, Trevor might mistake one of us for the other.

"Anyway, Trevor tried to laugh it all off," Kay had continued. "He asked me to meet him in Pacific Grove so he could explain. He scared me silly, so I told him no—I was flying to Seattle and then driving to Alpine. I knew what a liar he was, and I had to see what had happened for myself. That was when he suggested meeting me at Honoria's. It seemed that he was coming back up here this morning."

"That wasn't his original plan, though," I put in, grateful to be alive and doing something safe and ordinary, such as driving up the Stevens Pass highway at night without chains in what was turning into a blizzard. "He made that up on the spot because he wanted to—"

"Kill me." Kay had finished the sentence, adding a grim little laugh. "I'm sure his revised plan was to get me out of the way, and then fly back to Pacific Grove. Sheriff Dodge said the services are set for tomorrow."

I had nodded, thinking that now there would be two services. Honoria and Mrs. Smith would have to face the task of burying Trevor. Maybe, I hoped, they could bury the past with him.

"I absolutely refused to meet Trevor," Kay had continued, "so I stalled by staying with friends in Seattle. I called the sheriff's office from there to tell them about Trevor coming back to the area, and the next thing I knew, Dodge showed up at my friends' house. When I told him about Trevor's little plot, he decided we should head back to Alpine right away. He wanted to take me into town first, but when we reached that turnoff to Honoria's, he stopped to see if Trevor had shown up yet. As soon as he saw Trevor's van, he backed up and parked across the drive, by the highway. He told me to get down on the floor and not move. I didn't argue. I get the impression that you don't mess with Dodge when he's chasing down a murderer."

I'd agreed, wondering what Kay would have thought if she'd seen the fear in Milo's eyes. He'd held me for what seemed like hours, but was probably only a few seconds. "Emma, Emma, Emma," he said over and over. Then he'd let me go, and made sure that Trevor was dead. After that, the sheriff was all business.

"It was a wild stunt," Kay had said, referring to the victim's false identity. "I don't get it."

"Motive," I'd replied. "There was no motive to kill you—not then, I mean—if you had stood by Trevor while he was in prison and resumed your supposedly happy married life after he got out. But Faye was a black-mailer. Once it was discovered that the dead woman wasn't you, then it was just a matter of time before her background and intentions were unearthed. Trevor—and his mother and sister—were willing to take the chance that you'd never hear of your own demise. Honoria and Mrs. Smith couldn't face Trevor being put on trial again for murder. This time he wouldn't have got off so lightly. There are no excuses for a man who slits the throat of a helpless woman. As ever, Honoria shielded him. Faye was to be cremated so that no one else could see the body. Once the services were over, the Whitmans could put the whole sorry mess behind them. They never reckoned with your derailing their deception."

Kay had nodded, a solemn, ironic gesture. "I wouldn't have found out if I didn't have a friend who likes to play with his computer, even on weekends. He works for the state police, and was looking up homicides with Washington–California connections. My name popped up, with a Pacific Grove address. He knew I'd lived there, but he also knew I was in Sacramento when the murder occurred. So he called me." This time Kay's laugh had been softer.

Though Kay insisted she was still in shock, I'd found her remarkably lucid during our journey back to Alpine. Maybe the shock was delayed, triggered by the contrast between the swirling snow and the stark lights of the sheriff's office. It didn't matter if Kay had asked for a jug of lab alcohol to calm her nerves. She deserved to ease the pain that Trevor had caused her, not only on this terrifying Sunday, but during the brief years of their unhappy marriage.

For it was Trevor, not Mitch, who was abusive. He had beaten Kay, as well as anyone else who thwarted his wishes. Milo had managed to get Trevor's criminal record out of California. The dead man had a history of assault, though he hadn't served time until his conviction for killing Mitch Harmon. When Milo had recounted Honoria's litany of her husband's alleged misdeeds, she was undoubtedly talking about her brother.

The sheriff hadn't yet returned to his inner office, where I sat nursing my paper cup of brandy and giving details to Jack Mullins, who was doing some of the paperwork.

"Dodge never had to shoot anybody before," Jack remarked, looking unusually grim. "I don't know if it's hit him yet, but he's going to take this hard."

"It was my fault," I said. "I shouldn't have been there."

Jack grew skeptical. "Look at it this way—if you hadn't been inside the house with Whitman, he might have seen Dodge approaching and shot him. The guy knew Dodge, and by the time the sheriff got close enough to be recognizable, the SOB wouldn't have missed."

I hadn't considered what would have happened if I hadn't been foolish enough to break into Honoria's house and get caught casing her studio. Jack was right. I had no doubt that Trevor would have taken Milo out. There weren't too many ways to rewrite the scenario. Somebody would end up dead—Milo, Trevor, or me.

"I'll point that out in *The Advocate*," I promised, giving Jack a grateful little smile. "I'll make Milo sound like a real hero when I write this story."

The words weren't quite out of my mouth when the door flew open. Vida stood on the threshold, with Bill Blatt behind her.

"*You* write the story? Emma, you've gone mad! This is *my* story! What do you think you're doing, undermining me like this?"

"But," I protested, "this would be a first-person account. 'Crazed Gunman Holds Editor Hostage.' You can write up the straight news account."

But Vida shook her head, the ecru high-crowned hat wobbling dangerously. "No, no. It will be an interview. You're too close to it, you don't have perspective—just like finding the body. You need someone who can be objective. Really, Emma, I'm surprised at you!"

I was too tired to argue. Maybe in the morning I could cope with Vida. I could use the same arguments I'd trotted out for Ed Bronsky—the personal touch, the unexpected insights, the incomparable style of Emma Lord. Bilge and more bilge. What the hell, if Vida wanted to cover every angle, let her. I needed a good night's sleep.

"We got sidetracked," I mumbled as Vida stomped over to sit in Milo's other visitor's chair. Bill Blatt deferentially bowed out of the office.

" 'We'?" Vida was scornful. "Nonsense! I never got sidetracked! The biggest clue was Will Stuart and the medical supply store. What kept putting me off wasn't *how* Trevor killed this Faye person, but *why*. I should have caught on when I heard about the money being withdrawn from Honoria's account, but we never learned who it was for, so I couldn't assume blackmail, could I? And we didn't know Kay was really Faye until last night."

Jack and I regarded Vida with perplexed expressions. "What about Will Stuart?" I asked.

Vida tapped her tortoiseshell frames. "His eyes, of course. He couldn't see well because he hadn't picked up his new glasses at the time that Honoria and Trevor were in the store. Even if he had been able to see properly, people can disappear in those aisles."

I remembered the elderly man who had been cruising the medical aids while I quizzed Will. The old guy had definitely been out of sight for part of the time. "So what did Trevor do? Sneak out the back?"

"Of course. He slipped into the rear corridor which led to the salon," Vida explained, her voice growing calm. "When we visited Honoria and her family in Startup, she mentioned that she'd had an earlier problem with her wheelchair. Then another, 'a few days' later, as she put it. That meant she had already taken the chair in to Will, while her relatives were visiting. She also said that Kay hadn't yet seen Alpine, implying that Trevor had. I suspect he wandered around then, while Will was tinkering with Honoria's chair. He must have learned that the back way led into the salon. I don't suppose it meant much to him then, but later, when Faye took Honoria's appointment, he planned the murder. No doubt he had the knife hidden in his jacket. All he needed was the towel, to keep the blood off his clothes."

"What towel?" I demanded.

Vida was trying not to look smug, but was failing, badly. "The towel from the back of Honoria's temporary chair. I should have guessed—I was sitting on the answer. My beaded backrests at work and in the car, you see. So comfortable. Will's such an old fussbudget, he rambled on about trying to give Honoria the proper support for her back. What could he use but a towel to pad her chair? He's too cheap to hand out blankets."

I groaned; Jack laughed.

"So what happened to the purse and knife?" Jack inquired.

"You and the sheriff ought to know," Vida retorted. "If you ever finish searching the garbage, I'm sure you'll find it in the trash that was hauled out of here. Trevor was carrying a shopping bag when he came into *The Advocate* after the murder. I suspect he had had the purse in it, with the knife inside. While he and Honoria were calling on Milo, Trevor simply dumped it into one of your bins and let the county do its job." Vida's eyes slid in my direction. "But you already guessed as much, didn't you, Emma?"

I nodded. "It took me a while. I began to realize what that empty shopping bag meant when I was watching the train go by this afternoon. I always wonder why they haul empty freight cars—it seems such a waste. But of course there's a reason. Then, subconsciously, I remembered the train whistling while Trevor and Honoria were in the office. The two thoughts merged just about the time I got to Honoria's house in Startup. Trevor could only be carrying that shopping bag if he'd had something in it. But whatever it was wasn't there anymore. Since he'd gone from Alpine Medical Supply to the sheriff's, it dawned on me that he must have been hiding the knife and purse in the bag."

"Wow." Jack rubbed at his dimpled chin. "It's a good thing we don't need that stuff anymore. The perp is dead."

"So's Dodger," I murmured. "I'm thinking that Trevor killed the cat and mailed it to the Marshalls."

Jack was now looking bewildered, but Vida was already nodding in agreement. "Exactly," she said. "He was cunning, in a childlike way. If what Billy tells me is true, the poor wretched fellow never grew up. He remained the dependent little brother all his life. It's sad, really." Vida paused, as if in memory of Trevor's twisted life.

"He knew that Toby Popp was courting his sister. No, no," Vida interrupted herself as she saw the question on my face, "I've no idea if Honoria was the woman who broke Toby's heart before he married Jane Marshall. That doesn't matter now, it's just another side issue. As I was saying, Trevor knew about Toby, and no doubt Honoria told her brother that her wealthy swain's former family was living in Alpine. It would spread suspicion around to mail the dead cat to the Marshalls. It was also the cruel kind of prank that a perverted, adolescent mind would invent. Trevor must have known that Honoria's original intention was to come to the salon to talk with Laurie. I'm guessing, but I think Honoria was acting as an intermediary between Toby and the Marshall women. If Honoria actually married Toby, she wouldn't want hard feelings. Imagine the demands Faye would have made if Honoria's husband was a billionaire! Worse yet—from Trevor's point of view—what if Honoria was driven to marry Toby to keep up with the blackmail payments? Trevor's rival for his sister's affections would be an extremely rich and powerful man."

"Martin Marshall," I said suddenly, then smiled wryly at Vida. "He called Laurie about Honoria's appointment. That's why Laurie pretended to be even dopier than usual. Stella knew she'd received a call, so Laurie couldn't deny it completely. But her stepfather must have wanted to talk to Honoria, probably to see if she could stop Toby from harassing the family."

Vida nodded. "I think so. Martin had probably seen Honoria arrive in town in her special car. There was work being done on those broken pipes right by the Clemans Building and City Hall. The job must have required Martin to be on hand with his heavy equipment, which is when he saw Honoria and the rest of them pull in. But Honoria didn't go into the salon, so he called Laurie to find out what had happened. Later, after this Faye person was killed, Laurie didn't want her stepfather implicated in any way, so she acted as if she didn't know who called. Of course Martin's concern had nothing to do with the crime. He was disturbed only about Toby."

"Another goofball," Jack said under his breath.

Vida ignored him. "By the way, I think I know what Toby meant in that ad he tried to place."

I was perplexed. "What was it?"

Vida shot me a reproachful look. "We both saw it. 'One down, one to go.' It probably referred to the foundations at Index. Don't you recall that the main house had been poured and framed, and that the secondary building was in progress? Toby may have been trying to get Laurie to move in with him. Or maybe he was merely bragging."

"You know, Vida," I said with asperity, "you might have told me all of this earlier. My ideas were way behind yours. You cut me off from your theories and conjectures. That's cheating."

Vida's expression was innocent. "But it's my story."

"You almost got me killed!" Forgetting my weariness, I grew angry. For the past week Vida had let me wander aimlessly through a morass of guesswork and side issues—Toby Popp's eccentricities, the Marshalls' fears, Becca's rocky romance with Eric Forbes, a dead cat in a plain brown wrapper. Except for Dodger, none of those things had anything to do with the murder. If I'd had any inkling that Trevor was the killer, I'd never have gone to Startup.

Or would I? Of course I would. Subconsciously, I had known who the killer was as soon as I saw the fading lights of the Burlington Northern caboose. But I hadn't foreseen the danger. It wouldn't have occurred to me that Trevor would fly back from Pacific Grove. I'd probably have gone right ahead and done what I did, maybe hoping to find some sort of evidence that would clinch the case for Milo.

"You should have told Milo," I muttered.

Vida glanced at the deputy. "He wouldn't have listened, would he, Jack? There was no evidence. I kept waiting for you people to have someone find the purse and the knife in the garbage."

"That's easier said than done," Jack admitted. "Some of that stuff from the Monday pickup was probably destroyed before Dodge gave the order."

"I must go," Vida announced, getting to her feet. "I had to rush over here after Billy called. I haven't yet cleared the table from my company."

After Vida closed the door behind her, Jack gave me a bemused look. "She's something else, huh?"

I nodded. "She sure is. Thank God."

Jack turned his attention back to the form he'd been filling out, but before he could phrase the next question, he heaved a big sigh. "I feel bad about the boss. Not just him having to kill Whitman, but this whole deal with his girlfriend. Ex-girlfriend, I should say. I never liked her much, but then I never knew her."

"None of us did," I said quietly. "Not even Milo."

"Maybe she'll marry this Popp dude," Jack mused. "He sounds pretty goofy, too. Arboria or Honoria or whatever her name is must like them that way. She sure stuck up for that crummy brother of hers."

"They had a very unusual bond." The paper cup was empty; I leaned down to put it in Milo's wastebasket. "Growing up, they must have felt as if the whole world was against them. Father figure in, father figure out. Mother absorbed in her matrimonial pursuits. I wonder if the other sister, Cassandra, felt the same way that Honoria and Trevor did, or if she cut herself out of the family circle early on."

"Talk about dysfunctional." Jack shook his head. "I thought my relatives were weird. I guess I won't say anything the next time my dad seals himself in the garage, or my sister cracks raw eggs on her head."

We returned to the paperwork. I kept expecting Milo to come into the office. He never did, and eventually, I headed home and went to bed. Alone.

Ginny Burmeister Erlandson had many souvenirs, dozens of snapshots, and endless anecdotes about her Hawaiian honeymoon. The rest of us listened patiently for the first twenty minutes on Monday morning, but then the phones began to ring, and visitors started to descend upon *The Advocate*. We put on our work faces and got down to business.

Carla caused the day's first disruption. "You promised to open the back shop, Emma. I don't see any sign of that happening. Now that Ginny's back, I've got plenty of time to spare."

Across my desk, Carla's olive skin was slightly flushed. She was right. I'd kept the back shop on the back burner.

"I'll call in a consultant this week," I vowed, looking up from Leo's new concept for Itsa Bitsa Pizza's weekly ad. "Whoever it is will be able to tell us what we'll need, what we can do, and how much profit we can expect. Then we can set some realistic deadlines. How does that sound?"

Judging from Carla's sullen expression, it sounded dubious. But she gave a nod of assent. "I'll check with you Wednesday for a progress report." Her words conveyed more threat than reminder.

By four o'clock, Vida had finished three murder-related stories. The first was an overview of the case; the second was a feature, giving thumbnail sketches of the Whitmans, while trying to skirt legal entanglements. The third was her interview with me. Like all of Vida's other straight news, it required a firm editorial hand to rid the prose of its House & Home style.

Emma Lord, *Alpine Advocate* editor and publisher, headed for Monroe Sunday to purchase a few necessities for her upcoming trip to Arizona. Ms. Lord plans to visit her brother, Ben Lord, who is a Catholic priest in Tuba City, and her son, Adam Lord, a student at Arizona State University. While en route down Highway 2, Ms. Lord stopped off at the home of Honoria Whitman, the well-known potteress, whose most recent award was the coveted . . .

I had my work cut out for me.

Just off the Money Creek Campground Road the Skykomish River rushes over big boulders where the steelhead rest before continuing upstream. The bank is littered with fallen trees, their roots sticking out of the water like skeletal remains. In winter, the river is often high and a murky white. It surges over the gravel bar, concealing the boulders and much of the underbrush that is caught on the bottom. But the experienced fisherman knows where the prey lurks, searching out the patches of slower water and working the hole carefully and quietly.

I'm not myself at seven A.M., and my footgear isn't suited for scrambling along snow-covered riverbanks. But Jack Mullins told me that if I wanted to find the sheriff, I'd better look for him by the big cedar snag near the campground. Milo was taking some time off after closing the Whitman case. It was normal, Jack said, that an officer who had fatally shot a civilian would go on leave.

The sun was up when I reached the straight stretch of river about a hundred yards from Money Creek. I could see Milo standing knee-deep in the current, his back turned to me. At the river's edge, I found a reasonably flat rock, brushed off an accumulation of new snow, and sat down. I knew better than to shout at the sheriff; any unusual noise could spook the fish.

After about five minutes and as many casts, Milo turned just enough to see me. Under the bill of his hunting cap, he seemed to look puzzled. I shook my head and held up a hand, indicating that my presence wasn't urgent. I might not be a steelheader, but I knew the drill. Milo had to fish out the hole before he could leave the river. I guessed that he'd arrived around five, at first light.

It was chilly, but the snow had stopped the previous night. There was some wind, which felt raw. The air smelled of damp and cold. Icicles formed on the bank upstream that overhung the river. Behind me a crow called out from the evergreens, its cry urgent and shrill. I waited.

Milo waded with the current, now abreast of the big cedar snag. He cast with great care, never taking his eyes off the line. I tucked my hands up into the sleeves of my duffel coat. And waited.

Ten minutes must have passed. I could see the sun, a pale globe trying to break through the gray clouds. Milo worked the hole deliberately, cautiously, trying not to get hung up in the network of branches that lay hidden under the tumbling water.

The river rushed by me, roaring in my ears. I respected its power, its danger, its unpredictability. Next year, this entire section of the Sky might be completely changed. A sudden torrent could take out the snags, wash away the banks, send new boulders hurtling through the chute. I settled my hood closer around my ears. And waited.

Milo had something on his line. He moved the graphite rod this way and that, then jiggled it experimentally. I couldn't hear him swear over the rush of the river, but I could tell he was angry. It was a snag, not a fish. With a sudden jerk, he freed the hook. It fluttered bare, the cluster of salmon eggs lost among the grasping branches. Milo reeled in and headed for dry land.

"Any luck?" I called as he trod gingerly over the rocks. His feet must have been numb inside the high boots.

"Not even a bump," he replied, his breath coming out before him in wispy puffs. "The river's too high. It's off-color. I saw bear tracks upstream."

Standing up, I nodded. Those were all good reasons for not catching the elusive steelhead. But an empty creel doesn't mean that the fisherman hasn't had a good time.

"What are you doing here?" the sheriff inquired, pulling a pack of cigarettes from his fishing vest.

I tipped my head to one side, feeling strangely shy. "I never got to thank you for saving my life."

"Ah." Milo offered me a cigarette. I took it. He flicked his lighter, first for me, then for himself. But he didn't say anything more.

"You did something wonderful—and terrible. Are you okay?" I peered up at him through a haze of blue smoke.

"It stinks." Milo started for the trail that led to the parking area.

My Jag was parked next to his Cherokee Chief. Milo opened the rear door of his vehicle and began breaking down his rod. "You don't just shoot somebody and walk away," he said, not looking at me. "It doesn't matter if the guy's a homicidal perp. You can't shrug it off."

"I know." I bowed my head. "Frankly, I feel guilty. You did it for me."

Milo's grin was lopsided, embarrassed, ironic. "No, I didn't. I couldn't see who was inside with Trevor."

It had never occurred to me that even in the candlelight, the sheriff probably couldn't identify the other person in the living room.

"Damn," I breathed. "And I thought you wanted to save me!"

Milo eased the rod into a cloth case, then tied it shut. "Well, I did. I mean, I would, if I'd known it was you."

A sudden thought occurred to me. I plucked at the sleeve of Milo's down jacket. "Hey—my car was parked there. You must have known it was me."

Milo still avoided my eyes. "I didn't see your car. I saw Trevor's van. It blocked out your Jag. I went off the drive, through the trees, just in case he was watching for me. Then I saw that broken window out back, and figured he'd gone inside that way. But it was kind of small for me to get through, so I decided to take out one of the picture windows in the front." As he spoke in his not-quite-so-laconic voice, Milo slid the rod in a rack, checked his bait box, and got his walking boots out of the Chief.

My guilt began to lift, but it was replaced by a hollow feeling. Milo hadn't shot Trevor Whitman for my sake. I had been a cipher, a mere symbol of the Endangered

Civilian. Trevor had been armed and dangerous. As usual, Milo had gone by the book, and it wasn't a romance novel.

"Oh, well," I said, more to myself than to Milo.

He was pulling off his hip boots. "I'm glad Honoria isn't coming back," he said, the remark seemingly from out of nowhere. "Whatever we had got lost the other day."

"You mean the murder?" A few snowflakes were beginning to drift down. The sun had retreated from its battle with the clouds.

Milo shook his head. "I mean the other night at your house." Finally, the hazel eyes rested on my face.

"Oh." I tipped my head to one side. "I thought you'd forgotten."

Milo gently cuffed my chin with his fist. "Hell, no! What do you think has kept me on an even keel the past couple of days?"

"How would I know? I haven't seen you since we were in Startup."

"You know something?" Milo said, gazing up at the ominous sky. "I like talking to you, Emma. You say things. *Real* things, not made-up conversation. Honoria always wanted to talk about *topics*."

I knew what Milo meant. Perhaps our romance, if that's what it was, lived in our verbal exchanges. It wasn't sexual sparring, which is filled with taunts, teasing, and provocative innuendos. Milo and I talked because we liked and trusted each other. Intimacy was grousing about our jobs, worrying over our kids, asking for lamb chops, and pointing out mustard on chins. We were comfortable together; we enjoyed each other's company.

"Will we ruin everything if we . . . ah . . . move to

another level?" I asked in a small voice. Already it
seemed that the specter of sex made me tongue-tied.

Milo was arranging my hood over my inelegant
haircut. "Could be. It happens. But how else will we
know?"

"Know what?"

"You know." He brushed my forehead with his lips.

"I know." For just an instant I pressed my face against
his chest. Solid. Trustworthy. Reliable. Strong. My cata-
logue of Milo's virtues made him sound like a used car.
Maybe that's what we all were—somebody else's discards, somebody else's newfound delight.

"You had breakfast?" he asked.

"No. The Venison Inn?"

Milo sighed. "Sure, why not? I've got to face the folks
eventually."

"They think you're a hero, Milo."

"Bull. They don't know shit about heroes."

Maybe not. But I did.

In Alpine, murder always seems to occur
in alphabetical order . . .

THE ALPINE ADVOCATE
THE ALPINE BETRAYAL
THE ALPINE CHRISTMAS
THE ALPINE DECOY
THE ALPINE ESCAPE
THE ALPINE FURY
THE ALPINE GAMBLE
THE ALPINE HERO

. . . and you can be sure Emma Lord, editor
and publisher of *The Alpine Advocate*, is there
to report every detail.

THE EMMA LORD MYSTERIES

by Mary Daheim
Published by Ballantine Books.
Available wherever books are sold.

READ ALL ABOUT IT!
The Alpine Advocate
Novels by Mary Daheim

THE ALPINE ADVOCATE

As editor-publisher of *The Alpine Advocate*, Emma Lord is always in search of a good story. But when Mark Doukas, heir to the richest old man in town, is murdered, Emma gets more than she bargained for.

THE ALPINE BETRAYAL

Dani Marsh—former Alpine resident, now Hollywood star—returns to Alpine for some location shooting in the Cascade Mountains, only to become embroiled in the murder of her ex-husband. Once again, Emma Lord's nose for a story leads her straight into trouble.

THE ALPINE CHRISTMAS

It's Christmastime in Alpine, and that means snow, carolers, Christmas trees…and murder. The discovery of one woman's leg and another woman's nude, half-frozen body in the lake leads Emma Lord and her House & Home editor, Vida, into a deadly holiday.

THE ALPINE DECOY

The arrival of a young African American nurse in Alpine is news enough in this predominantly white community. When a second newcomer—a young black man—is found dead, Emma Lord believes that something sinister is afoot.

THE ALPINE ESCAPE

When Emma Lord decides to take a few days off, she expects some time alone to do some soul-searching. Instead, she is caught up in a century-old mystery: her friends have found the skeleton of an unknown young woman in their basement.

THE ALPINE FURY

The Bank of Alpine has been an Alpine fixture for generations, but suddenly something fishy seems to be going on. Emma Lord decides to investigate—and finds the bank's sexy blonde bookkeeper strangled to death at a local motel.

THE ALPINE GAMBLE

The year's biggest news story is the development of a luxury spa around Alpine's mineral springs—and the controversy surrounding it. But even those who predicted that the spa would bring sleaze and "Californicators" didn't expect to be confronted with murder.

The Emma Lord Mysteries
by Mary Daheim

MARY DAHEIM

Available in your local bookstore.
Published by Ballantine Books.